A PLEASANT MEMORY

Maximillian brought his mouth to her throat and kissed her tenderly, and Penelope closed her eyes. Yes, she remembered this. The softening of her entire body, the tingle that began and grew so quickly. The pleasant tension. Warm and gentle lips caressed the column of her throat, the curve of her shoulder, until she felt herself melting.

Maximillian pulled slowly away, and Penelope watched as he dipped a finger into the brandy and brought it to the tip of her breast. A single drop fell, and he lowered his mouth to lick away the liquor, to draw the nipple deep into his mouth with a gentle breath. She felt herself relenting, giving in to the rippling sensations and the growing tautness. Yes, she remembered this. Her body rose to meet his mouth, her back arching of its own will. With every stroke of his tongue her body awakened a bit more.

"Maximillian!" She tried to sit up but with a gentle hand he forced her back down. "You can't."

"Trust me, m'dear?" he asked huskily.

Penelope closed her eyes as he continued to rake his fingers across her flesh. Trust him? How could she? He'd played false with her, pretending to love her, pretending to offer happiness and adoration and then changing overnight into a stranger. He'd changed into a man with cold, lying eyes she could not read. He'd become a husband she did not know at all. Trust him? "Yes," she whispered.

The Indigo Blade

Linda Jones

LOVE SPELL BOOKS   ◆   NEW YORK CITY

*This book is lovingly dedicated to the fellow members of
the Cheese and Whine loop, Beverly Beaver,
Kris Robinette, Lyn Stone, and Gay Thomas.
Thanks for always being there.*

LOVE SPELL®

April 1999

Published by

Dorchester Publishing Co., Inc.
276 Fifth Avenue
New York, NY 10001

ISBN 0-505-52303-5

The name "Love Spell" and its logo are trademarks of Dorchester
Publishing Co., Inc.

Printed in the United States of America.

The Indigo Blade

Prologue

1774

The prisoner would be delivered into Chadwick's hands well before dark, and in a matter of days the troublemaker would serve as an example to the damned rebels who were making this job so bloody difficult.

Captain Bradford Thurman considered himself to be a good soldier. He thought himself better than most, to be honest. But he preferred fighting the French to playing nursemaid to a bunch of ungrateful colonials. Where would they be without the British Army? Suffering at the hands of savages or fighting off French settlers, that's where.

Bradford glanced over his shoulder to check on the prisoner and the four guards who flanked the unfortunate colonial. He wasn't much of a troublemaker at the moment, thanks to the beating he'd received just that morning. An unkempt head hung, dejected, so that a fall of greasy hair shielded the rebel's face. His shoulders were slumped; he knew he was traveling to his death. The insolent colonial would think twice before arguing with a soldier in the British Army again, if he had the opportunity in his few remaining hours on this earth.

The prisoner had committed a third act of sedition. Twenty lashes on the first offense hadn't dissuaded him, nor had the fifty that had followed a few months later. This third transgression had sealed his fate. Tomorrow the dissident would hang.

The damned colonials were like children, to Bradford's logical thinking. Rowdy, whiny children who didn't know a good thing when they had it. Recently, a goodly amount of excellent tea had been wasted in a fit of pique by grown men not-so-cleverly disguised as natives! If that was not a childish act, what was?

Perhaps when they saw one of their own swinging on a gallows they'd think twice about the preposterous concept of independence.

The January afternoon was nippy, and the damp chill penetrated Bradford's uniform in a most unpleasant way. South Carolina was certainly not as cold as the northern colonies, but the humid air made the chill all but unbearable. The road they traveled was narrow and lined with a thick growth of trees, bare-branched hardwoods and evergreens growing together and intertwining their boughs so that in spite of the blue sky above, Bradford felt as though he passed through a long, winding tunnel. Wilderness, that's all this blasted country was . . . mile after mile of trees and water and more trees. How he longed for London. . . .

He saw the overturned wagon as he came around a bend in the path, and cursed beneath his breath as he lifted a hand to still the soldiers to his rear. An old man with unruly gray hair and clothing that resembled a collection of sacks draped around his body was kneeling by the wagon, his back to the soldiers as he muttered loudly.

"Make way," Bradford ordered. The wagon, a number of scattered baskets, the old man, and the skirted body he knelt over, blocked the path completely.

The man jumped, obviously surprised, and as he spun his stooped body around, the left sleeve of his crude garment swung free. He raised his one hand in greeting. "Praise be. The Lord has answered my prayers and sent these kind soldiers to assist me."

"We've not come to assist you, old man," Bradford said sternly. "Clear this road immediately. We must pass."

The codger appeared to be puzzled for a moment, wrinkling his nose and peering up through narrowed eyes that were topped by dark eyebrows stark on a too-pale face. The man's skin was, in fact, more gray than was normal for a healthy man of any age, and was blotchy in several places. Good heavens, the fellow was probably diseased.

"I see," the old man muttered in a gratingly coarse voice. "I'd better get busy, then."

"Rebecca," he said in a softened voice as he

turned his attention to the woman on the ground. "Open your eyes now, your poor old grandfather needs you." He knelt beside her again, lowering his body with obvious effort, and gently patted her face. "Wake up, dear."

The old man looked back at the squad of soldiers. "I don't think she's badly hurt," he said, as if they might have a care for the injured woman. "There's no blood, but she's got a lump on her head the size of an egg."

The woman the geezer so fondly called Rebecca stirred, and a long strand of dark hair fell into her face. What a homely one she was! Long face, long nose, large mouth . . . but as she rolled onto her back she revealed an admirable, shapely figure.

"That's right, Rebecca, we must move the wagon so these fine soldiers can pass."

There was no way a one-armed old man and a wounded girl would be able to right that wagon and move it to the side of the road, so Bradford grudgingly ordered two of his troopers to dismount and assist. The other two moved close to the prisoner, in case the rebel was foolish enough to think his reduced guard offered a chance of escape.

Bradford dismounted himself, eager to get moving again and to deliver the prisoner to Charles Town and Victor Chadwick.

The old man tried valiantly to assist the soldiers in righting the wagon, while the dazed girl sat forlornly in the middle of the road. She rubbed the side of her head, moaned softly, and played with a strand of hair that fell onto her full breasts.

"Out of the way," Bradford ordered as he moved

the one-armed man aside to take his place. He had no desire to rub elbows with a diseased peasant. The old-timer mumbled his thanks, moved clumsily aside, and asked gruffly after his granddaughter. Bradford gave all his strength and attention to the chore at hand, heaving until his muscles strained and an unpleasant sweat broke out beneath his heavy uniform. It was hard work, but he had the help of his soldiers. With a final mighty surge of effort, the wagon was righted.

"Thank you, sir, thank you," the old man said, and Bradford turned to find the man and his granddaughter, who had come to her feet and was amazingly tall, standing very near—and pointing a variety of weapons in his direction. The old man held a dagger with a wooden grip and a long, thin, well-honed blade, and the young woman had a .67-caliber pistol in each of her large, roughened hands. The miscreants were close, and the weapons were steady, and Bradford decided it would not be prudent to reach for his own.

"Common wayside bandits," he spat. "You're fools if you think you can take on soldiers of the British Army and get away with it. Threaten me if you like, but you're headed for disaster. My troopers will take care of you."

"These troopers?" With a wave of his hand the old man gestured with his dagger to the wide-eyed men who flanked their captain.

"Those troopers," Bradford said grandly, pointing to where his men guarded the rebel who was traveling to his death.

The old man turned his head slowly, and seemingly without a care. "What troopers would that be? Surely you don't mean those two unfortunate lads."

Reluctantly, Bradford turned his head and looked to the spot where his troopers and the prisoner had been waiting patiently and securely moments earlier. His soldiers had dismounted, been stripped of their weapons, and they had been quite efficiently bound and gagged. They sat, wide-eyed, with their backs against the trunk of a small tree. The prisoner was gone.

"How dare you . . ." Before he could finish, they came without warning from the woods, five gray-haired old men dressed as the thief before him was, in baggy and torn clothing and soft moccasins. They came with ropes and strips of cloth, and in a matter of minutes he found himself and the remainder of his contingent stripped of weapons and securely bound.

The one-armed man knelt before him, and that dagger danced wickedly, cutting the air and coming awfully close to Bradford's heart.

"Perhaps I should do to you what you had planned for the young man you were transporting to Charles Town. What was his fate to be? Hanging? Firing squad?"

Suddenly Bradford was afraid. These weren't ordinary bandits, and it wasn't chance that had brought him and his troopers to this meeting. These were hot-headed rebels, madmen, revolutionaries.

"I was delivering my prisoner to Victor Chadwick, who is an important member of the Governor's Council. What Mr. Chadwick had planned for him, I wouldn't know." Bradford lied, and prayed as he had never prayed before that he lied well.

The man smiled, revealing blackened teeth. "Is that right?"

Bradford nodded.

"I want you to deliver a message for me," the man whispered, and Bradford felt a surge of relief. He would survive this encounter. After all, he couldn't deliver a message if he were dead.

"Certainly."

The old-timer swung his arm and the dagger forward, swiftly, with great power, and the sharp-edged metal was embedded in the road not two inches from Bradford's crotch. The shaking began, an uncontrollable, deep trembling that started in his legs and traveled quickly up and through his entire body.

"Tell Victor to watch his back." Colorless eyes flashed, strong and powerful in a white-gray and oddly weathered face. "Tell him not to sleep too deeply at night, nor relax his vigilance when he thinks himself among friends, nor trust that his King and his soldiers will keep him safe."

Bradford nodded.

"Tell him," the old man whispered, "the Indigo Blade is coming."

Chapter One

"Why did I have to be the woman?" Deep in the forest, in the shelter of the trees, Beck stripped off the dark wig and revealed his own cinnamon-colored hair, which he ruffled with long, thin fingers.

Max smiled as he freed his left arm and whisked off his own coarse gray wig. With a gentlemanly flourish he whipped a linen handkerchief from a deep pocket in his tattered jacket and began to wipe the rice powder and lampblack from his face, knowing full well it would take a good scrubbing to rid himself completely of the simple disguise.

Beneath the rags of a beggar his heart was still pumping madly with the excitement of the encounter. He didn't even feel the cold anymore. "Because you're the only one of us who can still get away with shaving once a week. Dalton and Garrick have

16

those unfashionable little beards they refuse to part with, Lewis and John would make dreadfully ugly females—"

"And I don't?"

"—and Fletcher simply flat-out refused," Max finished. "You did a splendid job. Why, I do believe that captain was growing sweet on you before you pulled those flintlocks on him."

Beck snorted as he unbuttoned his dress and reached inside for his "breasts," hand-sized sacks of grain joined by a ribbon and dangling from his neck.

Max was almost ashamed of the elation he experienced. However, it was a thrill he couldn't deny, and it washed over him not because they'd saved a man from the gallows, and certainly not because the job had been well planned and executed—he'd expected nothing less—but for a different reason.

For all his talk of leaving the perils of his former life behind, there was still a strong appeal to the immediate presence of danger. That—together with the knowledge that he was meting out a justice that was rare and precious in this world—gave him a tangible thrill. He felt more *alive* at this moment than he had in months.

"Hey, gorgeous." John's familiar gruff voice reached them before the sound of footsteps. "How about a little kiss?"

Beck spun around. "That's not funny."

"No, it's not," Garrick said crisply as he followed. "But you must remember that John has dallied with many a woman uglier than you."

"Just that one . . . well, and maybe that other one," John mumbled.

They continued the lighthearted teasing as Beck quickly shed the dress and stored it in a sack along with the "breasts" and wig. Garrick and John removed their wild gray wigs and tattered clothing, and revealed their own more-dignified garb and well-groomed dark heads of hair. Garrick brushed the powder from his goatee and mustache, and briskly swept his hands over his fine jacket as if to shed entirely the persona he'd taken on for this mission.

By the time they'd completely cast off every shred of the disguise that they'd donned for the British soldiers, the rest of their crew was approaching. Fletcher was in the lead, gloomy as always, while Dalton and Lewis argued quietly in the rear.

"How did it go?" Max directed his somber question to Fletcher.

Fletcher snatched off his wig and combed back his own unruly black curls with one hand. "They'd damn near beat him to death." When he was angry, as he was now, his Irish accent became more prominent. "And he was just a lad, I tell you. A mere child, and they would have hanged him without a second thought."

They were all silent now, as they listened. His euphoria past, Max studied the men who surrounded him. They'd seen injustice in the past, been touched by it and survived. Outwardly they were all composed. But he knew them well enough to know that beneath the relaxed exteriors their hearts beat as his did—fast and furiously with anger at that inequity.

"You saw him off?" he continued.

It was Lewis who answered. "We saw him safely on board the schooner. He'll be well-tended, and he'll be safe from the likes of Victor Chadwick, once he arrives in Williamsburg and is delivered into the hands of a sympathetic ally."

Max nodded in approval. How had this begun? He was barely settled in his new home—a home he'd fought long and hard for—when he'd heard the rumor. A rumor that had quickly been proven as fact. A number of silk- and satin-clad Charles Town loyalists had sat at a finely laid table and discussed the news with as much fire and enthusiasm as they'd given comments on the moistness of the bird they ate. A man was on his way to the gallows for speaking his mind and inciting a crowd to do the same. To Max's way of thinking, it wasn't right. In fact, it was damned unfair.

"We can't go back, you know," Garrick said softly. His steady voice was clear as a bell here in the solitude of the woods. "We can't just stop."

"For once Garrick's right," John mumbled.

"This is just the beginning," Fletcher said as he stepped away from the crowd. "Tonight we made ourselves a part of it."

"Do you propose that we continue?" Max directed his question to them all, six friends and shipmates and fellow soldiers. They'd been to hell and back together in the past seven years, survived tribulations that had proven the destruction of lesser men. This was supposed to have been their reward. A new country, a new home . . . peace at last.

But there was no peace here. Max wondered if he would ever truly have peace, if he would recognize the much-sought-after tranquility if it ever visited him. Most likely not, since he'd known no true peace in his lifetime.

"We could form a militia," Dalton said sensibly. "War is coming, and we all know it. With what we know, we could put together an army that would send those redcoats running home with their tails between their legs."

"There are only seven of us," Lewis said in an unusually solemn voice. "What can seven men do?"

Max smiled. He already knew what he was going to do. He'd thrown that fact into the face of a frightened soldier a short time ago. In his heart he was committed already, but he hadn't counted on having his comrades with him. If they would agree to join him, they could cause quite a flurry among the smug loyalists and the King's men in Charles Town.

"More of the same?" he suggested. "I was at a dinner party when I learned about the lad who was to hang. The tidbit of conversation was thrown out so casually and debated so briefly, I wonder if Chadwick even remembers that he mentioned it. We have the money to fit into this aristocratic, loyalist circle, and the information we obtain would be invaluable."

"We have the money," Fletcher said, "and Max has the bloodline."

"And the voice," Dalton added.

Beck piped up. "And the education. No one will

ever guess that you aren't one of their own."

They waited for him to respond. Six men watched him expectantly.

"You all have money and plans," he said. "I won't hold any one of you to an endeavor you don't believe in with all your heart." Max protested, gave them every chance to withdraw—but damn it, he wanted them with him.

Dalton grinned. "I've waited this long to start my own shipping business. I can wait a while longer."

The rest agreed, with reservation but no hesitation.

"It won't be easy," Max said, prepared to offer them, once again, a way out if they wished it.

It was Fletcher who answered first, his low voice speaking for them all. "And who among us has had an easy life?" He thrust his hand out. "No matter where the winds take us, in our hearts we will forever be the League of the Indigo Blade. I for one can't walk away from this fight."

Five more hands quickly joined Fletcher's. Max placed his hand atop them all. "For Jamie," he whispered, and with as much reverence as the most heartfelt prayer the familiar vow was echoed in six separate voices.

"For Jamie."

"Have you heard the latest?"

Penelope wasn't surprised that her cousin hadn't bothered to knock before bursting into the bedchamber with her question. Mary was bright and bubbly and had much too much energy for her own good, and she rarely behaved in a mundane manner. Knocking on a door meant stopping and waiting for approval to enter, and that would have been quite an inconvenience.

"The latest about what?" Penelope, settled comfortably on the cherry window seat, lifted her head from the book she was reading. They'd been in the Charles Town house for three days, and already she missed the solitude and quiet of her uncle's rice plantation. She knew that Mary, on the other hand, loved Charles Town with her own special passion. The plantation had been much too tame for her liking.

"A mere two weeks ago, a number of dragoons were transporting a dangerous prisoner," Mary said in a hushed voice as she sat on the side of the bed. Her green eyes were shining, her yellow gown was sunny, her bright red hair was slightly mussed, and Penelope thought, as she often did, that her cousin looked more like a child than a twenty-one-year-old woman. "The man was to be hanged right here in Charles Town, but en route he was liberated by a gang of ruffians."

"What was he to be hanged for?" Penelope laid her book aside to give her cousin the full attention that was always required.

"Sedition," Mary whispered. "He's one of those revolutionaries who are so determined to stir up trouble. On three separate occasions he incited a crowd to a near riot with his ridiculous talk."

Penelope held back her opinion that a man shouldn't be executed for voicing his thoughts, because she knew it would be a useless exercise. Mary listened intently to every word her loyalist father uttered, and believed all he said without question. "I see."

"The captain of the dragoons said there were at least twenty men who ambushed them on the road and took the prisoner. The troopers put up a valiant fight, but the odds were insurmountable. Twenty against five," she said with wonder in her eyes. "The leader of the brigands was an extremely large and strong one-armed man with fiery red eyes and silver hair."

"He should be easy to find, with that description." Penelope couldn't stop the smile that spread across her face. Such drama! One arm, silver hair, and red eyes, indeed. By the time the tale reached Mary's ears, who knows how much of the telling was true?

"There was a woman involved," Mary said dramatically. "A tall, extraordinary beautiful woman, they say. An amazon who fought like a warrior alongside the leader. I suspect," she said in a lowered voice, "that they are lovers."

"Really," Penelope said just as softly.

"The captain suspects that they might be in league with the natives," Mary continued, "since they were able to move their forces through the forest without so much as rustling a leaf."

"Sounds most interesting."

Mary missed the trace of sarcasm in Penelope's voice and continued. "We should hear more about the Indigo Blade tomorrow night, at the Lowrys' ball."

"The Indigo Blade?"

"That's what he calls himself," Mary said breathlessly. "I can't believe Victor didn't mention it to you. The outlaw actually threatened Victor personally, giving a most frightening message to the brave captain as they fought."

The mention of Victor Chadwick wiped the smile from Penelope's face. "I haven't seen him since we arrived. I've had a bit of a headache, and really haven't felt up to receiving visitors." A headache would give her a few days' reprieve, but sooner or later she would have to face the persistent man who pursued her at every turn. Her uncle would never allow her to remain in this room, reading and drawing to pass the time, hiding from the unwanted attentions of a perfectly acceptable and marriageable candidate.

She couldn't avoid Victor much longer. Penelope knew she would not be able to excuse herself from the Lowrys' much-anticipated ball, and her tenacious suitor was sure to be there. Already she dreaded the inevitable meeting.

"And even if I had," she continued without showing her distress, "he knows I detest all talk of politics."

Mary leaned back on her hands. "I can't believe you haven't snatched that wonderful man up yet. You should be married and have two babies by now."

Inwardly, Penelope shuddered at the thought of marriage to Victor Chadwick. He was handsome, he was wealthy, and he held an important position in the government. But kind as he was, Penelope didn't return his ardor. She liked him as a dear family friend, but she didn't love him. The absence of love wasn't an argument she could use on Uncle

William. He would simply counter that a woman in her position didn't choose a husband for love, but for money and power. Victor Chadwick had both.

Victor's last letter had hinted at another marriage proposal, and Penelope wasn't ready for the confrontation that was certain to come. Last year she'd refused him gently, but still he'd persisted, citing the fact that he was now past thirty and she was a marriageable twenty-three. Perhaps her refusal had been too gentle.

Her uncle thought a joining of his family with Chadwick a splendid idea, but would he go so far as to force her to marry Victor? She'd been in William Seton's care for ten years, since just after her thirteenth birthday, and she'd come to care for him almost as much as she had for her own father and mother. He had welcomed Penelope and her brother Tyler, who'd been five years old at the time, into his home, and from the first day he'd treated them as if they were his own. She respected her uncle, obeyed him, and cared for him deeply. But in this, she would defy him.

Defy him. She dreaded the thought. Since moving into her uncle's home, Penelope had done her best to be agreeable. More than that, she'd done her best to be well-behaved, helpful, and unobtrusive. Tyler was a trial, and even at the age of thirteen Penelope had been aware of the fact that Uncle William would be within his rights to be rid of his brother's children if they became too much of a burden. The more Tyler misbehaved, the harder Penelope tried to be the perfect niece.

Her uncle was pleased that she had a talent for

painting, so she spent as much time as possible perfecting the small gift she'd been given. He didn't like to be disturbed in the evening, and to please him she took to retiring early so as not to disturb him in any way. She had been, since coming into his care, a perfectly agreeable niece. And now he wanted her to marry Victor Chadwick.

If only Mary were more Victor's type. Penelope had been aware for quite some time that her cousin adored the man and all he stood for, and would gratefully accept any attentions he sent her way. For a while Mary had flirted outrageously with him, bestowing upon him her brightest smiles and undivided attention, batting her lashes and looking at him in a way that would have had any other man groveling at her feet, but Victor could be blind when he chose.

Uncle William was not. On their last stay at the Charles Town house just a few months earlier, he'd berated Mary loudly for her inappropriate behavior, ending his tirade with the words Penelope dreaded hearing.

"Why can't you be more like your cousin Penelope?"

Surely Mary was as sick of the unfair comparison as Penelope was. Perhaps Mary wasn't genteel or serene or ladylike in the way her father wished, but she was bright and beautiful, like a butterfly who never stayed in one place too long, but flitted from one flower to another in endless and graceful motion. There were times Penelope wished she had some of her cousin's bravado, if nothing else.

"I can't wait for tomorrow night," Mary said in a

dreamy voice. "Our new gowns are fabulously beautiful, and it's been so long since we danced and laughed and gossiped in a crowd. I don't know that I'll remember what to do."

"I doubt that you've forgotten any of your social graces."

Mary's smile was wide and bright. "Maybe Victor will propose marriage."

"Bite your tongue!" Penelope snapped. Just hearing those words made her heart leap unpleasantly in her chest.

Some of the light went out of Mary's eyes, and her smile faded. "You shouldn't be ungrateful for his attentions."

"I'm not ungrateful." A touch of guilt assaulted Penelope as she said the words. "It's just that I don't love Victor."

Penelope wondered if she really knew what love was, if she'd recognize it when—or if—it came to her.

"You're twenty-three years old," Mary said sternly. "If you wait too much longer, you'll be an old maid and no one will want you, and then what will you do? Be mistress of my father's house for your remaining years? Be the dutiful daughter he always wanted me to be?"

Penelope waited for the flash of anger to pass. Mary had a tendency to anger quickly, but her bursts of temper never lasted long. She was just as quick to forgive and move forward, usually with a contrite smile.

"I want to get married, one day," Penelope said softly as she watched the rage fade from Mary's eyes. "I want children, and my own home . . ." She wanted what her parents had found and treasured before an untimely death had claimed them. The fever that had struck her mother and father down hadn't spread to Penelope or her little brother, but it had changed their lives forever by robbing them of two loving parents. "But I expect to love the man I take as my husband."

Mary sighed in obvious despair. "You can love anyone appropriate if you set your mind to it."

Penelope didn't think that was true, but it wasn't wise to disagree with Mary on the subject of love. Actually, it wasn't wise to disagree with Mary about anything at all.

Mary rose from the side of the bed and circled around it with a gentle, graceful movement, her pale hands gripping at the cherry bedpost as she swayed away from Penelope so that her yellow skirt swirled softly around her legs. "You're being so difficult that perhaps I shan't tell you about the newest and most eligible man in Charles Town."

Penelope knew that if Mary had something to say, nothing would stop her. Not even a small, imagined taste of revenge. "Oh, do tell," she pleaded with a wide smile. "I shouldn't arrive at the Lowrys' ball unprepared now, should I?"

"With my luck, he'll take one look at you and fall madly in love and I'll never have a chance to sweep him off his feet." Mary's words were only half-joking. While there were many men in pursuit of William Seton's only daughter, men who openly adored her and came calling at the plantation and here in town, it seemed Mary was only interested in the men who pursued the more sedate, more mature Penelope. It was a perverse trait Penelope did not understand.

"With you wearing that new green gown, I'm sure this eligible man won't have so much as a glance for me." Her voice was lighthearted, but Penelope believed her statement to be true. Mary was one of the most beautiful women in all of South Carolina, surely. She had been blessed with brilliant red hair, bright green eyes, and an expressive face. Penelope, with her brown hair and brown eyes, had often felt downright dowdy next to her cousin, and it amazed her that on occasion men were frightened away by Mary's beauty and high spirits.

"He built a magnificent house and moved in just a few weeks ago." Mary entertained herself by walking past Penelope's dresser and lifting each and every object there to study it briefly before setting it back down. A pair of earrings, a comb, a velvet ribbon, and a silver-backed hand mirror. "He's most handsome, I've heard, in an elegant and aristocratic sort of way. Fabulously rich." This statement brought an even wider smile to Mary's face. "He has a houseful of servants, and never misses a social event."

"He sounds perfect for you."

"He does, doesn't he?" Mary's often devious mind was obviously in motion. Penelope could actually see the cunning gleam in those green eyes.

"Does this perfect man have a name?" Penelope reached for her book. Mary's visits were tumultuous, could either be fun or disheartening, but were almost always brief. Already Mary was moving toward the door.

"Maximillian Broderick," Mary said as she opened the door to take her leave. She evidently liked the way the name rolled off her tongue, because she said it again, more slowly this time.

"Maximillian Broderick."

Chapter Two

Mary loved a party like this one more than anything in the world. The gathering together of the finest citizens of Charles Town in their most extravagant costumes, the brightly burning lamps and candelabras glowing with the flames of enough candles to light William Seton's home for a full year, the music that filled the room, and most of all the adoration that was inevitably heaped upon William Seton's only daughter. Every now and then, Penelope could hear her cousin's cheerful laughter above the din.

Penelope was not antisocial—not in the least—but tonight the talk seemed to be primarily of politics and the inevitability of war. It was a subject that divided her mind and her heart, but of course she could share her uncertainties with no one. The slightest hint of sympathy toward the rebels would be seen as defiance of her uncle, and she wouldn't embarrass him in that way. So, she was unusually reserved, and the minutes passed with unbearable slowness.

Oh, she'd spoken with several ladies who'd welcomed her and admired her gown, and she'd shared a number of dances with attentive young men who—for a few moments—left the subject of rebellion and the likelihood of war behind, but the reality hung over the room like a tangible and very disagreeable cloud. Others apparently ignored the unpleasant realities, but Penelope felt the pain of those possibilities too deeply to dismiss them entirely.

Two of her dances had been with Victor, who found himself divided this evening. He couldn't very well give Penelope his full attention when he was the darling of the moment in this loyalist crowd. It was rather a relief to find that he was preoccupied and somewhat out of sorts.

Penelope watched him from her position in the corner of the room. As he discussed politics with a number of planters and merchants, he truly came alive. His hands were used to punctuate his most important points forcefully, and his face was animated as she'd never seen before.

She brushed her fingers almost nervously over her skirt of rose-colored silk and tapped her closed lace fan in a soft rhythm that spoke of an unaccustomed nervousness. Uncle William was one of the throng who listened intently to every word Victor Chadwick had to say.

From a distance, Penelope heard Mary's laughter

once again, and she turned her gaze to the crowd. Dressed in imported silks of every color, the Lowrys' guests were the elite of the colonial city of Charles Town, the well-to-do, the self-appointed aristocracy of a colony in distress. Penelope had always preferred the quieter setting of her uncle's plantation, but she couldn't deny that there was a splendid charm in the city and its people.

Mary belonged here, in this magnificent hall with these aristocratic people. Penelope knew, had always known, that she did not.

At once, several heads turned toward the entrance, and Penelope couldn't help but turn her head as well.

The man who filled the doorway with his presence surveyed the room as if he were a pampered prince lazily inspecting his adoring subjects. His back was straight as a board, but still his posture spoke of indolence and boredom. Perhaps it was the position of an elegant hand that was half-covered with the ecru lace that fell from beneath a lavender silk sleeve. Perhaps it was the long-fingered hands themselves, or the placement of those long legs that were encased tightly in matching lavender silk breeches and white silk hose . . . but Penelope suspected it was the eyes. Even from her post in the corner, she could see that they were half-closed and dulled with apathy.

Golden blond hair, unpowdered as was the custom among the younger men, was gathered into a queue with a black ribbon, and but for the lazy eyes and a patrician nose that bordered on being too long, he was an attractive man.

Mrs. Lowry rushed to greet this late-arriving guest with a girlish enthusiasm Penelope found distasteful and a touch disturbing. Harriet Lowry had always been the very model of propriety and good taste, and this handsome man had her positively simpering. He smiled with little effort and took Mrs. Lowry's offered hand, bestowing upon the matron's knuckles a brief kiss.

This was, surely, Mary's much-talked-about Maximillian Broderick. In all her ramblings, Mary hadn't bothered to mention that the man was a popinjay, a fop who dressed in lavender silk and adorned himself with more lace than any one woman in the crowded room.

Before Penelope could return her attention to her uncle and Victor and the disturbing notion that they were somehow plotting her marriage, the youngest Lowry son, Heath, claimed her for a dance.

This was more abominable than any mission in India, more detestable than the longest siege or the stormiest night at sea, and surely more crushing than the infamous Black Hole of Calcutta.

Max smiled down at the woman who had all but accosted him, a petite redhead who hadn't taken a breath since she'd begun speaking. She was one of those contemptible females who twittered on and on without heed to the words that fell from their lovely mouths. Likely there was not a thought in her head beyond the silk dress on her back and the music in her ears and the curl of her hair. Her world did not, at this moment, extend beyond this room.

Mary Seton would be a fitting match for the man he pretended to be.

He hadn't had the opportunity to seek out Victor Chadwick as of yet. The man had been deep in conversation when Max had arrived, the focal point of a gaggle of loyalists. At one point while Max flirted and danced, the crowd Chadwick spoke to disbanded. He hadn't spotted the councilman since.

So far he had gleaned not a single piece of usable information. Overheard conversations were trivial and boring, nothing more than heated opinion or everyday gossip—nothing that would be of use to the Indigo Blade. He hid his disappointment well, but it wasn't easy. Surely this horrendous evening was not to be totally wasted.

Mary Seton continued to talk, and Max continued to smile while he tuned her out and listened to the conversations going on around them. He heard harmless chitchat for the most part, gossip and trivialities. Still, the murmur of politics filled the room, words filled with passion and half-hearted grumbling. Grumbling aside, this was a loyalist crowd, and no one was going to offer any real argument this evening.

Over Mary Seton's shoulder, Max saw that Chadwick was headed in his direction. There was a woman on his arm, but Max paid her little mind. He caught Chadwick's eye and lifted an indolent hand to wave the man over.

The verbose Miss Seton glanced over her shoulder to see who had stolen his attention. Her smile faded and then brightened almost immediately.

Chadwick's eyes were a touch too bright this evening, and he seemed to be having a difficult time maintaining his usually severe posture. The odor of rum arrived as the councilman did.

"Penelope, darling," Mary said, slipping a hand onto the elbow of the woman on Chadwick's arm. "Why, wherever have you been keeping yourself this evening? Mr. Broderick," she continued with an odd inflection, and without waiting for a response to her question, "this is my cousin, Miss Penelope Seton."

Max flashed an indolent grin as he reluctantly and dutifully shifted his attention from Chadwick to the woman at his side.

His heart surely stopped as he laid his eyes on her. Faith, he had danced all evening with beautiful women, but none could compare to the one before him. With her dark eyes and delicate features and regal bearing, she was absolutely exquisite. Flawless and comfortingly serene, perfect in shape and face. His smile faded. His facade slipped and drifted away for a moment, as his eyes held hers.

"A pleasure, Miss Seton."

She was annoyed when he took her hand and raised her fingers to his mouth, that much was obvious with a flash of her dark eyes and a thinning of her luscious lips. However, Max didn't allow her displeasure to force him to release her hand any sooner than he wished. He held onto her cool, delicate fingers much longer than was proper.

"Mr. Broderick," she said primly.

Mary Seton began to ramble on—again—but this time Max managed to tune her out completely. Her voice twittered in the background of his consciousness, a mild annoyance and nothing more. Chadwick turned a tight smile to Mary Seton, allowing Max to stare without caution at Penelope Seton for a moment longer.

She didn't flutter and fidget, she didn't speak, and she didn't turn her head or avert her eyes to avoid his penetrating stare. God in heaven, he would be content to spend the remainder of the evening lost in those dark eyes. Eyes that were touched with irritation at the moment, but beneath the vexation he saw more. He saw spirit and tenderness, intelligence and sophistication.

And he saw peace. His peace.

Heath Lowry, bless his soul, appeared and asked Mary to join him in a dance. A fat merchant came into view at Chadwick's side, and with an offered glass of rum and a gravely voiced question, he whisked the councilman away, leaving Max alone with Penelope Seton. With a gentle strength, she removed her hand from his and walked away with nothing more for him than a curt nod of her head.

He followed.

As Penelope passed an open doorway, Max stepped forward and took her arm, and with a gentle maneuver he drew her beyond the portal and into a small, unoccupied corner of a dimly lit library.

"Mr. Broderick!" Her voice was indignant, prim, but he could hear the heat that accompanied her admonishment. There was fire beneath the cool exterior, passion in her every breath. Penelope Seton was not like any other woman he'd ever known, not in looks or temperament.

"How dare I?" he whispered, happy to finish her thought for her.

"Yes," she answered softly. "How dare you?"

Penelope was against the wall, and he pinned her there without touching, without coming too close. "I dare because there are some things a man cannot say in the company of a hundred strangers."

"Mr. Broderick . . ."

He continued as if he hadn't heard her, certain that if she walked away now he would never have this opportunity again. This good fortune would not pass him by; he wouldn't allow it. "I could tell you that you're the most beautiful woman in the world, but you've heard that before, I'm sure." She didn't smile and she didn't frown, but maintained that calm and slightly exasperated front as if she were indulging a naughty child. Max didn't allow that to dissuade him. "So I tell you, in these few cherished moments away from the crowd that will surely close in upon us in a moment or two, that I love you quite madly." The words that came so easily from his mouth were unplanned, natural, and—amazingly—true.

He'd managed to shock her. Her eyes flashed, and her lips parted in surprise. What would she do, he wondered, if he covered those lush lips with his own? Shriek. Faint. Kiss him back. Perhaps all three.

"What kind of a game are you playing with me, Mr. Broderick?"

"No game, Miss Seton," Max said with a smile. "Although I will confess to you and to you alone that on occasion I have been known to be less than truthful, *this* is not one of those occasions."

"So you make a habit of falling in love quickly," she said sensibly. "I have no doubt you fall out of it just as quickly."

"I wouldn't know," he said truthfully. "I've never been in love before. I don't know how long it will last. I only know that it is quite an extraordinary and staggering affliction." Staggering—that was a correct assessment. A blow to the head couldn't have shaken him this completely.

She tapped his sleeve with the tip of her folded fan, a gentle admonishment for his behavior. "Perhaps what you mistake for love is a bit of bad beef or fish from your supper," she said lightly, taking it all as a game, still.

"No," he said seriously. "You don't believe me, do you?"

"No, I don't."

Ah, she didn't believe him at all. She was annoyed, perhaps even a bit amused . . . but then she did not know yet that this was a momentous occasion. He knew it, though. All his senses were on alert, making it a moment of clarity he would never forget.

"Will you take me more seriously if I tell you that I've never said those words to another woman? That I've never told another woman that I love her? That's the truth, Miss Seton, for until I saw your face I didn't know what love was."

Again, she tapped his arm with her fan. "I'm sure you find this a clever game, Mr. Broderick, but you'd have a more receptive partner in my cousin Mary, or Elizabeth Lowry, or any one of a dozen

Linda Jones

young women who seem to share a great admiration for—" She looked him up and down, slowly and with calculating eyes, her perusal pausing briefly, perhaps, at the excess of lace on his cuff and cravat. "—for men such as yourself."

This wasn't going to be easy. Penelope Seton wasn't going to take him at his word and fall into his arms with any declarations of her own. He couldn't simply claim this magnificent woman as his own, as he wished. A part of him was frustrated . . . and another part rejoiced. Nothing worth having came easily. True treasures were fought for and won at any and all cost, and Penelope would be no different.

"May I call on you tomorrow?" he pressed. Much as he would like, they couldn't hide in this corner of the library forever. The party went on just outside the open door, merriment and music, voices boisterous and soft melding into a music all its own.

"I don't think—"

"Even if you say no," he interrupted, "I'll seek you out. You can't stop me, not even if you have the entire British Army posted outside your door."

Finely shaped eyebrows raised cautiously. "You're an outrageous man, Maximillian Broderick."

"Perhaps." Max didn't feel outrageous at the moment, though he had to admit that his overwhelming passion for a woman he'd just met was unusual. Declaring it immediately was probably unwise. No, he didn't feel outrageous or unwise. He felt wonderfully, remarkably, good.

40

His attention was drawn away as Burton Lowry stepped into his library, an unlit cigar in one hand and a glass of cognac in the other. Another man, one unknown to Max, followed closely. Their voices were lowered, but Max caught a few very important words of that conversation.

"Just as I was about to leave the house," Max said loudly, forcing a return of his nasal whine, "my valet found a stain on my waistcoat. You can imagine my distress."

Penelope simply raised her eyebrows again. If she was surprised at the change in his voice or the direction of the conversation, she showed it only with her eyes. She didn't say a word, bless her.

"Broderick," Lowry said, turning about to face the couple in the corner. "I didn't see you there."

"Miss Seton and I have been having a fascinating discussion about the selection and care of good imported silk."

Lowry's eyes glazed over, and his lip curled slightly in what could only be disgust. "Interesting," he mumbled.

"I must be going," Penelope said, stepping quickly past Max and, with a swish of her skirts, heading for the door. Once there, with the festivities waiting before her, she turned about and gave him a smile. A smile that spoke of secrets and curiosity, a smile that—in Max's fertile and hopeful imagination—whispered of a thousand nights yet to come.

"Tomorrow afternoon," she said softly.

Max nodded once, unable to speak.

She was a picture framed in the doorway, a vision

he would not soon forget. A wave of something powerful and heretofore unknown washed through him. He recognized it for what it was. Possession. The realization that this was *his* woman.

Her voice remained low, and for his ears alone. "Two o'clock."

Chapter Three

The carriage rocked slightly as it made the turn, and Penelope swayed into her cousin. Mary jumped, apparently startled by the contact.

"Sorry," Penelope whispered, trying not to disturb her uncle, who appeared to be half-asleep already.

Mary was unusually pensive, perhaps even troubled. She didn't smile and immediately forgive her cousin, as she generally did. Penelope reached out and tucked an unruly strand of red hair behind Mary's ear.

"Didn't you have a good time?"

"Of course I had a good time," Mary answered, her voice as low as Penelope's. "I'm just tired, that's all."

Penelope slipped her arm through Mary's. "Where did you disappear to after that dance with

Heath Lowry? I looked for you everywhere. . . ."

"I was overheated and went for a walk in the gardens," Mary answered testily.

"Alone?"

"Yes." It was more a breath than even a whisper. "Alone."

"It's awfully chilly for a long walk in the garden," Penelope observed.

"The room was crowded and overly warm," Mary said curtly. "I needed fresh air, chilly or not."

For a few minutes all was silent again. There was only the creak of the wheels and the steady clop of the horses' hooves against the road. It was almost enough to lull Penelope into an uneasy sleep herself.

"What did Mr. Broderick have to say to you?" Mary asked, her words quick and soft.

"What?"

"I saw the two of you slip into the library while I was dancing with Heath." Mary's tone was accusing and somewhat petulant.

"It was nothing, really," Penelope said, uncertain as to what she could share with her cousin. "He's a . . . a very strange man."

That was the truth. Strong hands dripping with lace, eyes that were lazy one moment and piercing the next, a voice that went from hypnotic to whining in a heartbeat.

"He's the richest and the most handsome man in all of Charles Town, and he was besotted from the moment he laid eyes on you." Mary sighed, perhaps in resignation. "Why didn't he look at me like that?"

Penelope often had a hard time knowing if Mary

wanted to be comforted or ignored. Tonight, in this restless state, she assumed her cousin needed consolation of some sort. "I saw lots of adoring glances cast your way tonight," she said softly. "Why, when I danced with Heath Lowry, all he did was talk about you and ask about your plans while we're in town. I wouldn't be surprised if he called on you before the week is out."

"Heath is a child."

"He's four years older than you," Penelope said.

"And still he's a child," Mary said haughtily. "I'm not interested in children, I'm interested in procuring a husband. Preferably a man, Penelope, and not a boy."

"And what if you fall in love with a mere boy?" Penelope's voice was light, teasing, but her mind immediately went to Maximillian Broderick and his outrageous avowal. It was an absurd notion that you could simply look at a person and fall in love. Surely you learned to like a person first, to admire and respect that person, and then—perhaps—love would come.

"I won't," Mary said decidedly. "I would never make the mistake of falling in love with a man who wouldn't make a proper husband."

To Penelope, who was usually by far the more sensible of the Seton cousins, Maximillian Broderick's extreme opinions on love made more sense than Mary's. A person didn't coldly choose love. Penelope expected that if she were lucky, love would find and embrace her one day, but she didn't expect it was as easy and quick as Maximillian made it sound, nor as calculating and unemotional as Mary seemed to think.

"I don't think you choose love," Penelope said softly, unable to shake completely the memory of warm lips against her fingers. "I think it chooses you."

Mary shook her head as if she disagreed, but for once she said nothing.

Penelope leaned back in her seat, grateful that Mary had decided to let the conversation die. When she closed her eyes, she saw Maximillian Broderick leaning slightly toward her, a sparkle in his blue-gray eyes and an impossible declaration of love on his lips.

They were closed in his study, the drapes shut tight against prying eyes in the night, a single candle burning low.

"There's a village north and west of Charles Town, Cypress Crossroads by name."

The six men before him waited expectantly.

"There are a good number of agitators in that village," Max continued. "And Chadwick's had his eye on them for some time."

John piped up. "There's a very nice tavern there," he muttered, his voice muddy and thick. "Good ale, clean mugs, good-looking bar maids . . ."

"So you know where this village is," Max interrupted, not anxious for a rousing and too-long description of the Cypress Crossroads tavern.

John grumbled his assent, and Lewis nodded his head.

"At dawn on the day after tomorrow, there will

be a raid. All weapons will be confiscated, and anyone who resists will be shot."

"They will most definitely resist," Lewis said solemnly. "They're a headstrong lot, those villagers."

It was as he'd suspected, from the gleeful plans he'd overheard. "Not if there's nothing to take. Not if the good people of Cypress Crossroads are prepared."

It was Fletcher who nodded first, knowing what Max had in mind. "They'll need an underground shelter or a secret room or perhaps both. Something the British soldiers won't be able to find, but that the villagers can get to in a hurry when the time comes."

"I'll leave it to you. You'd best leave first thing in the morning. Take Beck and John with you. Dalton, too, if you think you'll need him."

"We'll need all the hands we can get," Fletcher said glumly. "I take it you have other plans?"

How much could he say to these men? His comrades, his family, men he'd trust his very life to. In spite of all this, he hesitated before answering. "I'm infiltrating the Seton household tomorrow," he said steadily. "It's an excellent way to get close to Chadwick, as he's a devoted friend to William Seton and his family."

How devoted? he wondered. When he'd first seen Penelope, she'd been on Chadwick's arm. Ah, that feeling of possession he'd experienced was rearing its ugly head.

"Infiltrate how?" Garrick asked suspiciously.

"William Seton has a niece, Penelope. I'll be calling on her tomorrow afternoon." Max kept his voice steady, cool to the point of iciness.

"So while I'm digging a cellar, up to my elbows in mud, you'll be romancing some poor unsuspecting chit," Dalton said with his usual even and emotionless tone.

Max flashed a devil-may-care grin. "That's correct." Already he was questioning the powerful notions that had washed over him as he'd looked into Penelope Seton's eyes, the rush of intense longing that had coursed through him as he'd held her hand. It had been a moment of madness, surely.

But he could still see her lovely face, still hear her musical voice clearly in his besotted mind, while the evening's mundane memories faded away.

He directed his attention back to the planning of the mission. John was acquainted with the owner of the Cypress Crossroads tavern, who was a well-respected local leader. The tavern owner would serve as their liaison with the community, and by the time Chadwick's soldiers arrived, there would be nothing for them to confiscate but perhaps a useless rusty musket and a dull knife. They'd be greeted with cooperative, smiling faces. No one had to die, not this time.

One by one, the men filed out of Max's study, until only Max and Fletcher remained. Following the cacophony of seven voices actively planning the mission, the room was much too quiet for a long uncomfortable moment. The clock ticked, suddenly loud in the night. The candle's flame flickered. Max stared at the top of his desk, and Fletcher took a silent step forward.

"There's something you're not telling us," Fletcher accused. "Something's wrong."

"Nothing's wrong." Of the crew, Max had known Garrick the longest, but Fletcher had always had an uncanny ability to see right through him. To see right through them all. Fletcher answered, when asked, that it was his mother's Irish blood that had given him a kind of second sight. Max knew that what enabled Fletcher to read people so well was simple quiet observation and reasoning. It was perception, not a gift from the fairies.

And Fletcher knew Max far too well to be fooled now.

"Nothing's wrong," Max said again, "but there is a small, very minor, inconvenient complication."

Fletcher sighed and sat on the edge of Max's walnut desk. "A woman." He breathed the words, low, as he might have a curse.

Resigned, Max sat in the leather-covered armchair behind his desk. He relaxed for the first time since glimpsing Penelope Seton, thrust his ridiculously lavender-clad legs forward, and a true smile crossed his face. "Yes, a woman."

Fletcher grumbled something foul, but Max's mood could not be spoiled. "She's quite remarkable," he continued, for some unknown reason compelled to do his best to convince Fletcher of Penelope Seton's worth. "Beautiful, sweet, intelligent . . ."

"What did you do, spend the entire evening mooning after some maid when you should have been hounding Chadwick?" Fletcher snapped. "I'm not wasting my time risking my life while you go off—"

"Five minutes," Max interrupted softly. "I spent no more than five minutes in her company."

Fletcher groaned. "And that was enough to convince you that this Penelope Seton is some paragon of womanhood?"

"No," Max whispered. "It didn't even take five minutes. I only had to look at her." His earlier doubts fled, as the memory of that first glance came back to astound him with its clarity and power.

This time Fletcher did curse aloud, his words low and filthy but very clear. Max allowed his friend the outlet, smiling as he waited for the Irishman to finish.

"You've been too long without a woman," Fletcher finally said reasonably.

"I have," Max allowed.

"Let me take you to this house I know."

"No." What ailed him couldn't be cured by another woman, couldn't be erased by an emotionless pleasurable act. God in heaven, he didn't want to be cured of this particular ailment.

"You can't allow yourself to be taken in by a calculating female, not now."

"Penelope is not a calculating female," Max said defensively. Too defensively, perhaps. "And there's no reason for you to worry about my involvement with her. I can keep my personal life and the work of the Indigo Blade separate."

"You've become infatuated with the niece of a loyalist, and you can sit there and tell me it won't interfere with your enterprise?" Fletcher scoffed.

"Are you lying to me, or are you really so blinded by your ardor that you can't see what a folly this is?"

Max could always count on Fletcher for sound reasoning. In the heat of battle, in the midst of a storm, in their darkest hour, Fletcher had always been the voice of sanity in an insane world.

"Don't forget that through Penelope I can infiltrate a loyalist household and perhaps get close to Chadwick," he reasoned. "Even if I find that I'm wrong and Penelope isn't all that I believe her to be, this is still a good move."

"I don't know about that. It could jeopardize everything."

Max wasn't ready to admit that the Irishman might be right. But he was able to admit to himself that it didn't matter, not in the least. He would court Penelope Seton, he would look into those eyes and touch that hand again—and he would handle the consequences as they came.

It was afternoon when Penelope came downstairs. She'd taken great care in choosing her gown for the day, finally settling on a green silk print dress with a ruffle at the neck and the sleeves. It was becoming without being ostentatious. Flattering and yet simple. She wouldn't want anyone to think she'd gone to any trouble over Maximillian Broderick's impending visit—even though she had spent more than an hour choosing this particular gown.

He would likely look at her today and realize that last night's flirtation had been a whimsy, and nothing more. Perhaps he'd had too much sweet wine to drink, or had been carried away by the music and the dance, and today he would look into her eyes with that piercing stare of his and see that she was just an ordinary woman, unworthy of instant adoration. Still, his visit was likely to be entertaining, a much-needed diversion.

Her uncle came out of his study so quickly and crisply, she was certain he'd been waiting and watching for her.

"Penelope, my dear," he said, taking both her hands in his and kissing her cheek. "You look especially lovely this afternoon."

Her uncle William was not much taller than she, and in the past few years his middle had expanded and rounded and his hairline had receded greatly. He wore powdered wigs much of the time, but not at home.

"I can't believe I slept so late in the day," she said with a genuine smile. "Too much excitement last night, I suppose." Maximillian Broderick's face immediately came to mind.

He patted her hand. "I'm sorry we old men stole Victor away for so much of the evening. Why, you likely didn't see him nearly as much as you would've liked."

"I had a lovely time," she said without elaborating.

"I'm going to make it up to you," Uncle William said with a sly wink. "I've invited Victor for supper this evening, and I've promised to give you two some time alone."

He'd promised whom? Victor, of course. There would likely be another unwanted proposal of marriage, and she'd have no choice but to refuse. Not only would Victor be hurt, but her uncle would be furious with her as well. It was a scene she was anxious to avoid—or delay.

"Well, we can have a grand party this evening," she said with a wide smile. "You see, I was just on my way to tell you that I've also invited a guest to dine with us. He'll be calling on me this afternoon, and I thought it would be just lovely if he could stay for supper."

Her uncle's smile faded away. Frown lines appeared on his forehead, and his mouth puckered unpleasantly. She was well acquainted with his obvious look of displeasure, though it had never been directed at her. Tyler and Mary were usually the recipients of this scowl.

"I had no idea." Still, William Seton was a gracious host, and would not refuse her or her guest. "Who have you invited?"

"Maximillian Broderick," she said, hoping that the odd Mr. Broderick wouldn't decline her invitation when it was put to him this afternoon. "He hasn't been in Charles Town very long, and I thought it would be most kind of you to entertain him. It's our responsibility to offer the poor man a meal, don't you agree?"

"Poor man? He's as rich as any ten successful merchants in Charles Town!" Uncle William's face turned red and his eyes narrowed, but luckily he didn't suggest that she uninvite Maximillian.

"I only meant that he's surely in need of friends, being new in Charles Town and without any family."

He had no choice but to agree with her, though he seemed to do so grudgingly.

The thought that came to Penelope was devious, and wasn't like her, not at all. She would have thought the plan formulating in her mind unkind, if she'd believed a word of Maximillian's assertion of love. Fortunately, she didn't. He was using her as a diversion, no doubt, so surely he wouldn't object if she used him to scare off Victor and his unwanted attentions.

Not that she would tell him of her harmless scheme, of course.

By the time Maximillian arrived, promptly at two o'clock, Penelope was more than happy to see him. She was elated.

Mary watched, motionless and silent. They didn't know she was there, most likely wouldn't have known even if she'd leaned from the second-story window and waved her arms frantically.

Penelope and Maximillian Broderick had been in the garden most of the afternoon, talking and laughing. Walking arm in arm in the sun, sitting side by side in the shade. The day was cool, but not cold, and they both wore long velvet capes that brushed together frequently. Even that unconscious contact was somehow intimate.

They sat now, in dappled shade surrounded by early-blooming wild roses. They touched often, ever so lightly and quickly as if by accident. Hand to hand as they shifted on the bench, shoulder to shoulder as Maximillian leaned toward Penelope . . . and it was no accident, of that Mary was certain.

Maximillian Broderick plucked a rose from a nearby bush, carefully removed the thorns, and then placed the rose behind Penelope's ear. His hand lingered, perhaps brushing her ear with those long fingers.

It wasn't fair. Why should Penelope have everything? Penelope Seton was nothing, nobody, an orphan, a poor relation Mary tolerated magnanimously. And everyone loved her. Mary's own father, the servants at the plantation, Victor, and now Maximillian Broderick.

Mary placed the palm of her hand against the glass and closed her eyes as Penelope laughed again.

She'd tried to do what was right, she really had. Her father forever compared her unfavorably to her older cousin, and she'd been taught again and again that nothing she did was ever quite good enough. She wasn't as smart as Penelope, not as ladylike, not as desirable. Penelope and Tyler had moved in, and William Seton's love and attention had been unfairly divided. Mary was never allowed to forget that Penelope was a paragon she should admire and emulate.

In spite of all that, she'd tried to do what was right. She'd tried to accept and love her cousin, and there had been times when she truly did cherish Penelope—but last night everything had changed.

Last night in the Lowrys' garden, while the ball was in progress just a short distance away, Victor had kissed her at last. She'd believed, for a few precious moments, that he had finally come around. That he loved her. That was why she hadn't protested when he'd touched her so intimately. That was why she had allowed him to thrust his tongue into her mouth, and to move her even farther into the shadows.

He'd tasted and smelled of rum and cigars, a manly and rather unpleasant combination she still remembered so vividly that it was as if it was forever a part of her. Perhaps it was true. The very idea made her stomach roil.

When Victor had lifted her skirts she'd been afraid, but she hadn't said anything. Cold air had whipped beneath her skirts, even colder fingers pushed and prodded, and she'd uttered not a word of protest. This was proof that he loved her, of that she was certain, and so as he spread her legs even wider and freed his manhood, she kissed him back with all the ardor she could muster.

It had hurt, but she'd bitten her tongue and accepted the pain and the invasion without protest. The act had been painful at first, and then merely uncomfortable, but it had been mercifully quick. She'd tolerated it all, welcomed it, because it was proof that Victor had finally realized that he loved *her*.

That illusion had kept her happy, as long as it had lasted. Unfortunately it hadn't lasted long. Victor had told her, still huffing and sweating from the encounter, that after he and Penelope were wed he would like to continue their relationship. He found her, he said, an exciting woman. He would teach her, he said, how to please him and how to please herself.

She'd protested then—hadn't she? Softly whispered protests that he must love her, objections that had stuck in her throat. She'd been stunned and hurt and she couldn't quite believe what she'd been hearing. How could he even consider marrying Penelope after what had just happened?

Victor had even reminded her, as he straightened his trousers, that if she told anyone what had happened it would reflect more badly on her than on him. She was a vixen, he said, and no one would believe that she hadn't tempted him beyond reason with the intention of tricking him into marriage.

At that moment she'd known the truth—that Victor didn't love her at all, and that no one ever would.

On the trip home, she'd tried to ignore the ripped underclothes beneath her fine gown, the soreness and the stickiness between her legs, the pounding of her heart that threatened to burst through her chest. She wanted to scream and cry, but didn't dare.

Penelope, serene and safe at her side, had spoken naively of love and of choices while Mary had fought the screams and the tears that were building inside her. It was then that Mary had realized how she hated her cousin.

In the garden below, Maximillian Broderick leaned close and whispered into Penelope's ear. Penelope laughed, and when she turned her head Mary saw a bright and brilliant smile.

It wasn't fair.

Chapter Four

Penelope couldn't remember the last time she'd had such a fine day.

Maximillian had arrived, resplendent in royal-blue silk and a silver waistcoat, with flowers and compliments and a dazzling smile for her and her alone. He'd watched as she'd painted a simple watercolor of a cluster of flowers, and then she'd blushed as he declared it a masterpiece. When the day grew too cool, they retired to the parlor for a cup of chocolate and a game of backgammon. Throughout the day they'd talked and laughed, and the hours had flown by so quickly she couldn't believe how fast the afternoon disappeared.

Even now, sharing their dinner with her uncle and Victor Chadwick and a sulking Mary, Penelope was uncommonly happy.

Maximillian was seated at her side, and when the

discussion at the table deviated to politics, he turned to her and they had their own soft conversation about music and art and roses.

There was something hypnotic about this man. He had not professed again to love her, but he had given her his undivided attention since his arrival hours earlier, and there were times she was certain they communicated without words, that he could look at her with those hypnotic eyes and know what she was thinking. She found it not odd at all, but strangely comforting.

"Mr. Broderick." Her uncle's voice snapped sharply from the opposite end of the table. "You have nothing to add to this conversation?"

A subtle change came over Maximillian's face. The bright eyes dulled, the lids drooped as he turned to face William Seton. "Faith, my good man, you're discussing politics, and Penelope and I have agreed that the topic is much too dull. We have resolved, in fact, not to discuss politics at all."

He gave Penelope's uncle a weak, lazy smile.

"How can you have no interest," Victor returned without patience, "in something so important as the possibility of revolution? Have you no allegiance to your king?"

Maximillian withdrew a fine handkerchief from a lace-trimmed pocket in his waistcoat, and stifled a yawn with linen and lace held daintily to his mouth. "Pardon me," he said as he returned the handkerchief to its place. "You see, the mere mention of politics and I begin to fade like a plucked daisy in a dry vase."

Penelope laughed at this outrageous comment,

and Maximillian turned a blank expression to her, eyebrows slightly raised and chin lifted obstinately. "Are you laughing at me, m'dear?" The lifting of the corners of his mouth was so slight, Penelope was certain no one but she saw it. It was a smile meant for her and her alone.

"You're an amusing dinner companion, Maximillian. How could I not laugh?"

He took her hand and lifted it to his lips. "Laugh at me all you like," he said softly, and without the artificial lilt that had been in his voice a moment earlier. "I can forgive you anything."

As his mouth lingered warmly over her fingers, she felt something of the emotion he had no doubt mistaken for love. It was a kinship and a longing, a recognized connection that she felt with no one else in this world combined with an insatiable need to know more. It was exciting and comforting at the same time.

The intoxicating mingling of emotions could easily be mistaken for love, she was certain.

When the meal was finished and at last the diners stood, Uncle William turned his full and undivided attention to Penelope, and she realized with a sinking heart that she'd likely not gotten away with her little subterfuge after all. She'd only delayed the inevitable.

"Penelope, Victor would like a private word with you, if you can tear yourself away from your . . . guest." Her uncle had always been a blunt man, and this evening was no different. "Mr. Broderick, it's been a pleasure having you in my home," he said without a grain of sincerity. "Now, if you'll excuse us, we have some family affairs to discuss."

Penelope's smile faded as Maximillian looked down at her. The day had been wonderful, but Uncle William and Victor were about to ruin it. How could she thank this man she barely knew for a day worth remembering—for touching her heart, for looking at her now as if he understood how she felt?

"Nonsense," Maximillian said grandly, and he gave her a small, private smile before turning to face Victor. "This day has been much too trying for Penelope, and she's certainly not up to delving into any family affairs this evening. Perhaps in the morning," he suggested with a wave of his hand.

"I have an engagement that will keep me occupied in the morning," Victor said bluntly.

"I really am quite exhausted," Penelope said.

"Tomorrow afternoon, perhaps," Victor suggested testily.

"Mercy, that won't do at all," Maximillian said with another graceful wave of his hand. "Penelope and I have planned a picnic for tomorrow afternoon." He smiled down at her once again, a wide false smile unlike the other. "Isn't that right, m'dear?"

Somehow he knew what was going on, and he was doing his best to rescue her. At that moment, she did love him. "I have already promised Maximillian that we'd spend the afternoon together," she lied.

"Well, it looks as if your family business will have to wait for another day," Maximillian said as he took Penelope's arm and led her from the dining room. Without pausing, he escorted her to the foot of the staircase that led to the second floor.

"Will you be all right?" he asked without affectation.

"Yes, thanks to you," she whispered. "How did you know?"

He placed a finger beneath her chin and held it there, firm and soft, demanding and affectionate. "Because you tell everything with your eyes. When I see fear there, I must do whatever I can to take it away."

She thought, for a moment, that he would kiss her. He wanted to, that much she could tell, and against all reasoning she wanted him to. Out of gratitude perhaps, she mused, or curiosity, though she'd never before been curious about the feel of a man's mouth against her own. Before she could decide exactly why she wanted Maximillian to kiss her, she heard her uncle and Victor approaching, and apparently so did he.

"Hurry along," he whispered, "before they come to their senses and demand that I leave you to your blasted family affairs."

She turned her back on his smile and hurried up the stairs.

"Noon," he said as she ran toward the sanctuary of the second floor and her bedchamber. "I'll be here tomorrow precisely at noon."

In spite of a late night, Max was up with the sun, berating himself for not participating in the Cypress Crossroads venture and wondering if the endeavor went well. At the same time, he looked forward to another day in Penelope's company.

Fletcher was right. No matter how he fought it, his budding relationship with Penelope was going to interfere with his work—and his work was going to interfere with his relationship with Penelope. He'd always been single-minded and unfailingly dedicated, but this situation was already tearing him apart.

What was right? That was not always an easy question to answer. This fight for freedom was right, of that he was certain. Claiming Penelope as his own was right; he felt it in his heart. His heart demanded that he dedicate himself to both causes, that he throw caution to the wind and reach for all he desired.

At least he didn't have long to wait to find out the details of the Cypress Crossroads adventure. John, Dalton, and Beck had stayed behind—in disguise of course—but Fletcher had made his way home in the wee hours of the morning.

The ladies Beck had hired to see to the kitchen and the upkeep of the big house were happy to accommodate Max when he asked them to prepare a magnificent picnic lunch for him and his lady friend. The same ladies were shocked when he decided to forego breakfast at the vast and finely furnished dining room table in favor of carrying two cups of coffee to the livery to share with his stableman.

The others had rooms in the house, luxurious chambers on the third floor. But not Fletcher. He'd never been one for fancy places or people. He preferred the stable and the company of his beloved horses to an elegant chamber in a courtly mansion.

While the others slept in comfort, the ornery Fletcher bedded down on a cot in a tiny room that had been added to the stable just for him.

Max wasn't surprised to find his friend already tending to the horses.

"Coffee?" he asked as he stepped into the shelter.

Fletcher didn't turn around, nor did he seem to be surprised at Max's appearance. "In a minute."

Max waited for Fletcher to finish his chores, smiling as he watched his friend's back. Fletcher had a small fortune of his own, but no one would ever know it to look at him. This seemed to be all he wanted in the world: a roof over his head, fine horses all around, and a bottle of whiskey hidden somewhere close by.

"How did it go?" Max asked as he handed Fletcher the warm china cup.

"Flawlessly," Fletcher said woodenly, as if he'd expected nothing else. "The villagers were most co-operative. A cellar in the tavern was converted to an arsenal, as was a secreted room in a farm at the edge of town. I expect Chadwick and his soldiers had quite a surprise when they marched into Cypress Crossroads this morning and found that the sleepy little village was not what they expected. I imagine they're madly rummaging about the hamlet as we speak, searching for weapons and revolutionaries they will not find. How went your afternoon of romance?"

Max grinned. "Flawlessly."

Fletcher shot him a black glance. "You always did have a maddening propensity for purposely playing with fire."

Max thought of asking the Irishman if he'd ever been in love, but he knew what the answer would be—a harsh laugh and the insistence that no love beat in Fletcher Huxley's black heart.

"I dined in Victor Chadwick's company," Max said coolly. "And while I did not participate in the conversation, I did happen to overhear that he's expecting additional troops to arrive by ship at the end of the month."

"That information might be useful," Fletcher grudgingly acknowledged.

"When Dalton returns from Cypress Crossroads, I want him to get in touch with his friend from Williamsburg."

"The one who transported the boy who was to hang?"

"The very one."

Fletcher grinned and sipped at his cooling coffee. "If the ship transporting those troops was to be met at sea by a number of privateers, and if that ship and her occupants were stripped of arms and sent limping back to England, they wouldn't be much good to Chadwick at all, now would they?"

"Not at all," Max said primly, slipping into the persona that allowed him to pass among the loyalists without question.

Charles Town was beautiful, a paradise of palm fronds and flowing water and flowers of every color, a city of many fine houses, a busy harbor for ships of every size.

Never had it seemed so beautiful to Penelope as it did today. Maximillian had arrived on her doorstep promptly at noon, with a driver and footman and a very large basket containing enough food to feed a dozen hungry people.

They'd traveled north at a leisurely pace until she could no longer see the bay or the familiar ships or the fine homes of Charles Town. The carriage stopped in a deserted field surrounded by trees, and on a quilt of greens and blues the footman had laid out a feast.

And now they sat, the bright sun warming them on this mild February day. Maximillian seemed content to watch her as she sketched their near-wild surroundings, and she found she was amazingly content in his company. His footman and driver—an odd couple if ever she saw one—waited a good distance away. They shared their own meal and soft conversation, though now and again their openly curious eyes turned this way.

Their occasional perusal didn't bother Penelope. She wouldn't allow anything to spoil this afternoon. She was very aware that she wouldn't have many more days like this one, days free and happy, hours simply to sit and enjoy a beautiful day and the company of a man who had somehow worked his way into her heart.

"What's wrong?" Maximillian asked softly.

"Nothing." Penelope laid her paper and chalk aside, and turned her full attention to her companion. "What makes you think something's suddenly wrong?"

His ever-present smile faded. "The light in your eyes grew dull, your chin dropped in what appeared to be defeat, and something akin to a frown marred the perfection of your mouth. Your hand stilled, your breath quickened, and I knew that something had stolen the happiness that had been so much a part of you just a moment earlier."

Had anyone ever watched her so closely or known her so well? Penelope shifted and turned to face Maximillian, her feet tucked beneath her, her hands on the soft quilt that cushioned them from the hard ground; she leaned forward just slightly. She could confide in this man, she knew it. In her heart, in her always sensible mind . . . in a place within her so deep she hadn't yet completely fathomed it.

"I'm afraid it has to do with Uncle William's family affairs."

"I suspected as much."

"You see, last year, Victor Chadwick asked me to marry him."

A fire flashed and quickly died in Maximillian's eyes, clear eyes that were an odd color that was not gray nor blue nor green, but somehow all three. Those eyes changed with his mood—and the color of silk he wore. "I do hope you said no. I can't for the life of me imagine a woman like you married to a dull toad like Chadwick."

"I said no," Penelope said, "but I don't think Victor understood. When I told him I wasn't ready for marriage, he seemed to think that if he asked at a later date my answer would be different. I wish I'd had the nerve to tell him then that I have no desire to marry him, ever." If she had just a smidgen of Mary's courage, she wouldn't be in this mess. "And of course Uncle William is determined to see me married to the man of his choosing. He admires Victor, his politics and his power, his money. This time when Victor asks, I don't think my uncle will allow me to say no."

The fire was in Maximillian's eyes again, and this time it didn't fade quickly away but burned deep, becoming a part of him. "I can't allow that to happen."

"I don't think there's anything you or I can do to avoid it. If I defy Uncle William and refuse Victor again, he's likely to disown me. Tyler, too."

"The brother you speak of with such love."

"Yes. It would be devastating to Tyler—"

Penelope was silenced when Maximillian lifted his hand to her cheek. His fingers were warm, and his caress was so tender it nearly brought tears to her eyes.

"Marry me," he whispered.

"What?" Her own response was quick and soft. Surely she hadn't heard him correctly.

"Marry me." The smile was back.

"I hardly know you." It was true, and at the same time it was a blatant lie. Whom did she know as well as this man she'd met just two days ago? There was no one else she could share her dreams and fears with, laugh and cry with—no one. The connection had been immediate and disturbing, and she couldn't deny the affection that continued to blossom.

"You know how very much I adore you, that you captured my heart the moment I laid eyes on you, that we share a bond that's rare and wonderful. Isn't that enough?"

"I don't know . . ."

"Marry me, Penelope Seton." There was such wondrous passion in his voice that it touched her heart. "Throw caution to the wind, defy your uncle and Victor Chadwick, live dangerously."

His hand still at her cheek, Maximillian waited for an answer.

"I must be honest with you," she said, placing her hand over his. "I don't know that what I feel for you is love. I wish I could be as sure as you are, but I've always been a cautious one."

"I'll make you love me," he whispered.

"And if I say yes," she said quickly, "I might very well come to you with nothing. Uncle William may offer no dowry to a man who is not of his choosing. He might toss me out with nothing but the clothes on my back."

"I don't care."

"It might be quite a scandal."

"I love scandal." He was confident, smug even, but without warning the mask fell away and she saw a glimpse of raw pain and longing. "But if we're going to be perfectly honest with one another before finalizing our plans, there's something I must tell you."

Penelope steeled herself for the worst. He had a wife and a dozen children in England. He was dying of a horrid disease. He didn't really love her . . .

"I am the youngest son of an earl, a very rich and powerful man with an estate north of London. My mother was a kitchen maid on that country estate." Maximillian's words were clipped and harsh, filled with anguish, and Penelope would not have interrupted for all the world. She wanted to know more about this man, and she recognized his need to tell the story, to be certain that no secrets came between them. "Of course he never married her, even though his third wife and mother to his sixth and seventh sons was long dead. She was seventeen when I was born, twenty-eight years ago. He was fifty-three."

His hand dropped from her face, but she wasn't ready to let him go. Her hand remained atop his even as it fell, and she slowly and boldly wrapped her fingers through his.

"While he never legitimized me, he did recognize and abide me. After my mother died, when I was six, he took me in. I had a room with the servants, and I was tolerated as long as I stayed silent and invisible." He stared at her with such intensity she could feel the pain. "My father saw me clothed and fed, he made sure I received the finest education any bastard deserved, and in return all I had to do was stay out of his way."

He held her hand tightly.

"And all was well, until I went to London. You see, of his eight children, all sons, I am the one who bears the strongest resemblance to my father. My presence in London embarrassed him, and more importantly it mortified my eldest half-brother and heir to the title. I found I rather enjoyed being the torment of my fine family." The smile that crossed his face was a bitter one, a poor attempt on his part to dismiss the importance of his story. "I drank too much, I dallied with the affections of the daughters and wives of my father's acquaintances, and eventually I gambled away every cent I had."

"You don't have to do this." For all that she and Maximillian were very different, she could see the similarities in their childhoods. An ocean apart, they'd spent years without a mother's love, years trying to fit in. To be, as he said, invisible. The difference was, Maximillian had found the strength to rebel.

"I do." He brought her fingers to his lips and then dropped their joined hands into his lap. "My father's solution to his troublesome bastard was to ship me off to the East India Company, where I would either make my fortune or perish. It was quite clear that he preferred the latter possibility."

"But you are stronger than you allow others to see," Penelope said. "You surprised him, didn't you?"

He gave her a small smile. A real one. "That I did. I made my fortune, but in the end I had no desire to go back to London and resume my role as the family black sheep. It wasn't home—it was hell. I wanted something fresh and new."

"Something like Charles Town."

"And you, if you'll have a bastard for a husband."

Penelope brought their joined hands to her lips and kissed Maximillian's fingers as he had hers. The simple brush of his mouth against her hand brought her such comfort, and she wanted to offer him whatever solace she could at this moment. More than that, she wanted very much to know the man behind the fine manners and silk, and she was certain at this moment that there was a man very much worth knowing behind the facade.

"I find, as I sit here contemplating the future, that it matters not at all."

"We'll never discuss it again," he added brusquely. "It's been years since I spoke of my father, and if his name never passes these lips again, I won't regret it. Broderick was my mother's family name, the name he always insisted I use. It's the name I offer you, Penelope."

If she'd had any doubts earlier, they were now gone, whisked away by the glimpse of a man worthy of a life's devotion.

"Ask me again," she whispered, squeezing his hand tightly.

"Penelope Seton," he said huskily, "will you be my wife?"

"I will." There was not a single doubt in her mind, no regrets or recriminations.

"We'll be married tomorrow," he said with a smile.

Penelope laughed. A real true and unfettered laugh. "Tomorrow! Impossible. It will take at least a month to make the arrangements. The posting of the banns, a proper gown, and of course I must have Tyler here for the wedding, and he's still at my uncle's plantation."

"Impossible," Maximillian said seriously. "I can't wait a month to make you my wife."

"Three weeks?"

"One," he countered.

"Two," Penelope offered with a smile as wide as his own. "The banns must be posted for a fortnight."

Maximillian seemed at least to consider this compromise. "I could arrange for a waiving of the banns, you know," he offered quickly. "A fortnight." He sighed after a moment's consideration. "Seems like a terribly long time at the moment, but as I've waited a lifetime for you, m'love, I suppose I can wait two more weeks." He rocked up on his knees, and with that simple movement he towered above her. "A kiss to seal the bargain?"

"Yes." Before the agreement was out of her mouth, he was touching her, his lips over hers, his arms protectively encircling, and a warm and wonderful feeling washed over and through Penelope as he joined their mouths gently. The kiss was not demanding or harsh, but warm and intoxicating in the most extraordinary way. The kiss lingered. Penelope was in no hurry to break away, and apparently neither was Maximillian.

What a wonderful feeling this was. She was safe in these arms, she was loved, and she had just agreed to take as her husband a man she had already begun to love.

Chapter Five

"You're doing *what*?" Fletcher thundered.

"He's getting married," Garrick said with a distinct lack of emotion. "In a mere two weeks, I might add."

Lewis piped up, his usual lighthearted voice tinged with irritation. "Garrick and I were the first to be told, you know. And all we could do was nod submissively and wish the happy couple our best." He turned his cool eyes on Max. "Does this mean I have to be the driver all the time? Twenty-four hours a day, seven days a week, Lewis Turner the driver? And Garrick a footman!"

This was much the same reaction they'd gotten in the Seton household, when together he and Penelope had broken the news to her uncle. Disbelief, followed by irritation, which would soon be followed, if the chain of emotions stayed true, by horror.

"Good God!" Beck shouted. "Lewis is right. It's bad enough now, having to pretend to be servants while the cook and the maids are here, but at least they go home once supper is prepared, and they have a day off once a week. What's your bride going to say when we go riding off into the night? What's she going to say when the butler refuses to answer the door or when she finds out that I, who am supposedly in charge of the kitchen, can't boil a pot of water without assistance?"

Max had thought of all this, the numerous problems his marriage would create, but simply didn't care. In a fortnight, Penelope would be his wife. Nothing else mattered. She was all he'd ever wanted from life, and yet more than he'd ever expected to have. Obstacles be damned. "She'll have to be told, eventually," he conceded.

"You trust her that much?" John grumbled.

"I do."

"An engagement," Dalton suggested sensibly. "A nice, long, romantic betrothal. Shall we say two years?"

Max couldn't help but smile. "No."

They were all talking at once, all arguing, all violently opposed to this marriage. They seemed to think, to a man, that he'd lost his mind.

When there was a lull in the conversation, a low pitch in the roar that filled the room, Max spoke. "I love her. I want this marriage more than I've ever wanted anything in my life. More than respectability, more than money, more than justice. When we decided to come to these colonies to start over, I expected the fortune I made in the East to buy everything I'd ever need. A home, a position, and one day a suitable wife. I never expected this, but I refuse to turn my back on a heavenly gift because it comes at a bad time.

"I love her, and I need her."

Max's declaration silenced the men arguing before him. Dalton and John even had the good grace to look a trifle ashamed, but it was Garrick who broke the new and strained silence.

"Then you shall have her," he said softly.

"I didn't expect Uncle William to take this so well," Penelope said as she lazily brushed her hair. Dressed for bed and sitting atop the mattress, she stared at an unusually pensive Mary. "He didn't take it well initially, but he has come around nicely, don't you think?"

Mary, still fully clothed in a dark green day dress and shoes of embroidered damask, was settled on the window seat, and her face was as blandly indifferent as it had been all evening. "You're marrying the richest man in Charles Town," she said softly. "Of course Father's come around nicely."

Mary hadn't been her usual cheerful self since the Lowrys' ball. Considering that she'd always been moody, Penelope had dismissed the uncomfortable situation until now—but Mary had never maintained a sour disposition for this length of time. She should be dressed for bed herself, and sitting with Penelope on the bed as they discussed plans for the wedding. Instead, she positively sulked.

"Is something wrong?" Penelope asked bluntly. "You're not upset by my impending marriage, are you?"

"Upset?" Mary gave a tight smile. "Why should I be upset?"

"I don't know."

Mary cocked her head, and a soft curl danced across one cheek. "Do you love Maximillian Broderick?"

Penelope set her hairbrush aside and gave the query her full attention. Did she love Maximillian? This had happened so quickly, and there were times she was afraid to ponder the question too closely. Her courtship was a whirlwind she rode on aimlessly and happily unaware. "I can feel myself falling in love, a little more every time I see him, a little more every time he smiles at me or makes me laugh." It was true, she knew as she said the words aloud.

"He just seems so witless."

"Not all the time," Penelope said defensively. "There are moments when I see glimpses of a very different man from the dandy Maximillian appears to be." Moments when she saw untold depths of emotion in his eyes, intelligence, caring, true love.

"What if you're wrong? Maximillian Broderick may very well be nothing more than a very rich fop with nary a thought in his head beyond his wardrobe."

"I don't believe that's true." Penelope knew there was something more to the man who would be her husband, a depth of feeling no one had seen but her, a man to cherish.

"Victor will be very upset."

Penelope had given very little thought to Victor Chadwick, but Mary's mention reminded her that she still had to face him. Oh, Uncle William would break the news to Victor, but she would have to meet with him herself, eventually. "I don't really care. You know I never felt anything for Victor beyond friendship. Oh, Mary, perhaps he'll turn his attentions your way now that . . ." She stopped suddenly.

"Now that you're promised to another?" Mary snapped. "How flattering it is to be forever second choice. If you must know, I wouldn't have Victor Chadwick if he got down on his knees and begged me to be his wife."

Penelope ignored the bright tears in Mary's eyes, because she knew her cousin did not want or need sympathy at this moment. "I didn't mean—" How could she have been so thoughtless? Mary, who on occasion seemed to have not a care in the world, was sensitive where Victor was concerned and always had been. "You're right, of course," Penelope said sensibly. "He's not nearly good enough for you."

Mary stood quickly and left the room without so much as uttering good night, and a confused Penelope was left staring at the door her cousin closed forcefully behind her. Where was the bright and happy girl she knew?

This surely had something to do with Victor. Mary might say she wouldn't have the councilman for a husband, but Penelope knew how much her cousin admired him. Did Mary think Penelope was somehow wronging Victor by choosing to be Maximillian's wife? Or was she afraid that even now Victor wouldn't pay her the attentions she craved? Whatever the reason, Penelope was certain Mary would be her cheerful self very soon.

By the light of a single candle, she crawled into bed. Snuffing out the flame, she sank deep into the mattress and pulled the coverlet to her chin.

Not even her emotional and unpredictable cousin could ruin this day for her.

Married to Maximillian Broderick. It was an unexpected and wonderfully suitable turn of events. Who would have thought, when she watched him enter the Lowrys' ballroom, that she would, a mere two days later, find herself betrothed and smitten?

After two weeks, she would no longer be sleeping alone. She and Maximillian would share a bedchamber and a bed and all the intimacies a husband and wife were meant to share. The thought excited and frightened her. She had no mother to instruct her, and her aunt had been gone these many years. She'd heard the servants talk, and she knew—in essence—what happened in the marriage bed.

But in reality she didn't know what to expect. Her life was insulated, and she was and had always been sheltered and chaste. Maximillian's kiss upon their agreement to marry was the most intimate touch she'd ever known.

Penelope closed her eyes and drifted toward

sleep. If that kiss was any indication, marriage was going to agree with her admirably.

"Word of the League of the Indigo Blade has reached Boston," the man whispered, though there was likely not a living soul for miles around. The trees muffled any noise the two of them might have made, and the night cloaked their movements in darkness as they moved toward the rendezvous point.

Max absently stroked his false beard. The disguise he'd worn had enabled him to walk unobserved through the farming community where this man had been held prisoner by British soldiers for more than a week. "We've done nothing spectacular."

The man laughed softly in obvious surprise. "Nothing spectacular? You've saved half a dozen patriots from Victor Chadwick's hands."

"Three, to be honest," Max said blandly.

"Four, now," the man said gratefully. "And we've heard stories of a village that would have been ransacked without your assistance. I just want you to know your efforts are appreciated."

Max nodded, anxious to get this rebel on board the sloop bound for Boston.

"Who was that woman?" the man continued after a short span of silence. "The very tall one who was in the fray. She's one of yours, I guess."

Max smiled. "Rebecca?" Beck would be mortified to realize that he passed so easily for a homely woman. "Yes, she's one of ours."

"I thought so. Remarkable woman," the man said with obvious awe. "Is she married, by chance?"

Max laughed. He couldn't help himself. His laughter echoed through the forest, and the man he escorted jumped in his saddle and looked around suspiciously.

"You needn't worry," Max assured him. "The others led the British soldiers in the opposite direction. While you're sailing for Boston, those lobsterbacks will be up to their knees in swampland.

"Let's just say," Max returned his attention to the question at hand, "that there's a man in her life."

"I hope he understands what a remarkable woman he has."

Max decided to allow the subject to lapse. He was willing to fight and perhaps to die for these rebels and their cause, but he couldn't give too much away. He trusted no one beyond the circle of the league. And Penelope, of course, whom he trusted with his life and his heart.

What would she say to the news that her husband was the Indigo Blade? Word of the mysterious man and his league was out now, thanks in part to Chadwick's public rantings about the rebel who was making his life so difficult.

The idea of infuriating Chadwick brought another smile to Max's face.

He'd found himself smiling frequently in the past two weeks. Every spare moment was spent in Penelope's company, sitting in her uncle's garden, walking down crowded streets and along the river, talking about everything and finding a new fascination in every small detail of life. Penelope loved her brother with an admirable unbending devotion, she respected her uncle and appreciated everything he'd done for her and Tyler, even though in Max's mind the man was undeserving of such respect. She painted for her own pleasure, but had a true artist's eye for form and color. She was beautiful and seemed not to know it. She was kind and expected the same of everyone around her. She had a sweet tooth and liked the color blue and invariably rose early in the morning.

All these details and more he'd learned in the days since he'd asked her to be his wife. The more he learned, the more deeply he desired her.

He forced away thoughts of his beloved when at last they came to their destination. The waiting sailor, another seagoing friend of Dalton's, had weighed anchor at a dark and deserted spot on the river, and Max handed the rebel into his able hands. Only after they'd sailed did he remove the black wig and bulky jacket that was padded to make him appear much larger than he really was. He wiped the blacking from his teeth, and raked fingers through the long strands of his hair.

In two days, the waiting would be over, and Penelope would be his wife at last. The anticipation matched any he'd ever felt, even though what awaited him now was not gold or danger or revenge. Penelope offered a different reward. Love, home, family . . . comforts he'd never known and yet had secretly longed for in his heart. He'd seen them all in her dark eyes.

Mary had seen Victor step into her father's study just a few moments earlier. She paced beyond the door, her lip caught between her teeth, her skirt in her hands so it wouldn't impede her movement.

Her father was in the stables seeing to a lame horse, and would no doubt be with the stable boy a good half-hour more. Penelope was blithely packing her things into a trunk to be collected by Maximillian Broderick's servants, in order that her new home be prepared for her arrival. In two days, the much-anticipated wedding would take place, and Penelope would be the happy bride of the richest man in Charles Town.

She stopped pacing when she caught a glimpse of Victor standing beside her father's desk. He tapped his fingers impatiently against the fine polished wood. Poor Victor; he'd never been very good at waiting. He'd waited for Penelope for more than two years, and it had done him no good at all. Sweet little Penelope had blindly and happily deserted him for that half-wit Broderick.

Victor impatiently ran his fingers through his hair, brushing back a long and limp dark strand. She'd always thought him the most handsome of men, strong-featured and tall—though not quite as tall as Penelope's husband-to-be—with shoulders too broad to be refined and hair as black as night. She'd always been fascinated by his mouth, which was broad and cruel and tempting.

She stepped to the open doorway and watched without further deception. He saw her immediately, and lifted dark eyes to her. They hadn't spoken since the night of the Lowrys' ball, since the night he'd taken her virginity with all the care and love he showed the desk beneath his fidgety fingers.

"My father has been detained," she said calmly.

"Perhaps I can entertain you while you wait?"

Mary stepped into the room, gratified to see that Victor was uneasy. His nervousness gave her a feeling of power. She liked it.

"That won't be necessary."

She smiled, and that simple reaction caught him off balance. "But I have nothing else to do."

"Mary," he began hesitantly, "I've been meaning to speak to you about the night of the Lowrys' ball. The incident in the garden was a most unfortunate mistake. I'd been drinking, and I'm afraid . . ."

"Are you apologizing, Victor?" Her eyes were purposely wide as she stepped closer. She licked her lower lip and reached out to touch the sleeve of his black jacket, running her fingers over the expensive fabric. "I don't recall asking you to apologize."

She stood on her toes to kiss him square on the mouth. At first he was so shocked he didn't move at all, and then he began to respond, with anxious lips and then a hungry tongue. His mouth was hard and wet, and Mary fought the urge to pull away. Instead, she copied Victor, met every thrust of his intrusive tongue with one of her own.

"You promised to teach me more," she whispered as she took her mouth from his. "You promised to teach me how to pleasure you and myself." She took his hand in hers and lifted it to her breast, to lay it where he had grabbed her in the Lowrys' garden. She wondered if Victor could feel the tremble of her hand or the fierce beating of her heart. If he did, he gave no sign.

"Mary!" he glanced quickly toward the open door. "Your father might return at any moment!"

She smiled. "Yes, he might." Victor couldn't have Penelope—but he could have her. And this was his weakness, she knew that now. Physical sensation, need, sex. Mary knew she could give Victor something Penelope never could or would, and as she did so she could make him want and need her. She could take this power she felt and make it grow into something more.

Victor grinned. He didn't have a warm smile. His lips moved and tightened, his eyes narrowed to mere slits, and he brought that animalistic smile toward her for another kiss. "Not here," he whispered. "The carriage house tonight, after I've finished with your father."

She mimicked him, flicking her tongue in his mouth and tasting the very maleness of him. The smells, the taste, the pain of that encounter in the garden washed over her without warning, and she knew a moment of panic. She buried the terror deeply, before Victor knew she'd felt anything at all.

Victor Chadwick was a cruel, ruthless man. Demanding, coldly precise, selfish. For as long as she'd known him he'd been pursuing Penelope with unwavering and passionless devotion.

With a self-indulgent force he'd taken from Mary the virginity a woman of her stature was expected to offer her husband on their wedding night, and he'd left her broken-hearted and cold and alone afterward. Sometimes she recalled that night with such terror it brought tears to her eyes.

But in her heart she knew Victor was meant to be hers. There was more for them than pain and apologies that came too late. There had to be.

She loved him.

Chapter Six

This, of all nights, the rebels of Charles Town had chosen to raise their voices in protest, and the simple demonstration had quickly turned ugly. Rocks had been thrown by demonstrators, British pistols had been drawn, and when a stone had struck one soldier on the side of his head, sending him reeling, shots had been fired. Two of the dissenters now languished in Victor Chadwick's prison. Heath Lowry had been shot making his escape and was now missing.

In the darkness of the stable, Max donned his costume for the evening, as did the others. What horrid timing. Tomorrow was his wedding day, and he would likely not get a minute of sleep tonight.

"I don't like this," Fletcher said lowly as he squirmed in the red coat of the Queen's Regiment of the Light Dragoons. Dalton's privateer friend had stolen the uniforms from a Boston fortification only a few weeks before.

"Neither do I," Garrick said as he stepped into tall black boots. "Our faces are not properly disguised."

"It's dark in and around the building where Chadwick houses his prisoners, and we'll be in and out before anyone has a chance to take a close look at our faces. It's like the blackened teeth and the empty sleeve. These uniforms, the powdered wigs, that's what they'll remember."

"I hope you're right," John muttered beneath his breath.

There was no time to formulate another strategy, and they all knew it. Chadwick had angrily declared that he'd send his prisoners before a firing squad in the morning. He had no right to do so, but of course a small detail such as legality wouldn't stop a man like Chadwick.

What could the League of the Indigo Blade do but liberate the prisoners and replace them with a couple of Chadwick's own guards? Wouldn't Victor be surprised to throw open the doors to his small brick prison in the morning only to find two or three of his majesty's soldiers, bound and gagged?

Max could only hope that Heath Lowry, the son of a loyalist merchant and the only one of the protestors wounded, had found his way to a safe place. There were more rebels in Charles Town than loyalists, so there was a good chance the lad had found his way to a friend.

On seven of Fletcher's finest horses and in enemy garb, they rode toward the prison. It was late, and the few citizens they encountered had nothing but curses and spittle for the redcoats they hated. Max and his men provided no reaction to the insults, but rode with their shoulders squared and their eyes steady and straight ahead.

The people they passed were a reminder that the sentiments of rebellion grew with every passing day. Whispers of liberty and patriotism, of freedom, were becoming louder and more frequent. There would be war before long, and it wouldn't be easy or short-lived. War, just when he'd found a semblance of peace in Penelope.

The two guards who were posted outside the prison were alert and well-armed, but as Max had predicted, they saw no further than their familiar uniforms.

Garrick, who had been chosen earlier for this assignment, dismounted and faced the guards with the arrogant bearing of an officer. "We're here to relieve you of your charge." He waited patiently for the guards to unlock and open the door. They didn't, of course.

"We have orders to hold these rebels until morning," one of the guards said hesitantly.

"I have orders of my own," Garrick said contemptuously, reaching into an inside pocket to withdraw a sheet of paper and wave it before the guards. One guard took the folded paper, while another set his rifle aside to lift their single lantern. Lewis and Dalton dismounted, smoothly, simultaneously, and the guards' only reaction was to lift their eyes momentarily.

John and Beck were next. Max and Fletcher waited, still mounted, to the rear. In a heartbeat, the guards were surrounded, and before they could make a sound—perhaps before they even knew of the danger—they were disarmed and immobilized.

"Not a sound," Garrick said, his pistol pointed at one guard's heart. "We'll take those prisoners, now, if you don't mind."

The shorter guard was relieved of his key, and the prison door swung open a moment later. The sheet of paper Garrick had handed to the guard fluttered to the ground, unheeded.

When all were safely inside, Max and Fletcher dismounted. Max scooped up the paper from the ground, unfolded it, and shook the dirt from the once pristine page, and by the light of the moon he once again glanced over the painstakingly elaborate lettering.

It took no more than five minutes to liberate the rebels, bind and gag the unfortunate guards, and lock the prison door once again. The lantern had been extinguished, and Max was certain the men they rescued could see his face no more clearly than he could see theirs. That was, as always, for the best.

"In spite of our current state of dress, we're friends, of that I can assure you."

They nodded solemnly. "These four gentlemen," he gestured to the men who surrounded them, "will take you to a place where you'll be safe until transport to a more friendly haven can be arranged."

"I'm not leaving," one of them said softly. "This is my home."

"I suggest at least a temporary absence," Garrick added sardonically. "I have no wish to attempt this rescue endeavor on each and every night. Chadwick will be actively searching for you by morning, I can assure it."

How could you argue with a man who wanted only to defend his home? Max couldn't. Tonight, the men would be delivered to safety in Cypress Crossroads. After that, their fate was in their own hands.

Max had a feeling that before long no one would be truly safe.

Dalton took one rebel onto his horse, and Lewis the other. Garrick and John followed, and the group rode away with dignity and aplomb as if they had every right to be parading through the darkened streets of Charles Town.

When they were out of sight, Max drew the dagger from his belt. The short and sharp blade grew wickedly from a wooden handle that was engraved with the image of an indigo plant. There was even a brushing of the blue dye washed into the wood. He held the note to the prison door, and with all the force he could muster, he drove the blade through the note and into the door.

The words that were illuminated in the moonlight were large and flowing, the message short and to the point.

Chadwick—you possess nothing I cannot take away. It was signed, with a flourish, *The Indigo Blade*.

The noise beneath her window, soft and indistinct as it was, disturbed her. All was completely quiet but for Penelope's heart, so she sat up warily, certain the rustle was not a figment of her imagination. And then the answer came to her.

Maximillian.

She sprang from her bed. He likely wasn't having any better luck finding sleep than she, on this the eve of their wedding.

The window opened noiselessly and she leaned forward, listening to the silent night and waiting for the sound to come again. It did, a rustle in the bushes beneath her window.

"Maximillian?" she whispered.

She saw movement, a tall figure staggering through the shrubbery. It took her but a single glance to know that the man beneath her window was not Maximillian.

He heard her voice, though, and lifted his head. Hair paler than Maximillian's shone in the moonlight, and a familiar face was awash with anguish.

"Heath Lowry?" What on earth was he doing beneath her window in the middle of the night?

He lifted a hand slowly. "Help me," he whispered, his voice loud in the still night air.

Penelope didn't think twice. She grabbed her velvet cloak and tossed it over her shoulders as she hurried silently down the stairs in bare feet. She exited through the side door, stepping into the cold night air and searching for Heath once again.

He was sitting amidst the bushes with his back against the brick wall of the house and his head in his hands.

"What's wrong?" she asked, taking a single step forward. He was breathing heavily, his legs trembled, and she could see the dark stain at his side that could only be blood. "I'll get my uncle." She spun away, but Heath's harsh utterance stopped her.

"No."

Penelope turned in time to see Heath lift his head. It wasn't simply the moonlight that made him appear pale. He was badly hurt. "I've been shot, Penelope," he whispered. "Damned British soldiers."

"A doctor . . ."

"No. I can't trust anyone." His eyes were beseeching. "Not my family, not my friends. I don't know who to turn to. People say they sympathize, but how can I know that they're telling the truth?" He tried to rise, but fell clumsily back into place. "Can I trust you, Penelope?"

"Yes." Her answer was immediate and sure. "Of course you can trust me."

There wasn't time to panic, and like Heath she didn't know where to turn for help. "First we must get you inside. It's much too cold out here. The carriage house will do nicely."

She stepped into the shrubbery, ignoring the chill of her bare feet and the snag of a number of twigs. "Come along," she said, offering her arm and, as Heath rose, every ounce of her strength. He leaned against her as they stepped away from the house and toward the rear of the property.

"What happened?" she asked as they moved slowly across the damp grass.

"Didn't you hear the news?"

"No. I've been very busy this week. I'm getting married tomorrow—today," she amended.

"There was a demonstration, and a skirmish," he

said weakly. "It was meant to be a peaceful protest, but tempers flared. Words were shouted back and forth, and then Timothy threw a rock, damn his hide. A soldier fired, and then more rocks were thrown, and then . . . It was chaos, Penelope."

"I didn't know your sympathies were with the rebels," she said as they reached the carriage house at last.

"You're not going to turn me in, are you?"

Heath was too weak to do anything about it if she did decide to go to her uncle or to Victor. He could barely stand, in fact. "Of course not," she assured him. "You're my friend, Heath. I would never do anything to harm a friend."

The carriage house here was smaller than the one on the plantation, being just large enough for the carriage and a single wagon. The interior was pitch black, cavernous and foreign. There was a lantern stored in the far corner, behind the wagon if she remembered correctly. She hoped her memory wasn't faulty in that respect.

She saw Heath settled on the floor, and then she felt her way to the far corner, hands against the wall, until she found the lantern. She lit it, and then she set about finding what she could to tend his wound and returned to his side.

The injury was nasty, black and red torn flesh, and the sight of the wound in the lamplight turned her stomach—but she was careful not to show her squeamishness. Her distress would only disturb Heath, and that wouldn't be good for him. Not now. She could be strong when she had to.

"I didn't say anything for such a long time," he

said weakly as she cleaned his wound. "My father is a staunch loyalist, like your uncle, and I didn't dare to disagree with him, not aloud. I was afraid to oppose him, afraid I'd lose my family for politics."

"I know what you mean," Penelope said as she cleaned away fresh and dried blood.

"Then you want freedom, too?" There was a touch of surprise in Heath's voice.

"I don't know," she whispered. Until this moment, politics had seemed a distant and rather boring subject, the discussions of loyalty and freedom abstract concepts her uncle and Victor discussed at great length.

But this was real. Blood and pain, a son defying his father . . .

"I believe with all my heart," Heath whispered. "Independence, a new nation. I'd personally like to send every last one of those redcoats back to England where they belong."

"You shouldn't talk—"

"Sometimes a man has to stand up for what he knows is right, no matter what the cost." Heath took labored, deep breaths and stared away from her as she tended him. "Men are going to die, Penelope, and I might be one of them."

"Don't say such things . . ."

"I don't want to die, but I can't live like a coward, hiding behind my father's money and power, accepting what I'm told when I know what's right. I can't hide any more."

The bleeding had stopped, and Heath seemed to

be resting easier. "Tomorrow I'll have to find you a doctor."

"No." Heath shook his head and closed his eyes. "I just need to rest here for a few hours. I'll be gone before the sun comes up."

"You can't possibly go anywhere in your condition." Goodness, he was badly hurt. He needed rest, good food, and proper care. Care she couldn't give him.

He reached out blindly and found her hand. "I can, and I must. Thank you, Penelope. I won't forget this, I promise you."

"Heath?"

He opened one eye, and in spite of it all he gave her a crooked smile. "Yes?"

"Take care of yourself," she whispered, and then she left him to sleep.

Chapter Seven

The wedding was a fantasy, a wondrous page out of a magical story book. The church was decorated in white and gold to match Penelope's wedding dress and the silk suit her groom wore. White flowers and gold bows filled the church, and an extravagant number of candles burned brilliantly all around, even though it was the middle of the day, and soft light broke through the church windows.

A violin, a viola, and a cello played a canon by Pachelbel to set the mood for the many guests. Maximillian had made all the arrangements himself.

This was more than a marriage ceremony for Penelope, more than the simple promise to take Maximillian as her husband. It was the beginning of a new life and she knew, as she spoke her vows before friends and strangers and the man she was beginning to love, that after today her life would never be the same. That knowledge was frightening and exciting, thrilling and comforting.

Surely no bride had ever been more adored. The love Maximillian professed shone clearly in his eyes, and his smile told her more than the words he spoke with such quiet passion. What more could any woman ask for?

After the ceremony they rode in Maximillian's finest carriage to William Seton's house. Married at last, it seemed they'd both become suddenly shy. They held hands and said little on the short ride, and Maximillian kissed her—twice.

Though peeved that she'd chosen Maximillian over Victor, Uncle William had still found the graciousness to throw a wedding party at his home. A cautious man, always, he was not blind to the fact that Maximillian Broderick had quickly become an important man in Charles Town. The fact that Maximillian refused to discuss politics at all, and the fact that he expressed greater concern over the cut of his clothes than the state of the colonies, were overshadowed—in Uncle William's calculating eyes—by his wealth and social standing.

It seemed to Penelope that everyone in Charles Town had crowded into her uncle's home: old friends and acquaintances, as well as those who were simply curious about the couple who'd met and married so quickly. Yes, everyone was here, she noticed, but the Lowrys and Victor Chadwick.

There were muted whispers all around, and she knew Heath was most likely the subject of many of those quiet conversations. Poor Harriet Lowry was probably worried sick about her youngest son. Penelope hoped that Heath had, at the very least, found a way to get word to his family that he was well. Family was important, and surely they could put their political differences aside in this trying time.

True to his word, Heath had vanished before daylight. Penelope had slipped quietly to the carriage house as the sun rose, with a bite to eat for the wounded man, but he was already gone. The blanket she'd covered him with was neatly folded and returned to the back of the wagon, and all signs that anyone had spent the night in the carriage house were gone.

Penelope, standing at her husband's side and observing the crowd, gripped his arm tightly and smiled when she spotted Tyler stalking across the room. "I swear, I believe he's grown three inches since I left him at the plantation."

Fifteen years old and convinced he was a man, defiant in all matters great and small, a young man who had always taken great pleasure in teasing his sister and his cousin, Tyler Seton was the light of Penelope's life. He was growing so handsome. Tall, lithe, with dark blond hair and bright blue eyes much like their mother's, he already had the makings of a ladies' man.

And he never walked. He ran, he charged, and today he sauntered arrogantly.

"I'm so glad you arrived before the ceremony," Penelope said, greeting her brother with a hug and a kiss. Uncle William had promised to make the arrangements to bring her brother to Charles Town for the wedding, but Penelope had worried needlessly that Tyler wouldn't arrive in time. It had been a great comfort to see him sitting sullenly in the church.

Tyler turned accusing eyes on Maximillian. He looked the groom up and down, taking in the white silk and polished shoes, the lace cravat and immaculately groomed hair that made his own locks look quite haphazardly arranged. "You could have done better," he said as he turned back to Penelope.

"Tyler!"

"He's quite right, m'dear," Maximillian said lightly, apparently not in the least bit offended. "I'm not good enough for you, but then again what mortal man would be?" He turned sparkling gray-green eyes to Tyler. "But as you are her brother and protector and clearly have her best interests at heart, I will tell you this. I will care for Penelope and cherish her as no one else can. I give you my word, she's in good hands."

Tyler's eyes narrowed. "She'd better be."

Mary crept up behind Tyler and gave him a big hug before he could slip away. Her smile was as bright as Penelope had seen since the Lowrys' ball—since the night she'd met Maximillian.

Every man in the room had kept an eye on Mary this evening. Every man but Maximillian, Penelope amended silently. Mary was beautiful, as always, but tonight she sparkled. Her red hair was flawlessly styled, her blue gown suited her perfectly, and her smile was genuine.

Penelope wanted the best for her cousin. If only Mary could find this kind of happiness.

"I thought you would never arrive," Mary said as she kissed Tyler on the cheek. Since he already stood six feet tall, she had to stand on her toes to manage the feat. "You whisked into the church just in time, not a moment too soon. Is Father going to allow you to stay for a while?"

Tyler would have accompanied them to Charles Town weeks ago, if he hadn't had an argument with Uncle William just days before their departure.

Tyler smiled widely. "If I behave myself, I'll be allowed to stay until you and Uncle William return to the plantation."

"I see," Mary said, wide-eyed. "Behave yourself? Why, you might as well not bother to unpack." She laughed, and half a dozen admiring male heads turned in her direction. At that moment, Penelope was certain that whatever had been tormenting her cousin for the past few weeks had been resolved, and that all would be well.

Tyler was here, Mary was happy, and Penelope was married to a wonderful man who clearly adored her. What more could she ask for?

After she'd received the well wishes of every prominent citizen of Charles Town, when the guests were well-fed and glowing with the consumption of too much fine wine, her husband took her arm and placed his mouth near her ear.

"I have waited as long as I possibly can. It's time to go home, my love," he whispered.

"Yes," she answered with a smile. "Time to go home."

*   *   *

It was a moment Max knew he'd remember all his days, a worthy memory to banish his nightmares, as he carried his bride into the house. It was more than a house, now, more than a building filled with fine furnishings and treasures from around the world. It was home.

The only real home he'd ever known, a place for the heart to rest and rejoice. A place for family.

He carried Penelope through the vacant foyer and directly to the spiral staircase, up without pause to the second floor and the bedchamber that awaited.

Luxurious with gold and white and mahogany, the room was lit by a low blaze that burned in the hearth. Unlit candles sat on a table beside the bed, and flowers from the garden had been haphazardly arranged in vases on the dresser and the mantle above the fireplace. For all their protests, his friends had seen that everything was ready for him and his bride.

"It's the most beautiful room I've ever seen," Penelope said softly as he placed her on her feet. Her eyes roamed over the fine furnishings, at first avoiding but finally resting up on the tall, wide bed.

She was nervous. Of course she was nervous. He had no doubt but that this was a right and honorable union . . . but Penelope still had her doubts. About love, about marriage, about the way of a man and a woman in the bed she so studiously avoided looking at.

Max closed the door, and Penelope jumped—just a little. He noticed, of course, as he noticed everything about his bride.

"I've known you less than three weeks," he said, unable to hide the wonder in his voice, "and yet I feel like I've waited for this moment forever."

Penelope turned her eyes to him then. Lifting her chin, she stared up with big, dark brown eyes that were endlessly deep, eternal in their mystery.

Max placed his hands on her face, cupping her cheeks and making sure she didn't look away. "I love you," he whispered. "For my very life, I would not hurt you."

"I know," she whispered.

He kissed her lips before dropping his hands to her shoulders, tasted her sweetness and innocence, promised her more with the passion that was building within him. Her response was gentle, a softening of her mouth, the gradual parting of her lips.

His fingers touched the column of her neck, skin so soft and silky, tender skin that none but he had caressed. Beneath his fingers, she trembled.

He kissed her there, where a vein throbbed with every beat of her heart. She was his. His wife, his love, his soul. And he was hers with every fiber of his being.

He removed her wedding dress, his fingers slipping with deceptive indolence through the ties as he kissed her lips and her neck, his hands cautiously pushing the fabric away so he could feast his eyes on her.

She was lovely, more lovely than any sight he'd ever beheld. The gently rounded shoulders, the well-shaped arms and legs, the curve of her hip, all was perfection. When he stripped away her chemise to leave her completely bare, she raised her hands to cover her breasts, and blushed.

"No," he whispered, and he took her wrists in his hands and slowly drew them down. She didn't resist. "Let me see all of you. You're so very beautiful."

His bride stood before him, naked, shy, and unafraid.

Once again he lifted her in his arms, and this time he carried her to the bed, leaving the silk and lace and linen of her wedding clothes discarded on the Persian carpet.

She was the only good thing in his life, the only pure and unsullied part of him. And she was, already, a part of him.

"I want to make this, and every other part of our life together, perfect."

From her place in the center of the silk-covered bed, she smiled up at him. "I know."

He lowered his body over hers, kissed her waiting mouth again, and lost himself in the feel of her flesh beneath his. She was soft and giving, warm and yielding, so tempting it took every bit of discipline he could muster to maintain this leisurely pace.

Eager as he was, he would not rush this. It was a moment to be savored, a memory of a lifetime. He allowed his fingers to trail a leisurely path up her side, over silken curves until she quivered. Her breasts he stroked gently, brushing his fingers over nipples that hardened at his touch.

"Maximillian." She whispered his name with damp and swollen lips that brushed his own.

"Yes, my love."

Her hands rose from the satin-covered bed to rest upon his arms, the fingers light and tentative. "I do love you." She breathed the words that brought a smile to his face. "I do."

"I know."

This was not what she'd expected. Maximillian's hands dancing over her body, his lips loving her with words and touch, her own body responding in the most wonderful way.

She was warm—no, hot—all over, to her bones and her very heart. Her body quivered everywhere, inside and out, and with every touch and kiss she wanted more. With every word whispered she became more Maximillian's wife. She was apprehensive, still, but her nervousness had gradually changed to a rather pleasant anxiety—an anxiety that was developing into eagerness as each moment passed.

She meant the words she'd whispered moments earlier. Love. A connection that couldn't be denied, the realization that without Maximillian her life was empty and meaningless. The knowledge that this was meant to be, that it was genuine. Together, she and Maximillian were on the threshold of something wonderful and unknown.

The fire that burned on the opposite side of the room threw off just enough light for her to see Maximillian's face clearly. The aristocratic lines, the hooded eyes, the wide, wonderful mouth. A few locks of his perfectly groomed hair, gold in the half-light, fell from his queue to brush his cheek, and she reached out to touch a strand. He caught her hand and brought the wrist to his mouth, kissed the tender skin there and then allowed his mouth to travel up her arm, kissing, tasting, teasing as he went, leaving behind tremors of pleasure that lingered warmly on her flesh.

And then that mouth stilled over her breast. His hot breath touched her, and then Maximillian closed his lips over her breast and gently drew the nipple deeper into his mouth.

Her body's reaction was intense and uncontrollable. She arched off the bed as bands of power shot through her body, cried out softly in a plea for more.

When Maximillian lifted his body from hers, she missed the divine heat and pressure. Her hands reached out and found him, his sleeve and his hair, the silk and linen he shed quickly until her searching hands found hot and hard flesh.

He was magnificent, warm skin over finely sculpted muscles he hid beneath his fine clothes. Hard and hot and beautiful. Penelope found she loved to touch her husband, to trace the curves and dimples of his skin, and he responded to her gentle touch with a moan that came from deep within.

When he returned to her they lay together flesh to flesh, heart to heart, and his mouth came to hers with a new frenzy. She could see and feel him losing control, and it excited her to know that she had this kind of effect on him. She welcomed the impatient kiss, relished it, and answered in kind.

With his knees, Maximillian gently spread her legs until she cradled his body between her thighs. His mouth didn't leave hers as his hand swayed gently over her skin, as he slipped his hand between her thighs to caress her intimately. She was shocked for a moment and her body stiffened, but

Maximillian didn't still the fingers that stroked her flesh and fanned the flames of the blaze that had already taken control of her heart and soul.

"Yes," she whispered as she felt the first push of his manhood against her quivering flesh. He pushed inside of her, slowly, gradually, driving deeper as her body adjusted to his. She was aware of the moment he broke through her maidenhead, but there was no pain. Just pressure, and a surprising fullness.

Her body adapted quickly, accepting the fullness more easily than she'd imagined was possible.

Maximillian began to move, above, within, stroking tenderly and plunging deep. He rocked his hips, finding a rhythm that was slow and easy and perfectly wonderful . . . but soon it seemed too slow, too easy. Her hips rocked as his did, searching, swaying.

Ribbons of pleasure as bright as any light shot through her. The golden ribbons began where she and Maximillian were joined, and then trailed through her body like rays of the brightest sun.

Maximillian began to move faster, to plunge deeper, and Penelope lifted her hips to accept all of him. The ribbons quivered and tightened, and without warning a burst of intense pleasure washed over and through her. She held onto her husband as if for dear life, afraid to let go, at the same time afraid that if she didn't, this furious response would destroy them both.

She clung to Maximillian as he pushed deep one last time, held on as the waves of her response died and he allowed himself his own release. Her clasp was strong as he shuddered above her, and he gave her everything he had to give—his seed, his joy, his love.

Depleted, they collapsed on the bed, arms and legs entangled, hearts beating wildly.

She was exhausted and elated, complete in this hot entanglement. She'd been so nervous, so afraid, when Maximillian had carried her into this room, but at this moment there was no fear within her.

Penelope found her breath, a true feat. "So"—she exhaled softly—"that's how it's done."

Maximillian laughed. Not a twitter or a silly chuckle, but a low rumble from deep within his chest. "Yes, that's how it's done," he said, coming up onto one elbow to look down at her. "At least, that's one of the ways in which it's done."

"There are others?" She couldn't imagine . . . but then she'd never imagined anything like the act that had just occurred.

"Yes," Maximillian whispered. "My love, we've just begun."

Chapter Eight

"Max."

It was his whispered name that woke him, as a large, stilling hand was placed on his shoulder. Garrick stood above, leaning slightly over the bed, his solemn face lit by the flame of the single candle he carried.

Max was immediately awake. "What is it?"

"Come with me." Garrick spun away, leaving Max in the darkness with a sleeping Penelope. She hadn't so much as stirred as the whispers broke the silence, she was sleeping so soundly. He kissed her shoulder and then pulled up the coverlet to conceal that bared temptation before he slipped from the bed.

Garrick wouldn't disturb him on his wedding night unless something momentous had occurred. Max dressed quickly, stepping into his breeches and pulling on the wrinkled linen shirt he'd tossed to the floor a few hours ago. He glanced at Penelope once more as he left the room.

It wasn't only Garrick who was waiting in the passageway. They were all waiting, and there wasn't an easy face in the lot. Not even the normally jovial Lewis was smiling. Dalton played with his knife ominously, and there was pure thunder on Fletcher's face.

They didn't wait for him to ask what had happened.

"Chadwick got his hands on Heath Lowry early this morning," Garrick said lowly.

Max nodded solemnly. "In the study. I don't want to wake my wife." Fletcher and Dalton exchanged a cryptic glance.

"I'll stay here," Dalton offered, sheathing the knife in his belt and nodding once to Fletcher.

"No." Max didn't know what was going on, but he didn't like the mood, and he didn't like the thoughtful way Dalton had caressed his knife. "I want everyone in the study. Now."

He worked his way through them and led the way down the spiral staircase. It wasn't necessary to look back. Though they followed silently, he knew everyone was with him.

Inside the study, Max lit a pair of candles and placed them on his desk. Garrick set his candle on a table by the door as he entered, and the soft light flickered over solemn faces as the League of the Indigo Blade filed, one by one, into the room.

They surrounded the desk Max stood behind, and for a long moment, all were silent.

"Well?" Max prompted.

Garrick glanced to one side. "I can't do it," he whispered.

"I can," Beck said indignantly. "Your *wife*," he all but spat the word from his mouth, "handed Heath Lowry over to Chadwick."

Max's first reaction was staunch disbelief. "And who told you this? Chadwick? He's angry because Penelope married me."

"It was Lowry himself," Fletcher said darkly, "who denounced her."

There was a surge of disgust and disbelief within him, a cracking apart of everything he believed— everything he wanted to believe. Penelope was the one untainted aspect of his life, of himself, a pure and good and decent woman he'd taken to his heart. Lowry must've lied—they were all lying. "Are you sure?"

"Without question," John mumbled. "Lowry said Penelope Seton tended his wounds and promised not to betray him, and then she turned around and gave him over to Chadwick."

Max still didn't believe it. His sweet, innocent wife wouldn't turn a wounded man—or any man— over to Chadwick. Her uncle was a loyalist, true, and Chadwick was a family friend, but Penelope didn't care about politics. And he knew, with everything he was, that it wasn't in her heart to send a man to prison.

"We'll just have to liberate Lowry and see what he has to say."

"It's too late," Lewis whispered. "He's dead."

"What?" Max could barely force the words from his mouth.

"A few hours ago, by the light of a bonfire." Garrick spoke up at last. "Lowry accused your wife as they tied him to the whipping post outside the prison. He damned her to hell as a sergeant with hamlike arms delivered a good number of the hundred lashes Chadwick had ordered. The lashing continued even after he'd passed out, perhaps even after he'd expired." Garrick's voice grew progressively colder and harder. "The lad was sorely wounded to begin with. He never had a chance."

"It's a mistake," Max insisted softly, though already he didn't believe his own protestations.

Fletcher stepped forward, so that the light from the candles on the desk gave his face an eerie cast. "It happened like this. Lowry stumbled about, wounded, hiding where he could and trying to make his way to a place of safety. He didn't know where to go, who to turn to. It was pure chance that he ended up on the grounds of the Seton house. Penelope discovered him, tended his wounds, and then went to her good friend Victor Chadwick for advice."

Max shook his head. "She wouldn't."

"Lowry declared it and Chadwick confirmed it," Dalton said. He touched the blade of his knife again, caressing the handle, and Max now realized why he'd wanted to stay behind. His bride might very well be dead if he'd left Dalton above stairs alone. "What else do you want? A signed confession from your *wife*?"

No one had said the name aloud, but Max knew

111

Jamie was on the minds of every man in the room. Jamie was certainly on *his* mind, at the moment.

Jamie, who had been the romantic of the crew, a young man who was generous with his smiles and his dreams.

Jamie, who'd died a horrible death, tortured and lashed by command of the nawab of Bengal. Jamie had lost his life because a seductress—the daughter of the nawab and a woman Jamie swore he loved more than life itself—had betrayed him.

Revenge on the nawab had been the first true mission of the League of the Indigo Blade. They'd taken his palace, put his ambitious brother in his place, and watched as the usurper beheaded the former ruler. Justice was done, the new nawab had gratefully rewarded the league with treasures to add to their already substantial wealth—but it hadn't brought Jamie back.

The woman who had divulged Jamie's hiding place to a vengeful father had pleaded for her life, crying, sobbing that she'd only betrayed Jamie because she'd been so very frightened. She didn't know, she said, that her father would kill him. She'd even professed to still love him. They'd allowed her to live, and her uncle, the new nawab, promised to see her wed to a strict husband who would keep her humble.

But Jamie was still dead.

Max cradled his head in his hands, hiding his eyes, trying to shut out the images from the past and the present. Try as he might, he couldn't shut out the truth. While he'd loved Penelope, while she lay entwined in his arms laughing and declaring her love, a man she'd betrayed had died. While he'd dreamed impossibly of love and family and new beginnings with Penelope, a man had gone to the whipping post by her hand. He knew too well what a horrible death that was.

"Have you told her who you are?" Fletcher whispered, with a coldness that sent a chill up Max's spine.

"No, and she can never know now who we are or what we do," he said softly. He could feel his heart hardening. How else could he survive and do what had to be done? "We must watch her at all times." The words he had to speak were more difficult than he'd imagined. "She can't be trusted."

The men were silent as they waited for him to continue. "She'll need a ladies' maid. John, doesn't that tavern owner in Cypress Crossroads have a widowed daughter?"

"Helen," he confirmed.

"Would she be interested in the job?"

John nodded once.

"Good."

He wanted to believe that there was no malevolence in his wife's heart, only ignorance and a lack of concern. He wanted to believe that she didn't know what would happen to Heath Lowry—but she knew Chadwick as well as anyone else, and surely she'd known of his ambitions and his hatred for the colonial rebels.

"There's one more thing you should know," Fletcher said. "Lowry's body still hangs on the whipping post, a message to those who would oppose the king. There was a protest when word got out that Lowry was dead, but no one dares approach the body."

"Then *we'll* cut him down." He couldn't save the man his wife had condemned, but perhaps he could give Lowry some dignity in death.

Garrick shook his head slowly. "Impossible. The soldiers are watching and waiting, a dozen of them. They're waiting for the Indigo Blade."

There was something yet they had not told him, Max could see it on their faces. "And how do you know that?"

"The note you fixed to the prison door—Chadwick pinned it to the post above Lowry's head in much the same fashion. He even used your knife."

Max placed his hands against the desk and let his head drop so that he stared at them. So, this was his fault as much as Penelope's. She'd turned the boy over, that much was true, but Chadwick had wasted no time in sending him to his death. Chadwick hadn't waited a day or two before carrying out the sentence, because he couldn't take the chance of losing this prisoner. Max knew, with a sinking heart, that his arrogant challenge had cost Lowry his life.

What a fool he'd been to believe that he could find peace here, in a new country, in a new home, with Penelope. He was a bigger fool even than the one he pretended to be, a blind, besotted imbecile.

No more.

"I want Helen in place by the end of the day," he said without emotion. "I want to know exactly what my wife does, who she speaks to, what she reads, what she eats, and when she sleeps. Mrs. Broderick will not make a move without my knowledge."

John nodded in agreement.

Max fixed his eyes on Dalton. "You won't harm her," he insisted lowly. "And that goes for all of you. I will kill any man who touches my wife."

With those words a wedge was driven between him and his comrades. Max felt it, as surely as he felt the hardening of his heart, a distance that had not been there before, a breaking of trust. Not only did he no longer have his dreams of peace with Penelope, he no longer had this family he'd made for himself.

"She offers us a valuable link to the loyalist community in Charles Town," he continued without emotion. "I imagine Victor Chadwick will be a frequent quest for dinner in this house."

John grumbled.

"And we won't kill him, either," Max insisted. "Not just yet."

Her entire body ached, but it was a wonderfully satisfying ache, more a reminder of the night that had passed than a true pain.

Penelope lay very still in the rumpled bed, wondering where Maximillian was and fully expecting him to come happily through the door at any moment. She took the quiet minute to study her surroundings, the bedchamber she'd had little chance to survey last night.

It was, true to Maximillian's personality, lavishly furnished. The four-poster bed was of finely carved mahogany, as were the wardrobe and the dresser. Tall windows were dressed in gold satin that pooled on the floor, and the bedcover that was rumpled and askew matched the draperies perfectly in color and texture. There was a huge gilt-framed mirror on one wall, a landscape on another. The rug was most certainly Persian.

Penelope finally rose from the bed, deciding that Maximillian hadn't simply stepped out of the room for a moment. She was disappointed, but surely this was a sign of kindness and not neglect. He'd slipped away quietly and allowed her to continue sleeping. Perhaps he knew how tiring the night had been, how exhausted she was.

Exhausted but happy.

For most of her life she'd expected little and taught herself to be happy with what she had. After all, she was a poor relation who owed everything to her father's brother. The roof above her head, the clothes on her back, the safety and care of her little brother. Never in her wildest dreams had she expected to find love so quickly. Never had she expected that a man like Maximillian could love her so completely. And now, everything she could possibly want awaited her. A devoted husband, a wonderful home, children.

Most of her things were already neatly arranged in the dresser and the tall wardrobe, and Penelope chose a simple outfit for her first day in her new home: a plain chemise and petticoat, a linen gown in a becoming shade of blue, plain white hose and soft leather shoes. As she dressed, she couldn't help but wonder if she already carried Maximillian's child. It was certainly possible, after the night that had passed. Three times he'd made love to her, each time more gently than the last, each time more wonderfully.

When she was fully dressed and had styled her hair in a simple bun, she drew back the golden drapes to discover a small terrace overlooking the gardens. She opened the glass-paneled doors and stepped into a morning that was bright and fresh and cool. Beyond her stretched a wonderful garden, a collection of native flowers and palms that was somewhat wild—but was contained and arranged beautifully. Meandering trails were cut through the garden, S-shaped paths she looked forward to exploring as she looked forward to exploring the entire house.

It was the growling of her stomach that gave Penelope the courage to leave the elegant bedchamber on her own, to search out Maximillian and then the kitchen. There were a number of closed doors on the second floor, and a stairway to the third. She took the spiral staircase to the ground floor in search of her husband.

She remembered little of this Georgian mansion from the night before. Maximillian had carried her through quickly, and her mind had been . . . well, she'd been distracted. She saw now that the entire house was as lavishly furnished as the bedchamber. Persian and Baku rugs, fine porcelain vases and figurines, tasteful and expensive furniture. There was a grand and glorious vastness about the rooms she explored. She stepped quietly through the foyer and the magnificent grand hall at the front of the house. She quietly explored the library, a quaint parlor, and finally a dining room that would easily seat thirty.

A young gentleman with reddish-brown hair found her there, stepping into the room with an air of authority and apparently not at all surprised to find her investigating. "Is Madam ready for breakfast?" His words were clipped and so cold that Penelope felt an unexpected chill.

"Yes." She stepped forward with a small smile. Perhaps he wasn't thrilled about a new mistress appearing so suddenly. Perhaps he expected she would be a difficult task master. She'd do her best to put him at ease. "I'm Mrs. Broderick."

"I know who you are, madam."

"And you are . . ."

"Beck," he said, with no evidence of a softening disposition. "Beck Andrews. I'll be back shortly with your breakfast."

"I'd like to locate my husband first," Penelope said before he could whisk himself from the room. "Do you know where he is?"

The chilling Beck smiled at last—if you could call the tightening of his lips a smile. "Mr. Broderick never rises before noon." ·

"You're mistaken. He was already gone when I awoke."

Beck's eyes were cold and lifeless, but she was certain she saw a flicker of something as he answered. "I imagine he's in *his* chamber, madam." She recognized that glint now as amusement. At her expense.

"I see," she said calmly. "And which room would that be?"

"Second floor, first door to your right."

This time he left so quickly there was no chance for Penelope to interfere. Not that she wanted to, she assured herself as she left the dining room and headed for the gently curving stairway.

Penelope had assumed she and Maximillian would share a bedchamber, and she was hoping, as she grasped the smooth handrail and climbed to the second floor, that the hostile Beck was wrong. She prayed that the first door on the right would open to a room that was empty, that she would find the bed untouched and Maximillian would come around the next corner with a smile on his face.

She laid her fingers on the handle and pushed softly, making no sound, shifting her weight to open the door a crack.

She recognized Maximillian's golden head resting upon a fat pillow. His body was hidden under a thick green coverlet, and matching drapes were closed tight against the morning sun. The clothes he'd quickly removed last night were now folded neatly on a chair near the bed, and his shoes were side by side on the floor.

Penelope made not a sound, but Maximillian stirred and rolled slowly toward her. "What *is* it?" he asked testily. "It had better be something damned important for you to wake me at this ungodly hour."

Penelope stepped quietly into the room. He was barely awake, and probably didn't even realize who it was at his door. "Good morning," she whispered as she walked to the bed. There, she sat on the mattress beside her husband. "I thought we might have breakfast together."

"Gad, m'dear," he said primly. "I don't eat breakfast. Nasty habit, rising at the crack of dawn to ingest untoward amounts of victuals." His eyes were narrowed as he looked up at her. " 'Tis a meal you will have to accustom yourself to taking alone."

Penelope reached down to brush away a strand of golden hair that clung to Maximillian's cheek. He stiffened slightly at her touch. "I was surprised to find you gone from the bed this morning, and even more surprised to find you here," she admitted.

"Surely you don't expect that we will sleep in the same bed. Faith, m'dear," he said tiredly. "I couldn't possibly get a moment's rest with another body tossing and turning as you do."

"Do I?" she asked softly, more than a little disappointed.

"I'm afraid so, and I do need my rest, so if you'll hurry along . . ." He waved her off with an indolent gesture and then turned his back on her. A moment later she heard a soft, muffled snore.

Max raised up on his elbows as the door finally closed. Damnation, how could Penelope look so innocent and be so treacherous? How could she touch him and speak to him with such softness, after what she'd done? He knew the answer. The woman had no heart.

He needed to rest, but didn't really expect sleep to come. Even though it had been near dawn when he'd finally collected the remainder of his clothes from Penelope's room and come to this bed, he knew true, restful slumber was a luxury he would not enjoy for some time to come.

Unable to believe what his own men told him, he'd searched out the colonials who'd heard Heath Lowry's accusation for themselves. He'd gone in disguise, in gray wig and tattered clothing, to question the rebels on behalf, he told them, of the Indigo Blade. They all told the same story, and they'd all heard the tale from Lowry's mouth. One had even heard Chadwick confirm it.

So there was no doubt.

He'd been unable to snatch Lowry's body from the British soldiers, but in the night—after protests from the citizens of Charles Town—the soldiers had cut the body down. But not before Max had gotten a good look at what his wife's treachery had spawned.

Max tried to sleep, but rest wouldn't come. He wondered, as he lay there, if he'd ever sleep again with Penelope living under his roof.

It had taken all his strength not to reach up and place his hands around her neck as she'd sat on the side of his bed. It had taken every ounce of his resolve not to take her by the throat and ask her if she realized what she'd done, if she cared.

She had to believe that he was the man he pretended to be. Shallow, vain, self-centered. It would likely be the most difficult role he'd ever played, but he had no choice. He couldn't allow Penelope to see who he was. Couldn't afford the luxury of confronting her with even a portion of the truth. His horror, his disappointment. Allowing Penelope to see who and what he had become in the name of liberty would endanger not only his life, but the lives of men who trusted him. If she would blithely turn a family friend over to Chadwick, she was capable of any treachery.

He would use Penelope to get close to Chadwick and the other loyalists in Charles Town. He would play the foppish devoted husband in public and the disinterested fool in private, and no one would ever question that there was anything more to Maximillian Broderick.

No one.

"I'm a genius," Victor whispered in Mary's ear as he wrapped his arms around her waist.

Her laughter was soft, but true and deep. "I never doubted it."

Even though they were in her father's study, and they both knew William Seton might appear at any moment, he planted a kiss behind her ear.

This was her time, the time of her life when everything was going her way. Victor was falling in love with her, of that she was certain. Her body held an irrefutable power over him, a stronger control than she'd imagined possible. He needed her now. Soon, he wouldn't be able to live without her.

And Penelope, who was likely ignorantly happy at the moment, was about to embark upon the most trying time of her life.

If Penelope and Heath had entered the carriage house ten minutes earlier, they would have caught Mary Seton and Victor Chadwick in the midst of a most inappropriate act. Instead, they'd arrived as the lovers were dressing. Together, half-clothed and huddled together in the dark, Mary and Victor had heard almost every word of the conversation. Enough to convince Heath, when Victor confronted him a short time later, that Penelope had been the one to betray him.

Mary hadn't understood Victor's plan, not at first. This supposed disloyalty would make Penelope a heroine to William Seton and his loyalist friends, and Mary couldn't comprehend why Victor was anxious to lay the credit on her cousin.

It didn't take Mary long to understand Victor's motivations. Penelope's beloved Tyler was an unforgiving revolutionary at heart. She'd heard countless arguments between her father and her little cousin, loud and passionate arguments about that very subject.

And, too, the mood of the colonies was changing. The common people were uniting in their dreams of freedom and rebellion, and soon Penelope Broderick wouldn't be able to walk the streets of Charles Town without an armed guard for protection. Overnight she'd be transformed from Penelope Seton, beloved by everyone, to Penelope Broderick, hated traitor.

It was unfortunate that Heath had not survived his lashing. Victor had assured her that he'd never meant to kill the young man. Punishment for such behavior was necessary, he explained, to keep the rebels at bay. It was Heath's own fault that he was dead. She could almost make herself believe that was true. Perhaps soon she would.

"I wonder what Broderick will think of the news

that his wife turned poor Lowry in?" Victor asked bitterly.

He was still perturbed about losing Penelope, and that knowledge angered Mary more than she dared to reveal. Why did he continue to care? There was nothing Penelope could give him that she could not. "That popinjay," she said calmly, not allowing her displeasure to show. "I doubt he cares one way or another."

"What does she see in him?" Victor snapped. "I will never understand it."

Mary stepped out of his grasp and walked to the window. This would be a long and memorable day for her cousin, the beautiful and virtuous Penelope. "He's a fool, and he's going to make her miserable."

"I hope so," Victor said harshly.

Mary's response was a whisper. "So do I."

Chapter Nine

It had been a dreadfully long day. After leaving Maximillian to his sleep, Penelope ate alone in the large dining room and then took a walk in the garden. She explored the grounds, puzzled by Maximillian's behavior but not particularly worried. In the afternoon, she'd unpacked the rest of her things, and then taken a long nap. She hadn't seen her husband all day.

Until now. They stood in the formal dining room, she in the imported yellow silk gown she'd changed into for supper, Maximillian in a perfectly cut suit of pale blue velvet. Impossibly, he was embellished with more lace than he'd worn for the wedding.

The servants were lined up for her introduction, six men and one woman. There wasn't a smile to be seen.

"Come along, m'dear," Maximillian said tiredly. "The lads are waiting to meet you."

Nervously, she stepped forward.

"Dalton Archer." Maximillian indicated the first man in the queue with a wave of his hand. "Our butler, and an indispensable member of the household."

Penelope smiled at the man, who had dark blond hair and narrowed blue eyes and a neatly trimmed mustache and goatee. Of medium height and wide build, and dressed in a simple black suit, Dalton Archer looked like no butler she'd ever seen. He looked, in fact, more like a ruffian trying to pass himself off as a gentleman. He did not return her smile.

"Lewis Turner," Maximillian said, moving on down the line. "You've met Lewis, m'dear. Our extraordinarily reliable driver." Lewis Turner, the man she remembered from her jaunts with Maximillian, returned her smile. It was wide, cold, and totally ungenuine. His pale wavy hair was pulled back into a thick braid, and his suit was as simple as the butler's. There surely wasn't a subservient bone in his tall, lean body.

"Beck Andrews," Maximillian continued, turning to the youngest man of the assemblage, the chestnut-haired servant she'd encountered this morning. He looked no friendlier now than he had then.

"Mr. Andrews and I have met," she said softly, trying the smile once again without effect.

"Splendid," Maximillian said with a yawn. "John Rayburn," he continued without preamble. "My valet. Without John, I wouldn't be able to dress myself in the morning, I swear it. The man is a genius with a cravat."

John Rayburn had long and thick dark brown hair, dangerous steel-gray eyes, and a wide, full mouth. A valet? At the present time, Rayburn's own shirt was slightly askew, and his hair was in mild disarray. If Dalton looked like a ruffian, John looked like his partner in crime.

"Madam," he mumbled lowly as he bowed slightly.

"Garrick Vinson," Maximillian said with a flourish, patting the next man on the arm. "You've met Garrick, do you remember, m'dear? He's the footman, though he often does odd jobs around the place. Why, you're likely to run into Garrick anywhere in the house, at anytime."

The thought did not comfort her. With black hair pulled severely back, a small mustache and beard, and dressed in yet another black suit of clothes, he looked nearly as much the English lord as his master. But his eyes were uncivilized, black and wide beneath winged eyebrows. The devil, Penelope decided, forgoing the attempted smile that had done her no good to this point. This was surely what the devil looked like.

"Fletcher Huxley," Maximillian continued, moving to the last man in line. "My stableman. Ah, I do so love my horses. I race on occasion, you know."

"No, I didn't know," Penelope said, turning away from the disinterested gaze of the stableman, the only one of the lot who appeared to be over the age of thirty, and the only one who had not bothered to dress in the requisite black livery for the occasion. He looked as if he'd come straight from the stables, with his tattered work clothes and mussed dark hair. He looked as if he'd as soon be spending this time with the horses.

"And Helen, the newest addition to the household," Maximillian said with flourish. "She is to be your ladies' maid, your constant companion, your friend and servant."

Helen, a mature woman with wide hips, pale hair, and a pleasant face, curtseyed and uttered a quiet greeting, but she was as surly as the rest of the lot.

"Your uncle offered us a wedding gift of three slaves," Maximillian said distantly, and with a slight wrinkling of his nose. "Most inappropriate offer, I thought. My first impulse was to refuse his gift."

"I'm sure Uncle William meant well." She defended her uncle gently. The servants had not moved, and they listened intently.

Maximillian gave her a lazy smile. "Yes, I'm sure he had good intentions. However, my time abroad has given me an extreme distaste for the practice, hence my first instinct to refuse. I realized, on reflection, that refusing would simply mean a return to the plantation for the poor wretches, so I accepted."

"If it disturbs you . . ."

He ignored her. "And I promptly sent them on their way. One man has quite a knack for barrel making, and I've set him up in business right here in Charles Town. The other two expressed an interest in leaving the colonies, and they are both on board an eastern-bound ship as we speak."

"You did all this today?"

His eyes bored through her. "Object all you wish, my dear. You own nothing now, nothing and no one. All you have is mine."

It had not been her intent to complain, not at all. She admired Maximillian's beliefs, his convictions. It was a good and noble thing he'd done. "I have no objections," she said softly.

Penelope wanted more than anything to get her husband alone for a few moments. She wanted to ask him why he was behaving so strangely, and why he felt compelled to remind her that by marriage she had put herself completely in his hands. Even more than that, she wanted to ask him where on earth he had obtained his household staff.

"Off with you all," Maximillian said, dismissing the staff with an exaggerated wave of his hand. "I'm famished."

The group broke up and scattered, all but Beck, who saw to the setting of the table, and Dalton, who came forward with a sheet of paper in his hand.

"Madam, this was left for you this afternoon."

She took and unfolded the single sheet of paper, recognizing Tyler's neat handwriting before she read a single word. "My brother was here? Why didn't he stay and visit?"

"You were resting, madam," Dalton said sourly. "I told him you could not be disturbed."

"For my brother," she said, forcing cordiality, "I can be disturbed anytime, anywhere."

"I'll remember that, madam," Dalton said curtly,

and then he spun around to stride impatiently from the room.

Penelope's good mood faded as she read the letter, a curt and biting missive that ended with an alarming declaration.

"I don't understand," she said, turning to Maximillian. Her husband seemed to find something fascinating in the cut of his sleeve, as he studied the blue velvet that was pale as a robin's egg. "Read this, please, and tell me what it means."

Maximillian took the letter from her, an annoyed expression on his aristocratic face. " 'Penelope,' " he read lazily, and then he turned heavy-lidded eyes her way. "Rather abrupt, wouldn't you say? No 'Dear sister' or 'Beloved Penelope?' "

"Just read the rest," she said impatiently.

" 'Penelope,' " he said, beginning again. " 'How could you? Since you refuse to see me, I must be satisfied to leave this letter, but I could not go without letting you know how I feel about your unforgivable actions.' "

Maximillian raised finely shaped eyebrows above lazy eyes that were so pale at the moment they seemed to hold no color at all. "Ah, yes. Unforgivable actions."

He didn't wait for an answer but continued reading. " 'I know your sympathies lie with Uncle William and the loyalists, but I never believed you could stoop so low as to betray a friend. I can no longer stay here. By the time you read this, I will be far away. I can never undo what you've done, as I can never forgive it. But I can and will leave behind a family I can no longer bear to live with, and

I can fight for what I believe in. Tyler.' "

He offered the letter back with one hand and stifled a yawn with the other. "Sounds as if the lad's run away from home."

"Maximillian, how can you be so calm? Tyler isn't old enough to be living on his own. He hasn't finished his education, and he's . . . he's just fifteen."

"Some are men at fifteen," Maximillian said with little care. "Some are not. Your brother seemed to me quite capable of taking care of himself."

This was the most frustrating conversation she'd ever endured. "And what's this about my betraying a friend? What does that mean?"

Maximillian had evidently found a spot on his lacy cuff, for he began studying and brushing at it. "Oh, that," he muttered. "I imagine he's talking about Lowry. It's all the talk about town today, you know. My wife the brave heroine." He glanced at her from hooded eyes. "I never would have thought it of you."

"Heath Lowry?" Penelope said softly. She felt a wave of unease, a coolness in her cheeks. "I didn't expect anyone would find out."

"Really?" Maximillian turned his back to her and walked slowly from the room, that damned cuff continuing to claim his attention. "It's not every day that you get to send a rebel to his death. I'm rather surprised you didn't tell me all about it last night."

He continued walking away from her, and she had to hurry to catch up. "What do you mean, to his death? What happened?" His long legs were carrying him away from her too quickly, and she was soon breathless. "Maximillian, will you please stop?" He did not. "I did what I thought was right," she said breathlessly, knowing now that she should have fetched the doctor in spite of Heath's protests. "I can't believe Heath's dead. Are you sure?"

Maximillian came to an abrupt halt, and she caught up with him in the foyer of her new home. His back was stiff and straight, his face fixed and expressionless as he turned to her. "We don't discuss politics, remember m'dear? The topic is of no interest to me." There was not a hint of warmth in his eyes, not a hint of longing or love in the face he presented to her.

"But—"

"Enough," he said sharply. "Good God." He looked her up and down with barely disguised disdain. "You bore me already." With that, he turned his back to her once again and walked away. This time, she didn't bother to follow.

Chadwick's reinforcements were well on their way back to England, with an armed escort. Four privateers had intercepted the vessel transporting the troops, boarded the ship, and taken command with very little resistance. Chadwick would wonder what had delayed his troops, but he'd not receive word of their fate for weeks, perhaps months.

It was small consolation.

Max sat in his study, a single candle burning on his desk, a map spread before him. Pockets of resistance had sprung up across the country, and South Carolina was no different. Those rebels needed guns, ammunition, financial support, and training. The League of the Indigo Blade provided it all.

"Maximillian."

He closed his eyes at the intrusive sound of Penelope's voice. God, the woman was stubborn. He'd avoided her all day, rebuffed her in the evening, and still she sought him out.

"What?" he answered sharply without turning to face the doorway. He rolled up the map as her footsteps sounded softly, footsteps that brought her closer and closer.

"I just wanted to say good night."

Her voice was sweet as honey, the dulcet tones of an angel reminding him of the false treasure he'd found and claimed, the life she'd offered and then taken away. The anger that simmered inside him grew until he was afraid he could no longer contain it.

"Good night, then," he said sharply, opening a drawer and tossing the map inside, then slamming the drawer with more force than was necessary. Still, he hadn't looked at her. God help him, he did not think he could bear it.

"Maximillian." Penelope's soft whisper was hesitant, a caress so sweet and uncertain.

Max's first instinct was to come out of his chair and strangle her. He'd been a fool to think her innocent and precious. He'd been a bigger fool to fall in love with her. At this moment, he wanted revenge for the way she'd deceived him as much as he wanted her to pay for Heath Lowry's death. Perhaps more.

But he couldn't relent, he couldn't let the anger

overcome the cold calm he'd forced himself to maintain. Not yet. He stilled the fury that burned inside him, and calling on all the resolve he possessed, he rotated his head slowly until he could see her beautiful, treacherous face. "Yes, m'dear?"

"Is something wrong?"

How could she ask that question? Did she have no soul, no conscience at all? "No," he lied smoothly.

"It's just that you're acting very differently today. Have I displeased you in some way?" There was an earnest quality in her voice, a sadness on her face.

"No," he lied again. "What more could a man ask for in a wife?" He lifted his hand slowly to touch her arm, to trail his fingers over fine silk and delicate lace. Much as he wanted to, he did not grab and shake her. His touch was light, his fingers barely touching her gown. He could feel no warmth beneath the silk. Perhaps there was none.

It was a small smile that crossed her face, a faint turn of her mouth that transformed her entire face. "I'm happy to hear you say that. I want us to have a good life together, Maximillian."

"I'm sure we will." Unable to take any more, he allowed his hand to fall away and returned his attention to a now-bare desk. "You come from a good family, your breeding is practically impeccable, and being associated with the Seton name will do wonders for my import business when I get it into full swing." He drummed lazy fingers on the desk and forced a yawn. "And I, of course, will be the perfect husband. You'll never want for anything money can buy, m'dear. Clothes, jewels, whatever your heart desires."

"I care little for such things," she said softly.

"It's all I have to offer." The words came quickly, too harsh and too true.

There was a moment of complete silence. No rustle of silk, no murmur of Penelope's soft breath broke the stillness. If he was lucky, she would run from the room without another word. Luck was not with him, on this night or any other.

"And what of love?" she finally whispered.

"Faith, m'dear," Max said lightly, "the courting stage of our relationship is over. We are man and wife, and need endure no more silly chatter of love."

Dead silence filled the room again, and Max dared not look at Penelope. Instead, he lifted a hand and brushed at the lace cuff. "Would you look at that? Another damned spot, and this my favorite shirt."

Out of the corner of his eye he saw his wife backing toward the door.

"Good night," she said, her voice unsteady and almost weepy. "Should I . . . should I wait up for you?"

He forced himself to look at her, to stare into her damp eyes, to stare into the dark and deceptive depths where he'd once been foolish enough to see love. If he touched her again, he would kill her. If he let down this shield, he would accuse her of treachery and she would know the truth—that he was not who he pretended to be.

"I performed my husbandly duties last night, did I not? Lud, woman, was that not enough for you?"

Her hand trembled and her mouth quivered, but she said nothing.

"I quite outdid myself on our wedding night, I confess, and I find I'm still quite fatigued." He lifted a limp-wristed hand and smiled softly. "Gad, I hope you didn't think I would provide such services each and every night."

"Of course not," Penelope said as she reached the doorway, finally as anxious to escape as he was to have her go. "Good night, Maximillian."

Max didn't drop his hand or his facade until Penelope had been gone for a very long moment. He listened to her step on the stairs, the rustle of her gown, and finally the closing of her door above.

She was amoral, surely, to stand before him so innocently after what she'd done. Evil and heartless and empty. She was a shell of a woman, a beautiful body without a soul, without a conscience. Without a heart. He could never show his true self to her, never offer his heart and his soul to a woman who had none.

Why, after a lifetime of hard lessons on the falsity of human nature, had he been fooled by this woman? Why had he believed in her?

Max doused the candle to leave himself in comforting darkness.

Chapter Ten

Penelope quickly went from confused to angry to numb, and the process took all of a week. Maximillian's puzzling and complete transition from loving suitor to disinterested husband was only one of her problems.

Uncle William did not share her concern about Tyler's departure. In fact, when Penelope called on her uncle the morning after receiving Tyler's letter to discuss the problem, he'd brushed aside her concerns and began a tirade concerning her husband's ungrateful response to his wedding gift.

She'd tried to turn the conversation around, but her uncle had seemed almost pleased to be rid of the responsibility of a rebellious nephew. He'd insisted there was nothing he could do and urged Penelope to put the youngster from her mind. She couldn't.

It had been there, in William Seton's house, that she'd heard the story that had circulated about Heath's death and her part in the capture. Her uncle had actually congratulated her, and when she denied the preposterous charges and shed a tear for the young man who'd died, he'd winked slyly and told her not to fret. He understood completely her reasons for preferring to remain anonymous. Penelope's heartiest protestations were met with a condescending smile.

She didn't understand why Heath had accused her, or why Victor had confirmed the story. Poor Heath. She would forever remember him as she'd last seen him, hurt and scared; so young, so devoted to his cause. It wasn't fair that he should have died in that way. It wasn't right, and Penelope was torn as to what to do next. She'd wanted to rush from the house and spread the word that she was innocent, but she'd also wanted to hang her head and cry.

Silent tears came, but try as she might, she couldn't convince her uncle, who was most proud of her supposed actions, of her innocence. Victor Chadwick, the only person who might clear her of this charge, was conveniently unavailable. He was out of town for a few days, Uncle William said vaguely.

Mary had been asleep, still, on that morning, though Uncle William told Penelope—when she asked—that Mary was aware of Heath's fate and of Tyler's action. Apparently Mary was no more concerned about Tyler than Uncle William was, to be sleeping so late in the morning. Nor, evidently, did she grieve for Heath as Penelope did.

After that short visit, Penelope went home. She hadn't left the house since.

The fine Broderick mansion was more a prison than a home. The servants never smiled in her presence. In fact, they seemed to despise her. Maximillian was not the man she'd married, was not the man who'd professed so convincingly to love her. He was cold and distant, concerned only with his wardrobe and his horses, and was usually absent or sleeping. He did his best to avoid her, of that she was certain.

Their differing schedules helped to keep them apart. Penelope kept to the routine she'd maintained all her life—rising with the sun and finding her way to bed soon after it set. Maximillian rarely rose before noon, and Penelope usually had no idea where he was when she retired. She heard him in his study some nights, while on other nights he was mysteriously absent.

So, a week after becoming Mrs. Maximillian Broderick, Penelope drifted through her day unhappily, waiting for word from Tyler, questioning over and over again the events of the night she'd found Heath Lowry beneath her window, and wondering when or if her husband would make an appearance.

When Dalton came into the parlor to very sourly announce Miss Mary Seton, Penelope put the book she'd been holding but not reading aside and came to her feet.

Mary was radiant, with color in her cheeks and

a brilliant smile on her face. "I came to see how married life is agreeing with you," Mary said as she stepped into the room.

Penelope took quick steps to reach the doorway and throw her arms around her cousin's neck. "I miss you terribly," she said, and she meant it. No one would ever know how deeply and regretfully she meant it.

"But you have Maximillian now, and he's much richer and much more handsome than I," Mary teased as she stepped back to break away from the hug.

"Is something wrong?" Mary's smile faded.

Right then, looking into Mary's sparkling eyes, Penelope made her decision. She wouldn't take her troubles to her cousin or to anyone else, wouldn't become the pitied, unhappy wife. Marrying Maximillian had been her decision—her mistake. She had no choice but to make the best of it.

"I've been very worried about Tyler," she confessed.

"La," Mary said with a wave of her hand. "Tyler will be fine. I expect he'll come back any day now, hungry and tired and done with his ridiculous ideas of revolution. A full stomach and a soft warm bed will seem heaven after a few days or weeks on his own."

"I hope you're right."

"I am." Mary was sometimes annoyingly confident, certain she was infallible in her beliefs. This time, Penelope hoped her cousin was right.

"And then," Penelope said, taking Mary's arm and

leading her to the sofa, "there's this preposterous story going around."

"Heath Lowry," Mary said as she took her seat.

Penelope nodded.

"Gossip." Mary dismissed the subject with another wave of her hand. "And besides, what do you care what a bunch of agitators think? You're a true heroine to the loyalists."

"It's not true."

"Well, it seems you get the credit anyway," Mary said lightly.

This was impossible. No one took her concerns or her defense seriously, not even Mary. Penelope reclaimed her seat, while Mary rose and started to examine the room. Every figurine, every vase, every piece of furniture came under Mary's wandering inspection. She talked as she roamed, providing gossip from their small circle of friends, plans for a new gown, her latest confrontation with her father . . . and Penelope soaked it all in. She hadn't realized how she'd longed for friendly voice. A smile, a laugh . . . this had been sorely missing from her day-to-day life.

At last Mary, who'd made a complete circle of the large room, stopped in front of Penelope. "You really are worried," she said sternly. "Is it Tyler?"

"In part."

"And that business with Heath . . ."

"Until Victor gets back to Charles Town, there's no way for me to clear my name."

"Victor arrived yesterday," Mary said with a small smile. "He came by the house last night, and stayed to visit with me for a while. We talked until quite late." Her smile widened. "When we last spoke of Victor, my words were unkind, but you know better than anyone how I feel about him. And now—oh, Penelope—I think maybe he's finally falling in love with me."

For Mary's sake, Penelope hoped it was true, even though in their last discussion of Victor Chadwick they'd agreed he wasn't good enough for the bubbly and beautiful Mary Seton. She guessed they'd been words spoken in anger, at least on Mary's part.

"That's wonderful."

"You're not jealous, are you?" Mary asked, her smile dying. "I mean, you could have had Victor for yourself, if you'd wanted him."

Mary had always had a soft spot in her heart for Victor, and Penelope really wished her cousin the best in this. "I don't think Victor and I were well suited at all, and in time he would have realized it, too. You, on the other hand, are just what he needs. Sunshine in his life, a smile and a laugh, someone to make him less . . . serious."

"I can handle that, I think," Mary said with a sly smile.

"Mary," Penelope took her cousin's hands. "I need to see him as soon as possible. I need Victor to clear my name."

Mary squeezed Penelope's hands. "I'll speak to him on your behalf this evening."

"You should have seen her," Mary said gleefully. "She is positively miserable."

The carriage house had become as familiar to Mary as her own bedroom. She could find her way from the house to the small building to the fine coach in the dark. There, upon the padded cushions, Victor had loved her. He'd taken her in the back of the wagon, too, and on the ground, and standing up. There was no longer pain when he took her, and on occasion she began to feel that there was something beyond the quick coupling they shared.

It didn't matter. What mattered was that he needed her, that he told her she was beautiful, that in her arms he lost control.

Victor had been away from Charles Town for days, and he'd missed her. He said so, and with great enthusiasm he showed her how very much. And then, as they sat in the dark, he asked after Penelope.

"Perhaps I should do as she asks and clear her name."

"Don't you dare!" Mary grabbed his head, threading her fingers through his already mussed hair. He'd dressed quickly once he was done with her, and she'd hurriedly redonned her simple linen gown. He was rumpled and warm and satisfied. She was empty and cold and annoyed. "Everything's going perfectly, and I won't allow you to ruin it all now with a fit of honesty."

"If it had been anyone else, if it had been a servant or a stranger or a slave, this would already be forgotten," he whispered, his breath still coming heavy and uneven. "But Heath Lowry was one of their own, the son of a wealthy man, a young man they watched grow from a child to an adult, and they won't forgive Penelope. Not ever."

"Good," she whispered, leaning forward to plant a kiss on Victor's mouth. His response was mild, lazy in fact, and she couldn't have that. Not now. She needed him to need her, to crave her above all else. She reached between their bodies to lay her hand over the manhood beneath his breeches, to stroke it until it grew stiff again.

"You're insatiable," he said, drawing his smiling mouth away from hers. "The perfect woman. A lady on the outside, a whore at heart."

Victor's words hurt, but Mary wouldn't allow him to see her pain. "The perfect woman, you say. Will you miss me when I'm gone? Father's talking about returning to the plantation soon. I thought that he would wait until the sickly season, until the summer was upon us, but he's restless and wants to go home. What will you do without me?"

He wouldn't let her go. In her heart she knew it to be true. Surely she hadn't endured night after night of *this* for nothing.

"I'll miss you, I suppose," he admitted casually. "You're uninhibited and pretty, and perhaps the most audacious mistress I've ever had. I doubt if the next one will live up to your standards."

He spoke so easily about other women, about another to take her place. Mary dropped her hand and pulled away. "The next one?"

"You don't expect that I'll live the life of a celibate after you leave Charles Town, do you?" There was an underlying cruelty in his voice and in the hand that grasped her arm and pulled her close. "Don't spoil this by becoming tiresome, Mary."

She allowed Victor to kiss her again, deep and

rough this time. She allowed him to move between her legs and spread her thighs wide. "Maybe I don't have to leave Charles Town," she said hopefully. "I hate the plantation, I've always hated it."

Victor turned dark eyes up to her, then looked thoughtlessly away. "Your father would never allow you to stay here without a chaperone."

"I wouldn't need a chaperone if I were married." Mary took his head in her hands and forced him to look at her. "Would I?"

"And who's the unfortunate lad who's asked?"

Mary threaded her fingers through Victor's hair, holding on tight. He smiled at her, that wicked grin she loved and hated, and as she held his gaze, he moved forward to rest snugly between her thighs.

"You could ask," she whispered.

His smile never wavered. "Women like you aren't meant for marriage. You're a mistress, a harlot, a woman for whom one man would never be enough."

"You would be enough," she whispered.

He laughed at her, actually laughed at her as he leaned forward to take her mouth again. "When I do marry," he promised with his mouth brushing hers, "I'll be certain to live in a mansion with a sizable carriage house. I've been thinking of asking Suzanne Fairfax," he said casually. "What do you say, Mary? I'll marry Suzanne, and you can be my mistress always."

"But I thought . . ."

"All would have been perfection if only Penelope had said yes to my proposal," he said as though he didn't hear her. "One Seton as my wife, another as my paramour. One to bear my children, another to bring me pleasure. We could have lived in the same house."

The impossible idea seemed to excite him even more.

There was no tenderness in his touch, and Mary knew now that there was no love, either. A whore at heart, he'd called her. Not the kind of woman a man would marry. He was actually thinking, as he met with her night after night, of asking that pasty-faced Suzanne Fairfax to be his wife.

Tears came to her eyes but didn't fall. Victor might not think so now, but he would miss her when she went away. She'd make certain of it. She'd love him so hard, so completely, that no other woman would ever satisfy him. Then he'd think twice about marrying some boring, shy twit like Suzanne Fairfax.

Her tears dried as she brought her lips to Victor's neck. She wrapped her legs around his body and held him fast, and whispered into his ear—not words of love but the words of an insatiable lover.

Yes, he would miss her.

Max didn't want to face Penelope, but he had no choice. For days he'd avoided her easily, sleeping into the afternoon, racing his horses or visiting his favorite tailor once he arose, fulfilling his duties as the Indigo Blade as Penelope slept. He only saw his wife over the supper table, where he prattled on about clothing and horses and she remained quiet.

He took a deep breath and entered her bedchamber, bothering with only the faintest of knocks as he swung the door open. Penelope sat before a mirror while Helen brushed her magnificent dark hair. They both looked his way as the door swung open.

Helen showed no emotion, but Penelope was obviously surprised to see him. Shocked, even.

"I hate to disturb you, m'dear," he said as he stepped into her room, "but there are important plans to discuss."

Penelope glanced over her shoulder to Helen. "I can finish here, thank you."

Helen curtseyed and left the room without looking directly at him, without looking back at her mistress. She seemed grateful for the chance to escape.

"Plans, you say?" Penelope resumed brushing her hair, staring at her image in the mirror and avoiding looking at him. "What sort of plans?" She was pale, tired, and clearly unhappy.

"The Huntlands' ball is tomorrow night, and I had planned to wear the beige silk. I thought you might wear your pale blue gown."

Penelope placed the brush down and turned to face him at last. "These are the important plans we have to discuss?"

"We've been married a mere three weeks," Max said, trying to instill a touch of horror into his voice. "Lud, what would people say if we clashed?"

"I don't want to go," Penelope said softly. She returned her attention to the looking glass and began to braid her hair over her shoulder. Her hands worked mindlessly, long pale fingers intertwining with strands of thick dark hair. "I . . . I can't go, Maximillian."

This was exactly what he'd been afraid of. Penelope had left the house only once since the wedding, and she'd had a single visitor—her cousin Mary who'd called on occasion. His wife was hiding here, and that would not do.

"Nonsense," he said tiredly. "You can't remain in this house forever, m'dear."

"You don't understand."

"I understand quite well," he interrupted a bit too harshly. "It's the Lowry business, I suppose."

She turned wide, desolate eyes his way, and he could almost sympathize with her. Almost. Such pain, such heartache in that simple glance. Was any of it real? He thought not.

"Faith, m'dear, you're the talk of all Charles Town," he said brightly. "A heroine or a traitor, a sinner or a saint, no matter what face you choose to wear, everyone will want to see it."

"I didn't . . ."

"Hush," he said, raising a stilling hand. "I don't want to hear about your politics, your beliefs, or your reasons or your excuses. They bore me."

"I know," she whispered.

"You will go to the Huntlands' ball, and you will have a wonderful time. I insist."

"I can't."

Max stepped further into the room. He didn't want to be close to her, he didn't want to touch her, he didn't want to stare too closely into those deceptively sinless dark eyes that pleaded with him. "You will go," he insisted lowly. "And you will smile and dance and laugh and gossip. You will play the happy bride for everyone in attendance. You will not cry, or plead, or wallow in self-pity."

He needed to mingle with the loyalists, to become Victor Chadwick's friend and confidant. He'd endured horse races and cockfights, dull evenings over cognac and playing cards. He was quickly becoming accepted in this crowd. The Huntlands' ball was important. People talked at these social events, and he had no choice but to be there to hear every uttered secret. Word had it the president of the council himself would be in attendance.

He wouldn't throw away everything he'd worked for because Penelope was afraid to face what she'd done.

There was defeat on her face, a dead calm in her eyes. "The pale blue, you say?" she whispered.

Max smiled at his lovely, treacherous wife. "The pale blue."

Chapter Eleven

Penelope was well aware that no one in attendance would dare to confront and accuse her of her supposed involvement in Heath Lowry's death. Not here, not now. This was primarily a loyalist crowd here at the Huntlands', and several members of the governor's council were in attendance. No harsh words were spoken, but she saw the indictment in the eyes of many old acquaintances, felt their condemnation in the cool way they said hello and then turned quickly away.

Maximillian was no comfort at all, not that she'd expected it of him. He was satisfied because they made a handsome couple, because their outfits were harmonious and the March weather was fine and his new shoes didn't pinch. He seemed to care for nothing else.

Shortly after their arrival, he'd deposited her in a

corner and sauntered off to entertain a simpering group of empty-headed females who were charmed by his shallow wit and lazy smile.

She hated him. For making her come to this dreadful ball, for not being the man she thought he was, for making her dream of a wonderful life and then taking it away. She, who had always been content to settle for whatever life offered her, was no longer satisfied with her lot. Maximillian had offered her a small taste of true happiness, and then made it vanish so completely she was no longer certain it had ever existed.

She would likely spend the entire evening in this corner. Maximillian was entertaining and being entertained, Mary was dancing with partner after adoring partner, and no one—no one wanted to be seen with the betrayer Penelope Broderick.

"You are lovely this evening." The deep soft voice came out of nowhere, and Penelope turned her head to see Victor approaching with a smile on his face. He must have just arrived, because she'd been looking for him since she and Maximillian had been announced. She had so much to say to him, she didn't know where to start.

"I can't believe your devoted husband would leave you all alone," he said sarcastically.

"Victor Chadwick." Penelope took a deep breath to calm herself. "I've been trying to get in touch with you for weeks."

"I know." He stood beside her and watched the ebb and flow of dancers before them. "I did receive a number of letters, and of course your cousin mentioned a time or two that you were anxious to talk to me."

"Anxious," she hissed. "Yes, Victor, you could say I've been anxious to talk to you." She saw no reason to delay asking the questions that had troubled her for weeks. "Why did you lie about my part in Heath Lowry's capture? Why did he lie?"

He cocked his head to look at her. "I did you a favor," he said with a smile.

"A favor?" she hissed. "My life has been ruined and you truly believe you did me a *favor*?"

"What I did was save you from the serious charge of aiding a criminal. What I did was save you from a long term in a very nasty prison. Why, a soldier was sorely wounded. You can imagine the charges I would have been forced to bring against you if he had died. Prison, Penelope. I don't think I could bear to see you hanging from a gallows." He sounded very unsure of that last statement.

"I don't know what you're talking about."

"You were seen," he whispered, "leaving the carriage house."

"By whom?"

His smile widened. "That I cannot tell you. Suffice it to say I have spies everywhere. How else was I to save you but to say that you came to me with the information that Heath Lowry was hiding in your carriage house?"

"And Heath?"

"Well," Victor said without care, "telling Heath that you had come to me was necessary in order to make the scenario believable. I found it was quite simple to convince Heath that you'd betrayed him, since no one but you knew of his location."

"I would have preferred to face the charges," she said softly. "And I insist that you make a public announcement clearing my name."

"You insist," he said coldly.

He was going to do nothing, and Penelope knew it as she studied his stoic profile. He was angry because she'd chosen Maximillian over him, and this was her punishment. What would he say if he knew living with Maximillian was punishment enough?

"One day you'll thank me," he said as he surveyed the crowded room with apathetic eyes. Those eyes hardened when he turned them to her.

"I will not." She, who had never stood up to a man before—who had never stood up to anyone before—held her ground and looked Victor in the eye. He had gone too far, and there was no one to defend her. Not her uncle—and certainly not her husband. She had no choice but to defend herself.

"Come with me."

Penelope was about to protest when Victor took her arm and steered her away from her somewhat comfortable and safe corner. "I have nothing else to say to you," she said, trying in vain to slip her arm from his. He held on tight, and the only way she might escape would be to make a scene, to yell at him and demand that he release her.

She was already the center of attention, and had no desire to make herself more so. They stayed close to the wall, drifting around small clusters of party-goers who turned their heads to watch as she and Victor circled the room. When they reached the opened doors that led to a small garden, Victor steered her through and into the night.

Lanterns had been set here and there to light the night for those who needed a moment of fresh air, so they were not lost in darkness. Still, the sound and the light from the festive ballroom were muffled, and Penelope was grateful for the moment of respite.

"I have a proposition for you," Victor said, releasing her arm when they were well away from the doors. He indicated that she take a seat on the wrought iron bench amongst the roses, and she gratefully did so.

"I can't imagine what sort of proposition that might be."

She glanced up at Victor, who had placed himself before her so that he could easily stop her should she decide to return to the crowded ballroom without him. He was smiling again, a perfectly smug and satisfied grin.

"Spy for me," he said softly.

"What?" Penelope came to her feet, ready to storm past him and run into the house, if that's what was necessary to escape.

"Listen to me for a moment." Victor placed his hands on her shoulders and forced her to sit once again. "I wouldn't ask you to endanger yourself, Penelope, you're much too dear to me even though you are wasting yourself on that foppish husband of yours." A trace of hostility crept into his voice as he spoke of Maximillian.

"Before you go further," Penelope said coldly, "allow me to make it clear that I will not assist you in any way. A spy! That's absurd!"

"Is it?" Victor was undaunted. "A bit of information here, an out-of-place statement there . . . you simply listen and report what you hear to me."

"I said no."

"It's the Indigo Blade," Victor said softly, and if possible there was more distaste in his voice than there had been when he spoke of Maximillian. "I was away for several days, following up on a lead that could take me to the mongrel. He's here in Charles Town, Penelope, living among us, and I think he's right under my nose. I can feel it. I'm so close. . . ."

"No," Penelope said again. "I have no interest in your problems, political unrest, or the Indigo Blade."

"You've heard of him?"

"Of course."

"He's a menace," Victor said passionately.

"A very clever menace, from what I hear," Penelope said, glad to see Victor squirm.

He appeared to be quite uncomfortable, pursing his thin lips and wrinkling his nose as if he smelled something bad. "Heath Lowry's death has become rather a difficulty for me, you see. The president of the Council is well acquainted with the Lowrys. Even though the boy was an agitator and deserved every lash of the whip, it's become . . . a small problem. If I could capture the Indigo Blade, the Lowry incident would be forgotten."

He turned humorless eyes down to her. "What can I say to make you reconsider?"

"Nothing," Penelope said calmly.

"I have a gut feeling this Indigo Blade is one of

us. He might even be here tonight. All I'm asking is that you keep your ears and eyes open, perhaps ask a few questions."

Penelope smiled up at Victor. Even though she had no interest in politics, she had more respect for a man like the Indigo Blade, a man who fought for what he believed in, who liberated condemned men and then disappeared into the night, than she would ever have for Victor Chadwick.

"Faith, m'dear, whatever are you doing in the garden? It's much too cool for you to be out of doors without your cloak."

Maximillian's voice was false and much too high—and a splendid sound to Penelope, at the moment. Victor looked over his shoulder and scowled, and she took the opportunity to rise and step around him.

Her indifferent husband had rescued her, and he didn't even know it.

"We should dance together at least once, for appearance's sake, don't you know," Max said as he led Penelope to the dance floor. The fingers he held were delicate and cool, all but lifeless in his hand.

When he'd seen Chadwick and Penelope speaking, it had disturbed something deeply buried and most unwelcome. It was jealousy, a possessiveness he didn't dare acknowledge. When he'd watched them step into the night together, his jealousy had exploded into a white-hot rage.

And now, charlatan that he was, he danced with his wife with a half-smile on his face and nothing—absolutely nothing—in his eyes.

The minuet was unbearably slow, and his wife moved with uncommon grace.

"What were you and your chum talking about in the garden?" he asked lightly, as if he didn't care.

Penelope looked up at him with a flawless and falsely innocent face. Good God, she was beautiful. Her dark eyes wide and trusting, her perfectly shaped lips inviting. The sight of her was as astounding as it had been on the night they met. At times he was certain this effect she had on him would wane. At other times he was certain he would never rid himself of the curse.

"Nothing," she lied.

"Really? I could have sworn I heard your good friend Victor Chadwick mention the Indigo Blade."

Her lips parted slightly, her chin quivered, and Max responded with a smile. Penelope had been caught in her lie, and she knew it.

"Don't tell me," he whispered with a smile. "You and your chum have the same fate planned for the Indigo Blade as you served up to poor Heath Lowry."

Anger flashed in her normally placid eyes. "I thought you had no concern or patience for politics."

"Intrigue is always interesting," he said blandly. "Back stabbing, treachery, the machinations of a devious mind. Lud, m'dear, when I married you I had no idea you were so deliciously cunning."

She said nothing, but stared up at him with accusing eyes. His wife was usually such a good little actress, but tonight her talent failed her. He could see the anger in her eyes and in the set of her lush mouth. "Remind me why I married you." she whispered hoarsely. "At the moment I can't recall."

"Faith," he said without missing a beat. "I'm moneyed, I'm not horribly ugly, and I'm witty and entertaining. What woman wouldn't marry me?"

She lowered her eyes to his chest and kept her gaze there for the remainder of the dance. So, he thought as he studied the top of her head, Chadwick was soliciting her to help him find the Indigo Blade. If he'd been closer he would have heard more—if he'd been stronger he would have waited a moment longer to hear her answer.

Would his lovely wife send him to the gallows? Judging by her history and the spark of fury in her eyes at the moment, the answer was an unqualified yes.

It seemed the minuet would never end.

Penelope closed her eyes and tried to ignore her husband's mindless chatter as the carriage traveled slowly toward home. Maximillian talked nonstop about a new tailor he needed to visit, a boot maker who was supposedly divine, and a scandalous bit of gossip he'd heard.

It took all her willpower not to turn to him and scream for silence.

For all the lovely trappings of her life, she had nothing. No love, no happiness, no joy. And there was none forthcoming, it seemed, as Maximillian seemed perfectly content in this pretext of a marriage. She had but one thing in life to look forward to. Children.

If only the wedding night had resulted in a pregnancy. She would find contentment in bearing and raising a child; she knew it with all her heart. Having a baby would make her days worthwhile, give her life purpose. She'd be a good mother, she swore it. A devoted and loving parent. And Maximillian? She studied his fine profile through hooded eyes, as he chattered on about a stallion Mr. Huntland had recently acquired.

Maximillian was too selfish to be a good husband, and there wasn't enough love within him to make a good father. She'd believed differently, once. How had she allowed herself to see more than there was in his eyes? To feel love in his touch? What a fool she'd been.

But Maximillian was her husband, and if she was to have the children she wanted so badly, he would father them. That meant he would have to visit her bed on occasion.

The wedding night had been wonderful, and she'd thought it just the beginning. She'd never known such heat and passion and pleasure existed, she'd never known she could feel so much a part of another person, not just in body but in spirit and heart. She'd thought those feelings would continue and even grow, but now she wasn't even sure that what she'd experienced was real. Maximillian certainly hadn't felt the same way.

Perhaps she'd done something wrong. Perhaps she simply wasn't good enough.

If she wanted children, he would have to lie with her again, and she had a notion that if she waited, for Maximillian to come to her, she'd die a lonely, old, and childless woman.

Gathering her courage, she scooted across the seat to sit close to her husband. Apparently startled by her move, he raised fine eyebrows and set dubious gray-green eyes on her. "Are you cold, m'dear?" he asked as she snuggled against his side.

"A little."

"Ah," he said simply, turning away from her to look out the window.

He was warm but unyielding. "Would you put your arm around me?" she whispered. "I'm still chilly."

With apparent reluctance, he did as she asked. "Lud, I'll likely wrinkle this jacket."

He was not making this easy, with his head turned away and his arm stiffly around her. There had been a time when he'd touched her easily. A hand over hers, a gentle kiss that touched her so deeply the memory still shook her. Now, he acted as if he'd rather not touch her at all.

Penelope placed her hand on Maximillian's thigh, and he practically jumped out of his skin. She didn't move her hand away, but very gently stroked his hard thigh through heavy silk. She wondered if he could feel her hand tremble, if it mattered at all that this was difficult for her.

When he looked down at her she met his gaze squarely, and with a subtle shifting of her body she raised up and placed her lips against his.

His lips were cold and still, and she quickly drew away.

"Faith, m'dear," he said huskily, "I don't think you're chilly at all."

"No," she whispered. "I'm not."

He brought his mouth to hers and kissed her, a very reluctant and tentative caress. You'd think they were strangers who had never touched before, the way he so warily kissed her. His entire body was rigid, his mouth hesitant and stubborn against hers.

"Would you like me to come to your bed tonight?" he asked as he broke the awkward contact.

"Yes."

In the semi-dark, she could not identify the expression that flashed across his face, but it seemed to be, in the dim light, a mirror of the anger and confusion she herself felt. For a moment he was silent, and she thought he would refuse her.

If he refused her now, if he rejected her overture, there was no hope for them—no hope at all. His rejection would condemn her to a lifetime of loneliness, and she held her breath as she waited.

"You need but to ask," he said in a buoyant voice that did not match his somber facial cast. "We'll soon be home. Retire to your bedchamber and prepare yourself, and I'll be along shortly."

He lifted and removed his arm, then, and returned his attention to the passing landscape.

The ensuing silence was so dismal, Penelope wished for more inane chatter.

Chapter Twelve

A waiting Helen had silently helped Penelope out of her gown and into a demure nightdress. Together they went through the motions of their nightly ritual without a word or a smile.

Penelope had tried to befriend Helen early on, but without success. Helen did her job, was always there when Penelope needed her, but she didn't like her mistress or her position, of that Penelope was certain.

She no longer cared, any more than she cared that the other servants in the household evidently found her repulsive. At the moment, she had only one care on her mind and in her heart.

Tonight her husband would come to her bed. She thought again of the wedding night and how remarkable it had been, and wondered if perhaps Maximillian could summon some of that desire for her, even now. Perhaps in the bedroom he would shed his coolness. Perhaps here she could close her eyes and pretend he loved her.

Helen was dismissed, and Penelope paced her chamber by the light of a single candle. A baby. She reminded herself of what she wished so desperately for as she waited. A baby to heap love upon and to love her in return. A smiling face, outstretched arms, someone to hold. A child would need her. This house would not be so horribly empty if it was filled with children, their laughter and their tears.

The blaze in the fireplace had been low to begin with, and as she waited, it died to nothing more than glowing embers. As the candle burned and the minutes passed, she decided Maximillian had changed his mind. He wasn't coming. Perhaps he'd never intended to come to her tonight, but had promised only to appease her for the moment. Was she such an inadequate wife that he couldn't bear to pass a single night in her bed?

She stood at the window and looked out over the garden that was drenched in nightfall. This was a prison as surely as Victor's would have been. Her escape, her supposed rescue from an unwanted marriage, had trapped her just as surely and unpleasantly as marriage to Victor would have. This was worse, in fact. She'd never thought herself in love with Victor, and so he didn't have the power to hurt her this way.

"And what do you see, m'dear?"

She turned to find her husband lounging in the open doorway, a bottle of brandy in one hand, a half-empty drinking glass in the other.

"I didn't hear the door," she whispered.

Maximillian brought a finger of the hand that grasped the bottle to his lips. "Shhhh. I am like a ghost, moving silently through the house and haunting those in it. Do I haunt you m'dear?" His words slurred slightly.

"You're drunk," Penelope said.

"I'm afraid not, dear wife, though I will admit I did my best." Maximillian stepped into the room and slammed the door behind him. Penelope jumped at the resounding thud. "Did you hear that, m'dear? I wouldn't want to be accused of sneaking about my own house, now would I?"

This wasn't at all what she'd had in mind. Maximillian was so different, so unlike the man she knew, that he frightened her. His anger was usually masked in coldness and sarcasm, but tonight she could see the fury that waited just beneath the surface. Could she bear for this man to touch her?

"Perhaps this is not the best night . . ."

"But it is." Maximillian turned the near-empty liquor bottle up and refilled his glass, and then he set the bottle atop the dresser, precariously close to the edge. But for the slight slurring of his words, the brandy had little effect on him. He stood quite steadily, and was still as finely dressed and well-groomed as he'd been all evening. "You might as well shed that dreadful shift before we get started."

There was no great anticipation, as there had been on her wedding night. Just an apprehension, a confusion, and a reaffirmation of her resolve. If she could have nothing else, she would have babies. She removed the nightdress and placed it across the armchair before her dresser, and walked slowly to the bed. Maximillian still had his back to her. Was he allowing her modesty, or did he simply not care to look at her?

He didn't turn around until she sat on the side of the bed, and when he did he studied her as he might an inanimate object, head cocked to one side and eyes scrutinizing. "You are likely the most superb woman I have ever seen," he said softly and without emotion. "Perfect in proportion and face." He came toward her. "Flawless beauty."

Maximillian sat beside her, his glass of brandy dangling from one hand while he reached out to touch her breast with the other. "Flawless," he repeated.

She could not breathe.

His fingers danced over one breast and then the other, more gentle than his words or his eyes. There was no anger in his touch. "Lie back," he ordered, and with a long expelled breath, she did.

He brought his mouth to her throat and kissed her tenderly, and Penelope closed her eyes. Yes, she remembered this. The softening of her entire body, the tingle that began and grew so quickly. The pleasant tension. Warm and gentle lips caressed the column of her throat, the curve of her shoulder, until she felt herself melting.

Maximillian pulled slowly away, and Penelope watched as he dipped a finger into the brandy and brought it to the tip of her breast. A single drop fell, and he lowered his mouth to lick away the liquor, to draw the nipple deep into his mouth with a gentle breath. She felt herself relenting, giving in to the rippling sensations and the growing tautness. Yes, she remembered this. Her body rose to meet his mouth, her back arching of its own will. With every stroke of his tongue, her body awakened a bit more.

He repeated the process, dribbling a single drop of brandy onto her other breast, spreading the cool liquid with a circling and lazy finger, and then lowering his head to take the nipple into his mouth. He kissed that sensitive flesh, lavished caresses upon her, until she forgot everything but the sensations that were coursing through her body.

"You like this, do you?" he asked as he trailed a brandy-dampened finger from the valley of her breasts to her navel.

"Yes," she whispered.

His mouth followed the trail of dampness, slowly, intimately, almost lovingly, and Penelope closed her eyes and reveled in her body's response. The warmth was intense, the touch of his mouth against her skin as intoxicating as any wine. And then he trailed a coolly moist finger across her flat belly, from the navel downward.

"Maximillian!" she tried to sit up but with a gentle hand he forced her back down. "You can't."

"Trust me, m'dear?" he asked huskily.

Penelope closed her eyes as he continued to rake his fingers across her flesh. Trust him? How could she? He'd played false with her, pretending to love her, pretending to offer happiness and adoration and then changing overnight into a stranger. He'd changed into a man with cold, lying eyes she could not read. He'd become a husband she did not know at all. Trust him? "Yes," she whispered, not sure why that answer came to her lips.

He laid his mouth on her belly, kissed the skin so passionately she knew at that moment that he had to love her, even if it was in his own, distant way.

By the time he left the bed to kneel before her, she was no longer capable of protest. Her body was practically screaming for him, and she waited impatiently for him to shed his own clothes, to come to her, to touch and fill her. Instead, he trailed a bit of brandy on her inner thigh and kissed it away, and then he laid his mouth on her in a shockingly intimate way.

"Max . . . Maximillian," she whispered, but he didn't stop. He pulled her closer, tenderly forced her legs further apart, and continued, his tongue dancing over her flesh slowly and then fast, gently and then hard.

She wanted to scream, she wanted to cry—but her body wanted exactly what Maximillian was giving her. He did not relent, and Penelope found she could voice no more protest. She rocked gently, closed her eyes, and was lost in a haze of sensations so unexpectedly powerful they ruled her body and her mind.

She was lost, lost and loved and cherished, until every fiber of her being exploded in a response more potent than she'd imagined possible. Maximillian held her as she lurched and moaned, and caressed her inner thigh as the impossible pleasure faded away and left her with her own harsh reality.

Her breath would hardly come to her, as Maximillian rose slowly to tower above her. "Happy now?" he asked coldly.

He hadn't put down his drinking glass, and as she watched, he lifted it to his lips for a long swig. He was completely and neatly dressed, his jacket was straight, his cravat was perfection. There wasn't so much as a hair on his head out of place.

"Well good night, m'dear. My duty's done, I'd say." He collected the bottle from the dresser and sauntered toward the door, not even bothering to turn and face her as he reached it.

"Aren't you going to stay?" Penelope felt remarkably vulnerable, hot, disheveled, and she was still quaking from the incredible and shocking experience.

"Whatever for?"

As he opened the door and offered a distant "sweet dreams," Penelope realized that her husband had not once kissed her on the mouth, had not once told her he loved her, had not once shown the slightest desire to be with her. And as she listened to Maximillian walk slowly down the passageway to his own bedchamber, hot tears came to her eyes.

Max made his way through the passage in the dark, every step and every breath an effort. The distance between his bedchamber and Penelope's had never seemed so great.

Once he was in his own chamber, he didn't bother to light a candle or a lamp or a fire, but took comfort in the black shadows that surrounded him.

He didn't sit on the bed or in the armchair near the window, but paced slowly.

He was hiding as surely as Penelope was, in the dark, in the bottle, in his own righteousness.

Everything he was and ever had been ached, his body and his heart, with a pain as sharp and cutting as the most finely honed blade. He'd lived his twenty-eight years proving again and again that no one had the power to hurt him—not his father, nor the older brothers who'd openly despised his very presence. Not the women who were more than happy to meet with him in secret, though they acted in public as if they did not know the earl's bastard. Death was a game. Love was a promise. All lies, and he couldn't hide from that truth no matter how dark the room.

Penelope was his wife, and yet he couldn't lay with her no matter how much his body ached. He knew it, had sworn to himself that he would not. If the shields came down, if he allowed himself to reveal how much he wanted her, tragedy would certainly follow. He would either kill her with his bare hands or be forced to admit to himself that he still loved her.

He finished off the last of the brandy and stripped off his cravat and silk jacket as he paced the unlit room. Love her? No. Surely not. How could he love a woman who was capable of such cold betrayal? A woman who showed one face to the world and another, darker face, when it suited her. He couldn't possibly love her.

God help him, he could deny it all he wanted, in the dark, by the light of day, to her face . . . but he did love his wife with all his heart. If he didn't love her, the betrayal wouldn't hurt so much. If he didn't love her, he might have accepted the fact that she would send a boy to his death without a second thought, that she allied herself with a cruel man like Victor Chadwick.

If he didn't love her.

He'd thought love a blessing, once, but now he knew it was a curse, and the cruelest punishment of all. It fogged his mind, it ruled his body and his heart, it permeated his every waking moment.

He was out of his room and in the passageway before he had time to think about his actions. The distance did not seem so great, this time. He was standing in Penelope's open doorway before he allowed himself a second thought.

She was lying sideways across the bed, as he'd left her, but she had wrapped the gold satin coverlet around her body. She clutched it tightly, grasping the satin desperately. The candle on her bedside table burned low, casting a soft light over the forlorn face she turned to him. Her eyes shone bright, much too bright. He would have thought them tears in her eyes, but he didn't believe Penelope was capable of shedding tears like a normal woman.

"Did you forget something?" He could tell she tried to keep her voice aloof, but a faint tremble betrayed her.

"Yes." He closed the door behind him and walked toward the bed, stripping off his shirt and tossing it to the floor, picking up the candle from the bedside table and blowing out the flame.

He wasn't so drunk or so besotted that he'd take

170

the chance of Penelope seeing the tattoo on his upper thigh, the image of a dagger etched in indigo.

"Maximillian," she whispered as he took the satin coverlet in his hands and peeled it away from her body. He could hear the confusion in her voice, the questions he couldn't allow her to ask.

So he crawled atop his wife and silenced her with a kiss, a deep kiss he'd been longing to give her for weeks. He covered her body with his own and thrust his tongue into her mouth, his anger and his passion and his love mingling until he couldn't separate the emotions that warred within him.

Surely she felt his arousal pressing against her, the indisputable evidence that he could not run from her, that no matter how incensed he was, how damned self-righteous, he needed her.

Ah, she smelled so good, so sweet and tempting and forbidden.

He wondered if Penelope would push him away— and he wondered how he'd respond if she did. She didn't know what it was costing him to be here, that he was paying for his obsession with a little piece of his soul. Would he allow her to push him away, if it came to that? he wondered. But he didn't have to wonder for long. She wrapped her arms around his neck as he pushed her to the center of the big bed; she kissed him back with a tentative softening of her lips and a darting tongue that danced with his own.

He could get lost here, in the dark, in Penelope's arms, in the body she offered. Here he could hide from the truth, from his heartache. In the shadows and the heat of pure sensation he could hide from everything but his love for this woman.

His heart and his soul, everything he was and believed in, for the moment it was all hers.

For now, he allowed himself to forget that the moment couldn't last.

Chapter Thirteen

She was such a simpleton for believing, even for a moment, that Maximillian had changed.

After the night of the Huntlands' ball, the night he'd come to her bed and loved her until dawn lit the sky, she'd expected that somehow—some way—the man she'd fallen in love with and married had returned to her. He hadn't said a word when he'd come to her bed, and hadn't allowed her to speak, either, but she was convinced there had to be love in such a powerful encounter.

Perhaps not, since she'd barely seen her husband in the days since, and on the few occasions they'd been in the same room, he'd been indifferent and easily distracted. The days grew progressively warmer as spring came to Charles Town, but Penelope found no joy in the arrival of her favorite season.

She could only hope that she now carried a child—a baby she could devote herself to, love and care for, as her husband refused to allow her to love and care for him.

The sketch on her lap was not what she wanted. Her fingers, or else her mind, were not cooperating this morning. The double doors of her parlor stood open to allow fresh air to circulate, and the garden beyond was her inspiration for the morning. She wanted to capture the beauty of the flowers there, but she wasn't happy with the results. Perhaps she was too distracted this morning even for simple flowers. She tossed the sheet aside and began again, sketching what her mind saw. Portraits had never been easy for her, but she'd painted Tyler and Mary many times.

In just a few strokes, Maximillian's face took shape on the paper. She knew the lines so well, the cut of his jaw, the line of his nose, the shape of the lips. But she couldn't get the eyes just right.

It wasn't simply that her talent for capturing that part of the face was not great, though she had to confess that might be part of the problem. A good portion of the problem was the subject. Maximillian's eyes were rarely the same. Lazy one moment, piercing the next. Hooded and sleepy, and then in an instant all-seeing. Gray-blue one day, more green the next, he had the eyes of a chameleon. How could she begin to capture something like that?

"I will not wait on the doorstep."

Penelope heard her cousin's familiar voice issuing a strident order that carried easily from the front door to the parlor. She had put the portrait of her husband aside and was smiling by the time Dalton and Mary reached the parlor. Dalton was staring at Mary with annoyance and something near fury on his face. She really would have to speak to Maximillian about finding something else for Dalton to do. He simply was not well-suited to his position.

"Thank goodness," Mary said dramatically as she floated into the room. A simple lace cap sat atop perfectly sculpted curls, and she was dressed in one of her favorite day dresses, a calico in blues and greens. "Why, I was certain this servant was going to bodily restrain me so he could announce me properly or some such nonsense. And this can't wait another minute."

Mary shot a prim and angry glance over her shoulder to a waiting Dalton. "You're dismissed," she said haughtily.

Dalton took a deep breath and turned sharply on his heel.

"What can't wait?" Penelope rose from the sofa and greeted her cousin with a kiss on the cheek. A breeze wafted through the opened doors, a fragrant and refreshing breath of fresh air.

Mary disengaged herself and walked through the opened doors into the stone-paved courtyard. "Father's decided to leave for the plantation next week."

Penelope followed her cousin outside, stepping into the sunlight. "I'll miss you," she said, and she meant it. Her cousin was the only person she could really talk to. Once Mary was gone, she would truly be alone. "Very much."

Mary spun around quickly, and there was a touch of panic on her pretty face. "Can I stay here?" she asked breathlessly. "Father's closing up the house completely and taking all the servants to the plantation. He won't return to Charles Town for months. This is such a big house, and I won't be in the way, I promise you, and . . ."

"Yes," Penelope said with a grin, not even allowing her cousin to finish voicing her request. It would be wonderful to have Mary living under the same roof, to have someone to share meals with and talk to, someone to lean on, just as she and Mary always had.

Mary's eyes widened. "Don't you even have to ask your husband's permission?"

"No," Penelope said quickly. Why should Maximillian object? He was rarely in the house, and when he was here he had little time for his wife. There was no reason for him to deny her, and in this she would stand her ground. She needed Mary with her, now. "He'll love having you here as much as I will."

"No!"

It was Dalton who first reacted to the announcement, with a step forward and a loud denial.

"I'm afraid so," Max said with a sigh. "There's no credible reason for me to refuse."

"The cousin's trouble," Dalton hissed. "She sees everything, touches everything, is never still. She has a tart mouth and sharp eyes, and . . ."

"Enough," Max said with a smile. "Do you really think two pampered ladies are too much for the League of the Indigo Blade?"

"Yes," Dalton said indignantly.

John and Beck laughed softly.

"It is a complication," Fletcher said quietly, and Max's smile faded as he looked across the desk to the dissenters. The lights in his study burned low, Penelope had been long asleep, and he himself had shed his fancy duds for a simple brown suit.

"That it is," Lewis agreed, and Max could hear the resignation in his voice. The others looked somber but voiced no further protest.

"Have you located the boy?" Max directed his question to John.

"Yep," John said softly. "The lad didn't go far, that's for sure. He's met up with a band of rebels not twenty miles from here."

"How is he?"

"A fine shot with a rifle," John said proudly, "a hot head and a loud mouth. A grand lad, he reminds me of . . . me. Are you sure he's your wife's brother?"

Max looked at the desk so they, perhaps, wouldn't see his smile. A simple "he's well" would have sufficed, but John's answer told him much more. "I'm positive."

"Too bad," John mumbled, his voice thick and indistinct, as always. "He might've made a fine addition to the league, in a few years."

"Perhaps he still might."

Tyler was well, and as much as Max wanted to he didn't dare share the news with Penelope to ease her worry. He could offer no plausible explanation for his knowledge.

He dulled his obsession for Penelope with this work, avoided being alone with her, tried to escape even thinking about her. But there were moments when she came to him. Unwanted and unbidden, she crept into his mind. The woman he'd thought her to be, not the woman she truly was.

"Are we ready?" He directed his question to Beck, who'd seen to the preparations for tonight's adventure. A small town across the river had formed a militia, and they needed guns, powder, and bayonets. Max had instructed Beck to include clothing, sturdy boots, and food to the shipment. In the long run, he imagined those staples would be more needed than the weapons.

And they were in this for the long run. War appeared to be inevitable, and the colonies were equally divided into three groups: the rebels who craved freedom, the loyalists who supported their king, and those who wanted only to be left alone to live their lives in peace.

Those who wanted no part of the conflict would suffer in this as everyone else would. Peace was an impossible dream, a fantasy men strove for and rarely found. Like love and happiness, like justice and fairness.

Fools, all.

The music was lovely, intricate and soothing pieces that allowed Penelope to forget her troubles for a while. The St. Cecilia Society was presenting an evening of Bach, and the stringed instruments on the stage performed beautifully.

She had spent a good part of the afternoon trying to convince Maximillian that she did not want to attend this concert. He, of course, insisted that they should be seen. At the moment, she was glad he had forced her to attend.

In their private box, Maximillian was seated beside her, his eyes closed, his long legs stretched out before him. His hands were very still, and white lace from a pristine cuff brushed long, idle fingers. He was dressed in deep blue satin tonight, as was she. It was important to Maximillian that they appear, in public, to be ideally suited, wonderfully happy, an incomparable match in every way. From this box above the crowd below, she had no doubt but that they appeared to be the perfect couple.

Maximillian snored softly, and Penelope jabbed him gently with her elbow. He started, glanced to her sidelong through hooded eyes, and then allowed those eyes to drift closed once again.

"You've married an imbecile."

The words were whispered into Penelope's ear, and she jerked her head around to find Victor Chadwick leaning over her. A quick glance at Maximillian showed him to be sleeping soundly once again. At least he was no longer snoring.

"What are you doing here?" she hissed.

"I'm here with the Fairfax family," he said softly. "I saw you sitting here with your—" he glanced briefly at Maximillian—"your husband, and you appeared to be so completely miserable I felt it my duty to see if I could assist in any way."

"As a matter of fact, you can," she whispered.

At her side Maximillian snorted softly, opened his eyes very briefly, and allowed them to drift closed again.

Penelope rose slowly, nodded to the exit, and followed a smug Victor through velvet curtains.

"You need me. I knew you would, one day." Victor took her hand. "I would do anything for you," he whispered.

"Then make it public knowledge that I had nothing to do with Heath's capture and his death," Penelope said succinctly. "There's nothing else you can do for me."

He was unmoved by her request. "Anything but that," he said as he bent to kiss her hand.

As his lips touched her knuckles, Penelope jerked her hand away. She was as big a fool as Maximillian to believe she could sway Victor in this. "Then we have nothing to discuss." She turned from him to return to her seat, but he caught her arm and pulled her back.

"Tell me, Penelope," he whispered hoarsely, "why did you marry that imbecile? I vow, the puzzle keeps me up nights, pondering until the sun rises."

Victor's fingers on her arm were too tight, his face so close she could smell his rum and cigars—and yet she was not afraid.

"Do you know what it's like to be truly loved?" she whispered, refusing to recoil. "To be loved so much that you can see and feel and all but touch it?" She didn't wait for an answer. "Maximillian loved me that way, and it was . . . it was irresistible." She wondered if Victor would notice that she spoke of that love in the past tense. "He swept me away with that love."

Victor released her, and without waiting for a response, she slipped through the velvet curtains and to her seat. As she sat down, Maximillian awakened with a start. He blinked to clear his sleepy eyes, and turned to her slowly.

"Where did you go, m'dear?"

"Nowhere," she whispered. "I've been here all along." His sleepy eyes did not challenge her.

"Lud," he said with a yawn. "I must've been dreaming."

He closed his eyes once again, but this time his hand rested on her arm. A few measures of soothing music passed, and his hand drifted toward hers. Before Maximillian drifted off again, he wrapped his long fingers around Penelope's wrist, effectively and softly manacling her.

She couldn't sleep.

Penelope paced in the darkness of her room, after trying for several hours to force sleep to come. She'd never been a fidgety one, but had always been able to find rest easily. In the past she'd crawled into bed, closed her eyes, and sleep came.

But not tonight, when her mind was spinning. Tomorrow Mary would be moving in. They'd spent the afternoon making plans and choosing a suitable bedchamber. Penelope had been hoping Mary would chose the room next door, but her cousin had chosen the small bedroom at the end of the hall, declaring that she'd fallen instantly in love with the sunny yellow room.

It wasn't only anticipation that kept her awake. At dinner, Maximillian had been more distant than ever. Brooding, indifferent, removed, it was as if he were irritated by her very presence. No wonder he went out of his way to evade her.

The portrait that continued to be a failure was an indication of how well she knew her husband. She knew him not at all.

She stepped through the parted curtains and onto the terrace. The moonlight shone on the garden below, turning the flowers gray and silver, the leaves inky black. Deep shadows filled the garden, hiding the bright colors that would be waiting there in the morning.

The sounds of slow-moving horses' hooves came to her, first a barely discernible echo and then a distinctly approaching noise. There was more than one horse, more than two or three. She stepped back into the shadows as the noise became clearer, slowing and then stopping, probably at the stables that she could not see from her small terrace. Voices carried clearly in the night, carrying to her soft words she could not discern, and even softer laughter.

There was a voice, a hint of laughter, that reminded her of the man she'd married, a Maximillian she'd once believed to be real. Why was he out at this time of night? Where had he been? No wonder he slept well into the afternoon, if he was this late coming home.

Penelope slipped quietly into her chamber. She hadn't even been aware that Maximillian had left the house, but had assumed he slept just down the hall. Gathering her courage, she went to her door and opened it, just an inch or so. The house was quiet, dead as always, the passageway black and unwelcoming. She did not hear one of the many doors to the outside opening or closing, but eventually she did hear the footsteps on the stairs. Slow, dragging footsteps coming her way. She opened the door slowly, so as not to make a sound, and stepped into the passageway in time to see her husband reach the second floor.

Her husband, and yet not the man she knew. The first thing she noticed was that he wore not a bit of lace. His clothes were dark and serviceable, and his usually well-groomed hair was hanging limply to his shoulders.

"Where have you been?" she asked softly, and she had the satisfaction of seeing Maximillian jump out of his skin as he spun to face her.

"Good God, where did you come from?" he whispered, taking a single step toward her.

"I couldn't sleep, and I heard horses." He waited silently for her to continue. "You didn't answer my question. Where were you?"

More furtive footsteps sounded in the hallway below. Before she could ask who was in the house, Maximillian came to her side, took her arm, and led her into her chamber. He closed the door very quietly behind them, and then stood before it, blocking the exit effectively.

"You should not pry into affairs that are none of your concern," he said coldly. "It might turn out to be very unhealthy, m'dear."

His voice had not risen above a whisper.

"Perhaps I consider my husband's whereabouts my concern," she answered just as softly. "Am I mistaken?"

There was a brief but telling pause before Maximillian replied. "You are." He made no move to leave, and in fact lounged against her door motionless and silent.

She'd made a point all her life of avoiding confrontations—with Uncle William, with Mary, with Victor—but she had no desire to walk away from this, to bid the cold man at her door good night and hide under the thick coverlet until morning came.

"I think I have a right to know where you pass your nights, since you don't see fit to pass them with me." The faintest hint of a tear stung her eyes, but she blinked it away.

Maximillian didn't move at all, didn't smile or frown or wave a dismissive and indolent hand. For a few very long minutes he didn't answer her, either. When he did, Penelope wished she'd stayed true to her nature and hidden silently beneath the coverlet.

"Perhaps you won't care for the answer, m'dear," he said with complete indifference. "Perhaps I considered you to be one of those women who prefers to remain blissfully ignorant of her husband's late-night activities."

Her heart sank, but what had she expected him to say? There was another woman, of course. No wonder he never came to her bed.

She thought of railing indignantly against him, of accusing him of cold neglect and heartless adultery and even of ruining her life. All were apparently true. But she didn't want to rail against him—she wanted answers.

"I thought you loved me, once," she said calmly.

Maximillian didn't move. She waited for a wide smile and flippant answer, a false face and an affected voice, but neither was forthcoming. "So did I," he finally whispered.

Chapter Fourteen

The sketches no longer satisfied her, and Penelope paced the parlor restlessly. This was her place, the one room in the house—other than her bedchamber—where she felt somewhat secure. The dining room and separate kitchen were Beck's domain, and Dalton was likely to accost her if she were bold enough to venture into the library or Maximillian's study.

Only once had she had the urge to explore the third floor, and that black-eyed Garrick had appeared out of nowhere to advise her to keep herself to the first two floors of her own house. She hadn't had the nerve to argue with him, and she hadn't had the urge to explore the third floor since.

But here in the parlor they left her alone. She read, she painted, and she brooded. She socialized with no one other than Mary. It seemed everyone in Charles Town had condemned her for a betrayal of which she was innocent.

Mary had been living in this house almost a week, and Penelope didn't see her much more often than she had when her cousin had been living in William Seton's Charles Town house. She slept here, and ate breakfast and sometimes supper with Penelope, but for the most part she kept herself entertained with teas and parties and shopping expeditions with her friends.

Penelope stared at the blank wall before her. The creamy expanse was broken by a single oil painting, a plain landscape in a gilded frame. The painting was competent but unexciting, and suddenly Penelope found it irritating.

She left her seat on the sofa and walked straight to the bothersome painting, taking it from the wall with a heave and a wave of satisfaction. Nothing at all was better than mediocrity.

She stared at the blank wall. Her life was as mediocre as the creamy area she faced, and she didn't know how much longer she could stand it. Her husband did not love her, those she had considered friends condemned her without asking for an explanation, and she was surrounded by a houseful of men and women who merely tolerated her. It was unacceptable, but she didn't know what to do.

Return to Uncle William's plantation? She found an appeal in that prospect. The plantation, her comfortable room and the people there, were more home than this cursed house would ever be.

But after defying Uncle William to marry Maximillian, how could she return to him that way?

She couldn't.

Penelope rummaged through her art supplies and returned to the blank wall. She penciled in a few plants first, the native plants of Charles Town that grew outside her window. Palmettos, wisteria, wildflowers took shape on the wall. She moved down the wall, impatiently moving a side chair out of her way. Here she sketched the dangerous swamplands they'd passed on the road from the plantation to Charles Town: cypress trees and still water, Spanish moss and lily pads.

By the time she was penciling in a bay view on the opposite wall, there was a smile on her face. How long had it been since she'd truly smiled? Ages, it seemed, though she knew it had only been weeks. The weeks had passed so slowly since her wedding to Maximillian.

When she stood back to survey the newest section, a gruff throat was cleared behind her, and she turned to find Dalton waiting in the open doorway. Even his surly appearance couldn't wipe the smile from her face.

"Dinner will be served in half an hour, madam," he said, his eyes taking in the sketches on the walls.

"I'm not hungry." Penelope turned to survey her work, to decide what she needed to add next. With a raised hand she turned slowly, envisioning the possibilities. The mural would eventually encompass the room, one scene melding gently into another.

"Should I call a physician, madam?"

She turned to find that a puzzled Dalton remained in the doorway. He'd taken a step into the room and squinted at the sketches on two walls.

"Of course not," she said with a smile. "But would you see about purchasing more paints? What I have won't be nearly enough for this task."

"Whatever you wish, madam," he said softly.

"Blues and greens," she said as she stepped to Dalton's side to survey the sketches from a distance. "Reds and yellows, and I'll need new brushes, too."

For once, the odd butler didn't frighten her. In spite of his size and the fact that he looked more like a pirate than a servant, he didn't disturb her at all.

He continued to stare at the walls. "May I ask, madam," he said softly, "exactly what it is you're doing here?"

She looked up with her smile fixed, her heart steady, and her eyes locked to his. "I'm taking my life back."

Penelope was so intent on her sketch that she didn't hear the knock at the front door. She didn't know she had a visitor until Dalton, with his usual bad humor, announced Victor.

And just when she'd decided how to lead the wisteria up one corner.

Of all the residents of Charles Town, Victor Chadwick was the last person she wanted to see.

"Good afternoon, Victor." She climbed down from her footstool and grudgingly put her pencil aside. "Dalton, bring us some coffee, would you?"

Dalton was hesitant to leave, but he backed away slowly and eventually left Penelope and Victor alone.

Victor studied the walls as Dalton had earlier that day, with a healthy dose of skepticism. "What on earth are you doing?"

"Painting a mural," she said, turning her back to Victor to survey her work. "What do you think?"

"I'm sure it will be lovely," he said dubiously.

She didn't care what he thought, didn't care if no one but she ever saw the finished project.

"Why are you here?" she turned around slowly to face him. "Surely this is not a social call. I did my best on our last meeting to make it perfectly clear that we have nothing to discuss until you're ready to clear my name."

"Can't I pay a call on an old friend?" he said with a false smile.

Part of taking her life in her own hands had to be refusing to believe everything she was told. She had to be as cynical and untrusting as Victor and Maximillian were, if she were to survive. "No," she answered with a smile as false as her guest's.

"All right," Victor said, his grin widening with true amusement. "I've come to ask you a favor."

"Surely not."

"Have you still not forgiven me?" he asked as if he had truly expected a warm reception. "Dear Penelope, I told you I did what I thought was best. Besides, everyone's put the incident from their minds but you."

"What do you want?"

He came closer and lowered his voice. "I'm hot on the trail of the Indigo Blade," he whispered.

"Not that again!" Penelope took a step back, stopping when the back of her leg brushed the footstool.

190

"I told you I have no intention of spying for you. Not that I could even if I wanted to. Thanks to your deception and my resulting reputation, I've found it advisable to refuse most invitations to balls and other social events. I've been seen in public only twice since the wedding, Victor."

"You don't even have to leave the house."

"I beg your pardon?"

Victor smiled widely. "A couple of weeks ago the Indigo Blade delivered a shipment of arms to rebels on the outside of town. One of my men was nearby, and he followed. He followed the Indigo Blade to this street and then lost him."

"That doesn't mean . . ."

"I think one of your servants is the Indigo Blade. What a perfect setup that would be. No one looks at servants, no one pays them any mind when they come and go. Listening, hiding around every corner," he whispered. "It might even be that man who directed me to you just now."

"Dalton? Don't be ridiculous!" But was it truly ridiculous? She herself had observed on many occasions that the servants in her husband's employ were out of place in their positions. Were they using her dim-witted husband for their nefarious purposes?

Even if she did suspect that was true, she wouldn't tell Victor. She had developed a quiet admiration for the man who fought for what he believed in, who rescued rebels and assisted villages the British Army harassed. She'd heard the stories, of outrageous disguises and brave deeds, mostly from Mary, who got the gossip from her friends.

"I suppose I could just arrest the entire household and interrogate the lot of you until someone confesses," Victor said sourly, "but that might not be wise at this time." His narrowed eyes were calculating and somehow dead. "There are those in power who are still perturbed with me over the Lowry affair, and it seems the council president himself is rather taken with your foolish husband. I'd rather not take such desperate measures . . . if there's an alternative."

Heath Lowry had died for his beliefs. Penelope would always wonder if she could have done something differently, if she could have kept Heath alive. Willing or not, she wouldn't have a hand in seeing that injustice happen again.

Before she could give Victor her answer, Dalton returned with a silver tray and two fine china cups brimming with hot coffee. He placed the tray on a piecrust table, and then positioned himself in the doorway.

"You may leave," Victor said, cutting a glance to the man in the doorway. Dalton, after a moment's hesitation, took a single step back.

"Dalton," Penelope said softly. "Come here."

The butler narrowed his eyes. He didn't like taking orders from anyone, not Victor and certainly not her. He wasn't deferential, or meek, or even competent. Was it possible that he was the Indigo Blade? He didn't care for orders of any kind, but he did step into the room only a moment after her softly spoken command.

"I'm thinking of adding people to my mural. What do you think?"

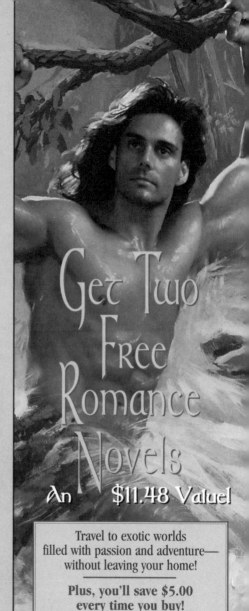

Thrill to the most sensual, adventure-filled Romances on the market today...

FROM  LOVE SPELL BOOKS

As a home subscriber to the Love Spell Romance Book Club, you'll enjoy the best in today's BRAND-NEW Time Travel, Futuristic, Legendary Lovers, Perfect Heroes and other genre romance fiction. For five years, Love Spell has brought you the award-winning, high-quality authors you know and love to read. Each Love Spell romance will sweep you away to a world of high adventure...and intimate romance. Discover for yourself all the passion and excitement millions of readers thrill to each and every month.

Save $5.00 Each Time You Buy!

Every other month, the Love Spell Romance Book Club brings you four brand-new titles from Love Spell Books. EACH PACKAGE WILL SAVE YOU AT LEAST $5.00 FROM THE BOOK-STORE PRICE! And you'll never miss a new title with our convenient home delivery service.

Here's how we do it: Each package will carry a FREE 10-DAY EXAMINATION privilege. At the end of that time, if you decide to keep your books, simply pay the low invoice price of $17.96, no shipping or handling charges added. HOME DELIVERY IS ALWAYS FREE. With today's top romance novels selling for $5.99 and higher, our price SAVES YOU AT LEAST $5.00 with each shipment.

AND YOUR FIRST TWO-BOOK SHIP-MENT IS TOTALLY FREE!

IT'S A BARGAIN YOU CAN'T BEAT! A SUPER $11.48 Value!

Love Spell ✦ A Division of Dorchester Publishing Co., Inc.

Get Two Books Totally
FREE —
An $11.48 Value!

▼ Tear Here and Mail Your FREE Book Card Today! ▼

PLEASE RUSH
MY TWO FREE
BOOKS TO ME
RIGHT AWAY!

Love Spell Romance Book Club
P.O. Box 6613
Edison, NJ 08818-6613

Dalton lifted a large, capable-looking hand to his breast. "Are you asking for my opinion, madam?"

"Yes," she answered with a smile. Her guest was fuming. "Victor, have your coffee before it gets cold. Dalton and I won't be a minute."

"I only have a minute, Penelope," Victor said sternly. "And I'm already late for a meeting." She supposed that was her clue to send Dalton on his way so he could try to persuade her to spy for him.

"Then you'd best drink your coffee." She turned her back on Victor and studied the mural that was slowly taking shape. "So, Dalton, what do you think?"

She heard Victor stride from the room, cursing beneath his breath. After the front door slammed, she looked up at Dalton. "I don't believe he cares for your coffee."

She witnessed something then that she'd never seen before, something she was certain few had observed. Dalton smiled.

"What do you want?" Mary asked haughtily. She didn't want Victor to see that her heart pounded and her blood roared and she wanted to cry and scream and hit him.

"I've missed you."

Of course he'd missed her. That was the plan, wasn't it? Soon he would realize that he needed her, that he couldn't live without her. Love wouldn't be far behind. "Well, I understand you'll be getting married in a few months. I'm sure Suzanne wouldn't approve of you meeting me like this."

The gazebo at the far end of the Broderick garden

Linda Jones

afforded them a little privacy—the darkness of night even more. Penelope and Maximillian had retired to their separate chambers hours ago, silent and dismal.

"Suzanne doesn't have to know." Victor sat beside her and placed a possessive arm around her shoulder.

If she gave in to him now she would be lost. If Victor thought he could come to her whenever he wished and she would give herself to him, he would have no reason to forget that milquetoast Suzanne and make her his wife. It was what Mary wanted more than anything, what she'd dreamed of for the past year—to be Mrs. Victor Chadwick.

"I can't," she whispered.

"Then why are you here?"

He tipped her face up so she was forced to look into his eyes. Surely he loved her, just a little.

"Because I've missed you, too."

Victor kissed her, thrusting his tongue deep into her mouth, pressing his lips harshly to hers. His breath came heavy and unevenly, his body tensed. She liked it when he lost control this way, when he moaned deep in his throat and trembled in her hands.

His hand slipped beneath her skirt, and that's when Mary drew away from him. "No," she whispered hoarsely.

"What kind of game is this?"

Mary shook her head. "It's not a game, Victor." That was a lie, and she knew it. Sex was a game, one she was just beginning to learn to play. "Before, I thought . . . I believed you loved me."

"I do love you," he whispered into her ear, nibbling on the lobe and trailing his lips down her neck. "I love you so much, Mary. Don't turn me away."

Those were the words she'd longed to hear. In her heart she'd believed from the beginning that if she played this game right Victor would come to love her, but she'd begun to doubt the plan.

"Say it again," she insisted softly.

"I love you."

She didn't protest this time when he slipped his hand beneath her skirt, didn't object when he gently lowered her to the floor of the gazebo.

"I love you, too," she whispered as he freed his manhood and spread her legs wide. "Oh, Victor, I've always loved you."

He pushed inside her, roughly and without so much as another kiss. Mary closed her eyes, knowing it would be over soon, knowing that she was about to have everything she'd ever wanted. Love, Victor, a happy life.

In moments, he shuddered above her, emptied his seed into her, and then collapsed over her body. At least this time she wouldn't wait and worry until her monthly flow came. It didn't matter, since Victor had finally realized his love for her and would surely make her his wife soon.

She wrapped her arms around his neck. "Say it again," she whispered with a wide smile on her face.

"Say what?" Victor's words were muffled against her hair, but he raised up slowly to look down at her.

"Tell me again that you love me." She lifted a hand to stroke his warm cheek, to brush her fingers over his damp, swollen lips.

"Really, Mary, don't be so naive."

"Naive?"

"You know the way the game is played." He withdrew from her and left her cold and empty. "I tell you what you want to hear, and you give me what we both want."

With a distant precision he straightened his clothing, tugged his suit back into order, and combed his hair back with both hands until he displayed no sign that a moment earlier he'd been heaving and sweating above her.

Mary saw everything with painful clarity as she watched Victor right his clothing. Her life was falling apart before her eyes, and she had no one to blame but herself. She knew, better than anyone, what he was capable of.

"You've never loved me, have you?" she whispered.

"No." Victor took a seat on the bench where they'd been sitting minutes earlier. "If it makes you feel any better, I have never loved anyone else, either. It's an emotion that becomes a crutch or a burden, and I have no room in my life for either."

There was no room in his life for her, she knew that now. No room but for this—a few unpleasant minutes when he used her body. Used her, not loved her.

"I don't ever want to see you again," Mary whispered hoarsely.

"Of course you do."

Still lying on the floor of the gazebo, lost in darkness, she shook her head slowly. "No. I don't want you to touch me, ever again. If you do I'll scream, and I'll tell everyone who will listen what you did to me."

His smile faded. "I never forced you."

"No," she acknowledged softly.

"If you tell you'll only be spreading the word that you're a jade, and as guilty of fornication as I am. Don't play the innocent with me now."

"I'm not. But I thought . . ."

"You wanted everything I gave you, don't deny it. I knew from the moment I kissed you in the Lowrys' garden that you had a great passion to share. Even in the dark I could see the fire in your eyes, and I could certainly feel the vitality and passion that radiated when I touched you. You're a natural-born slut." He stood slowly. "You won't turn me away. The next time you receive a note asking you to meet me here, or in the carriage house, or on the front lawn, you'll do it, because you need me as much as I need you." He reached down and took her hand, and jerked her to her feet. "Don't deny who you are, Mary."

A slut. Was it true? Her knees wobbled as Victor released her. She liked the kissing, sometimes, but the sex act itself was uncomfortable and unpleasant. She liked the power she felt when Victor came apart in her arms, but did that make her a slut?

He left her there to consider her options. She'd loved and wanted Victor for as long as she could remember—for as long as he'd been courting Penelope. She had sworn she'd do anything to make him love her . . . and she had done anything . . . and he didn't love her.

The tears started as she walked the dark path toward the house. What did she have awaiting her now? No decent man would have her as his wife. No one would ever love her. Victor would surely never love her—he probably despised her. At the moment, she despised herself.

It was dark, her eyes were filled with tears, and she tripped over some unseen hazard in the dark. She fell to her knees and caught herself with her hands in the soft earth. She was at the very edge of the path, and her hands were palms down in the soil of Penelope's garden.

For a few long moments she stayed there on her hands and knees, shaking uncontrollably, unable to find the strength to stand. She sobbed aloud, and tears fell from her burning eyes. She ached everywhere—her head, her heart, her knees—she ached especially where Victor had touched her.

What would become of her now?

"Miss Seton?"

She turned her head to one side to see a pair of sturdy black-clad legs and scuffed black boots. She wanted to order whoever it was to go away and leave her in peace, but she found she couldn't speak at all. If she opened her mouth, she would blubber like a baby.

Strong hands found her elbow and her waist, and the intruder lifted her to her feet.

She looked up into the meddler's face, ready to blast him for intruding on her privacy, and found herself staring into the narrowed eyes of Penelope's strange butler, Dalton.

"I'm . . . I'm . . ." The word "fine" refused to leave her lips. "I fell."

"I can see that." His voice was soft, a whisper that wouldn't disturb the night. "What are you doing out here this time of night?"

It was on her lips to tell him that it was none of his business when he slipped an arm easily around her waist to lead her toward the house.

"I couldn't sleep, and I thought a walk in the garden would help me relax."

"Ahh," he replied, and somehow she knew he didn't believe her.

Rather than taking her into the house, he led her directly to the separate building that was the kitchen, where he placed her in a hard-backed chair at a long, rough-hewn table. She sat there and watched him as he filled a bowl with water from a large ewer and collected a clean towel from the pantry.

He looked less like a butler than before, and he'd never filled that mold comfortably. Tonight he was again dressed all in black, but this was not the elegant black-and-white livery of the Broderick household. He wore tight, well-worn black breeches, tall boots, and a loose black shirt that fell open at the neck. His dark blond hair was untied and touching his shoulders, and when he knelt before her with the dampened towel in his hands, he fixed intense blue eyes on her face.

"You've never struck me as a woman who cries

easily," he said as he lifted the towel to wipe her cheeks gently.

"I'm not. I never cry."

"Then why do you cry now?"

Again, "it's none of your business" was on her tongue, but never made it past her lips. "Have you never been truly disappointed? I don't mean your normal, everyday frustration. I'm talking about a moment when you realize that nothing is as it should be. Has that ever happened to you?"

"Many times." His large hands were gentle against her face as he wiped away her tears.

"I'm sure you never cry," she said, trying for a haughty tone and failing.

"Perhaps on occasion," he admitted softly.

Once her face was wiped clean he turned his attention to her hands, holding each wrist while he bathed away the dirt gently and easily.

She wondered what would make a stoic man like Dalton cry. Had a woman broken his heart? When he turned those blue eyes to her again, she could see the pain there, and all of a sudden her troubles seemed small. Her heart was broken, she'd made a fool of herself, and she'd never have the one man she'd always wanted, no matter what sacrifices she was prepared to make.

But the pain she saw in Dalton's eyes seemed much deeper than any she'd ever known. She saw and even felt the agony, as if he spoke aloud. Death, rage, darkness. He'd known them all.

"Would you like to tell me," he asked as he finished with her hands and released her, "about the disappointment that brings tears to the eyes of a woman who does not cry?"

She could tell no one, not ever. Victor had proved himself right. She was a slut, a jade, an easy woman who would never have the things she wanted. Simple things, like love and a family of her own. She shook her head slowly, and Dalton stood.

"Then get to bed," he said gruffly as he cleared the bowl and towel from the table.

She stood quickly, and turned away from him with every intention of taking his advice.

"Mary," he said softly.

She stopped, not even thinking to correct him for his improper use of her given name.

"Yes?"

"It would be best if you refrained from late-night walks in the garden. Next time I might not be around to assist you."

"There won't be any more night-time excursions," she said, meaning it.

"Good."

Chapter Fifteen

"Lud, m'dear, whatever are you doing?"

The wonder Max conveyed with his voice was real. The stress of the past several weeks must have been too much for his wife, because before him was the evidence that she'd lost her mind.

"Painting," she murmured without so much as glancing over her shoulder to where he stood in the doorway. She was so intent on her project that he was surprised she responded at all.

"I can see that." He stepped into the parlor and found that Dalton had been correct in his reports. Each of the four walls was in some stage of destruction or renewal. Scenes were sketched in roughly, and here and there Penelope had begun to fill in the spaces with carefully applied paint.

He took a seat in a wing chair in the middle of

the room from which he could watch the process. Penelope paid him no mind at all.

She was truly talented. He'd known that to be true from the moment he'd seen her quickly sketch a simple flower, but he'd never seen her so intent upon her work. So dedicated. Oblivious to her surroundings, she stood perched on her footstool and dabbed with a bit of green paint, leaning close to inspect the area in progress. From this vantage point he could see that the scenes flowed with an effortless elegance across the room.

Her plain blue dress, a simple style with a high waist and a flowing skirt, was marked here and there with specks of paint, her sleeves were sloppily rolled up so as not to impede her work, her hair was falling in disarray from what had no doubt once been a neat bun—and she was breathtakingly beautiful, as always.

He took his eyes from her, wondering why he felt compelled to sit here and watch her. Curiosity? Perhaps. Love? God help him.

His wandering eyes fell upon a stack of papers that were haphazardly piled on the table to his left. Preliminary sketches for the mural that had claimed her attention for the past several days, he was sure. He took the sketches, placed them in his lap, and began to leaf through them. Yes, his wife was definitely gifted.

It was the last of the drawings that surprised him, three unfinished studies of the face he saw in the mirror every morning. She saw more than he knew, his wife. Each illustration showed a different face, one of the many faces he presented to the world.

He stood with the sketches in his hand. "You're quite talented, m'dear," he said as he came up behind her.

Startled, Penelope glanced over her shoulder. Her eyes were wide, and she teetered for a moment on the unsteady stool before tumbling backward. Max dropped the drawings and caught her.

The sketches fluttered to the floor as he stood there with his wife in his arms. Paint from her dress touched his cream silk jacket, and the small paintbrush in her hand stroked his cheek—just once. Beneath her simple dress she wore no busk, no stays, so that the body pressed against his was soft and yielding.

His body's immediate reaction proved to him that avoiding Penelope had been a useless exercise. Keeping his distance hadn't dulled his obsession, but fed it.

"Oh, I'm so sorry," she said, staring at his cheek and then his ruined jacket. A smile bloomed on her face, a very wicked and unrepentant smile. "I didn't realize you were still in the room, and when you spoke . . ."

"I startled you," Max said. "This unfortunate incident is entirely my fault."

He really should put her down, make a fuss over his paint-speckled silk, and tell her how very cumbersome she was.

But she felt just right, not cumbersome at all but warm and soft and secure. He wasn't ready to let her go.

Her smile died slowly. Poor Penelope, she was

surely as confused as he was. In spite of his best efforts, she saw his many faces. Did she wonder which of her husbands held her now?

With her thumb, she tentatively brushed at the paint on his cheek. "I am sorry, Maximillian," she said softly.

"It's quite all right, m'dear." Still he didn't release her.

"It's just that I so rarely see you anymore, and when we are in the same room you never stay for very long."

"I'm an impatient man," he whispered.

"Are you?"

He wanted nothing more at that moment than to carry his wife up the stairs and to her bedchamber, to make love to her by the light of day, to lose himself in her body and forget the differences that came between them.

Max lowered his lips to hers to kiss her tentatively. She tasted so good, smelled so wonderful, the kiss was an assault on his senses, an assault he was unprepared to fight against. Her mouth was receptive, inviting, and he almost forgot that on their last meeting he had all but told Penelope that he didn't love her.

She kissed him back, parting her lips slightly and moving her mouth in a tender exploration over his own. Maybe she didn't care that he didn't love her. Then again, maybe she was smarter than he knew and didn't believe his protests.

How was he supposed to live with Penelope and not love her?

Her eyes had drifted closed, but he needed to see

them, needed to look into those depths as he asked her what he'd never had the nerve to ask before.

"Penelope." He whispered the name against her welcoming lips, and her eyes opened slowly.

"Yes?"

Her betrayal remained between them, the secrets, the lies. Until the truth was spoken they could not have anything more than this shallow and painful sham of a marriage. She looked, at this moment, as if she wanted more—just as he did. "I have to know . . ."

"Madam, you have a visitor." Dalton's curt voice interrupted from close behind, too close behind. Maximillian cursed the man as he set Penelope on her feet.

He calmed himself, dismissed the rash act he'd been about to perpetrate for the sake of love, and turned with a much-too-wide smile on his face to greet Penelope's visitor.

Victor Chadwick.

He'd called here last week, according to Dalton. Dalton, who seemed to be suddenly taken with the woman he'd been so keen to do away with a few weeks ago. Dalton, who'd defended Penelope when Max had railed against the news that she'd received Chadwick privately.

Dalton was going soft.

"What a pleasure," Max said brightly as he approached an unsmiling Chadwick. The last time he'd seen Chadwick had been at a horse race at the edge of town, and before that he'd joined him at Huntland's house for a game of cards. The man had been unusually close-mouthed lately. It was most frustrating. "Dalton, tea all around."

"There's no tea, sir," Dalton said coldly.

Max sighed loudly. "Coffee, then." He turned to see Penelope's reaction. She was pale and fidgety and uncomfortable. Caught again.

"No coffee for me," Chadwick said solemnly. "And Maximillian, if you would indulge me, I need a private word with your charming wife."

Max forced the bright smile to stay in place. "Of course." He glanced at Penelope briefly. "You won't mind if I excuse myself. I really must change out of this paint-stained ensemble. My best imported silk, you know, and it's completely ruined."

"Go on, then," she said softly.

"I'll leave you to your intrigue and whispered secrets," he said lightly as he made his way to the door. In the doorway, he turned and grasped the handle firmly. He stared at Penelope, who had gone from warm and vulnerable to cold and unreadable. Ah, she had as many faces as he did, surely.

"Behave yourself, m'dear," he said softly as he closed the door.

Penelope stared at the closed door and cursed her husband to hell. If ever she needed him beside her it was now. Why didn't she have a husband who cared enough to stand up to Victor and tell him no, he could *not* have his wife alone for even a second? Didn't Maximillian know that she needed him here?

Of course not; he was much too concerned with his ruined clothing.

"What do you want, Victor?"

Victor cast a suspicious eye over the walls of her parlor. "I wanted to give you one last chance to reconsider your decision."

"Is this about that ridiculous spy business again? I've given you my answer, more than once."

Victor smiled, and she didn't like it at all. "The game has changed."

"I have no intention—"

"I have Tyler."

"What?"

Penelope frowned, sure she'd heard incorrectly. She hadn't been paying attention, that was it. She was still thinking about Maximillian and his most recent desertion. What did Victor mean he *had* Tyler? Here he stood, smiling smugly, asking her to do something she could never agree to, and what on earth did that have to do with Tyler?

"He was arrested with a band of miscreants who saw fit to raid my arsenal. Stealing is a serious offense. Stealing from me is extremely unwise."

She realized with a sinking heart that she hadn't misunderstood at all. "What do you want?"

"Since talking to you last, I have even more reason to believe that the Indigo Blade is working out of this very house. He lives here, perhaps disguised as a meek servant or a stable boy. Perhaps he's the husband of one of the cooks or housemaids, a man who might be found here at any time of the day."

She gathered all her courage to face the man who would stoop to such a deceitful level. "I think you're wrong."

Victor was much too calm. "The problem is that I don't know who he is, or what he looks like, as he so often employs those ridiculous disguises. Nor do I know for a fact how many men this rebel has in his employ." He began to pace in obvious excitement. "I hear four, and then I hear twenty. I hear he works alone, and then I hear he has an army waiting to take me on. I know he's here, but if I strike too soon, if I show my hand before I know exactly who this miscreant is, I might lose him completely." He stopped pacing and faced Penelope, looking her square in the eyes with frightening confidence. He knew she would do anything for her brother. "I want you to find out who he is."

"You don't need me for this," she insisted. "And . . . and I can't do it."

Victor smiled. "I couldn't bring myself to hang little Tyler. Why, he was almost a brother to me."

Penelope closed her eyes in relief.

"But I have my duty, Penelope. He'll be jailed in a dark dungeon, whipped in a public display to discourage others of like mind, broken so that when he is one day released, you won't know him." His voice was a whisper as he delivered the last of this dire threat.

There was nothing she wouldn't do to spare Tyler the fate Victor had so carefully planned. Tyler, who was hotheaded but innocent and young . . . as Heath Lowry had been innocent and young.

"How can I find out what you and your entire army cannot?"

"I expect you'll find a way."

Penelope closed her eyes against the room that suddenly swam and tilted. She couldn't do this . . .

she didn't want to have anything to do with Victor and his ambitious plans. . . .

"And by the way," Victor said casually, "is Mary still living here or has she returned to William's plantation?"

"What?" Her eyes snapped open. "How can you come in here and threaten me and then turn around and ask so casually after my cousin? How dare you?"

"Is she still here?" he asked, unmoved by her anger.

"Yes," she whispered.

He appeared to be a bit concerned, puzzled perhaps, as he turned and left her alone. "I'll call on you in three days, Penelope," he said as he reached the door. "I expect you'll have made some progress by then."

Victor closed the door behind him, and Penelope sank into the nearest chair—her energy drained, her newly reclaimed life in shambles.

What choice did she have but to do as he asked? A spy. She, who only wanted to be left out of this conflict, who only wanted to be left alone. No matter how hard she tried, how diligently she undertook this task, there was no guarantee she'd make any discoveries.

What would Victor do to Tyler if she did her best and was unsuccessful?

Her knees shook, and no matter how hard she tried she couldn't make them stop. Where was Maximillian? If ever she'd needed him, this was the time. She wanted to cry on his shoulder, tell him everything that had happened, and somehow have him make it all go away. The lies, the danger to Tyler—she just wanted it to go away.

She heard someone at the door, a soft step and a small movement of the handle.

"Maximillian," she whispered as the door opened slowly.

But it was Dalton who stepped into the room. "Madam, is everything all right?"

She could almost believe that the butler cared more for her welfare than her own husband. At least, Dalton appeared to be concerned.

"Yes." She studied this man who was, she was certain, no butler. He was defiant, impatient, brawny. His face had been browned and leathered by the sun, and he sported that unfashionable bit of facial hair. His hands were large and rough, the hands of a man who was no stranger to hard labor. Still it was flimsy evidence.

Was Dalton the Indigo Blade? And if she discovered that he was, did she dare give that information to Victor? Heaven above, she had no choice.

Outside the warm and secure house, a storm raged. Rain beat against the roof and windows, and lightning split the sky. Tonight there would be no excursions for the Indigo Blade, no delivery of weapons or secret meetings.

Penelope was distant over the evening meal, barely paying attention as Mary chattered on about a new bolt of fabric and the latest bit of gossip. Max had decided, grudgingly, that he might not have been present at all, for all the attention his wife paid him.

He'd been ignoring her for weeks, forcing the distance between them to grow, so why was he irritated that his plan had worked so well? It was the afternoon's kiss, he supposed, an innocent enough kiss for man and wife to share, but also more than enough to make him question his resolve.

Dalton came into the room with a tray of sliced Queen's cake for dessert, and Mary's rambling suddenly ended. She looked at the supposed butler with a slight shifting of her eyes, and no more, as if she were trying to observe him without being noticed. Her back straightened, and she lifted her hand to smoothe a wayward curl. Dalton looked sharply at everyone in the room *but* Mary. He didn't turn his eyes her way once, not even as he set a plate before her.

No wonder he'd objected to having her in the house, Maximillian thought as he suppressed a smile. He was sweet on her. The thought of Dalton Archer being sweet on anyone was difficult to imagine.

Max realized, as he watched, that Penelope followed Dalton's every move, watching and frowning, her dark eyes piercing and curious. Was she concerned about her cousin? Had she noticed the butler's odd behavior toward Mary? He didn't think so.

Beck entered the room bearing a silver tray that supported three china cups filled with steaming coffee, and Penelope's eyes followed him just as they had Dalton.

When they were alone, the three of them with their dessert and coffee, Penelope turned a falsely bland face to her husband.

"Maximillian," she said as she played with her cake, "how long has Dalton been with you?"

"Whyever do you ask?"

She shrugged her shoulders in a way that was surely supposed to be casual to the extreme—but he didn't buy it. "I'm just curious about the household staff."

"The entire staff or just my butler?"

Now they had Mary's full attention. "Dalton is a fine butler," she said defensively. "Unconventional, perhaps, but very reliable."

It seemed that both the Seton women were smitten with the handsome and *unconventional* butler. Max knew, reasonably, that he shouldn't be feeling these pangs of what could only be jealousy. Not after he'd done everything in his power to drive his wife away.

"Dalton has been with me for years, m'dear," he said lightly. "In England, in India, Dalton was at my side."

"I had no idea."

Max gave her a bored smile. "Until now, you haven't expressed an interest."

Dalton, who would have gladly killed Penelope on her wedding night, had been defending her of late—questioning what they knew to be true of her involvement in Heath Lowry's death, questioning her allegiance to Chadwick. What had his lovely wife done to sway the unmerciful man?

"It's just that your entire staff is, as Mary said, unconventional. Has Beck been with you as long as Dalton?"

Beck? The man still carried an openly hostile

grudge for Penelope's part in Lowry's death, as did Lewis and John. Surely she harbored no tender feelings for Beck. "No," he said simply, following his answer with a wide yawn. "Faith, m'dear, this is by far the dullest conversation I've ever endured."

He watched as Penelope turned her attention to her dessert, destroying it bit by bit and eating very little. What was she up to?

Maximillian and Mary had both retired long ago, and the storm that had begun not long after Victor's departure that afternoon continued to rage. Another storm raged within Penelope, a storm she could not escape as easily as the one outside this mansion.

Inside her warm bedchamber she was safe and warm, but she couldn't help but wonder where Tyler was at this moment. Did the same storm roar around him? Was he somewhere warm and secure?

She was dressed for bed in her plain shift, but she hadn't so much as attempted to crawl beneath the coverlet and find sleep. A single candle burned low, lighting her path as she paced on bare feet before the window.

What was she to do? If Victor was right and the Indigo Blade lived in this house, he could be anyone. Dalton, who was no butler. Beck, who hated her openly. John, who mumbled incoherently when he passed her, Lewis with his false smile, blackeyed Garrick, that gruff stableman Fletcher . . .

She had to have something to tell Victor in three days—and her first day was almost gone.

Carrying the single candle, she slipped to the

door and opened it soundlessly. The passageway was deserted and black, the house still. There was only the sound of the storm outside and her thudding heart.

Somewhere on the third floor, she knew, was evidence that the man Victor searched for was here. Weapons, the disguises the Indigo Blade was known for, incriminating notes and maps. All she had to do was find one piece of proof, and she could save her brother.

Garrick had kept her from the third floor once before. Was he the one who had something to hide? Exploring during the daytime hours was impossible. There was always someone about—watching her, following her—so her only chance was to explore while the household was abed, to sneak into the very rooms where they slept. A shiver worked its way through her body at the prospect.

And if she were caught? As she closed the door to her bedchamber and took the first steps toward the staircase at the end of the passageway, she found she didn't care. She would die for Tyler, if need be. She had nothing and no one else in this world to love.

The storm masked any sound she made, and she was very careful not to make any noise at all as she approached the stairway that led to the third floor. The candlelight flickered off the walls, gilt frames and oil paintings from around the world, polished tables and ancient vases, the trappings of her fine prison.

She had nothing to lose.

Her foot was on the first step, her face lifted to

the unexplored floor above, when she hesitated. If she learned that one of her husband's servants was indeed the Indigo Blade, she had no choice but to report her findings to Victor. Still, it would destroy her to betray a man she'd come to admire. A hero who saved innocents and stood up for those who would see these colonies free from England. But if she found nothing, Victor would punish Tyler terribly, and that would destroy her as well.

"Dalton's room is the third on the left."

She spun around so fast that the candle flickered and almost went out, but it quickly flared to life to illuminate her husband's angry face.

Chapter Sixteen

"But perhaps I don't need to tell you where his room is."

He should smile and inform his wife that her night-time activities didn't concern him at all, that any and all of the men living under this roof were ready and willing to serve her in every way, including visiting her bed if she wished it. But his blood was boiling and he couldn't fix the mask of the uncaring and flippant Maximillian Broderick that Penelope must know so well into place.

A crack of thunder shook the house; it sounded in Max's blood and reverberated through every throbbing vein. Standing on the bottom step of the narrow stairway that led to the third floor, Penelope jumped.

"Afraid of the storm, m'dear?"

She shook her head slowly.

"Afraid of me, m'dear?" he whispered.

Penelope hesitated before shaking her head this time. "I'm not looking for anyone's room. I was just restless. It's the storm, I suppose."

She seemed a horrible liar. Her dark eyes were wide, her soft lower lip trembled, and the hand that grasped the candlestick shook visibly. Ah, but he knew the opposite to be true.

He lifted his hand, offered it palm up, and waited for her to take it. "I would suggest that when you're restlessly wandering the house, you confine yourself to the first and second floors. Dalton sleeps with a knife, in case you haven't already discovered that fact in your restive night-time excursions, and Garrick always keeps a firearm close at hand. Wander into the wrong room and you'll likely make me a widower, m'dear."

After a moment's hesitation, she placed her hand in his and stepped down. Her trembling had lessened considerably, but her hand still quivered.

"I've never . . ." She stammered and blushed. "I wouldn't . . . How can you believe . . ." She looked up at him, her face soft in the mellow candlelight, her lips parted to defend herself from his accusations. He watched the strength come back into her eyes, felt the return of steadiness to the hand he grasped so lightly. "If you can believe that I would lie with another man, you know me not at all."

She told the truth, he could see it, and the wave of relief that washed over him almost buckled his knees. Maybe he believed this declaration to be true because he needed and wanted so badly to accept it. In spite of everything that had happened, she was his wife. She was *his*.

"Forgive me," he whispered.

She could have easily slipped her hand from his and made an escape, but did not. Her chilled fingers tightened. "What happened to us, Maximillian?"

There was no answer to her question, at least none he could voice. So he kissed her. A soft kiss, like the brushing of their lips in the parlor that afternoon, a tentative, uncertain caress. Her mouth warmed against his, her eyes fluttered closed, her body moved instinctively closer to his.

He could take her here and now, on the floor as the storm howled around the house. He could tell her how he loved her in spite of everything he'd done to prove otherwise, how he wanted her in his bed every night. Faith, she'd made a fool of him without even trying. . . . He took his lips from hers so suddenly and quickly she teetered on her feet and he had to reach out to brace her.

When Penelope was steady, he released her and turned away. "Good night, m'dear." He had almost reached the door to his bedchamber when she spoke.

"Am I doing something wrong?" Her voice trembled slightly.

He stopped with his hand against the door. "No, of course not," he said lightly.

If she would leave it at that he could make his escape. Penelope, of course, had no intentions of letting him off so lightly. "What must I do to make you love me again?"

She was coming closer. He could see the light

dancing on the walls as she approached, hear the soft sound of her bare feet against the rug that lined the passageway, feel the tightening of every muscle in his body as she came near.

"Perhaps I never stopped loving you," he whispered, certain she couldn't hear his soft words.

And then she placed a hand against his back. He savored the touch of her palm through his linen shirt, leaned back slightly to increase the pressure of her fingers against his spine.

"I could use a friend," she said softly. "I could use two strong arms to lean on. Maybe the love has gone, but there must be something between us. I can feel it, can't you? You're my husband, and I'm your wife. If we want anything more than . . . than what we have now, we have to try to make something of this marriage."

Maximillian turned and placed the two strong arms she needed around her. He tightened them as if she might change her mind and walk away.

"Let me stay with you tonight." Her voice was hesitant, as if she expected him to say no. Of course she was hesitant, after the hurtful things he'd said and done in the name of justice. It took courage for Penelope to face him and voice the facts of their less-than-perfect marriage, to ask for more. It was a courage he himself did not possess.

Max lifted her easily, so that her feet dangled inches from the floor and her candle tilted dangerously, and he carried her down the short expanse of passageway that separated his bedchamber from hers.

As Maximillian set her on her feet and opened the

220

door, another close flash of lightning split the sky and flashed brightly, illuminating her chamber and the untouched bed.

Penelope was not ashamed to admit that she needed her husband tonight, no matter that he didn't love or trust her, no matter that he'd just accused her of seeking out another man to take his place. She needed his arms around her, his warm body beside hers, and she needed him to make her forget, for a while, the impossible decisions she had to make.

She was tired of being alone.

Maximillian took the candle from her and blew out the flame, leaving them in complete darkness. She was about to remove her shift when he reached out to do that for her, to take the linen in his hands and lift it slowly over her head and then drop it on the floor. His hands touched her then, gentle hands that barely brushed against her flesh.

How could a man be so thoughtless one moment and so tender the next? She closed her eyes and allowed herself to enjoy the feel of his hands on her body, the exploring hands that brushed over her neck and her breasts, down her side and over her hip, as if he were memorizing every line, every curve.

The lightning flashed again, making the room bright as day for a heartbeat. For that flash of time she saw the man she married, a man who truly loved her.

"Maximillian." She whispered his name as she reached out to lay her hands at his waist.

"Yes, m'dear," he said hoarsely.

"Tell me there's no one else. That there are no other women. That when you leave me here alone at night you don't go to someone else for what I would gladly give you."

"Penelope . . ."

"Even if you don't mean it, even if it's a lie. I need to hear it."

He wrapped his arms around her and held her tight. "I neither need nor want any other woman. When I'm away from here I think of you, whether I want to or not. You're with me wherever I go." He led her to the bed and placed her upon it, dropping his arms from her aching body.

"I want to believe that's true," she whispered.

He returned to the bed without the breeches and linen shirt and slipped beneath the satin coverlet to take her in his arms. Their legs entwined, moving instinctively and without hesitation. Their arms reached out to hold and be held, and Penelope lifted her mouth for a kiss that made her forget, for the moment, that this man had hurt her, that he'd made her love him and then grown distant, had promised her perfection and delivered heartache.

He was here for her now, holding her with steady arms, protecting her from the stormy world outside this house—at least for tonight.

When she thought she could stand to wait no more, he rolled her onto her back and spread her thighs wide to stroke her throbbing body with exploring fingers. His mouth devoured hers, with thrusting tongue and demanding lips, as he drove her past the point of rational thought.

When he, at last, sheathed himself inside her, she

wrapped her legs around him possessively. There was nothing gentle in the way he loved her, nothing tame in the way he rocked above and inside her. He was as wild as the storm that roared around them.

There was no misunderstanding between them now, no accusations. There was simply his body and hers, his heart and hers, a wordless acceptance that they were wed not only by law, but by a bonding of the heart and soul.

She shattered in his arms, moaning against the mouth that was joined to hers, clutching desperately at Maximillian as he growled her name and drove deep and hard one last time. A distant flash of lightning illuminated her husband for her, ever so briefly—the unrestrained pale hair that fell across his face, hiding his expression from her, the hard, glistening body that was poised above hers.

How could she love a man who so often treated her with such disdain, with such cold distance? She didn't know how it was possible, but she did love him, still.

He fell gently across her spent body, covering her and protecting her with his body and his heart.

But for how long?

Mary lay beneath the covers, huddled against the storm. As she had twice before, as the long night passed, she reached beneath her pillow for the letters she'd tucked there. Letters from Victor, notes demanding that she meet him in the gazebo. To talk, he said, but she no longer believed him.

Tempted as she'd been, she'd ignored the last two letters from Victor, refusing to see him.

She'd been such a fool. Victor not only didn't love her, he loved no one and probably never would. She'd thought the joining of their bodies was proof of his love, but it had been much less for him.

He'd used her.

It hurt so badly, she assumed she must still love Victor in some way. Why? Why couldn't she choose to love someone else? Someone who wouldn't hurt her, someone who would love her in return.

She'd told Penelope often that a smart woman chose who she loved and rejected unacceptable prospects. So, why couldn't she chase memories of Victor from her mind?

Unbidden, she saw Dalton's face as he wiped away her tears and washed her hands, as he knelt before her and tended to her gently, with no idea of how much she was hurting inside.

He would surely think less of her if he knew.

Mary pulled a fat pillow over her head. The butler! Surely she wasn't lying in bed worrying about what the *butler* thought of her!

But he was a most handsome butler, she conceded as she moved the pillow from her face.

Penelope was sleeping soundly, and morning was lighting the sky when Max gathered his clothes from the floor, dressed quickly, and left the room. During the early morning hours the storm had passed, and this promised to be a bright and beautiful day.

Still, it was a day in which he could not tell his wife that he loved her, a day in which he could not share the deception that was a most important part of his life. A day in which he would look at the woman he loved more than life itself and wonder how she could do something so dastardly as she'd done.

"What's this?"

Max lifted his head to find a smiling man looking down at him from the narrow stairway where he'd found his wife last night. Dalton leaned against the banister with a taut nonchalance.

"*This* is none of your business," Max said coldly. He was certain there was nothing between Penelope and Dalton, but for some reason he felt the jealous rage from last night resurfacing.

He wished, not for the first time, that he cared for Penelope less—without the frenzy, without the passion, without the fierceness he was unaccustomed to. But he was learning there was no tempering his feelings where she was concerned.

Dalton came slowly down the stairs to meet Max in the passageway. "No one's likely to agree with me," he said softly, "but I think your wife's innocent of the charge against her."

"Do you?" Max faced the man who'd been at his side for seven years. "And what convinced you, pray tell? Did Penelope swear her innocence to you?"

"No." Dalton's smile was gone. "She's said nothing."

"Interesting. Then what changed your mind? You were ready to do away with her when you first heard of her betrayal, if I remember correctly."

Dalton was dressed for the day in the livery that marked him as a servant of the Broderick household, a conservative suit of clothes that could not restrain the fierce man he was. "Ask her," he whispered. "Let her explain."

"How noble of you."

"Ask her, and then look at her as she answers. You will know if she's lying or telling the truth."

That said, Dalton passed Max on his way to the staircase that curved to the first floor.

"Dalton," Max said darkly, turning to follow the man's progress. Dalton stopped at the top of the stairs and waited. "Are you in love with my wife?"

Dalton glanced over his shoulder, a wicked smile on his face. "No. Are you?"

Max turned his back sharply on Dalton and retreated into his chamber.

She knew now what she had to do.

Penelope sat before the mirror dressing her hair, wearing only her corset and petticoat as Helen gathered together the gown and shoes she would wear today.

It had been just past dawn when she'd wakened to find herself alone in a tumbled bed. Alone, and still warmed by the night's encounter with her husband.

She'd met the morning clearheaded for the first time since Victor had delivered his ultimatum, and the plan had come to her as she lay there wondering where her husband was and when he had left her bed.

This plan would take all her strength, all her convictions.

"Helen, I have something to ask of you." The words were quick, but sure, an order not a request.

Helen obviously cared for her mistress no more than the others in the house, and they usually passed their time together silently.

The older woman left her chore and turned to face Penelope with her normal sour expression on her face. "Of course, madam."

Penelope was well aware of her maid's political leanings. It hadn't taken much conversation to discern that fact. With a comment beneath her breath, a snort at the mention of the British, Helen had most definitely shown that she was no loyalist. As a servant and an obvious opponent of the British, if the Indigo Blade was living in this house, Helen would likely know who that man was.

"I have an important message for someone, and I believe you can help me get that message to him."

"A message for whom?" Helen asked suspiciously.

Penelope took the sealed letter from the drawer before her and stood to present it to Helen. "It is imperative that the man known as the Indigo Blade receives this as soon as possible."

Helen's hazel-brown eyes widened in surprise. "Madam, I don't know what makes you think—"

"I don't care how you do it," Penelope interrupted, offering the message to Helen, refusing to drop her hand and the offered note. Now was not the time to be timid, or kind, or reasonable. Tyler's life was at stake. "Just see that this is in the Indigo Blade's hands before Friday."

Helen took the sealed paper with trembling hands. "I'll do what I can, madam," she said softly.

Chapter Seventeen

Perhaps Dalton's suggestion had merit, and he should just ask Penelope about her part in Heath Lowry's capture. He'd almost done just that yesterday, after she'd fallen into his arms and a brief kiss had caused him to lose his senses. There were moments Max was certain he could look into Penelope's eyes and know if she spoke a truth or a lie—and there were other, more desperate moments, when he thought her to be most cleverly false.

There were too many doubts in his mind to ask her outright. How would he justify his interest after all this time? The devil-may-care Maximillian Broderick wouldn't be troubled by her actions, and had, in fact, insisted many times that he was bored by the subject.

What if she looked him in the eyes and admitted

with cold indifference that she'd willingly turned Lowry over to Chadwick?

What if she lied, and he saw the falseness on her lovely face?

Max picked at the lace cuff that hung from his royal-blue velvet sleeve. The truth or a lie. He didn't know which would be worse.

It was true that since the Lowry incident Penelope had done nothing to display any loyalist tendencies, nor had she shown a mercenary side to her nature. But he couldn't forget that the accusation had come from Lowry's own mouth, and a dying man had no reason to lie.

Had Lowry wondered as the lash struck his back again and again why a woman he'd called friend had turned against him? Jamie, with his romantic's heart, had surely wondered why the woman he loved would betray him. Had they both died with an unanswered *why?* on their lips and in their hearts?

He made his way to the open parlor door. Penelope had moved to another section of the wall, and dabbed absently with green paint at a penciled cypress tree. There was no need for the footstool at the moment, so if he startled her with his curiously doting presence there would be no need to catch her.

What a shame.

Penelope's hand stopped moving and fell to her side, but she continued to stare at the wall before her. Back straight, shoulders squared, she faced the wall as if it were an enemy. He waited for her to lift the brush and continue her work, but she did not.

He could ask her the damning question now, look into those telling eyes and ask her why she'd sent Lowry to his death. But he wouldn't like the answer. Heaven help him, he didn't want to hear the truth or a lie pass those lips.

Instead of walking away, he stepped into the parlor, surveying the walls, studying the project that absorbed his wife so completely. It would be magnificent when finished, he could tell already.

"Whatever possessed you?" he asked softly, and Penelope spun around as if she'd been caught in yet another lie.

"Maximillian," she said breathlessly, bringing her hand to her chest. "I thought you were gone for the day."

Ah, she was hiding something.

"Can't a man spend a few days at home now and again?" He gave his lovely wife a tired smile as he absently fluffed his lace cravat. "My horses are wearied, my tailor is fatigued, my bootmaker is haggard . . ." He waved an indolent hand and sighed for effect. "So I decided to give them all a holiday and spend some time with my wife."

Penelope didn't like the idea, obviously. She twisted her hands and briefly bit her bottom lip. He made his lovely wife nervous. "You haven't spent many days at home. Whatever will we do to pass the time?"

She hadn't been so reticent last night. In fact, she hadn't been timid at all. Surely she knew he wanted to pass the time in her bed. Loving her, laughing the way they had before the wedding and the betrayal.

"You said you needed a friend, m'dear."

"I do," she whispered.

Heaven above, he loved her to the point of pain, craved her smile and her touch, felt betrayed that she was not the woman he'd thought her to be. Was it fair to expect perfection, even from Penelope?

This turn of events astounded him. He had survived a barely tolerable childhood, storms at sea, war with the nawab of Bengal. He'd been attacked with blades of every length and breadth, firearms great and small, winds that would carry away the house above his head—only to discover that a *woman* held the power to deliver the greatest agony and the greatest joy.

"Oh, you're early." Her eyes went past him and to the open doorway, and Max turned to see Dalton and Chadwick entering his wife's domain.

"I came as soon as I received your note," Chadwick said with a tight smile.

Max turned his back on the guest and faced his wife. "But it appears you already have a friend, m'dear."

He didn't wait for them to ask him to leave, not today, but turned and sauntered past Chadwick and a sullen Dalton. He couldn't help but notice how smug and satisfied Chadwick was—or how tense his lovely wife had become. Something was definitely afoot, and it wasn't good.

As he pulled the door closed on Penelope and Chadwick, he turned angry eyes to Dalton.

"Innocent, is she?"

Dalton did not defend Penelope this time, but held forth a sealed note. "The meeting might have something to do with this."

Victor made himself comfortable on the sofa, but Penelope found she couldn't be still. She paced before him.

"You've found him already," Victor said with a satisfied smile.

"No," Penelope said softly. "But I have a plan."

"A plan," Victor said skeptically. "That wasn't part of the agreement."

She didn't allow his skepticism to stop her. "I've set up a meeting with the Indigo Blade for Friday night. Eleven o'clock in the garden."

"What makes you think he'll come?"

She spun on him, gathering all her courage. "What makes you think he won't?"

He laughed at her, and she wanted—more than anything—to reach out and slap his complacent face. But she didn't, of course.

"There's a gazebo at the end of the garden path," she continued undaunted.

Victor's laughter and even his smile faded. "I know."

"Be there at eleven o'clock Friday evening, and you'll have your Indigo Blade."

The last person she wanted to see, as she came down the stairs, was Victor Chadwick. If she'd come down a few minutes earlier, she would have been safely in the dining room having coffee and one of Beck's marvelous breakfasts; if she'd come down a few minutes later he would have been gone. But as it was, she stepped from the stairs just as Victor left Penelope's parlor.

"Mary," he said, trying and failing to summon concern in his voice. Why had she not seen his insincerity before? "I've been so worried about you."

"You needn't worry about me," she said calmly. "I'm doing quite well. How's your lovely bride-to-be?"

Victor had never been one for subtleties. Without another word, without asking for her permission, he strode to her, took her arm with strong, thin fingers, and led her forcibly to the front door.

"I need to talk to you," he said when she finally mustered the strength to protest meekly.

Outside, in the cool of a spring morning, Victor led her to the side yard of the Broderick mansion. Here they could not be seen from Penelope's parlor window, or the stables, or any of the windows from the oft-used rooms.

"Why have you not answered my letters?" he asked harshly, pressing her back against the brick wall and placing his body too close to hers. "Why did you leave me waiting in the gazebo?"

"I told you I don't want to see you again," she said firmly. "Now, let me go."

"You didn't mean it," he said softly, and then he pressed his lips to hers, rough and forceful, cold and demanding. She moved away until the back of her head was against the wall, and still he persisted, thrusting his tongue deep into her mouth.

She wanted it to stop.

Victor wasn't prepared for the hand that pushed

him away, and while he was surprised, he didn't move far.

"I did mean it," Mary whispered.

"But you love me," he insisted with a self-satisfied smile. "I'll expect to see you tonight," he added. "In the gazebo."

"No."

"Promise me you'll be there."

"No!"

His mouth moved toward hers again, his hand fell intimately to her hip, and Mary felt the panic rising in her. He wasn't listening to her, didn't care what she wanted or did not want.

"Promise me," he whispered.

"Miss Seton?" She recognized the gruff voice on the other side of the wall, heard the approaching footsteps through the grass. Victor cursed under his breath as he stepped away from her.

"There you are," Dalton said as he rounded the corner. Victor had taken several steps back, and Mary herself had moved away from the wall. She'd never in her life been so glad to see another human being. "Mrs. Broderick has requested your presence in the parlor. Immediately."

Dalton kept his eyes on her, didn't even glance at Victor. But he knew. There was a barely restrained anger in his eyes, a fury in the blue depths she read so well. Somehow, the man knew he was rescuing her.

"Miss Seton will be in momentarily," Victor snapped, dismissing the servant with his haughty voice and a wave of his hand.

Dalton looked at Victor then, and gave him a

scorching glance that was not at all humble.

"I'll escort you," Dalton said, still staring at Victor. "The ground's soaked, and there are nasty puddles to watch out for."

Without hesitation, Mary hurried to Dalton's side. When he offered his arm, she gratefully took it, and when Victor asked her, again, if she wouldn't agree to his invitation, she looked over her shoulder, smiled, and told him "no."

It felt good.

They were inside the house, the door closed behind them, before Dalton opened his mouth again. "Are you all right?" He led her through the foyer to the foot of the stairs.

She released his arm. "Yes, thank you. Tell Penelope I'll be right there. I would like to . . ."

"Mrs. Broderick didn't ask for you," Dalton said lowly.

"You lied?"

"I did."

Mary smiled up at Dalton, who always looked more a rogue than a butler, with his neatly trimmed small beard and piercing blue eyes. "Then I thank you," she said.

"Should I kill him for you?" His tone and expression stayed the same: stoic, harsh . . . beautiful.

"Would you?" she whispered.

"Yes."

For an angry moment she actually considered what Dalton offered, but then she placed an easy and stilling hand on his forearm. "No. I wouldn't want you to get into trouble, and I'm afraid you would if you actually killed Victor."

235

"No one would know it was me," he assured her.

She shook her head. "There's been enough death," she said, thinking of Heath.

He nodded as if he understood, and perhaps he did.

"But I am indebted to you," she insisted. A moment ago she'd been frightened and alone in her battle with Victor. Now, she looked at Dalton and felt warm and safe and . . . good heavens, for the first time in her life, she was truly *not* alone. "How can I thank you?"

"Tell me." He placed his hand over hers. "Do you love him?"

She had to think about the question for a moment, and Dalton waited patiently. "I don't know." Dalton deserved the truth, and so did she. "There was a time when I adored Victor more than anything or anyone, but right now I don't even know what love is."

"I can tell you what it isn't," Dalton said darkly. "It isn't craving something you cannot or should not have. It isn't groveling or hurtful, though I do believe it can bring incredible pain when it goes wrong."

"Yes."

"Sometimes," he added, "you have to let love go."

They were simple words, and she clung to them. Could she let the love she'd felt for Victor go? Looking at the man before her, she suddenly thought it possible. She also thought it possible she'd never loved Victor at all. She'd been enormored by the idea of love, the prospect of taking affection away from Penelope, but that wasn't love.

"Mary Seton," Dalton said gruffly, "would you swoon if the butler asked you for a kiss?"

"Not at all," she said softly, and then she closed her eyes and waited. Waited for harsh lips and intruding tongue, waited for a cold mouth pressed to hers. And she waited. And she waited.

The brush of lips against hers, when it came, was soft and warm. Dalton's mouth barely touched hers, but everywhere their lips met she tingled. She was very still, as those lips danced softly over hers, as they tasted and teased until her entire body quivered to her very bones.

She'd never known a kiss like this, had never known a kiss could be so pleasurable. At times Dalton's lips covered hers fully, at other times they brushed by as softly as a spring breeze.

He left her as easily and gently as he'd come to her, and she stood there with her eyes closed and her heart racing. Her knees were weak, her blood was racing. "Oh, my," she whispered.

When she opened her eyes, Dalton was gone.

Max settled the black wig over his fair hair, tugging to make certain it was securely seated.

"I can't believe you're doing this," Fletcher murmured darkly.

He couldn't believe it either. It had been two days since he'd received the note from Penelope, two days since he'd seen Victor Chadwick walk calmly into his wife's parlor for what had to be a damning encounter.

During those two days he'd avoided being in the same room with Penelope for more than a few minutes, afraid that if he found himself alone with her he would either tell all—or strangle her.

"It's a trap," Garrick said succinctly. "A sweet trap set by your very own wife, and you're walking into it with your eyes wide open like an innocent babe offering himself up to the hungry lions. You have no idea—"

Max lifted darkened eyebrows at his friend. "Getting a little carried away, aren't we? I know exactly what awaits me at the gazebo, and I'm well prepared."

"Are you?" John mumbled.

"Yes. You're to go about your business normally, and if Chadwick shows up . . ."

"*When* Chadwick shows up," Lewis and Beck said at once.

"If," Max said softly.

Dalton had been very quiet throughout the entire evening, but he spoke up now. "Let me kill him."

"Eventually," Max said as he slipped on the long dark coat that concealed two knives, a short sword, and a pistol.

"Tonight," Dalton said softly.

"No." Max had already decided that when Victor Chadwick died it would be by *his* hand. No one else's. "All of you get into the house. There's less than half an hour to the appointed meeting time, and for all we know Chadwick and his men are already waiting."

He flashed a bright smile, one that made his face feel like it would crack. He didn't feel like smiling; he wanted to run, he wanted to hide.

At ten o'clock, all his questions would be answered, whether he was prepared or not.

Chapter Eighteen

Penelope pulled the hooded cape tighter about her body as she quickly walked the path toward the gazebo. It was a chilly spring night, and a breeze cut through her lightweight wool cape and to her bones, making her shudder uncontrollably.

Then again, it wasn't really that cold. Maybe it wasn't the chill in the air that made her shiver, but the awareness of her actions and all that might yet go wrong.

What if the Indigo Blade didn't show up? There was always the possibility that he'd think this was a trap and stay away, and she couldn't discount the possibility that he'd never even received her note. She could wait out here all night, wondering what she could do next to save Tyler.

"That's far enough." The whisper stopped her well short of the gazebo, on a curve in the path.

"Who are you?" she kept her voice as low as his.

There was a brief pause, a few seconds of complete silence before the answer came. "I came in response to your invitation, Mrs. Broderick. Surely you know well enough who I am."

"Yes." She breathed in relief.

"Why have you called me here?"

Her heart beat much too fast, and she questioned again why she was doing this. She did not know this man, and she certainly didn't owe him anything—least of all a sacrifice of these proportions. But she'd made her decision.

"To warn you."

"To warn me?" She could hear a touch of humor in the hoarse whisper.

"Victor Chadwick knows—believes—the Indigo Blade lives in this house. If this is true, it's only a matter of time before he catches you."

She heard a rustle of leaves to her right. "And so you felt it your duty to warn me? Where is Chadwick now? Waiting behind the gazebo with his army?"

"He'll be here in an hour."

There was a long moment of silence, but she knew the man who had answered her summons had not departed silently. Finally, he spoke. "And you're supposed to keep me entertained for that length of time? How interesting. Whatever was Chadwick thinking?"

The stranger in the shadows was a frustrating man, like every other in her life. Could he not take this seriously? "I told Victor I was to meet you at eleven. I trust you'll be long gone by then."

"What do you want, Mrs. Broderick?" he asked again, the whisper deeper and harder to hear than before.

"I told you, I simply want to warn you of the danger at hand." Why was she doing this? The man obviously did not want or feel as if he needed her help. "Please accept my apologies for wasting your time, sir. I suggest you make yourself scarce before the hour has passed."

She spun away and started toward the house. In an hour, she would return and play the role of the waiting decoy for Victor, but she'd done all she could for the moment.

"Wait." There was a hint of urgency in his voice, enough to make her halt her progress.

Penelope heard him step onto the path behind her, stealthy footsteps as the stranger left the heavy foliage that had shielded him. If she turned, she would see the face of the Indigo Blade in the moonlight. She didn't move.

"Why?" he hissed. He was close, closer than she'd imagined.

A minute passed, and neither Penelope nor the man behind her moved. "I admire what you do," she finally whispered. "I think you're a commendable and worthy man, fighting for your convictions as you do. You shouldn't have to die for what you believe in."

"What's one more rebel head to your name?" he asked, and she could tell by the soft sound of that voice that he'd moved very near. "What difference does a little more blood on your hands make?"

It was more than she could take. Her fists balled

at her sides, and she lifted her chin in the darkness. "I had nothing to do with Heath Lowry's death."

"Why should I believe you?"

"Why should I care if you believe me or not?"

All was silent, and for a moment she thought herself to be alone. The man had silently walked away, and she would never know if he believed her or not. Despite her protest, she found she did care—very much.

And then he spoke from directly behind her. "If you had nothing to do with Lowry's capture and death, why would he denounce you?"

"Because he believed it to be true." Unshed tears came to her eyes, and she felt the anger and confusion she'd tried to bury rise within her once again. "Poor Heath! He died thinking I betrayed him, and I didn't. I couldn't have."

"Why would Lowry think you betrayed him?"

"Because that's what Victor Chadwick led him to believe." Her voice rose slightly, loud in the silent garden. "Victor lied to hurt me, to punish me for marrying another man." She couldn't tell even this stranger that on some days she was convinced marriage to Maximillian was punishment enough for all her sins.

"And you never protested?"

"I did!" Penelope started to turn to face the accuser behind her, but a hand on her shoulder stilled her progress. She shook his hand off, but did not turn about. "At least, I tried to tell the people who are important to me, the ones I love."

"Did you, now?"

She had been unable to speak of this to anyone,

and she found it a great release to share it all now, even with this stranger. And she found she wanted, very badly, for the man who stood silently on the garden path to believe her. "My uncle didn't believe me, my cousin didn't care, and my brother . . ." Her voice shook. "My brother ran away before I had a chance to explain."

The hand returned to her shoulder, comforting and steady, and this time she didn't shake it off.

"And your husband?"

"He never asked," she said. It hurt to admit it aloud, that Maximillian cared so little for her that the troubles in her life were nothing to him. A nuisance, a bother less consequential than a stain on his clothing. "He doesn't care."

"Then he's a bigger fool than he appears to be," the man replied.

"I did not come here to talk about my husband," Penelope said sharply. "Leave this house," she advised. "Take yourself to a place of safety and stay there until Victor's obsession with you has passed."

"I can't do that."

"Then I can do nothing more to help you."

The hand on her shoulder tightened. "Mrs. Broderick?" The whisper was close to her ear. "After all he's done to hurt you, why do you assist Chadwick in this endeavor?"

She swallowed hard and closed her eyes, trying to force away the tears and the night. "He has my brother."

"Tyler," Max whispered.

"You know him?"

There was such light in her voice, such hope, even now. "Yes, but I did not know he'd been taken."

"Arrested," Penelope said softly. "Tyler believes, as you do, in liberty and freedom, in revolution. He foolishly took up with a band of rebels who stole weapons from Victor's arsenal. They were caught. Victor says he'll have Tyler whipped if I don't do as he asks, he says he'll break his spirit . . . and Tyler's spirit, his heart, is what makes him so dear to me."

"Then you're taking quite a chance, warning me." Max wanted to spin Penelope around and take her in his arms and beg pardon for all he'd done, for what he'd believed. But there was not enough time for all that needed to be said, not here and now. Chadwick was coming, and they probably had no more than a few minutes.

"How can I trust the word of a man like Victor Chadwick?" He could hear the despair in her voice, and knew what torture this decision had been for her. "Even if I were to help him capture you, I don't believe he'd release Tyler, as he promises. He'd use Tyler again, and again, and I would be no better than a slave to his every whim. I can only hope that if Victor believes I'm doing my best to assist him, it will buy me time to find a way to free my brother."

He placed his free hand on her shoulder, so his gloved hands bracketed her hooded head, his thumbs at her neck, his leather-encased fingers folding over the dark green cloak that was almost black in the night. With the hood up he could see nothing—not her hair, not a glimpse of her face—but he could touch her, for a moment.

"I'll see Tyler freed."

"Will you?" There it was—the hope in her voice, the light.

"You have my word."

Penelope lifted a hand and placed it over one of his, there on her shoulder. She trembled, but just a little, as she folded her fingers over his. "I thank you with all of my heart, sir."

He bent to kiss her fingers lightly, to ask forgiveness silently for condemning her without ever giving her a chance to explain. It was a mistake she would likely not forgive, when faced with the truth.

"Mrs. Broderick?" he whispered as he lifted his lips from her fingers.

"Yes?"

"Penelope."

"Yes."

They stood there for a long and silent moment, hand in hand, heads so close together that if she turned her head a fraction she'd see and know his face.

Would she ever forget that he had condemned her without asking for an explanation, that he lied about his true self? Likely not. Would she listen to his inadequate explanations? Of course not. Perhaps she would listen to him now.

"You are a most remarkable and beautiful lady."

"I thank you for the compliment, sir, but you are the remarkable one. Rescuing rebels, leading Victor on a merry chase as no one else could. Devoting yourself to what you believe to be right. You have my deepest admiration."

Now was the time to tell her . . . but the sound of

approaching horses interrupted, and Penelope stepped forward and out of his grasp.

"Go," she whispered harshly, hurrying down the path toward the house. "That's Victor, I'm sure of it."

She didn't look back.

Huddled beneath her lightweight woolen cloak, Penelope sat on the gazebo bench, her hands in her lap as she waited. All was silent, though she knew full well she wasn't alone.

Her eyes had adjusted to the dark long ago, and she watched the bush Victor was hiding behind just a few feet away. Now and again she'd see the leaves flutter.

"Maybe he isn't coming."

His response was so low she could barely hear it. "You'd better hope he does."

She didn't. She hoped he was far away by now, saving Tyler, saving himself . . .

More than ever, Penelope wondered if she knew the man who called himself the Indigo Blade. When he'd kissed her hand, she'd seen a lock of long dark hair swing forward. The only dark-haired men in the house were John, Garrick, and Fletcher, but the man she'd met had seemed like none of these. John muttered and mumbled constantly, and this man's voice had been quite clear. Garrick was cold as ice, and she'd sensed great kindness and warmth in the Indigo Blade. Fletcher was earthy and coarse, and the man who'd placed his hands on her shoulders and comforted her was a gentleman. Of that she was certain.

Perhaps he didn't live beneath her roof after all, and Victor was looking in the wrong place for his quarry. She hoped that was true, and that Victor would never catch the man he sought so diligently.

After meeting the Indigo Blade, she respected him more than ever. He was strong and brave and noble, fearless in his beliefs, and clever in avoiding Victor. He was a man who was willing to fight and even to die for what he believed to be right, a man who aided those in dire need. Why couldn't her husband have just a few of those qualities?

Good heavens, she was fascinated with the man, after only a brief meeting and a brush of his lips against her hand. There was nothing to the feelings that bloomed inside her, she knew. She would never know the Indigo Blade, would likely never see his face, and would never hear his voice again. But for the moment, she found herself foolishly enamored of that soothing whisper.

How long would Victor insist that she wait? The minutes dragged past slowly, a silent torture. But then she was the only one who knew the Indigo Blade wasn't coming.

"Good evening, Mrs. Broderick." The familiar whisper came from behind her, breaking the silence of the night, and Penelope nearly jumped out of her skin.

Why was he here? He should be far away right now, safe from Victor and the soldiers who were waiting nearby.

"I'm very disappointed," he said, not waiting for her response. "I thought our meeting was to be private."

Penelope felt frozen, unable to speak, unable to move.

Victor jumped from his hiding place near the pathway entrance to the gazebo, leaping onto the path with a pistol in his hand. "He's here!"

Penelope waited for the rush of soldiers Victor had posted around the property, waited for the warlike shouts and the blasts of gunfire, but all was silent. Soundless, except for the tsking sound that came from the foliage behind her.

"I'm afraid your men have been otherwise detained, Chadwick. There's just you and me and the lovely Mrs. Broderick. What a sweet lure you chose, Chadwick. After all, what man could resist an invitation from a lady such as she?"

Victor stepped onto the gazebo, moving with a stealth Penelope had not seen from him in the past. He raised his pistol and took aim at the lush foliage. "Every man has a weakness," he said as his eyes searched the darkness.

"And Mrs. Broderick is supposed to be mine?" The whisper responded with a touch of humor. "Did you really think I would be so easy to capture, Chadwick?"

Victor used the sound of that voice to locate his objective, taking aim and firing.

Penelope covered her ears against the blast and shouted "No!" a protest that was lost in the explosion of the weapon.

As the roar of the pistol subsided, all was silent once again.

"I got him," Victor whispered triumphantly, and a wide smile bloomed across his face.

Penelope knew she couldn't let her revulsion show. She couldn't cry, she couldn't lash out at the man before her. For Tyler's sake, she remained calm.

"How can you be sure?"

Victor didn't answer, but left the gazebo to explore the grounds behind Penelope, to crash through the foliage in search of his victim. As minutes passed and he found no body and no wounded traitor, he became more and more impatient, cursing as he thrashed about in the dark garden.

Penelope clasped her hands together and held her breath. She prayed silently that Victor was wrong, that he'd missed his target and that the Indigo Blade was safely away from danger. Behind her, Victor continued to search, muttering and slashing at the thick growth of shrubs and flowers.

Victor cursed aloud, and she prayed silently, and the minutes dragged past. Too many minutes. Surely someone in the household had heard the shot. Where were they? She turned her attention to the house, just in time to see Dalton headed her way at a brisk walk.

"What's going on here?" Dalton asked, as he and the others came down the path. "I heard a gunshot." They were in varying states of dress, Dalton and Garrick still in their livery, Beck and John in loose shirts and tight pants and bare feet, Fletcher and Lewis in crude clothing worthy of the stables where they spent much of their time. They all spoke at once, excited and curious, so that it was impossible to make much sense of their words.

Maximillian lagged behind, joining the commotion several minutes after his servants. He was in his nightclothes, a long flannel nightshirt beneath a loose white banyon that floated around his body as he followed behind them all. With a wide yawn, he raised his hand to sleep-ruffled hair as if to make himself more presentable.

"Yes! I got him, all right!" Victor shouted, and Penelope closed her eyes against the tears she could not shed. Her plan had failed miserably, costing more than she'd imagined, adding to her list of sins. Heaven help her, she didn't want to see the Indigo Blade's body fallen in her garden. Why hadn't he run when she'd warned him?

Victor returned to the gazebo and offered his hand to her. "Blood," he said gleefully. "By God, I shot the Indigo Blade."

The blood on his hand was black in the moonlight, and even though she knew she should show no emotion, Penelope shuddered. Her stomach roiled and her head swam. If she were given to fainting spells, she'd likely collapse at Victor's feet.

"Come, on," Victor ordered, nodding toward the crew on the path. "Help me locate the body. This blood was on a palm frond, and a wounded man couldn't have gone far."

None of the men on the path moved.

"I demand that you assist me in this search!"

"Perhaps in the morning," Maximillian said with another wide yawn, and when he spun about the others turned as well. "Dalton," Maximillian halted in the middle of the path and glanced over his shoulder, "would you see my wife to the house? It's turned quite chilly, and she really shouldn't be out here in the night air. Its not healthy."

"Of course." Dalton turned to her and waited, and Penelope gratefully left the gazebo to join him.

"You can't just leave me like this. The brigand's done something with my men!" Victor protested.

"Those would be the soldiers we found bound and gagged outside the kitchen door, I suppose," Lewis said nonchalantly. "Since you've shown such concern, I'm sure you'll be glad to hear that they appear to be unhurt. Embarrassed, perhaps, but unhurt."

"A mere eight men to capture the Indigo Blade," Beck said lightly. "What were you thinking, sir?"

"Stop!" Victor shouted. "All of you stop right where you stand." He hurried forward. "Each and every one of you will be examined, by me, for a gunshot wound." His motions and his voice were desperate, excited.

"Are you suggesting that you perhaps *shot* one of my servants?" Maximillian asked tiredly. "Gad, the gentlemen in my social circle wouldn't take kindly to such a tale, Chadwick."

Penelope, and everyone else, knew that Maximillian's lazy words were a threat. Victor had already made a mistake in allowing Heath to die. He couldn't afford another blunder.

Max spread his arms wide. "Faith, they all look perfectly healthy to me." He crooked his fingers in a simple gesture of command, *come along*, before he turned and walked away.

"Watch your step, madam," Dalton said, offering

Penelope his arm. She took it, needing the support as her legs shook uncontrollably.

Far ahead, separated from her full view by the servants who rambled and chatted between them, Maximillian disappeared into the house. She saw no more than a flash of his rippling white banyon and then he was gone. Why could he not escort her into the house himself? He so carelessly gave her over to his butler, at a time when she needed his support—his arm to lean on, his shoulder to cry on.

Victor hurried past her with a curse, on his way to free his men.

Chapter Nineteen

Once the door was closed behind him, Max let the banyon fall to the floor, and he closed his fingers over the flannel nightshirt. The bandage beneath was damp with blood, but not soaked through. Damnation! Chadwick had the devil's own luck, to have found his target in the dark. It was just a scratch, a nuisance more than anything else, but it irritated the hell out of him that Chadwick had such luck.

He listened closely to Penelope's footsteps in the passageway, listened as she opened and closed the door to her own bedchamber.

How could he ever apologize for condemning his wife, the woman he loved, without so much as giving her a chance to explain? If only he'd gone to her when he'd heard the news and asked her what had

253

happened, they could have avoided so much pain and heartache.

Penelope would never forgive him, as he would never forgive himself.

John slipped into the room, opening and closing the door quickly. "Let's take a look at that," he said without preamble.

With care, Max lifted the flannel nightshirt to expose black breeches and the wound. "How is she?" he asked as John peeled away the makeshift bandage that had been slapped on as he'd quickly changed into these ridiculous nightclothes.

"Your wife?" John shot dark eyes upward. "She's distraught, teary-eyed, and sniffling. I guess she thinks you're dead. I mean, I guess she thinks the Indigo Blade is dead. Confusing, isn't it?"

John returned his attention to the scratch at Max's side.

"She was magnificent, wasn't she?" As John poked gently at his wound, Max actually smiled. "Magnificent, and valiant. A truly . . . Ouch!" His hint of a smile vanished with the pain. "Mind those clumsy fingers."

John glanced up briefly. "Sorry. Continue. You were talking about Mrs. Broderick. A truly . . . something."

Max scowled. "A truly remarkable woman."

"I think she's sweet on you," John mumbled as he rebandaged the scratch.

"Of course she is; she's my wife."

John looked up with a wicked gleam in his dark eyes. "I mean the *other* you."

It was true. Penelope had no idea who the Indigo

Blade was, and yet she cried for him even now. She'd admitted to her admiration, and then allowed a stranger to kiss her fingers without so much as a demure protest. A *stranger*!

"Chadwick has Tyler."

"No." John gasped, his humor fleeing quickly.

"He's using the boy to blackmail Penelope. I promised her I'd see Tyler freed."

"I'll find out where the lad's being held, and we'll have him out of that bastard's hands by tomorrow night."

"Yes. And make arrangements for Tyler to be housed in Cypress Crossroads for the time being. He'll be safe there."

Outside Max's window, Chadwick and his soldiers were making all kinds of racket, searching the garden for a body, and in the process destroying any semblance of a trail the Indigo Blade might have left. It was almost enough to bring a smile to his face. Almost.

"When are you going to tell her the truth?" John asked as he made his way to the door.

"After Tyler's safe," Max whispered. He had no choice but to wait. Penelope's brother was her one true weakness, and if Chadwick upped the stakes, Penelope would do anything to save him, sacrifice anyone . . .

Even her husband.

Penelope sat on the edge of the bed, still wrapped in her cloak. No candle burned, no fire blazed in the fireplace, but the moonlight breaking through the window illuminated the chamber sufficiently.

Even though the window was tightly closed, she could hear Victor and his soldiers searching for the man he'd shot, searching for the Indigo Blade as if he were a hunted, wounded animal.

Tears ran down her face, silent, desperate tears she couldn't stop. Why had he come back? Perhaps his appearance was meant to provoke Victor, another move in their dangerous game. And then again, perhaps he'd come back simply to prove to Victor that his extortion had been successful. Perhaps he'd believed by showing up he'd buy Tyler another day of safety, and for that she could only thank him.

But he was hurt, wounded, bleeding—perhaps even dead. Penelope looked down at her white hands, palms upward. More blood on her hands, he'd said. Only this time it was true.

"How's a body to sleep with that racket going on?"

Penelope glanced up to see her husband lounging in the doorway, dressed for bed in his flannel nightshirt with that Turkish-inspired banyon draped over his long, lean body.

"I'm sorry," she whispered, trying and failing to hide the tears in her voice.

"Not your fault, m'dear," he said as he stepped into her room. "It's that damned Victor Chadwick and his bloody soldiers."

She nodded silently.

Maximillian approached the bed slowly, and when he was close to her he reached down and pushed the hood back and away from her face. His hand settled warmly at her damp cheek. "Do you want to tell me why you are crying?"

If only she could. If only she could tell Maximillian everything. Telling him about Tyler would be a waste of time. What could he do? Nothing. He'd shown no interest in sharing her pain up to this point; why should she expect that to change now? All talk of politics bored him, as he liked to remind her.

Telling him that she shed tears for a man she didn't know would confuse and perhaps even anger him. He didn't trust her, didn't trust their tenuous love. After all, he'd already accused her of carrying on with the butler.

After a long interlude, she shook her head.

Instead of leaving her alone, as she'd expected he would, Maximillian sat on the bed beside her. "I hate to see your tears, m'dear," he said lightly. "Faith, they break my heart."

"Do they?" She looked at Maximillian, a man she loved and did not know, a husband who was a stranger to her.

"Yes."

He kissed her, softly, without demand, and she leaned into the caress and closed her eyes. When his arms went around her—strong, reassuring, and somehow tentative arms—she accepted this comfort and placed her head against his shoulder. Her body was taut as she held back the tears that wanted to flow.

Maximillian's hand settled in her hair. "But cry," he said softly, "if you must."

She slipped her arms around his waist and held

on. Her compassionate husband, unaccustomed to the role, flinched and became rigid as she held him, but as the seconds ticked by he relaxed, and his arms tightened.

She sobbed, just once, with her head against his shoulder and her arms holding on tight.

"It's all right," he assured her once again. "Cry, scream, rail against the world for awhile. You deserve it."

She didn't ask him what he meant, but allowed the tears she'd been holding back to fall freely. The sobs came, loud and terrible as if they were ripped from her very soul.

Maximillian held her, rocked back and forth with her body enfolded securely in his arms. With her face against his shoulder all was black, and yet the room was spinning. As her world was spinning, out of control.

As her tears slowed, so did the comforting sway. But the arms around her were secure and steady. Warm and comforting. Maximillian held her tight, as he whispered an assurance that all would be well.

She wanted to believe him, but she knew nothing would be well. Victor still had Tyler, and the Indigo Blade was wounded and possibly dying.

And there was nothing she could do.

Mary sauntered down the stairs, warm and well rested, truly happy for the first time in months. Perhaps years.

She wasn't yet ready to examine the reason for her happiness.

Even though it was late, Beck was just now laying out breakfast, and neither Penelope nor her husband was anywhere in sight.

Dalton was there, though, appearing shortly after she arrived in the dining room.

"Good morning, Miss Seton," he said formally.

"Good morning, Dalton." She couldn't help but smile. Beck snorted and left the room. "Where is everyone this morning?"

"Sleeping off last night's excitement, I imagine."

Her smile faded. "What excitement?"

"It seems Mr. Chadwick was in pursuit of the Indigo Blade last night, right here in the pleasure garden."

"And I slept through it?"

Dalton gave her a very informal and wide smile, revealing straight white teeth and a devilish side to his personality. "You must be a deep sleeper."

"Sometimes," she admitted. Last night she'd had wonderful dreams, sweet dreams she wouldn't have wanted to leave. But the Indigo Blade!

"There was quite a commotion beneath your window last night," Dalton said with a smile. "A shot fired, soldiers ambushed and captured. Why, it woke the entire household. *Almost* the entire household."

"I missed it," she said sullenly. "I slept through it all." Of course, she wasn't sorry to have missed seeing Victor, not sorry at all. It was a good feeling, not to be sad and tortured and miserably unhappy in the name of love.

But it would have been exciting to actually see the man who called himself the Indigo Blade!

Dalton pulled back a chair at the long table and waited for her to take her place. She walked toward him, this *butler* who'd been a visitor to her dreams last night, and took her seat.

"Perhaps," she said as he backed away, "you could tell me all about last night's adventure." She glanced over her shoulder to where Dalton stood by the door. And against her will, her heart skipped a beat.

Penelope dabbed at an imperfect flower in the mural, glad to have an outlet for her restlessness this afternoon.

She'd awakened well into the morning, after falling asleep, crying, in her husband's arms. Maximillian had removed her cloak and her shoes and her stockings, and had tucked her beneath the satin coverlet. And then, of course, he'd left her alone and returned to his own bedchamber. She hadn't seen him since, and it was well after noon.

Holding her and allowing her to cry was the first true kindness her husband had offered for quite some time. He had been, for the first days she'd known him, the friend she so often needed, the strong shoulder she wanted. How had he finally known, last night of all nights, how very badly she needed him?

The mural that would one day encircle the parlor was slowly taking shape. It would take several more weeks, perhaps months, before it was complete, but she was in no hurry. This was a task she loved.

But her arms grew tired, and she was having a difficult time concentrating today. She turned to place her brush with the others, and there—amidst the paints and brushes—was a stark white folded sheet of paper, sealed in red wax.

There was no name visible, but it was intended for her, she knew it. She took the paper between trembling fingers and held it for a long moment. It was from *him*. She knew that as well.

How had it gotten here? It hadn't been there when she'd started painting, and she'd heard nothing while intent on her work. The Indigo Blade or one of his company must have slipped into this room so silently she heard nothing.

She broke the seal and unfolded the paper. There was no address, no incriminating name at the top of the page. The words were simple, and with the reading of those words a burden was taken from her.

I am well. When my task is accomplished, you will be notified. If you need me for any reason, hang a yellow sash from your balcony and I will be there for you. Same time, same place. Be brave.

There was no signature, but for a small dagger drawn in the lower-right-hand corner of the page.

The Indigo Blade wasn't dead or dying; he was well. A smile came across her face. And he would free Tyler and let her know when the deed had been accomplished.

She could be brave, now.

"Faith, m'dear, I didn't sleep a wink," Maximillian said, stepping into the parlor and yawning widely.

While his eyes were closed and he held a hand to his mouth, she slipped the treasured note into the bodice of her dress.

Max's side ached and burned, he hadn't been lying about getting no sleep, and John had not yet been able to locate Tyler. And his wife had just very surreptitiously hidden the note from the Indigo Blade.

Ah, there were roses in Penelope's cheeks, a small smile forming on her lips. Would she tell him of her escapade? Of her secret encounter with that notorious rebel the Indigo Blade? He thought not.

"The Huntlands are having a dinner party tomorrow evening. I know you've been feeling less than sociable of late, but I think we should accept."

"Of course," she said, most agreeably.

The letter he'd written had obviously soothed her, as it was meant to. Garrick had delivered it himself, certain that he could sneak into this room and leave the note without Penelope ever being aware of his presence. Evidently he had succeeded.

"Your disposition is much improved today," he said, stepping into this parlor Penelope had made her own domain. "Why, last night I thought you to be inconsolable."

Her smile was constant. "No," she said, stepping toward him to lay a hand on his arm. "You consoled me very well, and I thank you."

"Faith, m'dear," he said, his irrational anger and his feigned inflection fading. " 'Tis surely a husband's task to soothe his wife when she is downhearted."

It would do his heart good if she would confide

in him now, if she would tell him of the blackmail and the meeting and the letter she'd secreted in her bodice.

He had no right even to wish for such a confidence, but he could not make himself stop. With this woman at his side he had so much . . . and so little. Too much of their life together was false. There were too many lies, too many secrets.

Penelope said nothing, but came up on her toes to kiss him quickly, a soft brush of her lips against his. It was a healing gesture, perhaps, as last night's commiseration had been a healing gesture.

But would Penelope want the healing to continue when she learned the truth?

Chapter Twenty

She could have gone to the dinner party with Penelope and Maximillian, putting on a pretty gown and a false smile for her friends. Mary Seton rarely declined a social invitation, but as Victor would likely be in attendance, she'd pled a headache and stayed in for the evening.

This was such a big house, with tall ceilings and large rooms and open spaces. Maximillian had expensive taste, in useful furnishings and decorative ones. Some of the porcelain was surely Chinese, and she'd never known anyone to be so extravagant with expensive fabrics. Every window was draped in heavy satin that pooled on the floor.

It was a good house to wander through on a quiet evening.

By the light of the single candle she carried, Mary wandered into the great hall, that rarely used room at the front of the house that was as formal as Penelope's parlor was cozy. It was a room built for balls and musical entertainments, for brightly lit days of celebrations.

Mary had always loved parties, crowds and laughter, dancing and flirting, but she was in no mood for such frivolity tonight. She needed time to gather her thoughts, and to do that she had to be alone. For now, she was glad for the quiet.

"Your headache is better?"

She spun around to find Dalton standing directly behind her, his hands behind his back, his livery as crisp as it had been this morning. Goodness, she hadn't heard a sound, and as he didn't carry a candle to light his way through the cavernous house, she'd had no warning of his approach.

"Gone entirely," she said softly.

"I see."

She couldn't see Dalton's face nearly well enough, so she took a step forward and held her candle high.

"To be perfectly honest," she said when his face was sufficiently illuminated, "I never had a headache at all."

"I thought not."

"Victor would likely be there," she explained, "and I have no desire to see him ever again, let alone share a meal at the same table."

What might have been the beginnings of a smile turned the corners of his mouth up. "I'm glad to hear it."

Dalton thought she had spurned Victor's advances and was afraid. Would he hate her if he knew all she'd done? The intimacies, the manipulations in the name of winning Victor's love, the deceit—the hate that had grown as Penelope discovered happiness and Mary had not.

Mary found she didn't hate Penelope anymore, didn't blame her cousin for all the troubles and disappointments that had come to her life. In fact, she felt sorry for her cousin. Penelope had problems of her own, difficulties she wouldn't discuss.

One day, when she had the nerve and another place to go, she'd tell Penelope what had happened the night Heath was captured. She hadn't realized what a burden the deception would cause. What pain for Penelope, and the Lowrys, and Mary herself. She hadn't known . . .

That was a lie. She'd agreed with everything Victor said, believing he'd come to love her, wanting more than anything the love that man was incapable of giving.

And now she cared nothing for Victor. Well, perhaps not *nothing*, but a bond had been broken, a burden cast off. She was learning to let love go, as Dalton had advised.

"Are you?" she asked. "Are you glad?"

"Yes."

"Why?"

His hint of a smile vanished. Gone completely as he lifted his hand to her face. "Because you deserve better than anything Victor Chadwick has to offer you."

But she didn't deserve better. Mary knew, even if Dalton didn't, that she didn't deserve anything at all.

The hand at her face, a gentle and undemanding

hand, was almost as exciting as the kiss—the light brushing of lips that had set her heart to racing. She'd dreamed of that kiss, of the weak-kneed feeling a hint of a touch had stirred to life.

Dalton moved closer, stepping in until he towered over her. He took the candle from her and set it on a table at his side, and then he slipped both arms around her and lowered his face to kiss her again.

She didn't object, but parted her lips to savor the sensations Dalton brought to life. As before, his mouth was gentle and teasing, but instead of disappearing this time, he stayed with her. His arms tightened, his mouth grew bolder, and soon there was nothing else in the world but the two of them and this kiss.

Her arms crept around him, holding on, searching for warmth and comfort. She'd never felt this way, as if she were floating, flying, soaring above the earth in Dalton's arms.

It was Dalton who broke away. Slowly and with a regret she could feel. "We should stop now," he said hoarsely.

Mary didn't want to stop, but she didn't have a choice. She didn't want Dalton to know what kind of woman she was, didn't want him to know that she'd done terrible things in the name of what she'd thought was love.

She didn't want him to know that she and Victor had been lovers. She wanted him to believe that she was good and pure and a real lady.

If this went any further, he'd know the truth. "We

can't do this again," she said sternly. "I don't know what you were thinking."

She slipped past him and ran in the dark to the spiral staircase, intent only on making her way safely above stairs to her chamber where she could shut out Dalton and Victor and be left alone with all her memories and regrets.

Perhaps tonight she'd dream of Dalton again; she could hope for that. It was all she could have.

"Mary!"

On the stairway, she turned to face Dalton. He stood in the foyer, candle in hand, his agonized face illuminated for her.

"You know this isn't right," she whispered.

"I'm not . . ." he began, and then he stopped suddenly. "I won't always be a butler."

She should tell him, in the haughtiest voice she could summon, that he was now and would always be beneath her, that she wouldn't stoop to his level, that she could never care for a servant—but she couldn't say any of that. She wouldn't hurt Dalton for all the world. Perhaps the truth was the best medicine.

"It's not you," she said, taking a single step down. "You're kind and strong and have a good heart. I'm not . . . I'm not good enough for you."

"Don't be ridiculous," he said with a hint of anger. "You're a sweet and beautiful lady, and I . . . I've come to care for you deeply, in spite of the fact that I know it's wrong. I fought it," he admitted. "I won't lie to you about that. I've told myself a thousand times that there's nothing for us. The life I lead isn't suitable for a lady to share."

"I've done things," she confessed. "Terrible things that I thought were wise and later found were foolishness."

"I know."

"You don't . . ."

"Chadwick," he interrupted, taking a step closer to the stairway. "In the gazebo."

"You do know." Her heart broke a little. She didn't want him to realize what kind of woman she really was. She wanted Dalton to forever see her as a sweet and beautiful lady.

"Yes," he whispered as he came closer, placing his foot on the bottom stair. "I saw what happened that night, I heard it all. Why do you think I haven't told you yet that I love you? I don't imagine you'll believe me, at least not yet. I plan to show you first what love really is, and then maybe I'll tell you."

"How can you even think you love me?"

"I don't know," he admitted. "I just know that I do."

"Dalton . . ."

He took another step. "I want to show you that what Chadwick did to you doesn't have anything to do with love. Love is shared and dazzling and . . ." He stopped suddenly, and she could see the confusion on his face.

"What's wrong?" She wanted Dalton to continue, to explain to her what love was.

"Until a few weeks ago I didn't even believe in love, and now here I am talking like a bloody poet. The truth of the matter is, I wanted to kill Chadwick for the way he treated you in the gazebo, and I almost did. I was following him to his horse with every intention of breaking his evil neck when I heard you crying, and I couldn't . . . I couldn't walk away."

"I don't know what I would have done without you that night." She would forever remember his arms around her, the gentle hands wiping away her tears.

His voice was strained as he answered. "I decided then that one day I would show you the way it should be with a man and a woman."

Her heart skipped a beat. "Did you?"

"One day, when you're ready, I'll show you what love is all about. If you'll have a mere butler." His confusion was gone and there was a hint of a smile on his face again. A smile that warmed Mary's heart and soul as she descended the steps that remained between them.

"Will you show me now?" she asked as she reached him. The candle he carried flickered, and Mary leaned over to blow it out.

In the dark, Dalton whispered. "Yes."

It had been quite late when they'd returned from the Huntlands' dinner party, but still Penelope was up with the sun. She immediately searched her chest of drawers for a yellow sash, and went to the balcony to tie it from the railing.

The bit of information she'd heard might be worth nothing—but then again, it might be valuable to the man who called himself the Indigo Blade.

She'd thought that perhaps Maximillian would stay with her last night. He'd been attentive of late, kinder than in the first weeks of their marriage, and she hoped that perhaps something had changed. But last night when they'd arrived home, he'd gone directly to his own bedchamber, claiming exhaustion. She had to admit, he was more pale than usual, and he'd almost fallen asleep in the carriage on the way home.

She hadn't minded Maximillian dozing off as the carriage rocked, since at the time he'd had his hand in hers and he'd rested his head against her shoulder. In moments like that she could believe that her husband did care for her, after all.

There was no time to dwell on the inconsistencies of her marriage. Tonight at ten o'clock, on the garden path, she'd meet once again with the Indigo Blade, a man who fascinated her more with every passing day.

Max, wearing the black wig and long coat he'd been wearing on his last secret meeting with Penelope, waited motionlessly behind a spreading, flowering plant that stood a good four feet high. He'd been waiting a half hour, taking his position well ahead of time to wait and observe, taking precautions just in case his wife had been effectively blackmailed by Chadwick once again.

Chadwick had claimed a few minutes of Penelope's time at the Huntland house on the previous night, and anything could have been said. Whispered plans, another trap, another threat to Tyler. Max hadn't lived this long by being careless.

As the town clock struck ten, he heard her steps on the path—stealthy, cautious steps. He looked past the leaves that hid his face, to see the figure in the dark hooded cloak hurrying in his direction.

He waited until she'd passed before he stood.

"Don't turn around."

She stopped suddenly, but did as he commanded and kept her back to him.

"You're truly well?" she whispered, the concern in her voice indisputable.

"Yes."

"I was so worried about you. I thought . . . for a while I thought you were dead. When Victor showed me the blood on his hands, the blood he'd wiped from the leaves where you'd stood, I was heartbroken."

Her low voice was filled with excitement and with relief. Did she truly care for a man she did not know? "As you can see, it was only a flesh wound."

"I can't see anything," she responded, and he knew that she wanted more than anything to turn and glimpse the face of the Indigo Blade. He couldn't allow that, not yet.

"Then you'll have to take my word on it."

"I do."

There was such awe in her voice, such undeniable admiration, it turned Max's stomach. Penelope trusted this man, this Indigo Blade, was with her life. She'd risked herself just to see that he was unharmed. One meeting, one note, and she was infatuated.

"Why did you signal for me? Just to *see* for yourself that I'm not dead?" he snapped.

"No." She breathed softly. "But I do thank you for

your note. It was a great relief to read those words of assurance."

Another woman would have turned to see the man she spoke to, in spite of his orders, but Penelope made no move. She was calm, confident, brave.

"Why are we here tonight?"

"I have news for you." A touch of excitement entered the voice she kept low. "You might already know this, but I couldn't be sure. Victor Chadwick said something at a dinner party I attended last night. He took me aside, and said that he'd spoken to Tyler that afternoon. That means my brother's somewhere close by, doesn't it?"

"Yes, it does. That's useful information." He was inordinately relieved that this meeting Penelope had arranged was about Tyler, and had nothing to do with her apparent fascination with a shadow.

"That's not the only reason I asked you here."

Max all but held his breath.

"There was a mention of a shipment of artillery that's expected tomorrow."

In the dark, Max grinned. His wife was turning into a little spy. He'd heard the comment about the shipment himself, of course, and plans for interception were already drawn up.

She recited the details he himself had heard, a touch of excitement in her voice, her only movement a small wave of her hand.

As Penelope finished delivering her information, Max stepped onto the path and came up behind her. "I thank you, Mrs. Broderick."

"Penelope."

"I thank you, Penelope," he said with a mixture

of pride and agitation, reaching out to lay his gloved hand on her arm. She didn't so much as turn her head to look at that hand.

Cool air swirled around them, whipping the hem of Penelope's cloak, slashing the strands of dark hair from the wig across his face. He increased the pressure of his fingers and stepped closer to buffer Penelope from the wind.

"If I can do more," she whispered, "even after you've rescued Tyler, I will. I can relay information such as what I heard last night, pass on messages if need be—I want very much to help."

"This is a dangerous game."

"I know."

Her arm was warm beneath his hand, and she made no move to step away. "Why would you want to continue even after the threat to your brother is past?"

He could almost feel the excitement radiating from her. "You've done something important with your life, never worrying about the danger, never shying away from what you know is right." There was a passion in her soft voice. "I want my life to be more than dinner parties and balls and painting pretty pictures. I want my life to extend beyond these four walls."

"A rebel in the making," he murmured, his mouth close to her ear.

"I don't know that I would call myself a rebel," she said, hesitation creeping into her voice. "I never thought much about the concept of freedom before. As long as I was warm and happy and secure, I didn't care who was in charge."

"What changed your mind?"

"You," she replied. "You're willing to sacrifice anything, do anything for what you believe to be right. My brother," she added. "who's foolishly passionate about the cause. Most of all"— she paused, and Max leaned close to catch her words—"I don't want men like Victor Chadwick ruling these colonies. I always thought his greatest crime to be dullness, but I know now that he's unfeeling and unkind, and four sturdy walls are not enough to keep a man like that out forever."

"He made a grave mistake when he took your brother."

"That he did," she said passionately.

He could so easily spin Penelope about, face her with his mistakes, and confess everything. He could beg forgiveness, declare his love and his stupidity. But he hesitated. Tyler was not yet safe, and Penelope . . . He had no idea how his wife would react to such momentous news.

"Penelope, are you there?"

Max glimpsed over his shoulder to see that Mary followed the garden path, a full skirt held off the ground, her eyes wandering as she stepped cautiously and searched for her cousin.

He ducked behind the foliage before Mary came completely into view.

"There you are."

Penelope turned slowly to greet her cousin.

"What are you doing out here at this time of night?" Mary asked, censure in her voice. "I went to your room to see if you were awake, since I couldn't sleep and I thought maybe you couldn't sleep either and we could talk. We haven't done that for ages, you know."

"I know."

"You weren't in your bed, where you should have been, so I went to your balcony to see if perhaps you were there. I saw someone in the garden, and I thought maybe it was you." She looked from side to side. "There was someone with you, wasn't there?"

"No," Penelope said calmly. "I'm alone. I couldn't sleep, and so I thought I'd take a walk."

"It's much too chilly for you to be out here." Mary took Penelope's arm and together they headed for the house. "Besides, I really, really need someone to talk to tonight."

Max watched the ladies walk away. Penelope glanced over her shoulder, just once, and the look on her face was forlorn and anxious at the same time.

An expression like that one was powerful enough to shake a man's very soul, and it told Max more than he wanted to know.

His lovely wife was smitten with the Indigo Blade.

As much as Penelope wanted to dismiss her cousin and return to the garden path, she knew she couldn't. And after a while, she was glad for this time with Mary.

They put their heads together as they had when they were young, whispering in the dark of dreams and of love.

Mary had not actually revealed any dark secrets,

but Penelope knew something had happened to her cousin. Something wonderful. She admitted that Penelope had been right all along. You don't choose love, it chooses you, coming out of nowhere like a thunderbolt from the blue and making everything marvelous and terrible at the same time.

Penelope even shared some of her reservations about Maximillian and their marriage, and not only had a burden been lifted, she'd seen things more clearly herself.

Maximillian did love her, of that she was certain, but something had happened to change his feelings. She wanted him to love her completely again, the way he had before the wedding.

Pride had kept Penelope from taking what should rightfully be hers, and she realized that now. She wasn't yet sure how she'd go about it, but she wanted Maximillian back—the way he was before the wedding, the way he'd been on their wedding night. Reclaiming her husband would be a part of taking her life back.

She wondered only briefly if her rendezvous with the Indigo Blade had as much to do with her resolve as did her discussion with Mary.

The meeting in the garden was a secret Penelope dared not share, not even with her cousin.

Chapter Twenty-one

After a short but surprisingly sound night's sleep, Penelope rose with so many things on her mind that she could barely think straight. Tyler's safety, her offer of an alliance with the Indigo Blade, her decision to reclaim her marriage as she reclaimed her life.

Maximillian was not cooperating in that aspect of her plans. He'd decided to spend this of all days racing one of his horses at the track north of Charles Town. He would be away from the house all day and, he'd informed her shortly after arising, would probably not be home in time for supper.

Making this the marriage she truly wanted might be more of a challenge than any endeavor she undertook to save Tyler or assist the Indigo Blade.

The day passed slowly, and but for Mary's company she would have spent the entire day alone.

Helen was not feeling well, Dalton had informed her. It was only a cold, he told Penelope when she asked, but Helen had decided it best to keep to her bed for the day. Penelope had no objections. She was, and always had been, perfectly capable of taking care of herself.

She dabbled at her mural for most of the afternoon, but her mind was elsewhere and she accomplished little.

With Mary's company, she enjoyed a pleasant supper. It was nice to see Mary her old self again. Happy, talkative, sharing a smile that touched not only her lips but her eyes.

Shortly after supper they retired. A lifetime habit of rising and setting with the sun didn't die easily, and after all the excitement of the past few days, Penelope was looking forward to a good night's sleep. Perhaps when she was well rested, more satisfying resolutions to her problems would come to her.

There was no need for a fire on this mild night, and Penelope began to undress by the light of a single candle. She unfastened the hook and eye at her throat, untied the ribbon there, and slipped off her shoes as she sat at the dresser to take her hair down. She'd removed the pins and was brushing her hair out when she saw it—the familiar rectangle of paper with a red wax seal.

Ridiculously, her heart skipped a beat as she touched the note. News of Tyler so soon? Or something else?

She broke the seal and revealed words that told her nothing.

The grand hall. Now.

Without bothering even to step into her shoes, Penelope flew silently from her room, the candle lighting her way through the deserted passageway and down the spiral staircase.

She rarely visited the grand hall. It was a large, cold room, a place for dancing should the day ever come when she and Maximillian wished to open their home to entertain.

The doors stood open to the grand hall, and Penelope stepped through on stocking feet and placed the candle on a table near the doors. The center of the room was bare, the pine floor untouched by all but the moonlight that broke through the parted draperies. Her single candle emitted little light, and the rest of the room was shadows, blackness. There were surely a hundred places for a man to hide.

"Hello?" she called unnecessarily. If the Indigo Blade was here, he would know she had answered his command. She walked forward until she was standing in the middle of the room, drenched in moonlight and suddenly afraid.

"You came." The whisper echoed from a far corner, and even though she knew she shouldn't, she spun to face that black recess. It took only a moment for her eyes to adjust to the darkness. He stood there, his head down so that all she saw was shadow and a fall of dark hair, his long black coat blending into the darkness.

"Yes," she answered.

"Turn around."

Hesitating only briefly, she did as he asked and turned her back to him. "Do you have news of Tyler?" She heard and felt him coming toward her. When he stopped directly behind her, his shoe scraped the floor, and the soft sound echoed in the hollow room.

"No." His breath touched her neck, and a shiver rushed down her spine.

"You've decided to allow me to help you?"

There was a short hesitation before he answered, and when he placed his gloved hand on her shoulder, Penelope jumped.

"No," he whispered again.

Her heart was beating so hard she imagined he could hear it, that the pounding would wake the entire household and they would rush to this room to find her with a man not her husband.

"Then why did you send for me?"

His hand left her shoulder and traveled slowly but certainly down her arm. "I wanted to see you again. We were interrupted last night, and I have much, much more to say to you."

"Oh."

He settled both hands familiarly at her waist, strong hands that held her gently but firmly before him. She should run, she should protest . . . but she did nothing.

"I thought about you all night, so much so that I barely slept." His face was close to her neck. She could feel his breath as he spoke, feel the words against her hair and her neck. "And when I finally slept, I dreamed about you. Should I tell you about my dreams, Penelope?"

"No." The word came out so softly she wasn't certain he would hear her, but she was incapable of anything more.

"Did you dream of me?" he persisted. "You in one bed, I in another, the same wonderful dream . . ."

"No," she said, more strongly this time. "Sir, you have misunderstood my feelings, surely. I do have the greatest admiration for you and what you stand for, but I'm . . . I'm a married woman."

Max smiled as he buried his face against Penelope's neck and hair. She smelled so good, felt so right—and she'd answered that question most properly.

But she was still here.

"Married women make the best mistresses," he said, nuzzling her hair aside so he could kiss her soft, luscious neck. Still, she didn't run. "And as your husband spends so much time away from home, you've surely given thought to taking a lover."

"I have not!" She tried to move away but he held her firmly in place. He held her so close to his body, in fact, that she was sure to feel his arousal pressing against her backside. He made damned sure she could feel it.

"Perhaps you should."

"Sir, you have sorely misunderstood . . ."

"What if I tell you I've found Tyler, and I'll rescue him . . . but there's a price to be paid."

Penelope stiffened in his arms, and he could hear her sharp intake of breath. "A single night in your bed, Penelope. Is that too much to ask?"

"Yes."

"For your brother's life?"

She stood very still, and did not answer for a long moment. "Don't ask me to make that decision," she finally answered.

"I won't," he assured her. "But I know how you feel about us, I know what you want from me, and I guess I thought it might be easier for you to take what you want if you could tell yourself you have no choice."

"I don't . . . I don't want anything from you." Her voice shook unsteadily.

Another lie. Would she never learn?

"Your heart beats fast, your breath comes hard, you can feel the rhythm of your very blood when I touch you." With one arm he pulled her against his body, while one gloved hand flitted to her throat to touch the quivering flesh there. "You might be unacquainted with such feelings, but they're signs of your desire. For me."

He took care that his touch was gentle as well as strong, that the leather of his glove barely fluttered over her throat.

"Don't be afraid," he whispered.

"Let me go."

"Soon."

He held her tight and tenderly kissed her neck once again. She did want him, that he could tell. Her skin was warm and flushed, and while she was afraid, she was not terrified, as she should be.

"I have a proposition for you," he said. "Come away with me. Leave that fool you call a husband and join the League of the Indigo Blade. Join me."

"No." She was just slightly indignant at the suggestion, when she should have been railing against him.

"I could carry you from the house right now, and no one would dare to stop me. I could make you my woman, in body and in heart, and when I was through, you wouldn't want to come back here, ever again."

"But you won't," she said, much too assured.

"What makes you say that?"

"I know you," she replied. "Against all reason, I know you. You can bluster all you like, you can try to shock and scare me, but you won't force me to do anything against my wishes."

"No," he acknowledged, "but perhaps I can change your wishes."

Penelope laughed nervously. A man who was not her husband held her a virtual prisoner and made improper suggestions, and she *laughed*.

"I assure you, sir, you cannot change my wishes in this matter. Truth be told, I'm flattered that you would go to so much trouble to attempt to seduce me, but it's a lost cause."

"Why?" What would he do if Penelope declared to him, right now, her undying love for her husband? Rejoice, first, and then try to find a way out of this mess he'd made for himself, he supposed.

"I am a married woman, sir. That's reason enough."

Not reason enough for him, damn it.

"Release me," she ordered. "Please."

Max spread his arms wide and Penelope fled. Quickly, without a word, silent on her stocking feet.

* * *

Penelope lay in her bed wide awake, staring at the ceiling above as she had most of the night.

Last night's visit had been disturbing, but through it all she'd been assured that the man who held her and made such outrageous suggestions was no threat. She couldn't explain her assurance to herself any better than she'd attempted to explain it to him. She simply knew.

What was more disturbing was the realization that he was, in part, correct in his assumptions of her. The shadowy man who called himself the Indigo Blade did appeal to her in an unacceptable way. When he whispered her name, when he touched her, she felt something altogether inappropriate. She was lonely, she reasoned. She needed love, she needed companionship.

She needed Maximillian.

So as dawn lit the sky, Penelope made her way to her husband's bedchamber. She couldn't sleep anyway, and she couldn't stop thinking about Tyler and the Indigo Blade and her marriage, the worries and heartaches mingling together and stealing her peace.

She wanted Maximillian back. The way he was before the wedding, the way he'd been on their wedding night. Reclaiming her husband was a part—a very large part—of taking her life back.

Without pausing, she opened the door to his chamber. He slept, the sunlight not yet touching his bed, his long body buried beneath a green satin coverlet. She hadn't heard him come in last night, so it must have been late when he returned, perhaps during one of her brief interludes of fitful sleep.

She closed the door behind her and stepped quietly to his side. He was deep asleep but restless, and completely unaware of her presence even as she reached down to brush a strand of golden hair away from his face.

In sleep, the fussy aristocrat was missing, and she was presented with the man she'd fallen in love with. She could see it all in him: A friend first, a man who adored her and laughed with her and then became her lover. A man of power and heart and great depth of emotion. This was the man she remembered, the man she wanted as her husband.

Uneasy in sleep, he turned away from her, throwing off the covers, moaning something she could not understand. Goodness, what a sight he was. Married all this time, and she had no idea her husband slept in the nude.

She straightened the coverlet with every intention of covering Maximillian to his shoulder, but the bandage caught her eye, a thin strip of linen that encircled his waist. She folded the green satin back. When had Maximillian hurt himself? She imagined a fall from one of his precious horses, or perhaps an accident he hadn't told her about. But why hadn't he told her? Why hadn't he complained of blood on his silk, or damage to his fine lace and linen?

There was a spot of blood on the bandage, a thin line of evidence that this was indeed an injury.

She folded the coverlet back even further, looking for any other signs of damage. The rest of his body was smooth and clean, muscled and taut . . . pristine until her eyes found the mark on his upper thigh.

At first, in the dim light, she thought it to be a birthmark or an irregular bruise, but closer inspection proved it to be something else entirely.

She'd never actually seen a tattoo before, though she had read about them. Usually they were associated with cultures other than the English, though there had been a fad in London not so many years ago. Knowing him as she did, she could imagine the proper Maximillian Broderick defying his father and getting a tattoo on his thigh where no one was likely to see it.

She smiled as she moved closer to study the mark. It looked to be a dagger, a blue dagger with a curved blade, a blue blade. Her smile faded.

An indigo blade.

She covered Maximillian easily, not so anxious now to awaken him.

It made perfect sense, so much so that she thought herself a simpleton for not at least suspecting the truth before now. The eyes that were never the same: They were her first clue. The depth she saw on occasion, the spirit behind the mask he wore. And of course, the way he'd turned on her after Heath Lowry had accused her of betraying him to Victor.

He'd punished her without asking, without giving her a chance to defend herself. He had condemned her with a self-righteous assurance and sentenced her to his own kind of hell. No wonder he'd softened toward her recently. She'd told him, as the Indigo

Blade, that she was innocent, and at last he believed her.

Not enough, apparently, to confide in her.

She knew now why she'd been so comfortable with the stranger in the garden, the man with the soothing voice and gentle hands. She understood, as well, why she'd felt no true danger from the man who tried to seduce her. It was no wonder she'd felt as if she knew this man who whispered darkly into her ear. She knew him very well.

Penelope pulled back her hand to punch Maximillian on the shoulder, to wake him from his restive sleep and confront him with the lies and the unnecessary condemnation. How could he claim to love her and then treat her this way? How could he so easily throw everything they had away? But after a moment she let her hand fall softly to the bed beside his head.

He was pale and restless because he'd been hurt. Hurt while convincing Victor that she'd gone through with her end of the bargain to save Tyler. Everything she'd said to him as he whispered to her in the guise of the Indigo Blade was true. He was noble and brave and honorable.

And she loved him, still.

But he had to pay for the way he'd treated her, for the deception and the lack of trust.

Maximillian had never trusted her, had he? He'd proven that, not only with his secrets but with his accusations. Did she know that Dalton slept with a knife beneath his pillow, indeed.

She very carefully arranged the satin coverlet around Maximillian, mindful of his wound as she tucked him in and silently wished him a good and restful sleep.

He was going to need it.

Mary rested on her elbow and watched the sleeping man at her side. My, he was magnificent. Hard and beautiful, manly and tender, the perfect lover.

Dalton had come to her room again last night, to take her in his arms and love her. This was true love, and unlike anything she'd ever shared with Victor. The act of coming together with Dalton was so very unlike the uncomfortable couplings with Victor that it seemed an altogether different act. Fast and furious one time, slow and languorous the next, and always the shared pleasure Victor had promised but never delivered.

She peeled the quilt away from his body. Gracious, he was splendid. Who would have known that a butler would have a body like this beneath his livery? Hard, sculpted muscle, sinew and pale coarse hair, and altogether so very much a man that she trembled to look at him.

She spotted the imperfection on his thigh, there just below the curve where hip became leg, and bent over his sleeping body to study it more closely. A tattoo! Who would have thought that Dalton would have a tattoo?

It was a small blue knife with an arced blade, and she reached out and almost touched it before she realized what she had found and her smile faded away.

He couldn't be. She returned her gaze to his

sleeping face. Dalton Archer, Maximillian's butler, the infamous Indigo Blade?

It made perfect sense. He was no ordinary butler, that was certain. He was too strong, too sure of himself. There was fire in his heart, passion in his every breath.

A small tattoo was hardly proof that her suspicions were correct, but there were surely ways to find the truth.

And Victor would give anything to have the Indigo Blade handed to him on a silver platter. Anything at all.

Max stared with a frown at the note in his hand. His wife's writing was refined, and flourishing, and cryptic.

Meet me at my uncle's house. Thursday evening, our usual time. I'll be above stairs.

There was no signature, but it had come from Penelope via Helen to John to Max's own hands in a matter of hours.

If Penelope wanted to meet with him, why not hang her yellow sash from the balcony and meet him on the garden path? Why request a meeting at her uncle's empty house? Ah, he didn't like this development.

If all went well, Tyler would be freed tonight. Lewis had located the boy on a ship in the harbor. Rescuing him would be difficult, but certainly not impossible. Once the boy was safely in Cypress Crossroads, Max would take his wife aside and tell her all his secrets, apologize, and ask her what the hell she was doing requesting a private meeting with a man she knew absolutely nothing about. A man who had made his libidinous intentions more than clear.

He was so intent on the letter he didn't hear her approaching the study. She rarely made an appearance in his domain, but on this afternoon she walked in with a brisk swish of her skirt and a wide smile on her face.

"I hope I'm not disturbing you," she said brightly.

"Of course not, m'dear," he said, slipping the note into his pocket.

She came directly to him and bent to give him a prim and quick kiss on the cheek.

"You're awfully chipper this afternoon," he observed dryly.

"Am I?" she replied as she stepped away from the desk. "I hadn't noticed."

She was positively glowing, damn her.

"I do hate to disturb you," she said demurely, "but I was considering taking a holiday, and I thought I'd simply mention it to you and make absolutely certain you have no objections." Her eyelashes fluttered.

"Holiday?"

"I'd like to visit Uncle William, if you don't mind."

"Whyever would I mind?" he said softly.

"Just a few weeks, I imagine," she said, turning her back on him with a dancelike twirl. "Perhaps a month or two."

"I see."

"I do miss Uncle William," she said with a honeyeyed tone.

"Do you?"

"Yes. I thought I might leave Friday." She was looking out his window, taking in a different view of the garden than the one her parlor offered, staring directly, if he wasn't mistaken, to the curve on the path where she'd met twice with the Indigo Blade.

"I'll arrange an escort. I'm sure Lewis and Garrick would be happy to accompany you."

She twirled around to face him. "Oh, that won't be necessary. I thought I might hire an escort rather than disturb your staff's routine."

"How thoughtful of you," he murmured.

"You're such a dear," she said brightly. "I knew you wouldn't mind."

She graced him with another sisterly kiss and sauntered from the room, and Max could only stare at her departing figure with a sinking heart.

Faith, his wife was apparently intending to decamp with the Indigo Blade.

For the first night in ages, Penelope had slept well from the moment her head hit the pillow until the sun rose. After all those years at the plantation, rising and going to bed with the sun, it was a schedule that still suited her.

She'd half-expected Maximillian to come to her last night, but of course he couldn't come to her bed until the wound at his side had healed sufficiently. He couldn't allow her to suspect who he really was.

Penelope found it amusing that her husband was so wonderfully, marvelously jealous of himself. When she'd asked so sweetly to visit her uncle, a muscle in his cheek had actually twitched. Over supper, as she'd sipped her wine with the most insipid and distant smile she could muster, he'd fumed.

What could he say? Nothing. He didn't dare confront her, not until tomorrow evening.

She was sitting before the mirror, brushing her hair, when she saw the note on her table. A familiar heavy paper with a red wax seal. Had he slipped into her room himself as she'd slept?

With shaking fingers, she broke the seal and unfolded the paper. She recognized the writing, as well as the signature sketch at the bottom of the page.

He's safe.

Penelope breathed a sigh of relief. No other words were needed to tell her that Tyler was out of Victor's hands, and was in some safe place Maximillian had chosen.

I am counting the hours until our rendezvous.

Ha! He was in for the shock of his life—which was no more than he deserved.

There was nothing more in the note, nothing to incriminate Maximillian or herself, no information that was not necessary revealed.

She took her own paper and pen and began a note to her husband—an answering note to the Indigo Blade.

You have my undying gratitude, she began. That much was true. *Your place in my heart can be filled by no other.* Also true. *Tomorrow night, my love.*

Penelope read the short note, deciding immediately that it was much too brazen. Goodness, she didn't want to scare poor Maximillian away! That

would spoil all her fun. With a sigh she folded the
letter she would not send and added it to the two
notes she'd received from the Indigo Blade, tied the
bundle in a blue ribbon, and placed it in her top
drawer.

Tyler was safe.

And tomorrow night she would claim her husband once and for all.

Chapter Twenty-two

It was an opportunity Mary couldn't resist. Dalton was engaged, as were the rest of the servants. The preparation for the evening meal or care of the horses claimed their attention. Maximillian and Penelope were both so preoccupied, he in his study and she in her parlor, that she was certain she could have danced a country jig and they wouldn't have noticed.

So she climbed quietly to the third floor.

Dalton Archer, butler by day and Indigo Blade by night? Was it possible? The very idea gave her a thrill and a surge of pride. She had recognized all along that he was different from every other man she'd ever known. Brave and strong, with a quiet intelligence and an honorable dignity.

In spite of her loyalist leanings, she was fascinated with the shadowy figure of the Indigo Blade, as was all of Charles Town. Who wouldn't be enthralled by such a courageous man?

She wasn't sure which chamber was Dalton's, though she was sure she'd recognize his possessions when she saw them. She understood Dalton better than anyone else she'd ever known, anticipated his every action. How he moved, how he was likely to react, when he would smile, when his blue eyes would twinkle. She read it all so well.

Very carefully, she opened the first door at the top of the stairs. It swung open to reveal a small but very finely furnished chamber, complete with a four-poster bed, an expensive rug, even a table and chair. Maximillian certainly provided well for his servants! The servants' rooms at the plantation were plain, serviceable units, with narrow cots and bare floors. The slaves' quarters were even worse. But this was as nice as her own chamber below.

It was not Dalton's room, though, but Beck's. There was an apron thrown across the back of a mahogany armchair. She stepped closer to the desk to look at the single sheet of paper there, and found a list of meals for the week. Nothing sinister about that.

She left the chamber as quietly as she'd entered it, and went to the next room.

This was most definitely not Dalton's room. There were a pair of nasty boots on the floor by yet another fine bed, and a few stray bits of straw on the expensive rug. Since Fletcher lived in a room at the back of the stables and rarely visited the house, this had to be Lewis Turner's room.

She didn't take the time to search any further, but

closed the door and went to the third chamber.

Mary knew, even before spying the neatly folded livery on the chest at the end of the bed, that this was Dalton's room. She could feel him here, sense his presence as she slipped into the chamber and closed the door. A smile crossed her face as she went to the bed and ran her hands over the thick cover. He slept here, when he wasn't with her. He dreamed in this bed; perhaps he even dreamed of her.

There was no time to lose herself in romantic and warming thoughts. She was here with a purpose. Mary went to the desk and opened the top drawer. A pistol was the only object there. That wasn't proof of anything, though she doubted many butlers concealed arms in their rooms.

There was nothing on the top of the desk, and so she turned to the polished chest. If she were the Indigo Blade, she thought as she knelt before the chest, this is where she'd hide any incriminating evidence. She lifted the livery, holding the clothing near her nose to inhale and absorb Dalton's scent, the familiar smell that filled her nostrils and made her want another of those long, sweet kisses.

She placed the clothing on the floor and opened the chest, and before her eyes was the proof she looked for.

A gray wig, a tattered coat, and a scruffy pair of pants were at the top of the pile. One of his infamous disguises. She lifted the items from the chest to explore further, and found what could only be called irrefutable confirmation that her lover was the Indigo Blade.

Knives, like the one tattooed on his thigh, were sheathed in leather and arranged in a neat row. The grips were wooden and washed in blue—indigo ink perhaps—and each knife had the image of the indigo plant carved into its handle.

She reached out and touched one, feathering her fingers over the leather and wood, slipping one and then another from its sheath to glimpse the sharpened metal. The blades of the knives she continued to study, one after another, were varied in length and in shape. Some blades curved, some were straight. One blade was short and fat, another long and thin. They all fascinated her, for a moment.

Surprisingly, she wasn't angry that Dalton hadn't confided in her. He had to be careful. He couldn't trust anyone.

Mary found that she wanted, most desperately, for Dalton to trust her enough to tell her who he was and what he did. She had done nothing to earn that trust, nothing but love him. But she was closer to Dalton than she'd ever been to anyone, and if he could confide in her, if he could share his life with her, she would be truly content.

She made certain the knives were exactly as she'd found them, that the disguise was replaced so that Dalton would never know that someone had searched his trunk. She placed the livery on top of the closed chest and backed away from the evidence, a smile on her face that refused to fade.

Max hitched his horse to a post near the rear door of William Seton's house. All was dark, black, and ominous—the house, the grounds, his heart most of all.

Why would his wife request a meeting with the Indigo Blade here? After their last encounter she was taking quite a chance, asking to meet the bounder in the privacy of her uncle's house. He could think of no good reason for this subterfuge, nothing he could bear to contemplate for long, at least.

The rear door swung in easily, opening into Seton's study. This was a house much simpler in design than his own, square rooms and straight lines, plain and simple furniture placed sparsely here and there. He had no problem avoiding the few obstacles in the study, even in the dark.

Once he exited the study, the stairway loomed before him. He could see a soft hint of candlelight from above, just enough to tell him that Penelope waited.

She'd "retired" early this evening, heading for her bedchamber directly after supper. What had she done, slipped quietly through one of the many doors or windows and walked to her uncle's house? Of course she had. It wasn't far, and getting herself a horse from the stables would have aroused too much suspicion.

And his lovely wife didn't want to arouse any suspicions, certainly.

He climbed the stairs slowly, silently, the light from above a beacon that guided him. The dark wig and long bulky coat were in place, and if he were seen from a distance the disguise would suffice. But if Penelope saw his face in candlelight, she'd know the truth.

He didn't care.

The light came from a room at the end of the hallway. The door was ajar, and light spilled warmly onto a bare pine floor. Penelope was waiting.

Max moved silently to the door and pushed it open with a gloved hand. Penelope stood near the window, her back presented to him. She was wearing her dark green cape, the hood up to cover her hair, the hem brushing the floor so that the draping lightweight wool was all he saw of her. His heart dropped to his knees.

He didn't think she could have heard him, but she spoke, startling him.

"You came."

"Did you think I wouldn't?" He stepped into the chamber cautiously, quietly.

"I didn't know." She turned then, slowly, cautiously, and Max prepared himself for the confrontation of a lifetime.

But Penelope was prepared for the secretive Indigo Blade. She had wrapped her yellow sash, the one she'd hung from her balcony to signal him, around her eyes so that she was effectively blinded. She took a tentative step toward him, one cautious hand lifted before her, feeling for a bedpost she found with two steps.

Gripping the post with one hand, she pushed the hood back with the other. Her dark hair was loose, waving like silk to disappear beneath the wool.

"I'm here," he whispered. "What do you want?"

Penelope smiled warmly, and his heart lurched. "After last night, surely you can guess."

"No."

Penelope allowed her hand to fall from the bedpost, and she took a step forward. "Speak again," she said, a hand fluttering blindly at the air before her, "so I can find you."

"Mrs. Broderick," he said gruffly.

"Penelope," she corrected, taking a small step.

"Penelope." It was enough. Her hand found his chest, and she planted herself before him. Fingers spread, palm against his chest, she used him to orient herself, as she'd used the bedpost.

"Take me with you," she whispered. "For a few days, for a fortnight . . . forever."

His worst fears were unfolding before his very eyes. Was she so anxious to escape him? "That's impossible."

"Last night you seemed to think it was very possible. You asked me to join you." Her hands rested comfortably at his chest, and her fingers moved ever so slightly across the linen of his shirt. "Surely you haven't changed your mind in the one day that has passed." Her face was lifted to him, a beautiful face soft and innocent in the candlelight. The sash covered her eyes, but her lips were turned up to him invitingly. "Don't you find me at all attractive?"

"Of course I do, but . . . but as you said last night, you're a married woman." How far would she go? God in heaven, she couldn't do this.

Her smile faded. "I'm a married woman whose husband does not love her."

How could Penelope doubt that he loved her?

Max cursed himself silently as he pondered that foolish question. He'd done everything possible to prove to her and to himself that he didn't. "You can't be sure . . ."

"I don't want to talk about *him*," she murmured hoarsely. "I want to talk about us. Do you feel it as I do? The energy in the air that surrounds us. The affection that makes my heart beat so fast I fear it will burst through my chest. I tried to deny it, but last night after I ran from you, I lay in my bed unable to sleep. I was so very lonely, and I wished often through the night that you were with me. I wished, too, that I was not a coward, afraid to take what I want most of all."

Max swallowed—hard. "Mrs. Broderick, this is inappropriate . . ." he began primly.

One of the hands that had been resting on his chest moved slowly downward, to settle at his waist. "I don't even know your name," she said, ignoring his protest. "I suppose I could simply call you my darling." Her smile came blooming back. "I like that, my darling."

"Penelope . . ." The hand at his chest rose slowly to find his lips, to brush warm fingers across his mouth in a curious gesture. Would she recognize him now? It would serve her right, to get the shock of a lifetime! But she didn't seem to recognize him, even as she brushed those gentle fingers across his jaw and explored the coarse hair of his wig.

"Tell me you don't want me."

"I don't . . . I don't want you," he said hoarsely.

Without restraint or pause, the hand at his waist slipped down to cover his rigid manhood, to stroke

302

the hard and painfully erect length beneath the coarse wool breeches.

"You lie, my darling." She voiced the accusation softly, coming up on her toes to bring her mouth to his.

She kissed him not with innocence, but with a wicked tongue that delved and thrust and tasted as she continued to stroke him.

He didn't know what game this was, but he was suddenly willing to play along. His body demanded it, while a portion of his brain reasoned that participating in her scheme would show Penelope good and well where teasing like this got her.

With a sigh of resignation, he grabbed Penelope and kissed her back, hard and demanding, with unrestrained passion that made his lovely and treacherous wife gasp. And then moan. And then melt. She accepted the assault so warmly, so damned easily.

"Wait," she said, breaking the kiss and taking her mouth and her hands from his body.

Max smiled. She needed a good scare. What was she thinking, to invite a stranger to meet with her this way? A stranger who had already made his intentions more than clear. When she pleaded her mistake, he'd grab her and kiss her again, maybe do a little delving of his own beneath her skirt, for good measure.

But Penelope didn't protest. She unhooked the clasps of her cloak, dropping it to the floor, revealing a simple high waist gown and hair that flowed like a dark river over her shoulders and down her back.

And then, with trembling fingers, she began to unfasten the tiny buttons at her bodice, to lay aside the cotton to reveal the swell of her breasts and lacy chemise beneath. He watched wordlessly as she peeled the sleeves and bodice away, as she stepped from the dress to leave herself in nothing more than petticoat and chemise and the yellow sash that covered her faithless eyes.

"You don't know what you're doing," he finally said.

"I do."

"Your husband . . ."

"Doesn't love me," she finished quickly. "Why do you continue to mention my husband? He lied to me on countless occasions, he rejected me again and again. Do I owe a man like that my unbending devotion?"

"Perhaps he has his reasons," Max said as Penelope reached up to push the shoulders of his jacket so that the garment fell to the floor.

"Are you married?" she asked, apparently unconcerned with what the answer might be.

"Yes," he answered, wondering what she would do. She stopped for a moment and then proceeded, blindly working the belt and buttons at his waist, tugging at his plain linen shirt as she slowly and adeptly began to undress him.

"Do you love her?" With the belt and buttons at his waist loosened, she slipped her hand into his trousers and found the hardened length of his manhood, gripped it with steady, brazen fingers.

"Very much," he replied.

Her hand stroked and teased, driving him to the

brink of madness. "Do you ever tell her of your feelings?"

It was becoming difficult to breathe—and even more difficult not to toss his wife on the bed and bury himself inside her. "Once," he admitted. "Long ago."

Penelope pressed her face against his chest and smiled, so that he could not see her reaction. She should have told Maximillian by now that she was well aware of his identity, but she rather enjoyed the incredulity in his voice, the confusion for a man who she knew now was rarely, if ever, befuddled.

And she had to admit this was—in a very wicked way—exciting. Her body tingled, her blood rushed hot and fast through her veins, and she wanted Maximillian as she'd never wanted him before.

She felt the moment he surrendered, felt it in his entire body as he gave himself over to her. Felt it in the hands at her clothing, easy competent hands that whisked away her chemise and her petticoat, gentle hands that stroked her skin. His hands settled over her breasts, and her nipples pebbled against his palm.

She ached for his touch, at her breasts and her mouth, between her legs. As if he knew what she wanted, what she needed, he answered her body's demands. He kissed her passionately and moaned softly. His fingers teased her nipples, flicking softly over sensitive tips and sending bursts of tingling energy through her entire body.

And then his fingers delved between her legs, touching her, easily and then hard, stroking until she was ready to come apart in his hands.

Linda Jones

Maximillian wouldn't allow that to happen, but pulled away just as she was about to find completion.

"Not yet," he whispered, lifting Penelope to carry her the two short steps to the bed. There he laid her easily on the mattress and gave her one quick kiss. He took her shoes off and dropped them to the floor, and then he rolled a stocking down, moving so slowly she was tempted to reach down and help him.

But as he removed the stocking he kissed the skin that was revealed, her thigh, her knee, her calf. His mouth found her breasts, tasting one and then the other, before he repeated the gesture with the other stocking. Kissing, teasing, stroking.

She heard his boots hit the floor, heard the quick rustle of clothing, and then he was above her. Bare chest to bare chest, his legs covering hers, his mouth devouring her once again.

She wanted him inside her, needed this joining, craved it with such intensity she could barely breathe, could barely think of anything else.

But not yet. Not now.

"Wait," she whispered hoarsely as he pressed his manhood against her, as he tensed and prepared to thrust inside her.

"*Now* you have second thoughts?" he said harshly. "For pity's sake, woman . . ."

"You didn't ask me," she said.

"I didn't ask you what?" She could hear the impatience in his voice, the ragged rhythm of his breath.

"If I love my husband."

306

He was very still above her. "I thought your actions made that very clear."

"Ask me," she demanded.

He hesitated for a long moment, and the body poised above hers was motionless as he complied. "Do you love your husband, Mrs. Broderick?"

"Yes," she whispered. "With all my heart and soul. With everything I am, I love my husband." She reached up and grabbed the coarse wig, sliding it up and off his head so she could bury her hands in his own fine hair. "I love you, Maximillian."

He removed the sash that covered her eyes, whipped it away so she could see his face. Candlelight flickered over his features, the harsh mouth and chameleon eyes, the firm jaw and patrician nose.

"You knew," he said, with such intense relief in his voice that Penelope felt a moment's remorse for her trickery.

She threaded her fingers through his golden hair. "Of course I knew. Faith, my darling, I will never love or want another man."

He kissed her then, a passionate and absorbing kiss, and pushed slowly and steadily to fill her. She tightened and relaxed around him, her body adjusting quickly to his possession. Ripples of pleasure radiated from deep inside her body, drove her to rock against his hips as he moved, to reach for more.

The pleasure began to build to an incredible level, to carry her away on waves of fierce sensation.

"Open your eyes," he demanded, and she did so

without question. "Look at me, and know who loves you."

Eyes locked with Maximillian's, her completion came as his did, endless waves of response so intense she cried out with a throaty moan.

He laid his head beside hers, protected her body with his own hovering gently above, barely touching his chest to hers.

"You have sufficiently repaid me for any wrong I might have done you in the past," he said softly into her ear.

Penelope grinned and slipped her arms around his neck. "I'm not so sure . . ."

He raised up to glare down at her. "Not sure! Do you know how it felt to watch you seduce another man?"

"But you're not another man," she said defensively.

"You knew very well what I'd think when I came into this room."

"And what of last night?" she countered. "You were testing me, weren't you?"

"Well, you seemed quite taken with a man not your husband," he said defensively. "What was I to think when you wept for a wounded stranger and did not see fit to share your pain with me?"

She kissed him easily, a tired, satisfied kiss. She'd had enough of fighting with this man, enough of accusations and arguments. More than enough. "Shall we make a pact, my darling?" she suggested. "You don't lie to me anymore, and I won't lie to you."

He hesitated before answering. "I won't tell you

anything that might put you in danger. When it comes to the league, there are some things you simply cannot know."

"In those particular cases," she said thoughtfully, "I will be satisfied if you withhold certain information or simply tell me the truth, that it would be dangerous for me to know. Yes, I would be satisfied with that. But in our marriage, in our personal life together, I cannot bear another lie."

"Agreed."

"Maximillian?" She tightened the arms around his neck. "Do you truly love me?"

He grinned at her, an unrestrained smile that she somehow knew was more Indigo Blade than Maximillian Broderick. "With all I am and all I ever shall be, I love you."

She felt him growing inside her, hardening and lengthening quickly. Her body responded, pulsing around him, coming to life again. Penelope was well aware that she did not know her husband—not as she should. Aristocratic Maximillian, dangerous Indigo Blade, he was a mystery to her and perhaps always would be.

She would happily spend a lifetime searching for the true nature of the man she'd married.

Chapter Twenty-three

The sun was rising as they rode toward home. Penelope was seated in front of Max, leaning back against his chest and taking in the breathtaking view before them. She was warm against him, snuggled securely in his embrace. This was surely heaven.

"When will you take me to see Tyler?" she asked sleepily. "We have to get some rest first, but I can't wait to see my little brother and hug him and wring his neck for making me worry so."

"I'm not taking you to see Tyler," he said, his voice revealing that he was as weary as Penelope. They hadn't gotten a moment's sleep in William Seton's house, but had passed the night making love, laughing, arguing, and making up. He imagined he'd have to apologize a few more times for not trusting Penelope, for not telling her who he was . . . but then again he expected another apology or two for *her* behavior last night. He couldn't help but smile. His wife had more strength and nerve than he'd ever expected.

She twisted her head to look up at him. "What do you mean you're not taking me to see Tyler? He's my brother, and I insist—"

"No," he said gently before she could argue any more. "It's too dangerous for you to know where he is."

"Too dangerous! That's ridiculous."

Through the night, she'd agreed easily that she did not expect him to reveal such secrets to her, and it would be dangerous—to her and to the people who'd agreed to hide Tyler—if she knew where her brother was. In reality, she was not taking this refusal well.

"Will you not take my word that he's well?"

Penelope didn't move. She was nestled cozily against him, and in spite of her displeasure on this one subject, she remained secure and content. "I haven't seen him in such a long time."

"Will you not trust me with your brother's safety?"

She took a moment to consider the question. "Of course I trust you," she finally said. "Goodness, you don't know what it's like to worry this way. I imagine the worst, always. One day you'll understand, when we have children and they behave foolishly and endanger themselves."

Max found himself smiling. "I want lots of children," he said softly. "Do you think you might already be . . . that perhaps we . . ."

She saved him from his babbling, answering serenely and surely. "Perhaps. I think I'd like a son first, and then a girl."

Ah, he could see it. Penelope carrying his child, a house full of babies, toddlers on his knee and in his arms. He'd never really thought of it before. He'd experienced a fleeting knowledge that one day his wife would bear a child, but he'd never imagined it so clearly that his heart reacted this way, thudding in his chest.

"I think I shall like that very much," he said thoughtfully.

As home came into view, Penelope shifted in his arms and glanced up, bestowing upon him a soft smile. "Do you realize we've never had this conversation before? Next I imagine we'll be discussing names for our firstborn." Her smile widened.

"Katherine," he said solemnly.

"Richard," she countered.

"Elizabeth."

"Anthony."

"Daisy."

"Horatio."

"Horatio! I think not."

Penelope laughed, and they continued the game until they stopped in front of the stable. Fletcher appeared, as if he'd been watching and waiting all night, and took the reins Max threw him.

"Fiona," Max said as he dropped to the ground and lifted his arms to his wife.

"Thomas," Penelope said as she came to him.

Fletcher shook his head in obvious disgust, and with a wide smile Max turned to his friend. "We're naming all the children we haven't had yet."

"Saints preserve us," Fletcher said in his most pointed Irish accent.

"Marguerite," he said as he took Penelope's arm and led her toward the house.

"Percival."

Max threw a glance to Fletcher. "Inform the rest of the staff that we're not to be disturbed today. If anyone knocks on my chamber door, there had better be fire or flood directly behind."

Fletcher grumbled his profane response.

Mary knew she couldn't tell Penelope what she'd learned about Dalton, but she had to speak to someone. She'd kept too many secrets, and it was beginning to weigh on her mind. Maybe now was the time to apologize to her cousin for her part in the deception surrounding Heath Lowry's death.

Not yet, Mary decided as she faced Penelope's chamber door. Perhaps never. She could only imagine what her cousin's response to the truth would be, and Mary found she was much too cowardly to risk losing Penelope's love and friendship—a love and friendship she'd once been so eager to throw away, but now treasured.

Penelope was usually up and about by this time of morning, but of course on this morning when Mary needed desperately to talk, her cousin was still abed.

Mary knew that if she'd spent the night in Dalton's arms, she wouldn't be feeling so restless. He hadn't come to her last night, but she understood. The Indigo Blade had more important tasks at hand, responsibilities that would take him away from her at night. She wasn't yet ready to confront him with her knowledge, but she wanted—she needed—to see him.

She rapped on the door, easily at first and then, when she got no response, a bit harder. Nothing. She swung the door open and peeked into Penelope's bedchamber to see that the bed was untouched, the gold satin coverlet in place, the many pillows fat.

Disappointed, she stepped into the room anyway. Penelope had apparently spent the night with her husband in his chamber. In his bed.

Penelope and Maximillian sometimes seemed so distant it was as if they weren't husband and wife at all. Perhaps they were just reserved around others, saving their loving glances and words for when they were alone. Goodness knows Penelope had never been overly demonstrative.

Mary knew that one day she would have what Penelope had. A husband, a fine house, any frippery her heart desired. She went to Penelope's bed and ran her hand over the coverlet. Never before had she touched such fine and heavy satin as this, until coming to the Broderick house. Her father had money, but he was unerringly frugal. All her life she'd been reprimanded for burning too many candles, for choosing the most expensive fabric, for always wanting more.

She could imagine very well Dalton as her husband, the two of them living in a big, wonderful house like this one. Sleeping together every night, ordering around their own household staff. Dalton

Archer was a great man. He would not play the butler forever.

Mary sat at Penelope's desk and ran her fingers over the ribbons there, satin ribbons in every color, bright colors that always looked magnificent in Penelope's dark hair and gaudy in Mary's red curls.

The drawer was partially open, and Mary reached down with the intention of sliding it closed. But a hint of blue ribbon caught her eye, a thin band of pale blue wrapped around a small bundle of letters.

She slid the drawer open and removed the bundle.

If she had not seen the seal—a wax seal bearing an image much like the tattoo on Dalton's thigh— she never would have continued. She slipped the letters from the blue ribbon and opened the first one. Why was Dalton sending messages to Penelope?

She grew cold as she read the letters. Meeting?

And then she read Penelope's note, a message Dalton had no doubt read and returned to her. *Your place in my heart can be filled by no other.* Mary was suddenly ill. *Tomorrow night, my love.*

The truth came to her with a painful clarity. Penelope wasn't in her husband's bedchamber, and Dalton wasn't fulfilling his duties as the courageous Indigo Blade. They were together. Kissing, touching, sleeping with their arms and legs entwined. Laughing at her. Laughing at her foolish dreams and the way she so easily gave her love.

The note that disturbed her the most was not the one Penelope had written, but the very short note that read simply, *The grand hall. Now.* She could envision too clearly Dalton waiting in the cavernous room, she could see Penelope sneaking down the stairway in the dead of night to meet him, to kiss and hold him silently where no one would see or hear. She'd probably been asleep in her bed, dreaming of Dalton while he loved Penelope as wonderfully and thoroughly as he'd ever loved her.

Penelope had stolen everything Mary ever wanted. Everything. Her own father's affection, Victor's admiration and love, the attentions of the wealthy Maximillian Broderick, and now Dalton.

This most recent loss hurt her more than any other, and she couldn't understand why. Dalton had never promised her forever, and he'd certainly never promised to be faithful. He'd used her, just as Victor had. He'd simply done a more adequate job.

Tears came to her eyes, but she refused to break down, refused to weep.

She didn't blame Dalton. This was all Penelope's fault, of that Mary was certain. Penelope, who presented an innocent face to the world but was a monster at heart. Penelope, who had taken everything Mary had ever wanted. She'd somehow discovered how much Mary loved Dalton, and she'd purposely set out to seduce him, to take him and his love away. *Penelope.*

Mary slipped the letters into the bodice of her linen dress, secreting the cold bundle near her heart, and then she studied the face in the mirror before her. She'd never seen her skin so ashen, her eyes so unnaturally wide and bright.

She had nothing. Nothing to gain, nothing to lose. She had no one to love, not her family, not

Victor . . . not Dalton. All she had was a sudden and burning desire for justice.

Everyone had to pay for their sins, eventually. It was time for Penelope to pay for hers.

It was most likely afternoon, though the dark and heavy drapes of Maximillian's bedchamber were closed against the sun so it was impossible to be sure.

Penelope found she did not care what time of day it was, not even *what* day it was, as her eyes drifted closed once again. She and Maximillian had curled up together beneath the covers hours ago, clinging to one another and the love they'd lost and found, and here they'd slept.

For Penelope, it had been the most restful sleep she'd found in a very long time. Questions were answered, and her life and her husband had been successfully reclaimed.

They still had so much to discuss, so many problems to solve, but none of those problems seemed terribly important at the moment. It was only important that she was here, with him. Love wouldn't solve every problem, she knew. But goodness, it made them all seem less important.

"Why are you awake?" Maximillian mumbled, pulling her close.

"I didn't mean to wake you," she whispered, snuggling against him. "Go back to sleep."

"I will," he answered. "Faith."

"What?"

"Faith," he repeated.

She came up to look at her husband, to stare fixedly at his closed eyes and tousled golden hair. "Faith, what?"

"Just Faith."

"Oh." She settled herself comfortably against his side. "James."

She'd never seen Victor's office before. It was, like the man who worked there, masculine and orderly and cold.

Mary paced before Victor's desk, the four condemning letters clutched in her hands. How dare he keep her waiting this way? Likely he was repaying her for refusing his last several requests for a late-night meeting.

"What a pleasant surprise," he said as he came sauntering through the open door. "To what do I owe the honor of this visit?"

Mary turned to face Victor, a man she'd loved and hated, a man who had encouraged her to participate in his intrigues and his so-called pleasures. He had a wide, humorless grin on his face, a grin so familiar it chilled her to the bone.

"Close the door," she said sternly.

The smile on Victor's face changed from mocking to lascivious as he slowly shut the door.

"So finally you come to me," he said smugly. "Do you miss me now, Mary?"

She stopped his advance with a raised hand. "Don't flatter yourself," she said indifferently. "Business brings me here, nothing more."

"I find that hard to believe."

Perhaps he found it hard to believe, but he wisely kept his distance.

Mary smiled at him, but she made sure it wasn't an encouraging smile. "You taught me well, Victor," she said, drawing on all her reserves to remain calm. "As you said you would."

She saw the gleam of hope in his eyes, and was more than happy to extinguish it. "You taught me that no man can be trusted, that every man will lie to get what he wants. You taught me that men are selfish lovers who allow their rod to lead them from one woman to another without a qualm."

Dalton had cemented that lesson, and in the process had hurt her more than Victor ever could.

"You taught me well," she finished.

All semblance of hope was gone from Victor's eyes. "Then why are you here?"

She offered him the letters, four notes still bound in a blue ribbon. "Your precious Penelope is having an adulterous affair."

He waved the letters before him. "I'm surprised, but how does that concern me?"

Mary wanted to enjoy this, to savor the moment when she would bring about Penelope's destruction. She couldn't tell Victor that Dalton Archer was the Indigo Blade. That shared knowledge would end the contest too quickly. She had a plan in mind, one Victor was sure to enjoy.

"What's the punishment for adultery?"

"It can be the death penalty," Victor said softly, outwardly confused, "but no one's actually been put to death for committing adultery in a very long time. A fine can be levied, perhaps a whipping ordered for a repeated offense."

"Something should be done. Why, I believe Penelope only married poor Maximillian for his money," she declared.

"I'm not surprised to hear that," Victor said sternly. It seemed Penelope's rejection still stung his pride.

She didn't care anymore how deeply Victor's feelings for Penelope were, how hurt he'd been by her marriage to another man. Mary's voice remained even and cool. "They rarely even talk, Penelope and Maximillian. They lead separate lives, each following their own direction." She sighed deeply. "It's no wonder poor Penelope was forced to turn to another man for affection."

"I still don't understand why you've brought this information to me," Victor said impatiently.

Mary smiled and took a single step closer. This was as close as she ever cared to be to Victor Chadwick. Even this was too close. He didn't make a move, but there was a kernel of fear inside her that he would lunge forward and grab her, touch her. If he touched her, she'd scream. She'd scream and she likely wouldn't ever be able to stop.

But in spite of that fear, her smile remained steady. She hesitated, not because she had doubts about her plan, of course, but in order to savor this moment. Victor waited, impatient, irritated, curious. Mary enjoyed making him wait, and more than that, she enjoyed the sudden surge of power she felt, knowing she held Penelope's future in her hands.

"The man she's cuckolding her husband with is none other than the Indigo Blade."

Chapter Twenty-four

The knock at his door was soft, but insistent, and after ignoring the intrusive tapping for several long seconds, Max rose, leaving Penelope sleeping peacefully in their warm bed.

"I said," he insisted as he opened the door a crack, "that we weren't to be disturbed but for fire or . . ."

"Flood," Lewis finished. "Fletcher informed us of that order, but this won't wait. We received word that Chadwick has arrested James Terrence."

"The man who puts out that weekly newspaper?"

"The very one. Chadwick's charging the man with libelous sedition against the king for an editorial he ran in last week's paper."

Max rubbed his face, tired, unable to think clearly. "Tomorrow we can . . ."

"Tonight," Lewis interrupted. "Terrence is sixty-two years old and in ill health. He won't survive long in Chadwick's prison."

Max sent Lewis to inform the others that he would be in his study momentarily to formulate a plan to rescue the elderly Terrence. He lit a candle and quietly gathered together his clothing, dark shirt and breeches, worn boots, black coat, and leather gloves, and he dressed without making a sound.

He shouldn't wake Penelope. She needed her rest, and telling her that he was leaving would only cause her worry.

But Max found he couldn't leave without saying good-bye. He didn't want Penelope to ever again wake in a lonely bed, wondering where he was and when he would be back. That was a mistake he'd made too often.

Fully dressed, he sat on the edge of the bed and placed a hand on her shoulder. Immediately, she was awake. Her eyes took in the dark outfit, and she knew. He could see the unwelcome knowledge in her eyes.

He didn't say a word, but bent to kiss her lips lightly.

She wanted to ask so many questions, he could see, but she said nothing as he lowered his lips to kiss her once more.

He was almost to the door when Penelope found her voice. "Be careful," she whispered.

It was a caution he would carry with him through the night, a reminder that he had more than just himself to account for now. He had Penelope, and little Horatio and Daisy and Faith and James to think about. He had wondrous days and nights to come. Love. Hope.

He met his glum-faced men in the study with a smile on his face.

After Maximillian left, Penelope found she couldn't go back to sleep. She'd had enough rest to catch up from last night's lack of sleep, and besides—she was worried.

The house was quiet, the other residents being either abed or gone. A number of them, she surmised, were with her husband.

Many of her questions about this odd household were now answered. The staff that was so inadequate and frightening—they were no doubt the infamous League of the Indigo Blade, the men who rode with Maximillian. That explained much: the odd hours they kept, the days her husband slept into the afternoon.

She accepted Maximillian's word that Tyler was safe, so she was able to worry about her little brother less. But what of her husband? Where was he now? Danger might be exciting when someone else was involved, but when it was the man you loved, it was simply frightening.

Penelope left the bed, wrapped herself in Maximillian's banyon, and slipped down the hall to her own bedchamber. There she lit a candle and began to gather garments from her chest and clothes presser. She placed the folded clothing neatly on her bed, gathering together her most frequently used items.

Her days of sleeping in a separate bed from her

husband were over. She'd make room in his dresser for her clothes, or perhaps move one of these fine pieces of furniture into his chamber. They had a real marriage now, and she wouldn't spend a moment longer than necessary away from Maximillian.

"Penelope?" Mary's voice was hesitant, lilting as she opened the door.

Penelope smiled brightly at her cousin. She would have told her visitor to come in, but of course Mary had never been one to wait for an invitation. She came in and walked straight to the bed, and Penelope resumed her chore.

"Going somewhere?" Mary asked sharply, observing the folded clothing on the bed.

Penelope spun around, intent on telling her cousin how very happy she was, how wonderful life was, how very much she loved her husband.

But an unexpected sight stopped her. Victor Chadwick stood in the doorway Mary had left open, his arms crossed over his chest, his eyes locked on her. She instinctively pulled the banyon tighter around her. "What are you doing here?" she demanded.

Victor placed a finger to his lips. "Let's not wake the others and make a nasty scene. It would be best if you came with me now. Quietly." He motioned with a raised hand, and two armed soldiers stepped smartly and silently to stand behind him. "We don't want anyone to be hurt."

She didn't even know who remained in the house. Helen, perhaps, who slept in a room off the separate kitchen and was surely too far removed to hear anything. Beck? Lewis? Any of the men who lived on the third floor. Perhaps they were all with Maximillian, and she had no choice but to face Victor alone.

Even if she were to rouse someone, they'd likely be caught unaware and be killed or wounded by Victor's soldiers. She couldn't, wouldn't, be a party to such violence.

"What do you want?" she said calmly.

"I want you to come with me," he said, lifting an inviting hand.

"No," she said, realizing that her defiance was only a useless display. Victor had all the power at the moment, the soldiers, the firearms.

"Mary," he said wearily, "help your troublesome cousin dress, would you?"

"Of course," Mary said demurely. "Leave us?"

Victor nodded once as he closed the door. "There are soldiers placed beneath your window, Mrs. Broderick. I suggest you be on your best behavior and hurry along."

When the door was closed, Mary took a dress from the pile on the bed and began gathering petticoats and underthings. She said not a word.

"Mary?" Penelope took a step closer to her cousin.

"Do as Victor says and hurry along," Mary said curtly.

"I don't understand."

Mary tossed a petticoat across the bed. "You don't understand!" she said angrily. "Don't play the innocent with me. I know what's going on in this house, Penelope, and does Victor."

Linda Jones

"You told, didn't you?" Penelope said accusingly, unable to believe that her own cousin would betray her and Maximillian this way. "Somehow you found out, and you went straight to Victor to share the news."

"Yes. Now get dressed."

"Why?"

Mary shook her head. "Why? You dare to ask me why? You're the one who's done wrong, sweet, pure Penelope. I should be asking you why you'd commit adultery with a seditious rogue."

Penelope bit back the automatic response that came to her lips. Adultery?

"I want to be the one to tell your husband," Mary continued, "that you shunned him for a rebel, that you forsook your wedding vows to take the notorious Indigo Blade to your bed. What do you think poor Maximillian will say to that?"

Penelope closed her eyes, thankful that Mary didn't, as she believed, know everything. Maximillian was safe, for the moment. It was up to her to keep the illusion alive, to keep him safe.

"You know as well as I that my husband ignored me from the day we were married. Tell him if you'd like. He'll no doubt be glad to be rid of me," Penelope said with an unwavering voice.

"Is that why you were running away with *him*?" Mary asked, pushing a small pile of clothing off the bed.

"Yes," Penelope answered.

"You don't deserve him," Mary hissed.

With great effort, Penelope her voice and her

326

demeanor calm. "Are you speaking of Maximillian or the Indigo Blade?"

Mary threw the selected clothing at Penelope. "Get dressed."

"I don't like it," Max muttered as he stalked into his study, tossing his gloves to the floor in anger.

"It was just a mistake," John muttered. "Nothing diabolical about that."

It was too easy to call the night's disaster a mistake, but Max didn't quite believe it. Not only was Terrence not imprisoned where they'd been informed, he hadn't been arrested at all. They'd awakened him from a sound sleep in his own bed, after searching for hours and wondering if they were indeed too late to save the old man.

"The information came from Chadwick himself," Max reminded the men who filed into his study. "In the past, he hasn't made mistakes like saying he's arrested a man when he has not."

"Maybe he meant to arrest him, and we just got there first," Lewis said with a shrug. "The old man is safely out of Charles Town now, so if Chadwick goes to arrest him later this morning, he'll get a nice surprise."

They liked that idea, but again, Max wasn't convinced.

There would be time for stewing later. Right now he wanted to climb the spiral staircase to his chamber, throw off these clothes, and crawl into bed with Penelope. He wanted to love her, to be a part of her body and soul and allow her to chase away the darkness and the uncertainty of his life.

She chased away the shadows.

The room was dark, but he found his way to the rumpled bed with no problem. "I'm home," he announced, and then he waited for her to rise from the darkness and beckon to him.

But there was nothing. No response, no movement. He lit a candle and saw that the disheveled bed was empty.

He'd expected her to wait for him here, envisioned her in this bed as he'd headed for home. . . .

Max carried the candle with him as he stalked to Penelope's bedchamber. She'd gone to retrieve a book, he thought, or her sketch pad, and had decided to stay in the familiar chamber while he was away. Without knocking, he threw open her door, and the sight that awaited him took his breath away.

Clothing was scattered across the neatly made bed and the floor: dresses and petticoats, shoes and busks, discarded without care.

"Penelope?" he whispered, expecting no response. All was silent, still, dead. "Penelope." His voice faded away as he walked into the room and surveyed the disorder.

Something had happened to her, something terrible—something that was entirely his fault.

He heard footsteps on the stairs, heard Dalton's gruff voice calling his name, but he didn't answer. At the moment he was incapable of speaking.

Soon Dalton was in the open doorway, a sheet of paper clasped in his hand. "Something's wrong," he said softly.

"I know," Max whispered.

"I found this on the desk in my chamber." Dalton offered the paper and waited for Max to come get it. "I'm sorry, Max, truly I am."

He didn't want to see what Dalton offered, but walked numbly to the doorway and took the note. The others gathered in the passageway, behind and beside Dalton, silently waiting as Max read.

Chadwick had Penelope. Max had known it somehow, as he'd seen the shambles in her room, as he'd stood there and whispered her name as if it were a prayer.

The note was addressed not to him, but to the Indigo Blade, and the instructions were simple. At a time and a place to be named by Chadwick at a later date, there would be an exchange made. The Indigo Blade for Penelope Broderick. Failure to comply with any instruction would bring about Mrs. Broderick's immediate demise.

All he could do was wait for further word from Chadwick.

In a lowered voice, Dalton told the others what was in the note, while Max stared at the words, reading them again and again. Nothing in the damning letter changed, no matter how desperately he wished it.

"Why was it left in your chamber?" Max asked, lifting his head at last.

"I don't know. Perhaps the place was picked at random."

"Chadwick doesn't do anything at random," Max said darkly.

At the far end of the passageway, a door opened noisily. "What's going on?" Mary asked, yawning as she stepped away from her chamber door. "I heard all these voices . . ." She stopped speaking when she saw the crowd.

Dalton swept past Lewis and Beck. "I have bad news," he said tenderly.

Someone had made terrible coffee, but Mary sipped at it without comment. A few candles burned as the sun came up and they sat—every member of the household—around the dining room table.

Dalton was beside her, constantly assuring and comforting her. Telling her everything would be fine, that Penelope would come back to them unharmed. He asked her time and again if she was all right, if she needed anything, and he was the one who had forced this awful coffee on her, insisting that it would do her good.

He was concerned about Penelope, but not frantic as she had expected he would be. Perhaps he didn't love Penelope any more than he loved her.

It was Maximillian who was so distraught it was painful to watch. At the moment he had his head in his hands, face down, loosened hair falling over his cheeks and to his shoulders.

She was glad for the curtain of that disheveled hair. When last she'd looked into Maximillian's eyes, she'd seen such pain there it hurt her. Would the agony go away when she told him that his beloved wife had been cavorting with the butler?

"Why has this happened?" she asked, looking from one sad face to another. Helen, the only other woman in the room, sniffled constantly, but had not yet given in to tears. Even the jovial Lewis was downhearted. Did they wonder why she didn't cry for her cousin? Best to get it all out in the open. "Why did Victor take Penelope?"

What excuse would Dalton come up with? How would he explain why the note was found in his chamber? She'd thought of that as she'd placed it there, after telling Victor that she'd place the message where the Indigo Blade would be certain to find it.

Perhaps Dalton would play ignorant, shrug his shoulders, and declare that Victor Chadwick must have gone mad, as there was no reason to take Penelope and leave that note in his quarters.

But as she waited for an answer, everyone at the table exchanged thoughtful glances—Dalton and Fletcher, Beck and Lewis, the mumbling John. Did they all know the truth about Dalton?

"Tell her," Maximillian muttered from beneath his fall of hair.

"Are you sure . . ." Fletcher began.

Maximillian lifted his head and they were all presented with an agonized expression that spoke volumes about his pain. Here was a man on the verge of breaking down, of falling apart. Mary wished that he would weep, that he would allow the grief to escape somehow instead of holding it in this way.

Those around her were obviously as affected by his anguish as she was. Helen allowed a small sob. Garrick lowered his eyes, unable to stand any more. No one could see such heartache and be unaffected, and eventually they all averted their eyes. All but Mary. She felt a rising anger mingling with her sympathy. Penelope didn't deserve to be loved this way.

Dalton took Mary's hand, and she gratefully took her eyes from Penelope's tormented husband. "Things here are not as they seem," he said kindly, taking his time breaking the news to her. "You have heard of the Indigo Blade?"

"Of course," she answered.

"He lives among us. He is here at this table."

She gripped his hand tightly. "I suspected as much. Why didn't you tell me?"

"I couldn't," he shook his head. "There were times I wanted to tell you everything, but I was not at liberty to divulge—"

"Not at liberty?" she asked incredulously. "I would imagine the Indigo Blade does as he pleases. Really Dalton, I never thought you were really a servant."

He looked confused, and then comprehension dawned on his face. "It's not me," he said. "I am dedicated to what we do, but I don't have the head for planning that our leader has. I have a tendency to rush headlong into situations without thinking things through."

"You're not—" She hadn't heard much past his nonchalant *It's not me*. "You're not the Indigo Blade?"

Dalton shook his head, and Mary looked around the table, studying the sad faces that surrounded her. Not Dalton, thank heaven. Not Dalton! But one of these men was Penelope's lover, the real Indigo Blade. She scrutinized each face, wondering how she'd gone so wrong, wondering which of these men Penelope loved so dearly.

And then her eyes lit on Maximillian again. He was truly tortured, agonized . . . heartbroken. Where was the lazy dandy she was accustomed to? Where were the lace and frills and fine manners?

"Maximillian," she whispered.

"Yes," Dalton answered. "Max is the one with a head for scheming and a flair for acting."

Mary stared at Dalton until he was all she saw. He tried to comfort her with a gentle hand to her face, with an attempted smile, but there was no comfort to be had. Mary knew, in that instant, that she would never know true peace again.

She forgot about the others in the room. She had to, if she was to get through this. "Dalton, I thought it was you," she proclaimed.

"Disappointed?"

She shook her head quickly. "No, never. It was the letters," she said, trying to explain. "I found them and I was so angry . . . I've never been so angry."

"What letters?" he asked, and Mary reached into her bodice to retrieve the blue-banded keepsakes.

"I thought you loved her," she cried out, "and I couldn't bear it."

Dalton took the letters and perused them quickly. "I don't understand."

All was silent. Mary looked bravely at the faces around her, faces that waited for her to explain. But she could only explain to Dalton.

She faced him, forcing the others from her conscious mind. "I know where she is," she confessed. "I know where Victor's taken her."

As she watched, the warmth vanished from Dalton's blue eyes, leaving her staring into the coldest ice. The comfort and caring fled, and she was confronted with a man who was as cold and unfeeling as Victor ever was. A dangerous man she did not know.

She couldn't remedy this mistake. Not ever.

"How would you know such a thing?" Dalton growled.

Mary wanted to drop her eyes, but that would be the coward's way. She gathered every bit of courage she possessed and looked squarely at Dalton as she answered.

"Because I helped him kidnap her."

Chapter Twenty-five

She'd expected prison, a damp and windowless room, but Victor and his soldiers had led Penelope to an inn at the edge of town, where she was given an armed escort to a small but comfortable chamber above stairs. There she'd passed what remained of the night of her capture and this very long day that followed.

Night had fallen again, she saw by the complete darkness outside her small window. A fire blazed in the stone hearth, her untouched supper cooled on a serviceable table, and a narrow bed piled high with blankets awaited.

Two armed soldiers stood guard at her door, making this comfortable room a prison as surely as any dungeon would be.

Penelope stood near the fire, her hands clasped before her as she dug deep within herself for the strength she needed to get through this. It would be so easy to break down now, to weep and wail and perhaps to faint away until all was said and done. Mary had betrayed her, and Victor held her captive, but Maximillian . . . Maximillian would certainly save her.

That knowledge gave Penelope strength and peace. There was no tangible reason for her certainty, no wisdom that others did not possess, but she was confident, still. Her husband was smarter than Victor, stronger, and he had right on his side. All she had to do was wait.

The door opened without a knock, and Penelope spun away from the fire to face a smug Victor Chadwick. He held a bottle of wine in one hand, two crystal tumblers in the other, and as he stepped inside her room one of the soldiers closed the door behind him.

"I do hope you're comfortable," he said with an aggravating and ordinary tone of voice, as if they stood in Uncle William's study or the Huntlands' grand hall.

She declined to respond, and still Victor made himself at home in her quarters, setting the bottle and glasses on the table with her supper and warming himself by the fire. "You haven't eaten. Is something wrong with the food? I can have the girl send up something else."

"I'm not very hungry." she responded calmly. "I prefer to wait to have supper until I'm home."

Victor turned to face her, his head cocked to one side and his smile firmly in place. "That might be a while, Penelope."

"I don't think so." Faith. She had to maintain her faith in Maximillian. Anything less would be a defeat for her, and a victory for the self-important man before her.

He studied her for a long moment, looking her up and down as if he'd never seen her before. "Wine, then. This is a fine bottle."

"No," she said firmly.

Victor sighed, but it was clear he'd not yet given up. "I never would have thought it of you," he said, stepping to the table and pouring himself a tall glass of liquor. "The genteel and reserved Penelope Seton Broderick taking a lover, and a man like the rascal who calls himself the Indigo Blade, at that. Really, Penelope, you disappoint me. If your husband did not satisfy you, you should have come to me."

She realized now why he'd been studying her so intently. A woman who would take one lover would surely take another. The wine, the private room instead of a prison . . . he apparently intended to seduce her.

If she played the prudish and devoted wife, if she railed against his outlandish suppositions, he might begin to suspect that Maximillian was the Indigo Blade. She couldn't allow that to happen, but the thought of allowing Victor Chadwick to touch her made her physically ill.

"It truly never occurred to me," she said sensibly. "I suppose I've always thought of you as an older brother, a trusted and dear family friend."

"I've always cared so very deeply for you."

As deeply as a man like him could care, which

she doubted was very deep or true. "As a friend."

She could sense his frustration before she saw it in his eyes and in the set of his mouth. "I wouldn't have asked you again and again to marry me if I'd cared for you only as a friend, Penelope. I wouldn't have taken your rejection without insult if I hadn't cared for you as much more than a *friend*."

Penelope simply shook her head.

"There could be more for us," he offered softly. "True, you're married to that nincompoop and you unwisely took up with a dangerous rebel, but I can forgive that. I can give you what neither of them ever can. We can start again. Tonight."

"No. Not tonight, not ever."

At last his smile faded. "I could simply take what you refuse to give. You're an adulteress, after all. Who would believe that you didn't come here with me of your own free will? Who would believe the protestations of a woman who has already made a dupe of her poor dim-witted husband? Yes," he proclaimed, as if the notion appealed to him. "I can take what I want."

The panic rose, quick and unexpected, at those words. No matter what, she couldn't allow her fear to show. Victor would like that, he wanted and expected it, and she knew, somehow, that he would find her panic exciting.

"You could," she admitted as she tried to force her heart to slow and her breath to come naturally. "But I will fight you, Victor, with all that I have. I don't want to be forced to do that. We were true friends, once."

"That word again," he muttered. "All right, perhaps we were *friends* until you went and ruined all my plans by marrying that dandy Broderick. Admit it," he said hoarsely. "You married him for his money."

"Perhaps," she replied. She was willing to let him believe that was true, if it turned his suspicion away from Maximillian.

"I never knew you were for sale, Penelope," he said angrily. "All your gentle protestations about not being ready for marriage, and all along you were waiting for a man whose wealth was impressive enough to sway you. I might have tried to raise the funds to buy you myself if I'd known."

He placed his now-empty glass heavily on the table. "Broderick has a bloody fortune, that I understand. But tell me, Penelope dear. What did it cost that damned Indigo Blade to have you?" he asked as he came to stand directly before her. "Perhaps I can match his offer."

"His heart," she said as Victor moved his mouth toward hers. She turned her head at the last moment, and his lips landed on her cheek. Cold, wet, repulsive lips.

"His heart." He spat with derision as he took her face firmly in his hands and held her in place. "What romantic foolishness. I thought better of you."

Holding her head tight so she could not move, he lowered his mouth to kiss her. Penelope spoke before he could claim her lips. "If you touch me, he'll kill you."

"He doesn't have to know."

"I'll make sure he knows, and I'll make sure everyone in Charles Town knows." Penelope's voice was sure and strong, in spite of her pounding heart and wobbly knees. "Most of the rebels there would be content to send you back to England where you belong, but the man they call the Indigo Blade will make you suffer. He will kill you."

Victor hesitated, his mouth a breath away from hers, his fingers digging into her face and scalp. "He can try."

"And if he doesn't, I will." God help her, she meant it. If she had a weapon now, she would use it without a second thought.

"You don't have the strength or the courage to take a life."

"I will," she swore.

She could see the doubt growing in Victor's eyes, the hint of fear. Perhaps he saw her determination, the will he did not expect from her.

"One man's heart isn't worth killing and dying for," he said in what she was sure he meant as a rational retort.

"Victor," she said, lifting her fingers to his to remove them from her face, to shove his cold and intrusive hands away. "One man's heart is the only thing worth killing and dying for."

He didn't feel the cold anymore. Night had fallen long ago and the air was damp and chill, much too cold for this time of year. Max had stopped feeling it long ago, as he had tried to stop feeling anything at all. How else was he to get through this?

He looked at Dalton, avoiding setting his eyes on Mary Seton. "Is everything in place?"

Dalton nodded once.

Max's anger and, even worse, his helplessness, rose to the surface again. "If he hurts her, I'll make him pay in ways he never imagined. I don't care who he is or how many of the king's soldiers come after me, by the time I kill the whoreson he'll be begging for death."

"He won't hurt her," Mary said softly, her voice cutting through the night and into Max's heart. "Victor's always been a little bit in love with Penelope."

Max spun on the red-headed woman who was huddled in her cloak against the unseasonable cold, hands tied before her, lips trembling. She'd barely spoken since leaving Charles Town, and she'd be wise even now to keep her mouth shut.

He'd never thought it in him to hate anyone this way, but he'd damned Penelope's cousin to hell a hundred times in the past twenty-four hours.

"I don't rest any easier knowing that the man who abducted my wife is infatuated with her." He was seething.

If only he knew where Penelope was at this very moment. Mary was in possession of a note, a note she was to deliver for the Indigo Blade tomorrow morning advising him to meet Chadwick and Penelope at the tavern in Cypress Crossroads.

Cypress Crossroads, where the people were friendly and unarmed. At least, that was what Victor had remembered from his foiled raid on the village. What safer place to meet with and dispose of the Indigo Blade?

It was a lucky break, the only one they'd had thus

far. Unfortunately, Penelope and her captors weren't there now. Mary had assumed the tavern was where Victor planned to keep his hostage until the appointed meeting time tomorrow evening. At least, that was her claim.

They could be anywhere.

During the course of the day, Dalton hadn't paid Mary Seton any more mind than Max had. In fact, he'd ignored her in an even more pointed manner. They brought her along on this excursion because everyone else was occupied . . . and just because she'd had second thoughts and expressed her regret, that didn't mean they could trust her. She was bound at all times, though it was likely not necessary. She was terrified of the swamp around them and the creatures who lived there. Even if she were free, she would be too scared to run in this wilderness.

Perhaps when this was over, he'd untie the ropes that bound Mary and leave her here.

When Victor left the room, slamming the heavy door behind him, Penelope breathed a sigh of relief and sat shakily on the edge of the bed. It was a miracle her legs hadn't buckled as she'd faced Victor.

Faced him and won.

She'd never known she had such determination inside her, perhaps because she'd never needed it before. Her days had been simple and easy, before Maximillian swept into her life, but Heath had been right. Some things were worth fighting, and even dying, for.

It was more than love that made her strong. In

the past few months she'd left behind a part of herself and discovered another. Her life would never again be contained by four walls. Easy and simple were wonderful for a child, but a woman needed more.

Maximillian had such conviction, such courage. With his money, he could live anywhere in the world. He could live a safe life, easy and simple, and assign no consideration to the needs of a budding nation.

But that wasn't her Maximillian. He embraced the world around him, saw injustice and challenged it, and would never be one to turn a blind eye.

Penelope wondered, as she slipped off her shoes and crawled beneath the covers, if the Indigo Blade needed an addition to his league—a loyal and devoted female who had recently discovered her own strength.

She hated this place. It was cold and dark and filled with things she could hear but could not see. The night had been endless, black and damp and so cold that Mary thought she'd never be warm again. At last the sun was rising, lighting the sky much too slowly for her liking and bringing the promise of warmth.

She hadn't slept, and neither had Dalton or Maximillian. She'd heard them throughout the night, moving about, whispering in low, somber voices. Even when all was silent, she knew they weren't asleep. They surely needed their rest, but an unnatural energy drove them both.

For Maximillian, it was an energy born of love.

For Dalton, it was an energy born of hate. Hate for her.

If she'd not been looking for deception at every turn, she would have asked Penelope to explain the letters. She would have gone to Dalton and asked him, outright, if he was the Indigo Blade. If she'd been able to trust anyone, none of this would be happening. Penelope would be safe at home, in bed with her husband.

And Dalton would still love her.

The way he kept playing with those knives when he looked her way, Mary was rather surprised he hadn't killed her yet. She should be more distressed at the prospect of her death, she supposed, but as she had nothing left to live for, it didn't seem to matter much. The pain would be with her until death, this pain of knowing she'd betrayed the only two people in the world who had ever truly loved her.

Mary couldn't help but wonder what would become of her if Dalton didn't kill her. She certainly couldn't return to Penelope's home, and she didn't want to return to the plantation, to her father's disappointment and disdain. When this was all behind her she could marry, perhaps, but who would have her?

No one.

There was only one person in this entire world who might have room in his life for her. Not as a wife, as she'd always hoped, but as a partner, a paramour. She'd never been able to make Victor love her and she never would, but he did want her, in his own way.

She shuddered at the thought, telling herself it was the chill of the swamp that made her bones shake.

Chapter Twenty-six

After a chilly ride, the Cypress Crossroads tavern was pleasantly warm, with a fire blazing and people gathered at the tables that were scattered about the long, narrow room. The man behind a crude plank bar recognized Victor as he led Penelope through the door.

"Mr. Chadwick." The hefty man greeted Victor with a smile as he closed the door. "What a pleasure to have you in my establishment once again."

There would be no help here, Penelope decided. The owner of the tavern was obviously acquainted with Victor, and the patrons paid the new arrivals no mind at all. No one seemed even to notice that Victor had a tight grip on her upper arm, or that four armed soldiers had been posted on the other side of the door.

At the table nearest the fire, a couple argued. An

old stooped woman berated her companion—no doubt her husband—emphasizing her words with an occasional rap of her gloved hand against the old man's shoulder. The old man responded, head down, with a muttered apology.

An elderly man with a shock of white hair—an old sailor, judging by his clothing—sat at a nearby table. He talked to himself in a monotone between sips of beer. The only word Penelope could make out was "hurricane."

Another patron, a man with wild red hair who wore a tartan plaid around his shoulders, flirted with the barmaid. Soft, endearing words spoken with a Scottish accent drifted to Penelope. The barmaid, a tall, dark-haired girl in a homespun dress, had her back to the door, but it was clear by the tilt of her head and her gentle sway that she was receptive to the Scot's words.

Victor chose a table at a distance from them all, and he seated himself with his back to the wall so he had a clear view of the door. He forced Penelope to sit down beside him, and beneath the table he kept a tight grip on her wrist.

"What now?" she asked softly.

"We wait."

Who did he expect to come through that door? She'd heard Victor instruct the soldiers to allow all to pass, but to be ready to enter the tavern at his shouted command.

Yesterday's confidence was waning in the light of reality. She had no doubt but that Maximillian would do his best to save her and himself, and she knew he was a better man than Victor in every way.

But Victor had a short sword hanging at his side and concealed beneath the table, and those four soldiers posted at the door were ready to do battle. What chance would Maximillian have against five armed men? Would he come alone, as the note had instructed, or would his league of followers be with him?

The stout proprietor of the tavern left his station at the bar and came to their table with a wide grin plastered on his face. he said. "What brings you back to Cypress Crossroads?"

Victor gave the man a cutting glance. "My reasons for stopping at your establishment are none of your concern."

"Of course," the man answered, apparently not at all offended. "I'll have my daughter bring you and your lady two tankards of my best ale."

"Fine," Victor snapped, his eyes returning to the door.

The proprietor turned away from the table and shouted at the tall woman who was still flirting with the Scot. "Rebecca!"

The barmaid shot a quick glance over her shoulder.

"Two tankards of our finest ale for Mr. Chadwick and his companion."

Rebecca leaned over to say a quick word to the Scot on her way to the bar, where she filled two tankards as her father had requested. Even from this distance, Penelope could see that she was a homely woman, big-boned with harsh facial features. A mouth that was too wide, a nose that was too long. There was something very familiar about that plain woman . . .

"Remember what I said," Victor whispered as the tavern owner walked away from the table.

"I do." How could she forget it? Victor had threatened that if she pleaded with anyone for help, he would punish not her but the person she appealed to. It was an effective warning, for Victor had brought only four men with him; four of his most trusted and obedient men, who would never think to protest any of Victor's actions. He had set himself up to do as he pleased with the Indigo Blade, and as witnesses he'd brought these boy-soldiers who looked up to him with a kind of fearful awe.

Rebecca walked to the table with pewter tankards in each hand and a small crooked smile on her face. There was something familiar about that face, and Penelope had never so much as passed through Cypress Crossroads. There was the chance, of course, that Rebecca had been in Charles Town and they'd passed on the street, but Penelope felt that she knew this woman in more than such a superficial way.

The proprietor's daughter placed the tankards before them and nodded shyly. Penelope whispered a thank you, while Victor ignored the unattractive girl. All of his attention was on the door.

Penelope stared up at the barmaid, eyes fixed on a face she knew . . . should know . . . *knew* very well. As her mouth fell slightly open, Beck winked at her.

* * *

Mary looked once again at Maximillian. He was dressed in his finest: royal-blue velvet jacket and trousers with a matching cape, lace cravat and cuffs, embroidered waistcoat, polished shoes with silver buckles.

The young couple who lived in this one-room cottage had disappeared soon after Mary, along with Dalton and Maximillian, had arrived. The others had been waiting, the men from the Broderick household who ignored her pointedly. While Dalton kept a wary eye on her, the others held a brief conference outside. She'd wanted so badly to say something to Dalton then, to plead with him not to hate her . . . but she'd remained as dreadfully silent as he had. Perhaps there was nothing left to say.

She had spent the past two hours or more sitting in a chair by a low-burning fire, watching Dalton and Maximillian, listening to their softly spoken words. Her hands were bound, but not her feet. If she got the chance, she could run. . . .

But Dalton would catch her if she did, and then what would become of her? Would he kill her with one of the knives he wore around his waist?

She had a feeling he would.

Maximillian was so obviously nervous; his body tense, he paced stiffly. Now and again he wrung his elegant hands, until he realized what he was doing and dropped them to his side. Their plan was simple, but everything had to come together perfectly.

"Let me help," she murmured, and two heads turned her way. It was growing dark outside, but the flickering firelight illuminated for Mary two fair heads, four eyes full of hate. "This is all my fault," she said when she got no response. "And I want to help make it right." She allowed tears to fill her eyes, tears of anger and frustration. "Please."

"No," Maximillian said forcefully.

She ignored Maximillian and looked to Dalton. He'd cared for her once. Maybe he didn't love her, maybe he would never forgive her . . . but maybe, too, he found it impossible to truly hate her after all they'd shared.

"I can help convince Victor that the Indigo Blade isn't coming," she said. "He trusts me completely."

"He's the only one who's fool enough to trust you," Maximillian answered curtly.

Maximillian turned his head away, but Dalton did not. He continued to stare at her as if he didn't know her at all, as if she were a stranger, or worse, an enemy.

"Gag her," Maximillian said. "We can't have her shouting a warning, and we can't leave her here."

Penelope took another look around the room. She only got a glimpse of the Scot's face, but it was surely Fletcher, the stableman. The sailor still had his head down, but when she caught sight of the small beard that was dusted and gray, she was reminded of Garrick.

The old man who was being constantly berated by his wife mumbled a response. Was that John, Maximillian's valet, beneath battered hat and disheveled gray hair? The woman who scolded him had, in profile, a sharp face with a prominent chin and high cheekbones. The old crone was Lewis Turner, surely.

Penelope turned her eyes to the door, watching and waiting as Victor did. She wasn't the only one who was anxious. Victor had not touched his ale, and he tapped his fingers restlessly on the table beside the tankard. He'd responded, when the bartender asked if there was something wrong with the ale, that he wasn't thirsty just yet.

Her own throat was parched and dry, but she was afraid if she put anything in her stomach it would come right back up again. She jumped at every noise: when a tankard was forcefully deposited on a table, when the "Scot" laughed. The old man moved his chair back, and it screeched across the floor. The sound cut to her very heart.

She'd always thought herself a patient woman, but this waiting was enough to drive even the most self-possessed person mad.

Without warning, the door opened suddenly, admitting a rush of damp, chilly air and a well-dressed and very calm Maximillian.

"Lud," he said as he slammed the door behind him. " 'Tis a night not fit for man nor beast."

Maximillian faced the table where she and Victor sat, his back straight, his gray-green eyes deceptively lazy, and as Penelope watched, he tossed his velvet cape back over his shoulders.

"There you are, m'dear," he said, stepping smartly to the table. "Faith, until I received the note I did not know what on earth had become of you. 'Tis good to see you looking well," he said in an unconcerned voice.

"*You* received the note?" Victor said in a low voice.

"Of course, my good man. 'Twas left on my pillow, after all." Maximillian whipped a sheet of folded paper from his waistcoat pocket and presented it to Victor.

Victor took the paper and unfolded it slowly. Penelope leaned to the side, just enough so she could read the letter.

Your wife is being held hostage by Victor Chadwick. She can be found tonight at the Cypress Crossroads tavern.

"This is his writing." Victor seethed. "I'd recognize it anywhere."

"Whose writing?" Maximillian asked casually. "The bloke didn't sign at all, just scribbled that dagger at the bottom of the page. Very inconsiderate of him, if you ask me."

Penelope lifted her eyes to his. He revealed nothing with that calm face and those lazy eyes, not even to her. Of course, he had yet to meet her gaze squarely.

"The Indigo Blade, you moron." Victor positively simmered, frustrated that his plan had gone wrong. "The man who's been trifling with your wife."

"Trifling?" Maximillian asked blandly, and with a slight lift of well-shaped, golden eyebrows.

Victor finally lost his temper. "The man who's been rogering your wife!"

Every head in the room turned their way, briefly.

Maximillian finally turned his eyes to Penelope. If she didn't know better herself, she'd believe he was actually surprised. Surprised, but not especially distressed. "Faith, m'dear," he said softly, and she could finally see the relief, the fear, the affection he hid from Victor so well. "Whatever would possess you to carry on in such a manner?"

Victor's fingers manacled her wrist, and the pressure there only got tighter. But for a moment, for now, she forgot that he threatened her still.

"Love," she answered.

Maximillian's eyes softened, and a silent message passed between them. All would be well.

"So you think yourself in love with this Indigo Blade chap?" he said lightly.

"Quite madly," she answered without hesitation.

Maximillian offered his hand, a strong, long-fingered hand draped with the fine lace that fell from his cuff. "Come along then. I'll take you home and see if I can't convince you to love me just as madly."

She lifted one hand to her husband, a hand he took and lifted to his lips for a soft kiss of reassurance and love. She gripped his fingers tightly, refusing to lose this tenuous connection, and his grip on her was just as firm. She would never let him go. Never.

Unfortunately, Victor maintained a tight grip on her other wrist.

Hands bound, Mary waited behind a tree and watched the posted soldiers as Dalton did. After Maximillian entered the tavern, Dalton had removed the gag, making her swear to silence.

"Let me help."

"We don't need your help," he said, never taking his eyes from the soldiers.

"I could—"

"We don't need your help," he repeated, and this time he did look at her. She almost wished he hadn't, those eyes were so cold. They shone with disdain just as clearly as they had once shone with love. "The plan is in motion."

"A potion in his ale," she whispered. "I heard Maximillian talking about John's special herbs."

He didn't answer, but turned his gaze to the soldiers at the tavern door. Unaware, they talked and laughed and watched the road for a suspicious character who might be the Indigo Blade.

When Maximillian had entered the tavern, they hadn't given him so much as a second glance.

"What if your plan doesn't work? What if the soldiers best the men who are only waiting for your command? If I'm inside I can help, I know I can." She wondered if Dalton sensed or heard her desperation. "I want to do this for you."

"Why?"

"Because I'm the only one who can."

She saw the rigid control break—in his eyes, in the set of his shoulders. He grabbed her arm and held her tightly. "Why did you take the letters to Chadwick?" he asked angrily. "I was ready to give up everything for you, and without so much as a word, you turned against me and your own cousin. You don't betray family. Not ever, not for any reason."

She tried to back away, but Dalton's strong hand held her tight, his fingers digging into her flesh. "Why did you do it?"

"I don't know." It was the truth. Jealousy, hate, and greed had consumed her and made her do terrible things. She'd thrown away her one chance at love, the one man who loved her, her chance for happiness . . . all for revenge.

The hand that didn't hold her in place raised slowly. Dalton grasped one of the knives Mary had discovered in his trunk on her excursion to the third floor, and his hand rose steadily until he held that knife between their bodies. "I loved you," he said.

"I still love you," she whispered, wondering if it would be enough to stop him—knowing it wouldn't be. She leaned forward to kiss him, to lay her lips over his one last time. The knife he held steadily pressed dangerously against her breast, but she didn't back away until the kiss was done.

The knife wasn't lowered. He would kill her after all, and Mary found she didn't want to fight what was to come. Dalton jerked her hands toward him, wrapped his fingers more securely around the knife, and with a lightning quick slash cut the ropes that bound her hands together.

"Run," he hissed. "And don't come back. If this goes wrong, Max will likely kill you."

Chapter Twenty-seven

Max stared at Chadwick's hand on Penelope, and with great effort preserved his facade of calm. Relieved as he was to see and touch her, they weren't out of this yet. "You may release my wife, now, Mr. Chadwick," he said idly. "I will take Penelope home and protect her from this Indigo Blade fellow."

"She's not going anywhere."

Max spied the full tankard of ale. "I may be mistaken, but I don't believe you have the authority to hold my wife against her will."

"My own authority is all I need."

Max knew that the four soldiers outside would be immobilized shortly. Dalton and the Cypress Crossroads volunteers were competent, driven, and dedicated to the aims of the Indigo Blade. He decided to give Dalton another moment more before making his move. They didn't need the roar of pistols and the clash of steel, though his men were prepared to meet such force if need be. But in a conflict of arms, anyone could be hurt—the tavern owner, the men of this village who had agreed to participate in this endeavor. Penelope.

If only Chadwick would drink the damned ale! A few of John's specially chosen herbs had been steeped in that ale, especially for Victor. This would all soon be over quickly and quietly. Max's fingers tightened over Penelope's warm hands, his heart thudding much too hard beneath fine linen and velvet. Yes, they would soon be rid of Victor Chadwick.

But only if he drank the ale.

"Let's discuss this over a drink, shall we?" he suggested with a smile. "I'm rather parched."

The words were barely out of his mouth before the owner of the tavern was at his side with another mug of ale. Max took a long swig before depositing the tankard on the table. Chadwick still didn't drink.

This standoff could last for hours, and Max wasn't sure how much more of this he could take.

Another minute, perhaps two, and he'd pull Penelope out of Chadwick's grasp and take the bastard on, one on one. Plans be damned, the sight of that man's hand on hers was enough to make him lose all control.

Penelope appeared to be unhurt, but until he could hold her tight, he wouldn't quite believe it.

Behind him, the door opened and closed quickly. He hoped it was not some innocent stumbling into this explosive situation, but that was likely the case. Did the arrival of a true tavern patron mean Dalton and his men had been delayed? Damn it, he couldn't stand this waiting much longer.

He didn't turn about until he saw Penelope's eyes go wide.

"Mary!" Chadwick was so surprised he let his grip on Penelope falter. She wrenched from his grasp and Max pulled his wife to her feet and into his arms.

Mary sauntered into the room with her cloak gathered close before her and her face deathly pale. Somehow she'd escaped from Dalton, and she was going to tell Chadwick everything. Damn her, she was going to ruin their chances for a bloodless victory tonight.

She didn't look his way, didn't respond when Penelope whispered her name. Her eyes were on Chadwick. "Let them go, Victor," she said softly. "This is a terrible mistake. I was wrong about everything."

"You weren't wrong," Chadwick said sharply. "Penelope herself admitted that she was involved with the Indigo Blade."

"Rogering, I believe you said," Max said angrily, releasing Penelope and forcing her to a position of safety behind him.

He didn't know what gave him away. Something as simple as a fleeting expression, perhaps, displaying the passionate anger foreign to the Maximillian Broderick Chadwick knew.

"You!" Chadwick said, rising to his feet so quickly he bumped the table and his tankard of ale teetered and sloshed, threatening to fall over and spill across the table. "It was you all along!" He drew a short sword from a scabbard that hung from his waist and pointed the tip of a sharp and deadly blade directly at Max's heart.

There was the screaming sound of chairs quickly forced backward, and the rasping sound of steel against steel as the disguised "patrons" of the Cypress Crossroads tavern drew their own concealed weapons.

Mary moved quickly, her cape whirling about her as she rushed to Chadwick's side. How quickly she chose sides, Max thought bitterly. She reached out a steady hand and laid it over his fingers and the hilt of the short sword. Did she want to help? "Don't," she said, her eyes on Chadwick. "If I ever meant anything to you, drop this sword now."

"Mary?" Penelope took a single step forward, but she was ignored by her cousin.

"We can sail for England, together," Mary continued. "I can't stay here, and after tonight, neither can you. Everyone will know you came here with the intention of killing the Indigo Blade, and like it or not, he's become a hero to many people. You can't deny your intentions. If you'd come to capture him, you would have surely brought along more than four soldiers."

The tip of the blade touched Max's chest, and that fact alone kept his men at bay. A lunge, a simple forward thrust by Chadwick, and he was dead.

"We can be happy there," Mary continued.

"Guards!" Chadwick shouted at the top of his lungs, cutting his eyes to the door. All was still for a long moment, and then he shouted again. Louder. "Thurman!"

His sword didn't drop, but his eyes took in the armed men around him, the Scot and the sailor, the old man and woman, and "Rebecca." He was weighing his odds, and evidently finding them not in his favor.

"You won't get away with this," Max said calmly. "Kill me if you must, but you'll be dead before you have time to draw the sword from my body."

"Where are my soldiers?"

"Detained," Beck said succinctly.

Chadwick spared a momentary shocked glance to the barmaid with the surprisingly deep voice.

"It seems we have a stalemate," Mary said softly and urgently, "so I suppose a truce of some sort is called for. There's no need for anyone to be hurt. Let us go." She turned a despairing face to Max, and then to her cousin. "We'll sail for England and out of your lives."

Penelope placed a steady hand on Max's arm. "Agree," she whispered. "Please."

A simple nod of his head, and he would be rid of Chadwick. But was that enough? Could he ever rest easy knowing the man who had kidnapped his wife was free? England was far away. Perhaps far enough. "Agreed."

Mary smiled, and as she let her hand fall from the sword, she lifted the tankard of ale that sat before Chadwick. "Let's drink to it, shall we?"

"Mary . . ." Max began, but he was too late. She lifted the mug of drugged ale to her lips and took a deep drink.

And then she handed the tankard to Chadwick. "Come on, Maximillian," she said, indicating his own tankard of ale. "This agreement won't be binding until we've all drunk to it." Her eyes met his then, so clearly and so solidly that he realized she had indeed heard them talking of poisoning the ale. "Everyone!" she demanded.

Tankards were lifted, including the one in Chadwick's hand. At last, he let his sword fall.

Mary seemed to hold her breath as she watched Chadwick drain his tankard, and with a smile on her face she sat in the chair nearest her. "Good," she whispered. She was obviously beginning to feel the effects of the potion. Her eyes drooped and she swayed back unsteadily. "Have a seat, Victor," she said thickly, "before you fall flat on your face."

"I am not . . ." he began, and then he raised a hand to his head. "Good heavens, what's wrong with me?" He did as Mary had instructed and sat heavily in his chair.

"Poison," Mary said, very gently taking Chadwick's hand in her own. "They put it in the ale."

"Poison?"

"I'm sorry, but it really is for the best. I couldn't let you kill Maximillian or hurt Penelope, and I know you, Victor. You wouldn't be bound by your word." Her voice was unsteady, the herbs or the moment overcoming her. "I couldn't allow you to hurt them anymore, and I know you would never be satisfied with only me and England. Dalton doesn't love me, and Penelope will never forgive me for everything I've done. I might as well be dead."

Penelope moved quickly and a little shakily to Mary's side. "What have you done?" she asked tenderly.

"I tried to fix this mess as best I could."

Chadwick, who had taken a much larger dose of the drugged ale, allowed his head to drop. His last conscious movement was to wrest his hand from Mary's.

Fat tears rolled down Penelope's cheeks, and Max was there to comfort her. He placed his arm around her shoulder. "It's a sleeping potion, not poison," he said quietly. "She'll be all right."

Penelope heard him and sighed with relief, but Mary was oblivious. "Forgive me. I never did tell you about Heath, and I should have. I should have trusted you with everything, Penelope. You always loved me."

"Everything's going to be fine," Penelope said as she brushed a red curl away from Mary's face.

"Tell Dalton that I'm sorry," Mary said as she lowered her head to the table. "Tell him I loved him from the moment he . . . he helped me up."

As Mary closed her eyes, Dalton and the Cypress Crossroads contingent burst into the tavern. Dalton's eyes searched the room until he saw Mary, so still, her head on the table, her eyes peacefully closed.

"Oh, no." His raised knife dropped to his side as he walked toward Mary. He looked at the tears on Penelope's face, and then at a very still Mary. "I tried to stop her—I really, did, Max. I released her so you wouldn't kill her, but instead of escaping, she ran straight for the tavern door."

"Dalton . . ." Max began but his friend wouldn't stop.

"We weren't ready to take the soldiers, and I had

to stand there in the woods and watch her walk into the middle of this. And now she's—"

"Sleeping," Max finished, taking a dazed Dalton's arm as he reached the table. "Thanks to John's special blend of herbs."

"Sleeping?" Dalton raised misty eyes to Max. "She drank Chadwick's ale?"

Max nodded once. "Just a sip." Thinking it was a deadly poison, she'd drunk deeply and then handed the tankard to Chadwick. Trying to make things right, she said. He'd always been unforgiving. Evil was evil, and right was right, and there was nothing in between. And now he was faced with this dilemma. Damn it, why was nothing in his life ever easy?

The relief that washed through Dalton was visible, almost tangible. Max released his arm, and he circled the table. "And this one?" Dalton grabbed a handful of hair and lifted Chadwick's head from the table. "This whoreson deserves to die."

Truer words were never spoken, but Max had to disagree vocally. It was the reason they'd decided a few hours ago to substitute the sleeping potion for the poison, the reason Chadwick was still alive. "But we can't kill him."

"Why not?"

"Because killing him here and now would bring the king's army down on these people's heads. They would pay for our revenge, and that's not right."

Dalton dropped Chadwick's head so it thunked hollowly on the table. "You're not going to let him go?"

"Not exactly." A small smile crossed Max's face. "Lewis had a splendid idea."

Lewis explained his plan to send Chadwick on a long voyage to India where he would be the *guest* of, or rather a gift to, the barbarous nawab of Bengal. They would send Victor with one of Dalton's enterprising associates, who would be sure to make the journey long and arduous. Max wrapped his arms around Penelope and nestled her against his chest.

Penelope was safe now, but could he keep her safe always? The coming years promised to be uncertain, and there were more men like Victor Chadwick out there—men worse than Victor Chadwick. He bent to whisper in her ear. "I was terrified." He'd never admitted his fear to anyone, not even as a child. Being afraid was one thing, but admitting to it made a man vulnerable. It felt rather like standing naked on deck during a hurricane. Exposed. Defenseless. But he wanted Penelope to know how he felt, what she meant to him. "Terrified," he repeated.

She lifted her head and smiled at him. "There were moments I was terrified, too, but there were others when I felt no fear at all."

"Is that a fact?"

"I knew you would come, and I knew we would leave here together." She was as serene as if she stood in her parlor dabbing at her mural.

"What confidence you have in me, m'dear."

Penelope slipped her arm around his waist. "What confidence I have in us," she replied.

Beck made a laughing suggestion that they give Chadwick a tattoo to remember the Indigo Blade by, a small surprise for him to find when he awakened in the hold of the ship that would take him to India.

"A tattoo like yours?" Penelope asked.

"We all have them, here and there," he answered, his voice as low as hers.

Penelope looked at the strange and marvelous crew that surrounded her. "And who is the artisan capable of performing such a task?" She studied the faces in the room, one by one, until her eyes finally rested on a grinning Dalton.

"Will he give me one?"

"Absolutely not!" Max answered, about the same time Dalton did. Behind him, Lewis and Beck laughed heartily.

As Dalton prepared to do his best—or his worst— to Chadwick, Max led Penelope to a far corner of the tavern. There, he gathered her in his arms and held her as he'd longed to from the moment he'd come through the door and seen her sitting at Chadwick's side. If he had his way, he would never let her go.

She did not tremble, and she did not cry. Her only tears had been for Mary, when she'd thought the ale to be truly poisoned. His delicate wife was evidently stronger than he'd imagined.

"Do you know how much I love you?" he asked softly.

"Perhaps as much as I love you."

"Perhaps."

Quietly, oddly content, they stood and watched as the League of the Indigo Blade shed their costumes. Wigs, padded coats, a couple of quickly discarded dresses, were all tossed into a sack.

With Lewis's help, Dalton gathered together the supplies he needed—a bone that was sharpened at one end and a vial of indigo ink—and sat at the table between the two unconscious victims of John's sleeping potion. He worked his magic first on the side of Chadwick's neck.

The indigo dagger Dalton fashioned there was long and narrow, and the tip ended just beneath Chadwick's ear. It was a tedious process and took quite a while, but everyone watched with a mixture of amazement and amusement.

It wasn't enough, apparently, to satisfy Dalton. A smaller dagger was etched above Chadwick's right eyebrow. During this process the proprietor of the tavern and the men of Cypress Crossroads who had stormed into the tavern with Dalton wandered away, one by one, until only Penelope, the sleeping Mary and Chadwick, and the League of the Indigo Blade remained.

Another tattoo was added to the top of Chadwick's left hand. Dalton might have continued, but Mary stirred and stole his attention.

Mary, who had taken a much smaller amount of the drugged ale than Chadwick, lifted her head slowly. Penelope took a step forward to go to her cousin, to comfort her in spite of—or perhaps because of—all that had happened. But Max pulled her back.

"I have to . . ." she began.

"Look," he whispered.

Mary, when she realized that she was not dead after all, came to her feet as quickly as she could, clearly with every intention of bolting from the tavern. Dalton stopped her with a swift and firm hand that found Mary's wrist and held her tight.

Lewis and Beck stood over Chadwick, and with a silent nod they each took an arm and hauled the marked man to his feet and away from the table. Chadwick's long journey had just begun.

Mary watched as Victor was dragged away, and then she lifted her eyes to Dalton, whose hand remained tightly at her wrist. "I didn't drink enough."

She was looking for the hate in those blue eyes, but hate wasn't what she saw. Tears filled Dalton's eyes, tears that didn't fall but simply glistened here. What would make a man like this cry? It wasn't as if—her heart lept with the possibility—it wasn't as if he loved her.

"I thought you were dead," he whispered. "For a split second, when I saw you lying there, I thought Max or Chadwick had killed you."

"I drank . . ."

"I know what you did, damn it," he said angrily, pulling her close. "If Max hadn't decided to substitute a sleeping potion for the poison, you would be dead."

"It wasn't poison?"

Dalton sighed and lifted his free hand to her cheek. "No, thank God. It wasn't poison."

It should have been poison. She should be dead right now . . . but Dalton's hand on her face was so gentle and warm and wonderful, she was glad to be alive, glad for this second chance.

But what would happen to her now? She couldn't

go back to Charles Town, and she had nowhere else to go but the plantation. She hated that place, had always hated it, but what choice did she have?

Right now, she just wanted to get out of here. She had to get away from Dalton and Maximillian and Penelope.

"Changes will have to be made," Dalton said softly, and Mary nodded her head, unable to speak. She didn't want to contemplate such changes. She looked at his throat, studied the vein that throbbed there, unable to look into those tear-filled eyes again. He was so very disappointed in her, still.

"You must learn to trust me," he continued, "with everything. I cannot have a wife who lies to me, who doesn't know without doubt that I would never hurt her."

She lifted her eyes slowly. "Wife?"

"You must learn serenity," he pronounced. "I will need that from you."

"Wife?" she repeated.

"If you'll have me."

She nodded slowly, and was rewarded with a small smile. Dalton sat heavily in the nearest chair, and pulled her with him, depositing her on his lap.

"I want you to understand who I am and why I'm here, before we go any further."

She melted against him and laid her head against his shoulder, safe at last. "I want to know everything."

He wrapped his arms around her, holding on tight. Whether the support was for her or for him, she didn't know. It didn't matter. From now on they would support one another.

"His name was Jamie . . ." Dalton began.

*   *   *

Penelope found she could not watch the scene unfolding in the corner, as Dalton pulled Mary onto his lap. It was too personal, and not meant to be shared,

Instead she fastened her eyes on Garrick, Fletcher, and John as they hesitantly approached their leader.

"Well?" John muttered. "What do we do with those four British soldiers?"

"They're just lads, really," Fletcher added. "One of them looked familiar, and do you know who he turned out to be? The captain who righted that wagon for us a few months back. Bradford Thurman, he said his name was."

"Really," Maximillian muttered.

Fletcher nodded his head. "He doesn't like you much, Max, and before I shoved the gag back in his mouth he made it clear that he doesn't care for the colonies, either."

Maximillian raised a rakish eyebrow.

"They're not hurt at all," Fletcher continued. "Just bound and gagged and scared half to death. They seem like nice lads, except for that Thurman fellow. I'd hate to have to kill them."

Garrick brushed absently at the powder in his little black beard. "What choice do we have?"

Maximillian pondered the question for a moment, and then he smiled as the answer came to him. "Make the choice theirs. They can sail for India with Chadwick, or they can sail for England on their word they will never return to these colonies."

"They don't look like deserters," Garrick said cynically.

Max only smiled. "Put them on a secure ship headed for home, and woo them with talk of living the rest of their lives in the English countryside, where they will marry country maids and make babies and happily forget that they ever heard of Charles Town and Victor Chadwick and the Indigo Blade. Tell them I have a feeling the army will be much too busy in the coming months to diligently look for four soldiers who come up missing." His smile faded. "And tell them that if they do come back, they'll bloody well wish they hadn't. I'll make sure of it."

They all approved of that solution, certain they could convince the young soldiers to be glad to head for home and leave the colonies behind.

But before they left to see to the soldiers, Garrick turned his black gaze on Penelope. "I understand we owe you an apology, madam," he said coldly. "We are not usually so quick to judge, I assure you, but . . ." There was a softening of his dark eyes. "Suffice it to say, I offer my deepest regrets for my mistake, and I am now and forever your humble servant." He took her hand, bent over it stiffly, and kissed her knuckles briefly before John nudged him aside.

"Don't you believe him," John said, taking Penelope's hand and giving her a wicked smile. "Garrick wouldn't know humble if it bit him on the ass." He lifted her hand for a kiss that lingered a moment more than was proper. "But as for what he said about being wrong and sorry and all that," he lifted his eyes to hers, "same goes for me, madam."

John stepped aside and Fletcher took his place. He, too, took her hand. Red-faced and obviously embarrassed, he shook that hand slightly. "I always knew these boys were fools," he said softly. "But I never expected to make myself a simpleton right alongside them."

She smiled at his apology, and when he saw her grin, he lifted her hand to his lips, briefly.

"That's quite enough," Maximillian said, taking her much-honored hand in his own.

"Lewis and Beck will want to apologize, I would think," John said as they made their way to the door.

"Saints preserve us," Fletcher said, and then they all laughed.

Penelope fell easily into her husband's protective arms.

"I have a feeling," she confided, "that life with the Indigo Blade is going to be an adventure."

"Will that be a problem for you?" Maximillian asked as if he dreaded the answer, as if he didn't already know. But perhaps he didn't. So much had happened in the past few days. Did he think she could ever prefer the safe and sheltered life she'd enjoyed before becoming his wife?

She drew her head away from his chest and looked him square in the eyes. The love was there, the love she'd seen on the night they met. It was deeper now, impossibly stronger. And it would grow stronger, still.

"I wouldn't have it any other way."

Epilogue

She'd made a lot of progress in the past month. Sections of the mural were complete, while still others were practically bare. It would take her weeks, perhaps months, to finish it to her satisfaction.

Of course, the mural would be progressing more quickly without her daily lessons, but Maximillian was insistent. If she planned to be a member of the league, she had to prepare herself accordingly. She rather enjoyed the swordplay, but the pistols still made her uneasy. Maximillian demanded, though, that she become proficient with both.

The season had turned almost on the very night a tattooed and unconscious Victor Chadwick had sailed out of their lives, the days becoming warmer, the nights wonderfully balmy. Perhaps that was merely coincidence, but there were moments when Penelope didn't think it was coincidence at all that

Victor and the last vestiges of winter left their lives at the exact same time.

"When people see this, they'll think you've lost your mind."

Penelope glanced over her shoulder to smile at Tyler. Once Victor was safely at sea, Maximillian had collected her brother and brought him home . . . where he caused turmoil daily. Tyler and Garrick butted heads on a regular basis, but at the same time, her little brother was becoming fast friends with John and Beck.

"I rather like it," she said defensively.

"I didn't say I didn't like it," he said as he stepped into the room and checked her progress. "I just think it's peculiar."

She couldn't argue with Tyler for long. She'd missed him so much she was likely to agree with most anything he said, or to grab him as he passed by and give him a big hug for no reason, at any time of the day. As long as no one else was around, he didn't seem to mind.

One day, Tyler would likely join Maximillian and his league, and after an initial burst of protective denial, Penelope accepted that when the time came it would be a good and proper action. No one was more passionate about liberty than her brother.

Tyler had learned, as the others had, that Penelope had nothing to do with Heath's capture. He had apologized quietly and sincerely for believing her capable of such treachery, and Penelope had forgiven him.

"Do you mind terribly having a peculiar sister?"

She put her brushes aside to face her brother. He

grew taller and more handsome, to her loving eye, every day. With his pale hair and blue eyes, he looked more like Maximillian's blood than her own. The three of them were becoming a family, gradually, not always easily—at least, they were the beginnings of a family.

"A moderately peculiar sister I can handle," he said with a sneer. "But that husband of yours is damned odd."

"Tyler! What a thing to say." She couldn't help but smile.

He lowered his voice. "I received a lesson this very afternoon on the importance of a properly tied cravat." He spoke with a touch of horror. "Maximillian, with John's assistance and Beck watching on, gave me a lecture on this important subject that lasted at least three-quarters of an hour." The sneer had merely faded.

"He means well," Penelope said, trying and failing to restrain her smile. Maximillian did love to bedevil Tyler at every opportunity.

When Maximillian, dressed in pale blue silk, stepped into the parlor, studiously examining the lace of his white cuff, Tyler left abruptly, with a mumbled insult Penelope couldn't quite decipher. They hadn't yet told Tyler that his dandy brother-in-law was the Indigo Blade, and the fiery young man had no patience for the foppish Maximillian Broderick.

Maximillian smiled widely when they were, at last, alone. "Your brother is a fine young man," he said as he surveyed the walls and her progress. "He has your fire and determination."

She'd never known she had fire and determination, until Maximillian had brought it out. "We should really tell him who you are," she said softly. "He'll be much happier."

"Soon," he agreed. "We should first give him time to adjust to the news that his cousin is marrying the butler, don't you think?"

Uncle William was mortified, and Tyler likely would be, too, when he heard. For all his talk of equality and freedom, there was a bit of a snob in her brother.

It would likely be a scandal, but for once Mary didn't seem to care what anyone else thought. This was her second chance, she said, and if Dalton would have her, she would defy anyone and everyone to have him. Maximillian had not completely forgiven Mary yet, but Penelope had hopes that he would, one day. After all, Mary had been prepared to make the ultimate sacrifice to save them all.

Maximillian, who still reminded Penelope on occasion of her cruel trick as she seduced the Indigo Blade, was not as quick to forgive as she.

Penelope watched as her husband paced her parlor nervously. He likely had another mission planned and was delaying telling her. He didn't like to worry her, and he most definitely did not like it when she asked to come along. After today, he would likely never allow her to ride with him.

"It's coming along nicely," he said, walking around the room and studying each detail of the mural. "When you're finished here, perhaps you should do something like this in my study."

"I don't think I'll have time," she said, stepping in

front of her strolling husband to halt his progress.

"No time?" He raised his eyebrows and wrapped his arms around her waist.

"With Tyler living here now, and the lessons you insist upon, why, once the baby comes, I won't have much time for painting."

He grinned, apparently not surprised at all. "Jessica," he said softly.

"Christopher," she countered.

He kissed her, brushing his mouth across hers lightly, sending shivers up her spine.

"There's just one problem," she whispered against that mouth.

"What's that?"

"I don't know if the father of my child is my aristocratic, gentle husband, or that hot-headed rebel they call the Indigo Blade."

"Ah," he said as if he understood completely. "What a quandary."

"I certainly thought so."

He tightened his protective arms. "If you had to choose, who would you want the man in your life and the father of your child to be?"

"I'm an incredibly selfish woman," she confessed. "I want them both."

"Faith, m'dear," Maximillian whispered against her waiting mouth. "You shall have whatever your heart desires."

Chapter One

1895

The man locked his doors! Here in rural Alabama, a hundred miles from nowhere, this paranoid Rory Donovan secured every one of his doors and windows at night. Every single one! Jackie knew it to be true because she'd checked, circling the plantation house and silently trying every door and every window.

Well, she wasn't going to give up just because the job wasn't easy. If only she had a set of false keys like the ones Mina used to carry, she'd be in that house right now, climbing the stairs to the master bedroom. In that room, she'd heard tell, a Fabergé egg lay on a bed of black velvet.

If she had that egg in her hands she could retire. The cottage she dreamed about would be hers, and she'd gladly leave this chancy profession to others who were more daring than she.

Jackie placed her hands on her hips and lifted her head to the gallery that encircled the second floor. Washed in moonlight, the two-story, square plantation house was colorless, hushed, and imposing. White-pillared and classic in design, it was a Southern castle, a monument to a time and a lifestyle long gone. There was elegance here, and majesty . . . and money.

There wasn't enough light for her to see very far beyond the gallery railing, and that concerned her for a moment. For all she knew, a sleepless resident of this house could be standing in the shadows above, waiting and watching. A smile crossed her face. It was going on three in the morning, so that wasn't likely.

Taking a deep and silent breath she approached one of the narrow columns that girdled the house. This was turning out to be a bit more work than she'd intended, but the prize that awaited her was worth any effort.

This was definitely her last job, she reminded herself as she clasped her hands to the white column and hoisted herself up. She'd said that before, once when she'd been almost caught, and again a few months later. She had enough money to get by on if she were very frugal. But in the end she'd always decided that the time wasn't right for retirement. Tonight, however, she meant it. Truly.

The black trousers had definitely been a good choice for these early-morning hours; she never would have been able to work her way to the second-story gallery in a cumbersome skirt. Her progress up the column was slow but steady, and when her arms and legs got tired she thought of the Fabergé egg. It was gold, she'd heard, encrusted with more gems than even the grandest lady would wear. Pearls, rubies, sapphires, diamonds. Ah, she absolutely adored diamonds.

A peek onto the gallery through the slats of the railing confirmed her suspicion that no one was about at this hour. All was as quiet and gray and peaceful there as it was below. A dismal thought occurred to her, but she brushed it aside. Surely Donovan was not so paranoid as to lock the French doors on the second floor.

Once she'd hauled herself up to the gallery, she sat with her back against the column she'd climbed, catching her breath and ordering her heart to be still. It took her only a moment to catch her breath, but her heart was slow in obeying. As she sat there, she thought about Rory Donovan and his fine house and his Fabergé egg. Sally had said that he'd won it in a poker game in Nashville, taking the prize with four aces from a Russian prince or duke or somesuch who'd thought—wrongly—that he had an unbeatable hand.

Some people had all the luck. It wasn't the first time Jackie had made this observation, and it likely wouldn't be the last. From her spot against the column, she looked down the wide gallery. Rory Donovan was one lucky son of a bitch. He had this plantation—Cloudmont, he called it—more than his share of money, and according to Sally he'd been blessed with the gift of beauty as well. He wouldn't miss the egg. At least, not for long.

Jackie rose to her feet silently and made her way to the nearest open French door. She peered beyond the lace curtains that danced softly in the breeze to see a small boy snug under his covers, a shock of hair unruly against his pillow and a tattered blanket clutched in little fingers. She smiled, but only for a moment.

She knew of entire families who lived in rooms smaller than this one. The bed was wide and had a tall, ornately carved headboard. The matching wardrobe would hold everything Jackie owned, and more. There was a fine rocking chair, a large rug, and a desk to hold rocks and books and other boyish treasures.

This was one lucky kid, Jackie reasoned as she made her way along the gallery to the next room.

The French doors before her were closed tight, and a quick look through a pane of glass showed her that this room was deserted. Sheets were draped over the contents, and in the moonlight the covered furniture looked vaguely like a family of ghosts. She shivered once and continued on, rounding the corner. Taking small, silent steps, she walked to the very end of the gallery and stopped just short of the next door. This was the place; she knew it. Even though she hadn't yet glimpsed the inside of the room, her heart told her that this was the place. A treasure beyond her wildest dreams awaited within.

She peeked around the door to see a scene similar to the one in the first room. All was gray and dark, but her eyes had adjusted to the night and she could see the room well enough. A man slept in a massive four-poster bed, the quilt pulled well above his waist, his hair tousled on the white pillow his head rested upon.

Sally had been right; from what little Jackie could see by the pale moonlight, he appeared to be a handsome gentleman. Rory Donovan had been blessed with regular, strong features and thick, slightly curly hair. His chin was square, his jawbone prominent, and his shoulders wide.

Without a twinge of conscience, she stepped around the open French door and into the room. Once she was inside, she stood very still. Some people were such light sleepers that the very presence of another person in their room awakened them, and before she went too far she had to make sure that Rory Donovan was not so sensitive.

She stepped into a shadow, watching the figure on the bed for movement and listening for a change in breathing before she moved on. It simply wouldn't do for Donovan to wake and catch her. Even asleep he looked far too strong, and far too fast to deal with.

When it became clear he hadn't been disturbed, she turned her attention to the rest of the fine bedchamber. It was a large room, airy and elegantly furnished and free of clutter. There was a dresser and a tall wardrobe fashioned from the same dark wood as the tall four-poster bed, a massive wing chair upholstered in a dark fabric, and against the far wall there was a glass display case sitting on a low table. That case held the object of her desire.

She crossed the room silently, her eyes on the egg

that had brought her here. Even by the scant moonlight that made its way through the French doors on two walls, it was magnificent, finer than she'd imagined, more exquisite than she'd dreamed. Gems formed an elaborate pattern on the golden egg, twisting and twirling in an almost exotic design. How could she not smile?

Here was her retirement, her way out of this crazy life, a chance to begin again.

A harmonica had been carelessly placed on the display case. She glanced back at the man on the bed. Did he play? She didn't know him, except from Sally's descriptions, but for some reason she couldn't imagine him playing such a thing. Sally'd said he was a charmer, a carefree man of the world, but in sleep he seemed much too serious and imposing for a such frivolous pastime as playing a harmonica.

She lifted the instrument with every intention of putting it aside so she could lift the glass cover, when something struck her as odd. She held the harmonica up so it caught more moonlight. Gold. The man had a gold mouth harp! Without another thought she slipped the harmonica into the front pocket of her trousers.

Her hands were on the glass cover when she heard Donovan stir. Just to be safe, she dropped down and placed her back to the wall, pulling herself into a tight ball and making herself as small as possible. She was in the shadow of the wing chair, well hidden. If Donovan should arise from his bed he wouldn't see her here. *He wouldn't*. She closed her eyes and said a little prayer. Who was the patron saint of thieves? Dammit, Mina would know.

Her prayer went unanswered. Rory Donovan sat up slowly, running lethargic fingers through his short hair, rolling one shoulder as if he had a crick in it. *That's it*, she thought. *Work out those kinks, lie down, and go back to sleep*.

Her silent instructions were no more effective than her prayer had been. Donovan sat there for a minute, and then he tossed his quilt aside and sat up, throwing his legs over the side of the bed and rolling his shoulder once more as if it pained him. He rotated that bare shoulder yet again, sending the muscles on his back into a undulating dance that was quite interesting.

All better, now, she thought. *Lie down and return to dreamland, Mr. Rory Donovan*.

He was an uncooperative mark, deciding instead to stand. Mercy! The man slept as God made him, bare from one end to the other. She followed the fascinating process as he unfolded himself from the side of the bed, stretching to an incredible height. Good heavens, the man was probably six-and-a-half feet tall! Sally had said he was tall, but Jackie had assumed he might reach near six feet. Since Mr. Clark, Sally's gregarious father, stood no more than five feet, six inches tall, and Sally was an inch shorter than Jackie at an even five feet, Jackie had assumed that anyone more than five feet, eight inches would qualify as "tall." But this was incredible; Rory Donovan was a veritable giant! Heaven help her, she couldn't allow this man to catch her.

He stepped to the door, where his long naked body was washed in moonlight. This was a disaster of major proportions. Not only was he tall, he was well-built. Regrettably, there wasn't an ounce of fat on the man. His legs were long and lean and hard, tailor-made for chasing clumsy or unlucky thieves, and as he again lifted a hand to his hair, she saw that it was large as well. Large and powerful. His back was to her—thank God for small favors—but she had already seen more than enough. Oh, she could *not* get caught here.

She watched, spellbound, as a sudden and gentle breeze washed over that unadorned body, ruffling the fine hair on his head and the curtains that framed him.

Jackie closed her eyes and tried her best to remember who the patron saint of thieves was.

He should be sleeping. It had been a long day, a hard day, and he hadn't had a good night's sleep in more than a week. Rory looked out over the well-tended lawn beyond the gallery railing, a sight that usually had the power to soothe him. This was home, after all, his land, his legacy, the place that harbored all his memories—good and bad.

Cloudmont was a well-run community, and a walk around the gallery, when he chose to survey his land in that manner, would show him a stable and barn and carriage house, all of it enclosed by a white Tennessee fence. The kitchen beyond the house and the covered brick walkway that connected the two buildings were silent at night. On that brick porch, pies cooled and jams were put into jars, and Rory drank his coffee there on many afternoons. Farther beyond were the smokehouse, the woodhouse, and Nell's raised cottage. The flower garden thrived, as did the vegetable garden. All was well here.

Tonight, Rory remained at the doorway rather than walking about the gallery and admiring it all. The sight didn't comfort him, not the way it once had. Yes, all was well here, but changes were coming. They were inevitable, but he wasn't ready. Just recently he'd decided to accept the fact that he might never be ready.

Kevin needed a woman's soft touch. The boy was six years old, and because Margaret had died long before his first birthday his son had no memory of her. No memory of the woman who had given birth to him, nursed him, cuddled him, and sung lullabies when he'd cried. The chills came, as they always did when he allowed himself to think of his late wife, and he ran an impatient hand over the goose bumps on one arm.

He should marry again, for Kevin's sake; he should do his duty and provide the boy with a family that consisted of more than an inattentive father-figure and a crotchety housekeeper. Nell did her best, but she ran the household and she was getting on in years; he couldn't expect her to take charge of Kevin full-time as well.

Nannies had come and gone in the past five years. Just in the past two years, one had married and moved to Virginia, another had gone to live with her ill sister, and three had simply quit, declaring their charge beyond redemption. Kevin was a handful, he would admit that much.

Marriage was the most logical solution, but Rory

didn't want to get married, not ever again.

Something odd tickled his nose, a hint of a fragrance that didn't belong. He closed his eyes and took a deep breath in an effort to identify the scent. It was pleasant, and made him think of beautiful women and soft hands. The tension left his body, and he let his mind wander free. For a few precious seconds he didn't think of Kevin or marriage or of anything but the faint odor that tickled his nose.

"Fiddle," he whispered to no one in particular. "I smell lavender."

Nicholas of Myra! It came to her in a flash, the memory of Mina saying a special prayer to the patron saint of thieves. Jackie said her own quick prayer as Donovan turned to face her. Before she thought to close her eyes she got enough of an eyeful to know that he was as impressive downstairs as he was up. She never panicked, but there was an unexpected flutter of fear in her heart.

She kept her eyes closed and held her breath, in the childish hope that perhaps if she couldn't see him he wouldn't see her. Soft footsteps approached, and she opened her eyes just enough to see the legs and feet coming toward her. The sight did nothing to still her heartbeat. Oh, she had a feeling she couldn't run fast enough. . . .

Donovan didn't discover her, though, but lowered himself into the wing chair that shadowed her. Blast! If she breathed too hard he would hear her!

He stretched out those long legs, leaned back in the chair, and took a deep breath. "Lavender," he murmured sleepily.

Jackie cursed silently in the shadow of the wing chair, barely breathing, making very certain that she didn't so much as move a muscle. Rory Donovan, bare as the day he was born, sat not much more than a foot away. A lift of her eyes gave her a view of his forearm so clear she could see the tiny hairs there. Straight ahead the scene was one of long legs and big feet stretched out forever and a day, long legs and big feet she would practically have to step over to make her way out of this room if he didn't get back to bed soon.

Nicholas of Myra certainly wasn't a very attentive or effective saint. It soon became obvious that Donovan had no intention of going back to bed. His breathing gradually became deeper and more even, the hand that hung over the arm of the chair relaxed, and once he whispered "lavender" again before he began to snore.

She'd dabbed a very small bit of lavender-scented water behind her ears almost sixteen hours ago. Another gift Rory Donovan apparently possessed, in addition to his good luck and beauty, was an uncanny nose. Fortunately for her he didn't quite trust what his senses were telling him.

Her breathing was slow and silent, and she remained motionless in her hiding place until every muscle screamed at her to move, and an itch appeared for no reason at the center of her back. She ignored the rebellion of her body and tried to think of something to take her mind off her discomfort: the ocean, a bawdy song Mina was fond of, the magnificent prize awaiting so near that, if diamonds had a scent, she'd be able to smell them the way Donovan had smelled her lavender water. That was the thought that finally soothed her. The smell of diamonds.

When she was certain Donovan was sleeping soundly, she stood slowly. Her muscles were tight and cramped from sitting for so long, but she ignored the pain. She could spare only a glance at the egg that had called her here. There was no time, and opening the case while Donovan slept this close-by would be too foolhardy for her to attempt. Besides, the housekeeper was usually up and about well before five, which didn't leave Jackie much time to make her escape.

Jackie stepped very cautiously forward, casting a brief sideways glance to the man in the chair. Donovan was sleeping soundly. Big and hard as he was, he looked very vulnerable at the moment, sleeping in his chair and dreaming of lavender. She very pointedly looked at his face and ignored the area between his legs, but since she'd never had the opportunity to study a man quite this closely and safely it seemed a sin to waste the opportunity.

Her perusal of the manly instrument God had given Rory Donovan was purely academic, she told herself as she glanced down. She stared for a moment, wishing the shadows didn't fall just so. Well, it certainly didn't *look* threatening in its current state.

Her curiosity satisfied, she looked at his face again—to make sure he wasn't waking up, she told herself. His peaceful expression hadn't changed. If she had more time she might have been compelled to watch him awhile longer, though why she felt that urge she couldn't say.

Holding her breath, she stepped past Donovan's legs, lifting her own feet much higher than necessary to make absolutely certain she didn't brush against him. She needn't have worried; he didn't stir.

At the French doors she paused and looked over her shoulder. Her eyes fell longingly on the Fabergé egg, and for an instant she wanted it so badly she was certain she really could smell the diamonds. The odor was crisp and clean and tantalizing, and it tempted her mightily. She sighed. Not tonight.

She turned toward Donovan once again, and a smile crept across her unrepentant face.

"I'll be back," she whispered, so softly that little more than a breath brushed her lips. Silently, she stepped out onto the gallery, blending into the shadows. "I'll be back."

Linda Jones

On A Wicked Wind

Hurled into the Caribbean and swept back in time, Sabrina Steele finds herself abruptly aroused in the arms of the dashing pirate captain Antonio Rafael de Zamora. There, on his tropical island, Rafael teaches her to crest the waves of passion and sail the seas of ecstasy. But the handsome rogue has a tortured past, and in order to consummate a love that called her through time, the headstrong beauty seeks to uncover the pirate's true buried treasure—his heart.

___52251-9 $5.99 US/$6.99 CAN

Dorchester Publishing Co., Inc.
P.O. Box 6640
Wayne, PA 19087-8640

Please add $1.75 for shipping and handling for the first book and $.50 for each book thereafter. NY, NYC, and PA residents, please add appropriate sales tax. No cash, stamps, or C.O.D.s. All orders shipped within 6 weeks via postal service book rate. Canadian orders require $2.00 extra postage and must be paid in U.S. dollars through a U.S. banking facility.

Name_____
Address_____
City_____State_____Zip_____
I have enclosed $_____ in payment for the checked book(s).
Payment <u>must</u> accompany all orders. ❏ Please send a free catalog.

Someone's Been Sleeping In My Bed

A Faerie Tale Romance

LindaJones

WHO'S BEEN EATING FROM MY BOWL?
IS SHE A BEAUTY IN BOTH HEART AND
SOUL?
WHO'S BEEN SITTING IN MY CHAIR?
IS SHE PRETTY OF FACE AND FAIR OF
HAIR?
WHO'S BEEN SLEEPING IN MY BED?
IS SHE THE DAMSEL I WILL WED?

The golden-haired woman barely escapes from a stagecoach robbery before she gets lost in the Wyoming mountains. Hungry, harried, and out of hope, she stumbles on a rude cabin, the home of three brothers, great bears of men who nearly frighten her out of her wits. But Maddalyn Kelly is no Goldilocks; she is a feisty beauty who can fend for herself. Still, how can she ever guess that the Barrett boys will bare their souls to her--or that one of them will share with her an ecstasy so exquisite it is almost unbearable?

_52094-X $5.99 US/$6.99 CAN

NO ANGEL'S GRACE

LINDA WINSTEAD

From the moment Dillon feasts his eyes on the raven-haired beauty, Grace Cavanaugh, he knows she is trouble. Sharp-tongued and stubborn, with a flawless complexion and a priceless wardrobe, Grace certainly doesn't belong on a Western ranch. But that's what Dillon calls home, and as long as the lovely orphan is his charge, that's where they'll stay.

But Grace Cavanaugh has learned the hard way that men can't be trusted. Not for all the diamonds and rubies in England will she give herself to any man. But when Dillon walks into her life he changes all the rules. Suddenly the unapproachable ice princess finds herself melting at his simplest touch, and wondering what she'll have to do to convince him that their love is the most precious gem of all.

_4223-1 $5.50 US/$6.50 CAN

Dorchester Publishing Co., Inc.
P.O. Box 6640
Wayne, PA 19087-8640

SANDRA HILL

Sweeter Savage Love. When a twist of fate casts Harriet Ginoza back in time to the Old South, the modern psychologist meets the object of her forbidden fantasies. Though she knows the dangerously handsome rogue is everything she should despise, she can't help but feel that within his arms she might attain a sweeter savage love.

___52212-8 $5.99 US/$6.99 CAN

Desperado. When a routine skydive goes awry, Major Helen Prescott and Rafe Santiago parachute straight into the 1850 California Gold Rush. Mistaken for a notorious bandit and his infamously sensuous mistress, they find themselves on the wrong side of the law. In a time and place where rules have no meaning, Helen finds herself all too willing to throw caution to the wind to spend every night in the arms of her very own desperado.

___52182-2 $5.99 US/$6.99 CAN

Dorchester Publishing Co., Inc.
P.O. Box 6640
Wayne, PA 19087-8640

Please add $1.75 for shipping and handling for the first book and $.50 for each book thereafter. NY, NYC, and PA residents, please add appropriate sales tax. No cash, stamps, or C.O.D.s. All orders shipped within 6 weeks via postal service book rate. Canadian orders require $2.00 extra postage and must be paid in U.S. dollars through a U.S. banking facility.

Name_____
Address_____
City_____ State_____ Zip_____
I have enclosed $_____ in payment for the checked book(s).
Payment <u>must</u> accompany all orders. ❏ Please send a free catalog.

Prince Of Thieves
Saranne Dawson

Lord Roderic Hode, the former Earl of Varley, is Maryana's king's sworn enemy and now leads a rogue band of thieves who steals from the rich and gives to the poor. But when she looks into Roderic's blazing eyes, she sees his passion for life, for his people, for her. Deep in the forest, he takes her to the peak of ecstasy and joins their souls with a desire sanctioned only by love. Torn between her heritage and a love that knows no bounds, Maryana will gladly renounce her people if only she can forever remain in the strong arms of her prince of thieves.